THE ORANGE TURN

Ronald K. Myers

THE ORANGE TURN

DOUBLE DRAGON

A DOUBLE DRAGON PAPERBACK

ISBN 978-1-78695-443-5

Double Dragon
is an imprint of
Fiction4All

Published 2020
Fiction4All
www.fiction4all.com

Cover art by Ronald K. Myers

CHAPTER 1

The earth shifted.

Puffy-faced pig people swayed sideways.

From the safety of his corporation-protected home, Chief Earth Officer John McQueen peered out the window. Although the shifting of the earth was a common thing, the neat uniformed guards had not walked past for over an hour. They had no reason to be late, but beyond the field of an ocean of blue grass, whirling wisps of white smoke swirled through shafts of dirty-orange beams of sunlight.

Something wasn't right.

Behind McQueen, the sound of the double doors to the library swished open. He didn't turn around. With his hand, he motioned for his bodyguard.

"Judd," he said, "come here. Look at that smoke. It's too clean to be coming from a steam car, burning coal."

Judd didn't come to the window.

Flames flitted around the borders of the blue grass, and a billowing cloud of thick white smoke mushroomed into the sky.

McQueen raised his voice. "Judd, come over here. Tell me what's burning."

An unfamiliar voice answered. "I'm not Judd. The Dinkies are burning wood virus."

McQueen turned. Standing in front of him, an unfamiliar, portly man stared into space.

"Whoever you are," McQueen said, "you must know there is no such thing as wood virus."

The man's face wreathed into a smile. "I know that, Chief Earth Officer." He flashed McQueen a secret wink. "We know the pig people don't know that, and we know it reinforces their fear of the fake wood virus."

This strange man gave McQueen an uneasy feeling. The intruder did not seem to have the assurance of a person used to command. As McQueen's eyes traveled down the man's body, for all to see and for all to fear, another sign of the man's ineptitude came into view. Holstered on his hip, was an illegal squirt gun.

McQueen gestured to the gun. "I hope that isn't loaded."

"It sure is." The man took out the squirt gun and sprayed water into his mouth. "When I'm thirsty it comes in handy."

McQueen flared up angrily. "That's just great," he said with sarcasm in his voice. "When a pig person sees you drinking unfiltered water, they'll do it, too."

"So what if they do?" The man made a feeble placatory gesture. "We'll just shoot them with the antidote. They'll die."

McQueen felt his cheeks grow tight with fury. "Warriors are not supposed to shoot a pig person when it's not necessary." He watched the man for a discernible reaction. Seeing none, he threw his hand in the air. "Sure, the pig people of Blue Town have to be constantly convinced to stay on the blue grass, but they're not to be sacrificed because a warrior is careless."

Puzzlement filled the man's face, and McQueen couldn't understand why. The antidote supposedly used to cure people, who had been exposed to the mutating water, wood, and green-grass virus, always killed the recipient. Although the poison antidote kept the threat of the viruses alive, he found it hard to believe this man had such a low value of other people's lives; and that was something McQueen didn't need or want. And, in addition to being his bodyguard, Judd was McQueen's friend. McQueen wanted Judd back.

Looking for his bodyguard, McQueen turned his head right then left. "Where's Judd?"

As if he had just remembered something important, the intruder snapped to attention. "Chief Earth Officer, Captain Sproat reporting for duty." His face lit up with excited delight. "I am your new bodyguard."

McQueen remembered the name, Sproat, but it didn't seem to fit the lard-like body that was standing at attention and holding his quivering hand to his forehead. His salute was not a crisp military salute a regular warrior would display. It was a sloppy gesture at best. Sproat's uniform, although the uniform of a warrior, it did not cover a healthy body. Except where his stomach puffed out and strained against the buttons of his shirt, the uniform looked like it had been slept in. A tube of loose fat sagged down like an overflowing bowl of dough and covered the man's belt buckle.

McQueen would take speed, quickness, and stamina over bulging muscles any day; and for a warrior, this man was a sickening sight. As a foreboding feeling entered McQueen's chest, he remembered Sproat was a name that had come up in evaluation reports. Sproat was a man hungry for advancement and the power that came with it, but his performance scores and physical tests were always far below average. McQueen had always voted to have him stay at the lowest rank possible; but the regular warriors had been on strike for over two years; and even though the Friends of the Earth Corporation had no one else to promote, McQueen was sure they wouldn't have sent such a failure to be the bodyguard of the Chief Earth Officer.

Still holding the salute, Sproat's eyes traveled around the room and fixed on an orange wall safe. "I'm here to get Judd's key." He gestured to the safe. "I was tole it is in an orange safe, and that you would show me how to open it."

Years ago, the key to the orange turn had been locked in the orange safe, but the key was too valuable to be left in a wall safe. Although many people believed the key was still in the safe, years ago, McQueen had taken the key out and hidden it in a secret place. Suspecting Judd was playing a joke on him, McQueen decided to play along.

"Sure," he said with mock cooperation. "I'll show you how to open it."

Sproat dropped his salute, stepped to the safe, and stared at its combination lock. "What do I do first?"

McQueen almost laughed out loud but held it in. "Okay, turn the dial three times to the left and stop at nine. Sproat turned the dial and looked to McQueen. McQueen rolled his hand in encouragement. "Do it again. You turned it too fast."

This time, Sproat turned the dial slowly. "Okay, what's next?"

McQueen turned from Sproat and searched for Judd. He could be peeking around a corner. He

8

wasn't. But McQueen was sure Judd would come out of hiding and burst out laughing. He turned back to Sproat. "Tap the dial once, stop at seven, turn around three times, and hop on one foot."

Sproat did what McQueen told him to do, spun around in bewilderment, and looked to McQueen for more instructions.

McQueen couldn't believe anyone could be this ignorant. The man had to be acting. It had to be a joke. "Okay, wink three times, take a deep breath, and hold it."

Again, Sproat did as he was told.

McQueen reached over and opened the unlocked safe.

Expelling air, Sproat leaned forward and peeked into the safe.

It was empty.

His face filled with disappointment. "Where's the key?"

Ignoring Sproat, McQueen yelled over his shoulder, "Okay, Judd, you can come out now."

Judd didn't come out of hiding. McQueen turned toward Sproat so he could give him the benefit of his full attention. "Are you part of a joke Judd is playing on me?"

Portly Sproat lifted his chubby hand to his sweating forehead and held a quivering salute. "No, Chief Earth Officer, I'm no joke. Your regular bodyguard was caught going off the blue grass. I have replaced him."

Judd would never have been caught going off the blue grass, and the key to the orange turn wasn't a key to be given to just anyone. Sproat was lying. If he wasn't acting, he should have never been a warrior. He should have been recycled. With extensive training and a lot of luck, this man might qualify for a job as a dish washer or a rickshaw cleaner. He was anything but a warrior. Sproat was no bodyguard. He had to be one of the pig people who had crossed the picket lines. He was a replacement warrior. Not caring for the good of all, this man wrapped himself in ignorance. This man was a scab.

McQueen didn't want to, but he returned Sproat's salute. "I'm sorry, Captain Sproat." Not wanting to look at him, he turned away, but Sproat's reflection remained in the window. "Scabs do not qualify for the bodyguard position."

Sproat's flabby face flushed with anger. Although it was military courteously to drop the salute once a superior officer returned it, he didn't drop his salute. He opened his mouth to say something but closed it.

In the reflection, McQueen glared at him. Right away, he noticed Sproat did not have the brash, clamorous arrogance of newly assumed authority other people had.

"Captain Sproat," McQueen said, "why wasn't I informed of such a change in my protection?"

Still holding the salute, Sproat's jaw muscles clenched under the fat on his face. With his twisted hand above his sweating forehead, he just stood there. After thirty seconds, his mouth moved. "Chief Earth Officer, McQueen, the Friends of the Earth Corporation felt it was in your best interest to have a new bodyguard as soon as possible."

McQueen continued to look out the window. Under a sky infusing with dirty-gray pallor, the ocean of blue grass in his private seven-acre back yard waved in the gentle wind. In the distance, at the edge of the orange warning signs, a line of dirty dumpy men, wearing crumpled, brown uniforms, walked through the tall blue grass, mashing it down with their fat feet.

In the reflection in the glass, McQueen watched behind his back. Sproat finally dropped his salute. "Is there something wrong, Chief Earth Officer?"

McQueen pointed to the men tramping down the grass. "What happened to security? The sentry has not passed by in over an hour. No one is permitted to walk on the blue grass of the Chief Earth Officer's residence. What are those men doing?"

Sproat bent forward and stretched his double-chinned neck to look out the window. "It's a training exercise," he said with his voice rising to a mouse-like pitch. "That patrol must have taken the wrong path."

Trying to clear the sight of the ugly men from his mind, McQueen jerked his head toward Sproat. "They look like the lard patrol. Is that the best we have?"

Sproat stuttered, but managed to speak. "Chief Earth Officer, since the warriors went on strike, they're the only men we can get."

McQueen raised his voice to a pitch of authority. "They are not doing their job!"

"But, Chief Earth Officer," Sproat objected. "I don't think a little bent over blue grass will hurt anybody." As if suddenly afraid, he shuddered. "Besides, bent over grass makes it easier to spot those rat-tailed Pygmies."

11

McQueen swung around and jerked his finger at Sproat. "The rat-tailed Pigmies did not ruin the land. The pig people did. In its slow recovering state, the land can only support a small population of the Pygmy race. Being ancestors of the ancient rain forest, the Pigmies can come and go without harming the feeble growths. They weave their small bodies amongst the plants without disturbing the growing cycles."

Sproat held up his hands and backed away. "I don't care what you say. Those Pigmies have big buck teeth that have poisonous venom. They should all be given the antidote."

The rat-tailed Pigmies rarely talked to anyone. When perturbed, their tails would come up in a threatening S posture. This threatening gesture had frightened many pig people away from the Orangeville experiment, and had kept them on the blue grass. When the Pigmies had talked to McQueen they were very intelligent and preferred to stay away from the ignorance of the pig people.

"Just because you're afraid of the Pigmies," McQueen said, "it is no reason to kill them."

Sproat's scared expression faded.

McQueen held out his arm toward an array of books in a vast opened plastic cabinet. "I don't have time to be opening and closing doors every time I need a book. You should know that the blue grass must be kept high enough to keep the pig people from seeing these books."

Sproat tilted his chubby head with a questioning slant. "What's the matter with letting them see a few books?"

McQueen shook his head in disbelief and slammed one of the plastic doors on the cabinet. It covered half of the books.

"Unlike the plastic pamphlets the pig people use," he said, "these books are made of paper. Paper is made from wood. If the pig people see the paper books, they'll know the wood virus is fake."

"I don't think any of the pig people will get this close."

"What makes you say that?"

"I have heard from various sources that pig people never go near your field."

"You've heard?" McQueen questioned. "A warrior cannot rely on isolated statements, connect them, and make preconceived judgments. A warrior must be ready for anything and everything. He must see and confirm things for himself."

"I think you're overreacting, chief."

The man hadn't known McQueen for more than a few minutes. There was no way he could be considered a friend and call McQueen, chief. McQueen slammed the other cabinet door and raised his voice. "Chief? I don't think you realize who's in charge here. All replacement warriors must show respect and keep up the virus farce."

Cowering, Sproat stiffened and stood at rigid attention. "I'm sorry, Chief Earth Officer, McQueen."

McQueen lowered his voice a notch. "Anything you do, no matter how trivial you may think it is, it may be the one thing that compromises the secret of the blue grass."

Now, Sproat's voice was high pitched and squeaky. "I know that, Chief Earth Officer."

13

Puzzled by the high pitch of Sproat's voice, McQueen wanted to ask him about it, but instead, he said, "I've heard the pig people are going off the blue grass. Are they?"

As if overheated, Sproat tugged at the tight collar of his baggy uniform. "Only a few people have ventured off," he squeaked out. "They are still afraid of the green grass and the water virus."

"They better be," McQueen said. "If they find out it isn't real, they'll be taking baths in the rivers and lakes."

"I don't think it will ever go that far."

"It may have gone too far already. In the last month, the sales of dry washing clay and bottled water have decreased thirty percent."

"Maybe the people are not washing as much."

"They might not wash as much, but they would never cut down on the amount of water they drink."

"Nothing like that has happened."

McQueen didn't believe him. "What's the matter with you?"

As if he were in a hurry to leave, Sproat stepped back and didn't answer.

McQueen studied the scab bodyguard. "What do you mean nothing like that has happened? I just told you the sales of bottled water had decrease thirty percent. If it continues to drop, due to the fact that people are no longer afraid of unfiltered water, the planet's natural resources will be greatly stressed. The social order will be shaken."

Sproat moved uneasy. "We have taken care of everything."

McQueen took a hard look at Sproat. "You better be sure. You can't let those pig people get close to the water. They'll poison it."

A disarming smile formed on Sproat's lips. "The canals seem to be clean and unpolluted."

McQueen wanted to believe him, but Sproat was smiling like an unemployed liar auditioning for work. He wasn't taking his job seriously. It was a warrior's job to protect the earth. Canals dug to divert the world's dwindling water supply to the river above Niagara Falls was a failed attempt to keep the hydro power plants running, but the canals did provide a nursery for vanishing aquatic life. To maintain the Friends of the Earth's master plan of keeping the earth on a recovery path, the canals had to remain free of *all* pollution.

"What do you mean the canals *seem* to be clean and unpolluted?" McQueen asked. "Those canals are the lifeblood of what is left of our forest and plant life. If they fail, the lands around the rivers and canals will dry up. Dumping chemical-laced crack water down holes thousands of meters deep has greatly depleted the water available every place the gas companies have drilled. With temperatures hot enough to melt plastic, we don't need any more dry lakes and plains taking over the earth."

Sproat didn't answer. As if he didn't care about his job, he lazily shrugged. What was worse, was that he seemed to be hiding something. McQueen wanted to know what it was. He jerked his finger at Sproat. "What is the real reason you are here?"

The fat under Sproat's jaw twitched, but he kept his mouth shut.

15

McQueen smacked the palm of his own hand with his fist. "I have given the Friends of the Earth Corporation more than long enough to settle the warrior strike. I've had it with scabs like you."

Sproat cringed but a grin betrayed his true feelings. "Without the approval of the corporation, you can't do anything about it."

McQueen felt distrust and hate for the man. "Oh, but I can, Captain Sproat. You seem to forget: I *am* the Chief Earth Officer. I can use my emergency powers."

Sproat reached up and placed his hand on McQueen's shoulder. It was forbidden for a warrior to touch a superior officer. McQueen snapped his head to the side and glared at the hand.

Sproat's lips curled into a sorry smile. He jerked his hand back. "Chief Earth Officer, McQueen," he said with his voice squeaking. "You have no need to worry. My men will provide you with the same quality of security your warriors have done for seventeen years. Your wife and son have nothing to fear."

McQueen raised his hand and shook his finger in front of Sproat's face. "If the secret of the virus has been let out and the pig people are going off the blue grass, we'll all have something to fear."

"Yes, Chief Earth Officer," Sproat said, and now his voice was very high, like someone was choking him.

McQueen dropped his hand and turned away. "You should have someone look at that throat."

"There's nothing wrong with my throat," Sproat said with a strained, but lower voice. "I just talk that way sometimes."

"I'd still have it checked."

Sproat put his chubby hand to his forehead and attempted to salute. "Is that an order, Chief Earth Officer?"

McQueen abruptly turned toward Sproat. "It's your throat. Do what you want."

Sproat dropped his hand and lowered his voice. "Yes, Chief Earth Officer."

Studying Sproat's dark eyes for a hint of what he trying to conceal, McQueen found nothing but ignorance. Maybe he could trick him into telling him what he was hiding. He crossed the room, sat in a plush leather armchair, and motioned for Sproat to come near.

Sproat strolled over and looked down at McQueen.

McQueen looked up at Sproat. "Captain Sproat," he said with exaggerated compassion. "The warriors have been on strike for over two years. Should I continue to let them strike and bring the men who just trespassed onto the blue grass before the board?"

Sproat's face relaxed. As if he knew something McQueen didn't know, he became extra calm. "There is no need to bother the board with a simple mistake. This afternoon, when you take your son for a walk, I'll have my men correct the situation."

"I would appreciate that," McQueen said; but every time he had taken his son outside, someone rummaged through his office; and the slob standing in front of him looked like just the sort of person who would do something like that. If it was him, and he was taking care of the scabs in the field, who had tramped down the blue grass, he wouldn't have time to sneak in. If his office wasn't disturbed today, then McQueen would have a pretty good idea the person rummaging through his office wasn't Sproat.

Sproat smiled a cocky smile and held a salute. "If you need me, Chief Earth Officer, just call."

McQueen placed his hands on the armrests of the armchair and pushed himself to a standing position. "I'll do just that."

Sproat dropped his salute, turned on his heavy heel, and hastened to the door. After he opened the door, he stepped out and intentionally slammed it. Two paintings of McQueen's father's farm, that his Dinky friend, Tommy, had painted, vibrated on the wall.

As McQueen crossed the room, his wife, Danielle, walked into the library. Her neat professional appearance always brightened a room. To others, she seemed unemotional. But McQueen knew she was always calm in a crisis. Now, something behind her intense brown eyes signaled she was disturbed.

She turned her cute body toward him. "John, that man didn't have to close the door so forcefully. I have a bad feeling about him."

Adjusting the paintings on the wall, McQueen nodded. "Me, too. In addition to slamming doors, when his voice rises, he sounds like he's lying."

"If he is, you'll have to prove it."

McQueen adjusted the painting or his father's farm, just a tad. It was level. He turned toward Danielle. "How can I prove anyone is lying when everyone on the board outvotes me?"

"I'm not sure,' Danielle said. "But if Sproat's charging people to let them go off the blue grass, he's going to be a wealthy man."

McQueen felt a bad feeling crawling up his back. He shivered and shook it off. "I have never seen a bodyguard or a warrior as unhealthy as Sproat."

"It's not your fault, John." Danielle flashed him a sweet smile and touched his arm. "They forced him on you."

McQueen felt his face flush with shame. "I have become a Chief Earth Officer in name only." He placed his hand on the door of the book cabinet. "I'm going to look up the best way to use my emergency powers."

Danielle held up one finger. "Remember, without the old warriors, you have no power."

McQueen didn't want to admit it, but she was right. "If I can find the old warriors," he said with determination. "I don't care what the price is. I'm going to hire them back. The old warriors will have no trouble keeping those pig people off the green lands."

Danielle turned her head to one side. Like a satin waterfall, her long black hair flowed over her perfect breasts.

McQueen didn't want to talk anymore, but Danielle continued. "Sproat couldn't have attained the rank of captain without some sense of duty."

"If he has any sense of duty, he doesn't show it."

"Maybe he just needs a little more time."

Peering through the window, McQueen studied the tramped down blue grass. "When the regular

19

warriors were on duty, Blue Town ran itself. Fear of the virus controlled the pig people. If Sproat can't control his own eating habits, how can he control Blue Town?"

Danielle flashed him a shy smile. "You could be suspicious for nothing."

In thought, McQueen rubbed his forehead. "I haven't seen Tommy in a long while. I should go to the Grotto, pay him a visit. If anything's going on, he'll know all about it."

"Don't let anyone see you going off the blue grass. It would be a bad example for the pig people to see a Chief Earth Officer who is not afraid of the virus. And it will be worse if they see you talking to a Dinky."

"I thought after seventeen years the people would learn to live with the earth and be ready to learn about the fake virus."

"It would be nice," Danielle said and placed her arm around his waist. "But the people and the earth are just not ready for it. They still act like pigs."

"Maybe someday they'll advance and learn how to care for the real world."

"Maybe our son will be fortunate enough to live in a town without blue grass."

McQueen slid his arm around Danielle.

She turned and embraced him. "When it happens, he'll be ready. You've trained him since he was a baby."

McQueen looked into her eyes.

As she spoke, the dreamy look of peace and happiness intensified. "I love your symmetric muscles," she said. "She ran her hand down his arms. "I love your strong arms, but most of all, I love how you move. You have the sinuous grace of a dancer."

McQueen felt his face reddened. "You mean you wouldn't rather be with a Humpty Dumpty shaped pig person?"

"Don't be silly, John."

"How about a Dinky?"

"Tommy's cute and he's okay for laughs, but he's too little." She flashed McQueen a beautiful and mischievous smile. "But he would make a good pet."

McQueen smiled a faint smile. Although Tommy had a sharp mind, he and his mutant friends were about half the height of other people, and their big floppy ears and round adorable eyes caused their faces to look comic. McQueen was going to remind Danielle that Tommy was just as intelligent as or more intelligent than most people; but not wanting to spoil the moment, he let it pass.

"Now that you've decided to stay with me," McQueen said, "what would you like to do?"

Danielle placed her finger to her lips and gave him a coy smile. "I would love to walk with you in the freedom of the green forest. We could listen to the sparkling springs, swim in the green lakes, and spend a few precious moments in the real world."

"If the Orangeville experiment works, we will have a sample of what the world should be like. We'll even be able to stand in the rain without being afraid someone will see us."

"Maybe if you took a few people to Orangeville, they would realize why they must stay on the blue grass."

"The Pygmies have permitted a few people to visit, but they only wanted to take from the recovering land. The Pigmies have told me that before we can even think about letting pig people live on the farms and in the forests around Blue Town, it will be twenty years."

"I didn't know it would take that long."

"Long ago it wouldn't have taken so long, but even though honesty lies in the heart of every person on earth, it has been buried by corruption and greed." McQueen waved his hand and gestured toward the blue grass outside the window. "If the people are going off the blue grass, this section of the planet may not recover at all." Feeling a pang of extreme discomfort, he continued. "If they find out there is no virus, eventually they'll find Orangeville. The bad part is that if they get that far and they break the dam, the water in the canals will overflow and wash away the new plants and aquatic life."

"But what about Niagara Falls?" Danielle said, and her forehead lined with concentration. "The water is still deep there."

"After we opened the gates and tried to get the generators operating, the canals went down a good meter. Normally that wouldn't be a problem, but more than ever the canals need water for plant and tree growth. If they don't get water and we get another heat wave like the one that melted the blue asphalt, the canals will become like the rest of the planet."

"You mean they'll dry up?"

"Many rivers and lakes have already dried up from global boiling and dumping crack water down into deep holes. Even though the cracking companies claimed the dumping was completely safe and had no effect on any environment, in every case, the loss of water caused droughts; and then the drying winds came."

For a moment, a sullen look appeared on Daniel's face. "I can't believe those cracking people are too ignorant to understand the mechanics of rainfall."

"To top it off," McQueen said with a rising hint of frustration, "heat lightning started fires that lasted for months." He paused and tried to get the horrible history out of his mind. "And it doesn't end. The dry winds still stir up red hot dust and smother the land."

"That scares me," Danielle said and shuddered. "If it keeps happening, the earth will never recover."

"Then, our only hope will be the Orange Turn."

"But we don't know who the other person is, and for all we know, that person may already be dead."

"Dead or alive, when, and if, the time comes, we'll just have to find him or her." He squinted one eye. "Are you sure you're not the other person?"

A sour look formed on Danielle's face. "I don't even want to think about that."

Turning toward the window, McQueen changed the subject. "There's a full moon tonight. If there's electricity, the TV signals might get through?"

"I sure miss those clear digital signals. Those pictures weren't grainy and didn't have a tiny sound."

"After the super nova, the virus, or whatever it was, wiped out all the computers and digital screens, we were lucky the museums had few old TVs. we could put into service."

"I wanted to watch the wheelbarrow people at the buffet."

"It's a shame entertainment has dropped to such a level." He let out a muffled spasm of amusement. "Have one of their stomach's exploded?"

I don't know. Since you left for the tour of the water plants, I have only been able to get ghost images, and most of the time it's a blizzard of snow."

"That's strange," McQueen said. "Just before I left, I could get a relatively clear picture. Although it rolled and flicked, it was almost clear. I even had limited use of the phones."

Suggestively, Danielle ran her finger down McQueen's neck and unbuttoned the top button on his shirt. "More debris in the atmosphere always stops the signals."

McQueen didn't acknowledge her sexual signals. "If the people are sneaking off the blue grass they are polluting the atmosphere again."

Danielle turned her head with a playful flick. "Maybe Sproat and his scabs are getting drunk on the job." She pulled away from him and swayed her sensual body. Making soft, feminine sounds that arouse his senses, she walked backwards, her teasing dark eyes enticing him to follow.

He watched her midnight-black hair glisten, and an impulse to pull her close surged in his chest. "Maybe we should talk about this later."

She reached out with both hands to draw him close.

As a wave of hot sensual energy whispered through his body, he took one step toward her.

Boom! The double doors to the room banged open. Sproat and twenty of his men rushed into the room and stood with their antidote guns drawn.

"McQueen!" Sproat shouted. "You are under arrest."

The lard-bellied man on Sproat's left pulled the lever on his gun and chambered an antidote bullet. "Arrest hell," he screamed, and jerked the gun at McQueen. "We're going to rip your little love nest apart."

Danielle jumped in front of McQueen.

The lard-bellied man fired the gun.

The antidote bullet sank into her chest.

She fell to the floor.

Sproat's nineteen other men took aim. McQueen ran through the library and out into the hall. Then he circled around and slunk behind Sproat's men. In the short time Danielle had been laying on the floor, her clothes had been torn from her body and turned inside out. They were looking for the orange turn key. McQueen wanted to pick her up and run. When he bent over to lift her from the floor, one of Sproat's men rushed toward him. The man had a horrible face. It was distorted, evil, brutal, and inhuman. McQueen wanted to at least lure that thing away from Danielle. He backed away.

Six of Sproat's men grabbed him and fastened restraint bands around his hands and feet. Sproat stepped in front of him. "Sorry for the earlier charade."

McQueen broke free and bolted toward the door.

The men grabbed him and slammed him against the wall.

The picture of his father's farm crashed to the floor.

Struggling and staring at the broken glass and the sliced picture, he stopped trying to escape.

Sproat placed his heavy foot on the broken glass and ground it into the picture. Smiling, he wagged his finger at McQueen. "No tricks, McQueen."

As if cowering in fright, McQueen relaxed and drew back. The men loosened their grips. He reared up and jerked toward Sproat. The men re-gripped and held him tight.

Sproat pointed to the orange safe. "You thought it was funny making me do stupid circus tricks to open that safe. Now it's your turn to do circus tricks. You're going to do what we tell you to do, and you're going to do it for a long time."

McQueen kicked his feet and wiggled his body. "Let me loose you stinking scabs. When I don't make my monthly address the pig people will wonder what happened to me."

"No problem." As if it were a footstool, Sproat placed his glass impregnated boot on Danielle's lifeless head and motioned to his men. "Search him."

His men patted McQueen's body. One put his hand in McQueen's pocket and pulled out a knife. "No key, only this."

For a moment, Sproat studied the knife, then waved his hand down. "He won't need that."

"Take anything you want," McQueen said and struggled against his restraints. "I'm not going to speak."

Sproat arrogantly leaned back. "You'll speak every month, and you'll give us the key. If you don't, your son will suffer the same consequences as your wife."

McQueen struggled against the restraining grasps of his captors. "When my bodyguard finds out what you've done, you'll all be recycled."

Sproat lifted his boot from Danielle's head. "Oh, your buddy, Judd." He laughed. "Tell him yourself. He's right outside." He motioned toward the window.

Outside, a steam car, billowing alarming volumes of white-gray smoke into the air, chugged over the tall blue grass and stopped in front of the window. The driver of the car turned and pointed to the two potbellied guards in dirty-brown uniforms standing on the steam car platform. Like hunters with a trophy kill, the guards held up Judd. His blue-faced, lifeless body's lower extremities had been browned by exposure to something hot, and his clothing had been torn to shreds.

CHAPTER 2

With the sun westering to a sickly pale-orange, just outside the blue grass boundaries and behind the empty rickshaws, Tommy, the mutant Dinky, stood behind a thick stand of green grass and peered through an opening in a line of blue spruce trees. Pig people, gathered in front of a dark blue plastic podium, cried out in a tsunami of adulation. In the distance, making his way to the podium, John McQueen's long, strong legs stepped with the precision of a majestic prince. When he stepped up on the podium, his smooth deltoid muscles formed a sinuous curve and accented the many metals that were embroidered across the major pectoral muscle of his chest. A single eagle feather, with a white tip, caught the light, reflected a brown-purple sheen, and stood upright at the back of his head.

A ways from the podium, a group of teen-age pig people, milled around, squinting their swine-like eyes. These puffy-faced Humpty-Dumpty-shaped teen-agers, with pig-like characteristics, wore their pants down around their behinds. As if they were malnourished, their bloated stomachs stuck out over their belts. The Friends of the Earth Corporation had tricked them into believing that wearing their pants in this unnatural restrictive manner was the latest style, but it was only a trick played on them. It not only made them easier to identify, it also marked them as young, naïve, and prime targets for propaganda and behavior control. While most of them watched McQueen, a few looked toward the forbidden green grass boundaries, excitedly waved their hands, and chattered as if some great event was about to happen. And it was. The wheelbarrow people event would be next.

McQueen raised his hand in a salute to a higher being.

The teen-agers spun around and faced the podium. As a sudden silence spread across the huge crowd, the pig people eagerly waited for McQueen to finish his monthly address. As he leveled a lingering gaze across the crowd, his coal-black hair hung smooth and sleek down his straight back. The tree gold stars on his shoulders shimmered in the sun and broadcasted that he was the Chief Earth Officer. He lowered his arm and stepped forward. The symmetric muscles on his strong arms gracefully moved under his smooth-fitting blue-spruce-blue uniform.

Before he could speak, a warrior guard yelled out, "Stay on the blue grass!"

All eyes turned toward the warrior. He had his antidote gun aimed at a pig person walking off the blue grass.

The guard shouted, "Pig person, if you do not want to be shot, stay on the blue grass."

The pig person took one step onto the green grass.

The warrior shot the antidote bullet.

It zinged through the air and stuck in the pig person's back.

The pig person reached around his chubby body to pull out the antidote bullet, but his body was too wide. He could not reach the feathered end of the bullet. Moaning, he fell to the ground. As the throng of pig people turned toward the fallen pig person, woman's screams were followed by the babble of voices.

Warriors in white plastic suits, with air masks covering their faces, ran to the fallen pig person, picked him up, placed him on a blue stretcher, and whisked him away.

Still peering through the opening in the blue spruce trees, Tommy was amazed at how the pig people had held fast to their sanity for so many years. Being forced to live in a continuous probability of being forced to stay on the blue grass forever, any normal person would have gone stir-crazy within a few months. But Tommy figured that like most people, familiarity becomes like an old shoe. Even though it is worn and hurts the person's feet, they refuse to wear a new pair simply because they are accustomed to the old ones and do not want to take a chance and change anything they are not accustomed to.

McQueen sadly shook head and began, "People of Blue Town, another one of our fine citizens has been shot for going off the blue grass. We all know that if the antidote doesn't work he will mutate into a Dinky. If you don't want this to happen to you—" Choking up with emotion because of the lie he was telling, he paused and looked down. With his face grimacing with pain, he looked up. "Don't let this happen to you. Please stay on the blue grass."

An assistant came forward and whispered in McQueen's ear.

McQueen nodded.

As he began his usual monthly address, Tommy wondered what was wrong with his old friend. Being the Chief Earth Officer for seventeen years and living in an ocean of safe blue grass had not aged him, but today his voice didn't ring with its usual bright outlook. It had a business like edge. Like a liar avoiding eye contact, McQueen bent his head downward and continued making his address.

Today, he didn't point beyond the rickshaws and warn the pig people that if they went off the blue grass they would be infected with any one of the viruses. Her didn't tell them that if they weren't saved with the antidote shots, they would shrink to half their height and mutate into Dinkies. Once a Dinky, the person was fated to lead a life of substandard quality. He or she would spend the rest of their lives as an agricultural slaves or performing some other demeaning work, like pulling a rickshaw.

With his large round eyes peering from under the brim of his floppy hat, Tommy leaned back against a blue spruce tree and waited for his favorite part of McQueen's address. He wanted him to point to the parked rickshaws and say, "If you want the virus to turn you into a Dinky and go humping around Blue Town, pulling your fat friends in those two-wheeled taxies, just go off the blue grass." But he didn't.

Tommy leaned away from the tree, cocked his big ears, and listened, more.

McQueen usually told the gathered crowd about how much longer the water virus, the wood virus, and the green-grass virus would be around. But this time he didn't. And he didn't tell the people how close the scientists were to finding a cure for the virus. His speech was lackluster. It didn't give the pig people hope. McQueen was not his usual self.

Whoosh! Behind Tommy, something brushed against the branch of the blue spruce tree. He turned around. Sludge, the mining Dinky, stood with his muscular leg hooked over a branch.

Although Sludge's head was covered with thin reddish-blond hair, it did not add to his looks. He was not handsome. When he talked, his mouth looked like it had a fat night-crawler hanging down the side of his mustached mouth that moved and jerked with each word. His skin broadcasted age lines that were records of the many years he had spent drinking and fighting, and the top of his muscular back was bowed from a life of picking and shoveling in the mines. His eyes were watery-brown, set in a face that had worn out many a combatant's fists.

In spite of his apparent lack of education, Sludge was a highly respected member of the mining work crew. When there was a cave in, and someone had been buried, Sludge was always the first to start digging and the last to quit. Even though he had a bad foot that he dragged when he stood on it too much, he had worked on his hands and knees and pulled many a Dinky from what would have been a dark grave.

As usual, Sludge wore his dirt-covered clothes, and his pants drooped below his small waist. He was smiling.

"What are you doing here?" Tommy whispered. "Did you come to watch the wheelbarrow people come to the buffet?"

"I jist come over to see what's goin' on with McQueen." Sludge made a face. "I ain't watchin' a bunch of pig people make their stomach bigger than they already are."

"I know it's not right," Tommy said, "but it's about the only excitement they have. Without it, the Friends of the Earth wouldn't be able to fool all the people all of the time. The free food and the wheelbarrow people entice them to buy into the virus deception without hesitation. It's a crucial tool in keeping people on the blue grass. It's visceral but it works."

"Quit usin' doze big words," Sludge said and craned his neck to get a better look at the people on the podium. "I thought all that the pig people came to hear was that useless information. Where's McQueen's spoiled family?"

Tommy's eyes swam across the sea of pig people and focused on the people on the podium. He hadn't noticed before, but McQueen's wife and son were not on the podium. "I don't know. They're usually here."

Sludge lifted his chin and gestured toward McQueen's tapping finger. "Does he got some kind a nervous disorder?"

Tommy studied McQueen's finger. It was tapping on the side of the podium. "Not that I know of . . . Wait!" he said, and watched the finger's rhythm. It sent out, *Dit-dit-dit, dah-dah-dah, did-dit-dit.*

"He's tapping Morse code." Tommy cupped his hand to his ear. "He's tapping out *SOS.*"

"So what?" Sludge said with his usual belligerent attitude. "It ain't nothin' to git excited about."

Tommy tilted his head in a questioning slant. "Don't you know *SOS* is a signal for help?"

"He's the Chief Earth Officer. He don't need nobody's help."

Tommy watched McQueen's finger. "Maybe he does. He's sending something else."

The rhythm of the code tapped out: *Prisoner in shelter, prisoner in shelter.*

"He's being held in the underground virus fallout shelter."

"You gotta have your signals crossed," Sludge said. "Look at 'em. He ain't in no shelter. He's standin' right in front of the crowd."

"They must be holding his wife and son hostage."

"You can't know that."

"I *can* know that, and I know that after dark, pig people have been going off the blue grass."

"No they ain't," Sludge said. "They can't get past the guards. Didn't you just see one get shot?"

"I did. But they're still going off."

As if trying to clear the thought from his mind, Sludge gave his head a vicious shake. "Ain't, no way"

Tommy flashed Sludge a blank look. "Haven't you seen them go off? Sometimes when a guard is stinking pee-pants drunk, passed out, and lying in his own vomit, the pig people just walk past him. Other times the pig people stand right next to the orange warning signs, pay the guards off, and step right onto the green grass."

34

Sludge clinched his fist and jerked it. "Ahh, haw!" he said as if he had just been enlightened. "That's why Sproat and his band of halfwits have a lot of money to throw around."

The omnipresent screech of the loudspeakers blaring "*Stay on the blue grass*," overpowered McQueen's address. The pig people covered their ears with their hands, but didn't move. Warriors rushed to the green grass borders and shouted at the teenagers, "Stay back!"

Sludge's face filled with disbelief. "Look at those idiots. Just because they have their pants down around their behinds, they think they can go off the blue grass."

Tommy gestured with an airy wave of his hand. "If green radiation gum drops were falling from the sky, they'd still try to go off. The warriors only keep them off the green grass when somebody's watching."

Sludge reached up and scratched the back of his dusty head. "If they still had the credits system, those guards wouldn't be collectin' nothin'."

"Yeah, but, McQueen thought it would be better for us they switched back to the paper money."

"So what's the difference? Sludge said, hunched his shoulders, and twitched his thumbs. "Money's, money. It still spends."

"Without credits, the Friends of the Earth can't trace how much anybody makes or saves. It's less control. I think McQueen knew that and figured it would give the pig-people more freedom."

Sludge let out a muffled snort. "Well, da next time you see your friend, tell him it ain't workin'."

Tommy held up his hand and signaled Sludge to be quiet. He didn't want a scab warrior to hear them. If they were caught, Sludge and he would be taken prisoner. Except for working in the fields and pulling rickshaws, mutants were not permitted to run free. Tommy pulled his floppy hat up off his ears, turned around, and looked beyond the trees. No one was close. But in the distance, two pig people walked off the blue grass, past the orange warning signs, and walked into the thick green foliage of Forbidden Forest.

Tommy placed his hand on Sludge's strong shoulder. "Did you see that?"

Sludge turned and looked beyond the trees. "See what?"

"Sproat and his men are letting people off the blue grass in broad daylight."

As the two pig people walked into the green grass and vanished into the forest, a smug look appeared on Sludge's face. "The great buffet ain't workin'. Those guards are makin' money night and day."

"McQueen would never let that happen. He knows the virus farce has to continue."

Sludge spread his hands. "Yep, that's why they're keepin' him in that shelter."

"We have to dig him out."

"What-ah-ya mean, *we?*"

Tommy gently shook Sludge's shoulder. "You have to agree, old friend, that with all the earth's sunsets and expectations, *we* are nothing without clean air and water."

Nodding as if he had heard it all before, Sludge replied, "Yeah, yeah, yeah."

"We'll go to the Grotto," Tommy said with his voice filled with elation. "We'll ask our friends to help us dig an opening in the old escape tunnel."

Sludge shrugged Tommy's hand off his back and. flashed him a humorless smile. "Then what?"

"Then, we'll get him out."

"And?" Sludge encouragingly rolled his hand.

"And, we'll get his wife and son out, too. It'll be good to be with my old friend again. He'll stop the warrior strike. He'll get rid of Sproat's scabs. When the old warriors come back, they'll keep those pig people on the blue grass."

Sludge's smile vanished. "That last earth shift caused a couple a cave-ins. We got tunnels to fix. We ain't diggin' him out, too."

Tommy turned to watch the end of McQueen's address. When he turned back, with the short strides of a Dinky and with his short arms hanging away from his muscular body, Sludge surreptitiously walked into the forest. He wasn't staying to watch the buffet spectacle.

Usually the conveyor belt, signaling the start of the buffet, wasn't started until McQueen had finished his speech. Without the promise of gargantuan amounts of food and the wheelbarrow people extravaganza, the pig people would not stay for McQueen's full address. But today, before he finished his address, the land under Tommy's feet seemed unstable, but it wasn't an earthquake. It was vibrations from the hand-turned crank of the conveyor belt. It was a signal that the buffet would be starting early. It didn't matter who was speaking, no one could compete with the tantalizing sight of the wheelbarrow people coming to the food-filled buffet belt.

McQueen cut his speech short.

The wheelbarrow people were on the way.

As food was heaped onto the belt, the crowd of pig people raised their chubby hands over their pig-like heads and roared in approval.

And here they came: Walking pigeon-toed, with strong, fat encased, arms gripping the heavy duty plastic handles of one-wheeled wheelbarrows that held their enormous stomachs. Huffing and puffing, they could barely see over their huge swollen stomachs. Tommy had often wondered how such stomachs were possible, but found out that from birth, pig people selected to become wheelbarrow people were constantly fed. At the age of twelve they were given their first operation, and another stomach was attached to their already ballooned stomachs. Tommy didn't know how many operations it took to become a wheelbarrow person, but by the size of their stomachs it had to be a lot.

A few meters before the buffet belt, one of the wheelbarrow people's chubby hands slipped from the handle of his wheelbarrow. The sudden jerk on his other hand caused him to turn sideways and tilt to the side. He tried to correct his tilt and right the wheelbarrow but he overcompensated. The wheelbarrow slipped out from under his belly. He fell back and plopped onto his back.

The crowd laughed with delight.

The TV cameras zoomed in.

The fallen wheelbarrow person tried to right himself, but the weight of his heavy stomach pinned

38

his hips to the ground. He could not turn over, and his arms did not have the strength to push his enormous body to one side. With tears in his eyes, he looked toward the buffet belt and held out his hand. "Help me. I need food."

But the main event was about to happen. No one helped.

The other wheelbarrow people had quickly waddled to the long tables and stopped. With their stomachs blocking their view and keeping their hands too far away from the food-filled conveyor belt, they all turned to one side, lowered their wheelbarrow-filled stomachs, and in insatiable expectation, they rubbed their hands together. Now, when the event began, they could see and grab big juicy hamburgers, soft buns, freshly cut coleslaw, thick crisp fries, pizza, fried potatoes, mashed potatoes and gravy, cookies, puddings cakes, and pies.

A pig person held up his hand on a switch and shouted, "Does everybody want to see a stomach explode today?"

As if trained to do so, in unison, the crowd yelled, "Yes! Yes! Yes!"

The pig person pushed the switch up.

The belt began to slowly move.

A short pig person picked up a leg of beef and held it in the air. Everyone watched. Then he bit into the leg so deeply that his teeth tore three days' worth of meat off the bone.

Everyone cheered and the wheelbarrow people began eating.

While shoveling and snarfing sounds filled the grand party atmosphere, slave Dinkies ran back and forth filling steaming cups of coffee, serving chilled mugs of beer and wine, and bottles of virus-free water. As the belt moved past, the wheelbarrow people grabbed food, voraciously stuffed it into their mouths, ate quickly, and begged for more. At the end of the conveyor belt, the overly made up wheelbarrow women's stomachs were not as big as the stomachs of the people who stood at the beginning of the belt. They didn't clog their mouths with as much food as the people at the beginning of the belt. They couldn't. Before it could get to the end of the belt, most of the food had already been eaten.

One extra-large wheelbarrow person, with triple chins, stood next to the middle of the belt, grabbed an entire pizza, and shoved it into his mouth.

Another wheelbarrow person, with two chins, waved a piece of fat pie in front of his face and shouted, "Way to go, Mush Mouth."

With grease dripping down their chubby chins and spattering on the front of their shirts, half the of wheelbarrow people applauded; and with fat-filled saliva flowing from their slobbering lips, the other half roared encouragement and kept right on cramming more and more food into their mouths and gobbling it down into their bloated stomachs.

While the wheelbarrow people continued to greedily gorge themselves in a contest to see who could make their stomach explode; and pig people used plastic poles to try and turn the fallen, whimpering wheelbarrow person off of his back, Tommy slipped away from the concealment of the trees and made his way back to the secret tunnel complex called the Grotto.

He was not afraid to walk through the tall forbidden green grass, walk under or touch trees, or wade through a stream. He knew the green grass, wood, and water virus wasn't real. It was only used to keep the pig people out of the forest and away from the water and all green growth. The walkways in Blue Town were covered with long canopies; and when it rained, the pig people stayed inside until the streets dried up. If they were let loose, or permitted to stand in a simple shower of rain, the truth about the virus would be known. Then, the pig people would cut down the trees, rip up the land, and pollute the waterways. Years of biological recovery would be reversed. The incubation of plants and the nurturing of the lakes, rivers, and streams would stop. The pig people believed that if the virus infected them they would mutate into midget Dinkies, be forced to become agriculture slaves, be forced to pull rickshaws, or work the wheelbarrow people buffet. The threat was a good control mechanism. Most of the pig people feared it, but now, more and more were becoming unafraid.

Walking toward the Grotto, Tommy circled McQueen's father's old burnt-down farmhouse. When Sproat's scabs had discovered the secret water tunnel entrance through the springhouse of the farm, they destroyed it. In its place, a pool, the size of a small lake, bubbled with greasy brine created from the dumping of chemicals used to force methane gas from deep in the ground. Now this brine fouled the once clear cool water that came from the springhouse and had forced the Dinkies to move the entrance.

After Tommy walked past the weeds that grew in the black ashes, he tramped up over the hill, and stopped at the new entrance to the Grotto. Here, underground, the little Dinkies who had escaped from the farms, the rickshaw taxi companies, and the wheelbarrow buffet lived in a secret society. At night or on rainy days they would come out and dance among the green grass, swim in the canals, and drink water that was forbidden to the pig people. Because the slave Dinkies served as visible examples of what the virus would do, the Friends of the Earth Corporation and Sproat's men always searched for the Dinkies who had escaped.

Tommy realized he and his Dinky race didn't maim or malign the earth. They didn't suck the life out it. They didn't just live on the earth, they lived with the earth. They weren't pig people who destroyed what gave them life. And that was one reason that even though McQueen knew about the new secret entrance to the tunnel complex, he would never tell the pig people or the Friends of the Earth Cooperation about it. Keeping the pig people on the blue grass was for their own good and for the good of the recovering earth. Pig people could never be told the truth about the fake virus. They were too ignorant.

This new entrance to the tunnel complex was at the edge of a sinkhole. At the surface, it seemed to be a harmless weedy depression in the gray shale. But below, old hand and knee coal mines had been refurbished into a thriving Dinky, underground city, complete with a labyrinth of tunnels, some cut by hand and continually expanded by the little mining Dinkies.

On the surface, solar flares increased the electric from the Aurora Borealis that constantly crept down from the far north. It was a fantastic sight, but it wiped out power for weeks and months at a time. When the Aurora Borealis receded and electricity was restored, radiation, magnetic fields, and the earth shifts interrupted electric motors and generators, causing their armatures to reverse and spin into bird nest tangles. But in the underground hide-a-way, chemical batteries and hydrogen generators fed electric lighting and heating technology and created a livable place for men Dinkies, women Dinkies, and children Dinkies. Although the tunnels were only about a meter high, it was not the hostile environment that would be expected in an underground environment.

At the mouth of the hole in the ground, Tommy stepped down onto the first ledge. He reached into the weeds and vines and pulled out the rope that was attached to an overhanging rock above the entrance to the first tunnel. He hung on and swung to a black stone ledge that hovered over a sinkhole. From this ledge, he clambered down twenty meters on a makeshift ladder. At the bottom, he stepped on secret stones. If an intruder climbed down the makeshift ladder and didn't know which secret stones to step on, the stone would swing out from under his feet. He would fall into mud up his waist.

In a pile next to the mud, the stench of rotting dead animals and garbage hung in the air. This unwanted smell was new here. It was awful.

Tommy felt something was wrong. McQueen had promised the Dinkies that they could live in the tunnels just as long as the virus secret was maintained. Sproat and his men didn't know where the entrance was. Without McQueen's knowledge they had been throwing garbage and dead animals into the entrance hole. They were using it for a dump.

Coughing, Tommy tried to clear his nostrils of the effluvium but he couldn't. He held his breath and walked to the end of the trail of secret stones. At an opening, about the size of a fireplace, he dropped to his hands and knees and crawled through. The tunnel inside was completely black. By feel alone, he carefully balanced along a long ledge until he came to the first room of the labyrinth of chambers and tunnels. One hundred meters farther into the complex, he crawled into a section so large that the strings of electric lights were dwarfed by its expansive space. From here, like the spokes of a wheel, many tunnels led through the earth. An underground stream flowed through one tunnel and waterwheels turned. Their shafts rotated into the sides of secret protective lead, iron, and gold shields that protected the low speed alternators from minor disruptions in the magnetic fields. But when the earth shifted and caused huge disruptions, little balance beams activated brakes that stopped the alternators and prevented the armatures from expanding into bird's nest tangles. The Dinkies' systems produced what couldn't be produced on the surface and what had previously ran the OvalCars: a constant voltage of uninterrupted electricity.

Just as he had done for years, Tommy walked to the head of the huge meeting room and picked up a huge wooden club.

Boom! Boom! Boom! He banged on a wooden barrel.

It was the signal for a meeting.

Beyond the room, grumbling Dinkies came walking from their various tunnels. Lights from little headlamps sent yellow lines of light slicing out the dark tunnels that didn't have electric lights.

From one tunnel, lights flashes and the familiar voice of Sludge rang out. "Who's ever poundin' on that barrel better have a good reason for stoppin' our workday."

"You tell him, Sludge," another voice rang out. "We don't have time for dumb, stupid meetings."

From the dark tunnel where the voices were coming, Sludge and another mutant stepped into the light. Sludge was on the right, covered with dirt, and he had a shovel slung over his shoulder. Another mutant Dinky walked at his side. Although he was black, he could have passed for Sludge's brother. Yellow Ring was just as dirty as Sludge; but he had a yellow scar that wrapped around his thick throat, and in the back of his neck was a huge fold of skin. He always had gumballs in his pocket and chewed them constantly; and when he did, the skin fold on the back of his neck, looked like an extra mouth. He walked with a limp he had gotten when he injured his leg working in the Patagonia tunnels.

As they walked closer, it was as if they were dirt magnets. Dirt and dust surround them. They walked up to the barrel and stopped.

Tommy looked at them and smiled. "Well if it isn't the gold dust twins."

Yellow Ring immediately sprang to the defensive. "Go ahead, Tommy." He shook his shovel at him. "Start your smart mouth. I'll bang it shut with the end of this shovel."

Tommy smiled and Yellow Ring smiled back. The harsh words were all in fun. A Dinky miner's type of fun, where they cut their best friends down with the rottenest things just to get the other's attention, just playful insults.

"What's the meeting gonna be *for*?" Sludge asked, and other Dinkies began to file into the great hall.

Tommy motioned toward the Dinkies who were brushing loose dirt off the floor and sitting down. "I thought you would have told them by now."

"Tell us what?" Yellow Ring impatiently asked.

Tommy put both hands on the top of the barrel and leaned toward Yellow Ring. "I'll tell you when everybody has been seated."

"You always gotta make us wait," Sludge said with his head leaning crookedly against the wall. "But it don't matter. They ain't gonna like your idea anyway."

"Come on, old buddies," Tommy pleaded to Sludge and Yellow Ring. "Give me a change to present my case."

"I guess, we kin," Sludge said. "You and McQueen used to treat us pretty good."

"Used to?" Tommy questioned, but didn't wait for a reply. Instead, he picked up the club.

Boom! Boom! Boom! He banged on the barrel.

The crowd stopped mumbling.

Where old slave irons hung, a few stragglers came through the tunnel and leaned against the wall.

Boom! Tommy banged on the barrel one more time.

As all the gathered Dinkies looked toward him, he stood behind the barrel, spread his arms, and held his palms up. "I have called this emergency meeting because our friend, John McQueen, needs our help."

The Dinkies seemed impressed and whispered among themselves.

A voice rang out, "McQueen's not our friend."

A murmur rippled through the crowd.

Sludge waved the back of his hand to encourage Tommy. "Keep talking."

Tommy stared into the crowd. "McQueen has been taken prisoner by Sproat and his scabs."

"He ain't no prisoner," Yellow Ring, yelled, tossed a red gumball up into the air, and caught it with his open mouth. "Sludge tole us he jist got done watching him stand on the podium and spout off his monthly lies."

"He was there," Sludge said. "But his son and wife were not. His bodyguard wasn't there, either."

Chewing on the gumball that had broken down in his mouth, Yellow Ring said, "So what? His spoiled family don't have to be right next to him every minute of his life. And that stupid bodyguard probably took the day off."

"That may be true," Tommy said. "But McQueen gave me a signal. He needs our help."

"What's he need our help for?" Yellow Ring asked. "He coulda run away after he got done tellin' his lies."

Tommy paused and studied Yellow Ring's face. He saw no compassion, only determination; and the fold of skin that looked like a mouth on the back of his neck looked mean and threatening. Yellow Ring popped another red gumball into his mouth, and the mouth on the back of his neck moved and lost its threatening appearance.

Tommy looked into the crowd for a sign of compassion. "While we speak, they're holding his wife and son hostage." Icy coldness greeted his eyes. He continued. "When McQueen gave his speech, he didn't say anything about the blue grass or the progress the scientist are making on the virus."

Chewing with his mouth open, Yellow Ring folded his hands across his chest and tapped his dusty little foot. "That don't mean nothin'."

Tommy swung his hand down with disgust. "But, I know McQueen. I grew up with him. There's something wrong."

"Sure there is," Sludge said. "Sproat and his men are letting those pig people off the blue grass."

"That's right," Yellow Ring agreed. "I seed 'em goin' in the canals and drinkin' the water, too."

"Before we know it," Tommy said, "it'll be like before the blue grass farce was started. We won't have a decent place to live." With a pleading look in his eyes, he looked to Sludge for help.

Sludge turned his back to Tommy and talked to the crowd. "We ain't da' people dat ruined da land. Doze pig people did it. I seed it. Everyone here has seed it. Let pig people on the green world and they destroy it." He turned toward Tommy. "Why do you think they're called pig people?" He turned back to the crowd. "We all know those pigs, up top, root around and ruin every living thing they touch. If we get McQueen out maybe he'll put them back where they belong."

With a wave of his hand, Yellow Ring dismissed Sludge's suggestion. "Yeah, go ahead, dig him out. Everything doze pig people touches turns to crap." He pointed to the slave irons hanging on the wall. "Yeah, just dig him out. Let him put those irons back on us. Let him turn this place into crap, too."

Tommy took off his floppy hat and used his red bandanna to wipe the sweat off his forehead. "McQueen won't turn this place to crap."

Yellow Ring looked offended. "How do you know dat?"

"He's not like the pig people. He cares for others. He cares for the earth."

A narrow-faced Dinky, with sad eyes, stood up and held his hat in his hands. "When the pig people still had computers, they weaponized the weather. Said it was for the defense of the nation. They created droughts and floods. For profit and power they sent great tsunamis toward their so-called enemies. The world never recovered from that great fiasco. Something is being dumped into the water ways again. The scientists report phosphorus levels are much higher than the pre-phosphorus levels."

Yellow Ring nodded and the mouth on the back of his neck looked like it had smiled. "So what? We already know about how they used the weather for weapons." He cast the narrow-faced Dinky an irascible scowl. "What are you worried about them being preposterous for?"

"Yeah," agreed Sludge. "Let them be funny. They're nothin' but a bunch of clowns anyway."

The Narrow-faced Dinky reached into his hat and took out a folded piece of paper. As if he hadn't heard what Yellow ring and Sludge had just said, he replied, "Just because they can't weaponize the weather anymore, they can still kill a lot of people."

Yellow Ring turned toward the crowd. "What are they going to do? Make people laugh to death?"

Realizing what Yellow Neck and Sludge had just said, the narrow-faced Dinky's eyes widen with comprehension. 'The word is phosphorus, not preposterous."

Sludge threw up his hand. "Well, talk so we can understand. Don't be using those high flatulent words.

The Narrow-faced Dinky nodded, unfolded the paper, and fixed his gaze on it. "Large amounts *phosphorus*—" He paused for emphasis and continued, "Large amounts of *phosphorus* is raising because of the zebra mussels. Just as before, they have changed the way the nutrients are being moved and the food web of our freshwater canals is not working."

"What do you mean not working?" Yellow Ring asked. "Those canals look okay to me." He popped a green gumball into his mouth. "If dem zebra mussels can live in dem canals, so can everything else."

50

As if he were reading from a book, the narrowed-faced Dinky lowered his head and raised his voice. "Zebra mussels have reduced the tiny animal and plant life that once floated in the water by filtering particles from the water and depositing them in bottom sediments."

Yellow Ring jerked his head with such furry that he looked like he was talking out of both mouths, but the mouth in the back of his neck didn't have a gumball jumping around inside. "Who cares about animals and plants," he said. "Specially ones you ain't never seed?"

Tommy couldn't understand why Yellow Ring was so closed-minded. He wanted to tell him how wrong he was, but he held his frustration. "The bigger plants and animals can't exist without the little plants and animals," he said. "It's a food chain."

"So what?" Yellow Ring said and smiled a cocky smile. "Who wants to eat a chain?"

Laughter waved across the crowd.

Tommy didn't know if they were laughing because of the fake mouth in the back of Yellow Ring's neck or his smart remark.

The narrowed-faced Dinky shook his head with disgust. "The changes in climate, over fertilization, and the dumping of sewage are causing the increased phosphorus."

Yellow Ring reached into his pocket for another gumball and shook his head with a defiant shake. "So what?"

The narrow-faced Dinky lifted his head. "This creates dead water zones. Colder and denser water stays at the bottom and cannot be replenished with oxygen by moving to the surface."

Sludge vigorously shook his head. "I ain't believin' none of that crap." He stood up. "The scientists said that ain't gonna hurt nothin'. In the end, it'll work its way out."

Pleading, the narrow-faced Dinky turned his palm up and talked directly at Sludge. "You can't believe what junk scientists are paid to say. And nothing worked its way out before."

As if he had the answer to the problem, Sludge wagged his head around. "Those dead water zones ain't dead. They just got too many living things in 'em. They're suckin' up all the oxygen."

"That's right," Yellow Ring said with his hand in his pocket. "All they gotta do is kill some ahh dem fish."

"That's what they said before," the narrow-faced Dinky said. "And look what happened. We had to dig canals to direct the water away from the phosphorus and make new living zones. Now these zones are the only ones left on the planet. We can't let the people off the blue grass. They'll ruin the new zones, too."

Sludge raised his voice and yelled directly at the narrow-faced Dinky. "What are you? Some kind of scientist? Those canals were built so that the great Orangeville dam could be built. Everybody knows that lake is just a vacation resort for McQueen and his scab buddies."

The crowd roared in agreement.

Wait!" Tommy said, and waved his hands in the air. "That's not true. We have to dig him out."

A Dinky, who had been sitting quietly with his head down, raised his hand. "You're trying to make us believe McQueen can be our protective mother." He raised his head and flashed Tommy a superior grin. "We don't need another mother. We have already been born."

The narrow-faced Dinky agreed with Tommy. "We have to dig McQueen out."

With a mischievous look on his face, Yellow Ring looked directly at the narrow-faced Dinky. "What do you mean *we?*"

The narrow-faced Dinky put his hat back on his head and sat down.

Tommy knitted his brow in thought. He was losing the argument. "Look!" he said, "you all know McQueen has helped us keep this complex secret."

"It ain't no secret no more," Yellow Ring said and lifted his hand to throw a red gumball into his mouth but didn't. "Those pig people are throwing dead animals in our entrance. They ain't nothin' but ignorant hogs."

"What are they trying to do?" Sludge said. "Stink us out of our home?"

A Dinky with a long face and a comb-over rose to his feet and stood in a crouched over position. His forehead furrowed as if he were in pain. "I think we're still safe."

Yellow Ring squinted at him with suspicion. "How do you figure that?"

The Dinky ran his hand over his comb-over hair. "If they knew it was our entrance, they wouldn't be throwing dead animals into it."

53

"We don't know that for sure," Yellow Ring said. "Sproat and his band of scabs ain't got no brains. What little they had, they killed with booze."

Lowering himself to the floor, the Dinky with the comb-over muttered, "That's one more reason we have to dig out McQueen."

A Dinky with extra big eyes stood up. Jerking his hand next to his face, he said, "When the pig people tried to ruin the world with computers and atomic tests, Mother Nature fought back." He smiled a big I-told-you-so smile. "She cooled the earth's molten iron core, and that changed the magnetic fields, erased everything the pig people had saved on tapes, disks, computers, and sticks. Mother Nature will fix the earth again." In a dismissive gesture, he waved his hand down and tilted his head. "We don't have to dig anybody out of anything."

Yellow Ring gave a resigned shrug. "If they wanna ruin the world up there, let em."

"That's right," Sludge chimed in. "Let them rot in their own filth. We'll be safe down here."

Tommy picked up the club and pointed it toward Sludge. "What one person does, affects everyone. We must keep the pig people from destroying what livable space the world has left."

As if he were flicking the statement away, Sludge lifted his hand and flicked his fingers backwards. "They already destroyed it for us. That's why we live down here."

Yellow Ring wagged his head around in arrogant circles, and the mouth on the back of his neck opened and closed. "We ain't gonna help nobody who lets pigs turn our entrance into a stinkin' dump."

From far in the back of the crowd, a hunched over Dinky rose up and shouted, "McQueen let warriors go on uncontrolled strikes." He swung his fist down. "Bottle water services have been lost for weeks. The scab replacement warriors are rampant with incompetency and inadequate command." He jerked his fist at Tommy. "Can you stand there and say McQueen is doing the job of Chief Earth Officer? Can you truthfully say that he is keeping an orderly society of pig people?"

Another Dinky stood up in the center of the crowd. "McQueen's not doing his job. He's not a real Chief Earth Officer. He has no power."

Yellow Ring reached into his bulging pocket for another gumball. He pulled his hand out too fast. Red, white, blue, and green gumballs flew into the air, spattered onto the hard-packed dirt, and began rolling down the incline of the tunnel floor.

He bent over and tried to pinch the gumballs between his thumb and finger. They slipped out and kept on rolling. He swung his hand down and tried to scoop them up, but the gumballs continued to evade his grasping hands. He took a fast step forward and bent over. A machine-gun-like stream of gas putted from his behind.

"That's it, Yellow Ring," Sludge said and laughed. "If you can't catch 'em, shoot 'em."

The crowd of Dinkies broke into a ripple of laughter.

Yellow Ring straightened up. His ears reddened and he snarled at Sludge. "Quit actin' like some kinda nut." As if he had just remembered

55

what he was doing, Sludge whirled around, ran ahead of the rolling gumballs, and stopped. Then, he placed his shovel in front of the gumballs and scooped them up.

The laughter eased.

A Dinky, leaning against the wall, pointed at Tommy. "McQueen's not in his right mind. His old youth camp brain-washing has caught up with him."

Tommy waved the small end of the club back and forth in a negative motion. "It isn't his fault."

The Dinky leaning against the wall, stepped toward Tommy. "Well, it ain't our fault. He's in charge. All he cares about is that treasure he has the key for. It *is* his fault?"

Another Dinky, wearing a pinstriped suit, stood up and shouted. "Because McQueen won't keep his promises and wants all the treasure for himself, we have to smell dead animals."

As if he were digging the air in front of his face, the Dinky against the wall waved his shovel. "We can't exactly waltz in there and get him out. We'll have to dig another entrance."

In the middle of the crowd, a Dinky wearing Ben Franklin glasses stood up. "That's right. After his friends dumped brine into our old entrance, he didn't help us dig a new one. We don't have time to dig a new entrance and dig a tunnel just to get a worthless Chief Earth Officer out of his own shelter."

"Tell it like it is." Yellow Ring jerked his shovel at Tommy. "Why should we help McQueen? He couldn't make it as a warrior, so they made him a Chief Earth Officer. He can't be trusted."

At the back of the room, a Dinky jumped up, took off his skullcap, and waved it in the air. "Where has McQueen been? He was supposed to be our friend. He was in power when the scabs blew up our water tunnel. Now he's letting them destroy another entrance."

The Dinky at the wall jerked one hand into the air. "He's just a pig person." He put his other hand to his face and pinched his nose with his fingers.

"Orant! Orant!" He grunted like a pig. "We ain't gonna help no pig people."

"McQueen has shown he doesn't care about us," Sludge said. "We don't care about him."

Yellow Ring waved his shovel in the air. "We ain't got time for this dumb, stupid talk. McQueen has the key to the greatest treasure ever found. We can't afford to sit around like he does. Everybody hast to git back to work."

The crowd roared in approval, turned, and began funneling back into the tunnel system.

Boom! Boom! Boom! Tommy banged on the barrel.

No one stopped.

He pleaded, "There is no treasure. Won't anyone help?"

Walking away, Yellow Ring looked back over his shoulder and shouted, "Tell McQueen to use that key. With the treasure he'll get, he can buy his way out." He continued walking, looked down, and stopped. He bent over, picked something up, and showed it to Sludge. "Look! A gumball."

As the others walked away, one Dinky with a black and white collar stopped and turned toward Tommy. A look of sadness appeared on his face.

"Will you help?" Tommy asked.

The Dinky didn't shake his head yes or no. With the look of a tired salesclerk, he said, "Where there is darkness the light will shine. Don't worry about surface evil. Eventually it will change to goodness. Our responsibility is the evil that is within our immediate surroundings."

Tommy lowered his voice and pleaded, "But I need help now."

Drooping his shoulders and shaking his head, the Dinky shuffled away and blended into the blackness of the dark tunnel.

"Thanks for the help, friends," Tommy said to an empty room and left.

Climbing out of the entrance hole, Tommy thought about how he could get McQueen out of the shelter. If he had to dig a tunnel himself, it would take weeks. Sproat might move McQueen by then. He might even have him killed by then. Tommy needed another way to get him out.

CHAPTER 3

After his monthly address, McQueen was unwillingly taken to a windowless holding station. Sitting in a plastic prisoner chair, he waited for Dinkies to come with rickshaws and wheel him and the lazy guards back to his home and the shelter.

As his eyes adjusted to the dim light of the hallway, the pungent odor of urine and a whiff of decomposing flesh seemed to bounce off the filth-flanked walls. Next to the wall, gray fur, on leather-like skin, wrapped around the bones of a rat that had died long ago. A ways down the hall, a guard staggered through the weaving bodies of his fellow guards and stopped a few meters from McQueen.

Moving in a foot-sliding slouch and looking like he had just got his bearings back, the guard made his way toward McQueen. When he looked like he was going to fall flat on his blood-flushed face, at the last second, he thrust his hand against the cement block wall and caught his balance. Teetering, he took careful steps and lifted each foot higher than necessary.

When he was in front of McQueen, he stopped and held himself up against the cold concrete wall. McQueen looked up at him. Grease, oozing down from the roots of the tall hawk-faced man's slicked back hair, made his forehead seem wet.

He peered down at McQueen. "Hey, old buddy, how much money did we collect today?"

McQueen realized the guard was so drunk that he didn't know to whom he was speaking. "They haven't counted it yet," McQueen lied. "How much did they get yesterday?"

Expressing bafflement, the guard squinted one eye and rubbed his unshaven chin. "I'm not good at numbers." He wrinkled his sweating forehead. "But what's the difference. We have more than enough money, now. But our old buddy, Sproat, always says it's not enough. He wants more."

McQueen stood up. He hoped he could convince the drunken guard to tell him what they planned to do with him. "You look like you're worn to a frazzle." He gestured to the chair he had just gotten up from. "Sit down. Take a break."

The guard kept his hand on the wall. "Frazzle." He laughed a sputtering laugh. "I'm worn to a frazzle." Being careful not to fall over, he lowered himself into the chair. "That's better." He sucked in a fat stomach-expanding breath of air. "Thanks, buddy. I'm worn to a frazzle."

"Any time," McQueen said. "Do you have any idea what they are going to do with McQueen?"

The guard shook his head slow and easy. "I've never seen McQueen. They said he was going to make all the pig people stay on the blue grass, so they threw him in that shelter."

This was new to McQueen. He wondered how many pig people the guards were letting off the blue grass. He wanted to know more, but he would have to keep this drunk talking. "Could McQueen really make them stay on the grass?"

"I don't know." The guard ran his hand across his greasy forehead. "It doesn't matter anyway. The people go off just about whenever they want."

McQueen fumed in silence, but asked, "But don't you control them?"

The guard laughed and jerked his hand into the air. "Pretty soon we won't be able to control them at all. Sproat's money making days will be over."

McQueen wished the forced control Sproat had over him would end. He looked at the guard with hope in his heart. "Then Sproat will let McQueen out?"

The guard's eyes grew wide. "No way. McQueen has the key to the orange turn. They say it opens a big underground treasure chest."

McQueen knew Sproat wanted the key, but he wanted to know what he would do to get it. "How's he going to get the key from McQueen?"

With the back of his hand, the guard wiped the slobber from his mouth. "He's gonna starve it out of him, ain't going to feed him a thing." He slumped down in the chair, weaved, and started to fall.

McQueen reached out and shook the guard's arm. "But what will the pig people say?"

The guard caught himself and sat up with a jolt. "Sproat can't let him out. He'll tell the Friends of the Earth Corporation what we're doing. We'll all be recycled." He waved his hand in a circle. "Nobody lives through recycling?"

"I don't think he would recycle everybody."

The guard squirmed in the chair. "Yes he will. He wants that treasure for himself. If he keeps the pig people on the blue grass, Sproat will never get near it."

"But everyone knows there is no treasure?"

The guard's voice barked with agitation. "Yes there is. If McQueen don't tell him where it is, Sproat's gonna let him starve to death."

"You've got to be joking. Sproat wouldn't really do that."

As if he had just ran a foot race and was completely exhausted, the guard breathed with labored breaths. He didn't answer.

McQueen had just made his monthly address. He wouldn't be expected to make another one for a full month. That would be enough time to starve to death or make him so weak that he wouldn't know what he was doing. Again, he put his hand on the guard's arm and shook it. "Would Sproat really starve McQueen to death?"

The guard's breathing slowed. Barely audible, he said, "What?" His chin drooped and rested on his chest. He was falling asleep.

McQueen raised his voice and shook the man. "Would he let him die?"

The guard jerked his head up off his chest. "Sproat has the Friends of the Earth Corporation are paid off. Except for keeping people from getting recycled, Sproat does anything he wants." He let his head fall to one side. In a drunken stupor, he muttered, "If Sproat says McQueen hasta die, then he hasta die."

"But what will Sproat do with McQueen's son?"

The guard didn't answer. He had passed out.

A pair of guards walked down the hall, stopped in front of the sleeping guard, and laughed at him. Then, they escorted McQueen to a waiting rickshaw and transferred him back to the hallway that led to the virus containment shelter in his corporation-protected home.

At the door to the underground containment shelter, four guards picked McQueen up and threw him through the open doorway. Trying to resist, he tripped on the door threshold, flew across the room, and landed face first. Still moving, he skidded across the hard concrete floor and banged his head against the stone wall. He held his aching head with one hand; and with his other hand, he pushed himself to a kneeling position. When he turned around and looked up, Sproat stood there with his chubby hands on his flabby hips.

McQueen pleaded, "Can't you find a better place to keep me prisoner?"

Tapping his foot in front of McQueen's face, Sproat folded his arms across the top of his fat belly and he looked down at him. "You'll be just fine in here."

McQueen put one foot forward and stood up. "What did you do with my son?"

"That's privileged information," Sproat said and looked to the red-headed guard who stood in the doorway. "Your guard, Tony, doesn't even know that."

Looking for a hint of weakness that might help him escape, McQueen stared into Tony's green eyes. Sometimes guards with red hair had good-humored intelligence. Although this guard had red hair, his eyes showed no intelligence. With his eyes sparkling with stupidity, the guard waved his antidote gun around as if it were a toy. "If we want you to know anything, we'll tell you."

"But I'm the Chief Earth Officer," McQueen objected. "If the Friends of the Earth Corporation find out what you're doing, you'll all be recycled."

Pain and concern filled Tony's face. "They wouldn't recycle me?" he said and looked to Sproat. "Has anyone lived through that?"

Sproat flashed Tony a big cocky smile. "No one is going to get recycled." As if he had just run up three flights of stairs, he slumped into a plastic chair. "My best friend is in charge of recycling."

Now McQueen knew why the scab warriors were so incompetent: Regardless of their ineptitude and poor physical condition, every one had been given a fraudulent diploma and graduated from warrior school.

Tony's face relaxed and he slouched against the doorway. "Maybe we should bake him in front of a hot fire like we did to his bodyguard."

Sproat frantically waved his hand in a negative gesture. "We won't have to do anything like that, yet."

"Well, Johnny McQueen," Tony said with arrogance in his voice. "Be a good boy. Get back down on your knees and do what we tell you to do. Maybe we'll let you live."

McQueen didn't get on his knees. Knowing that Judd had been held in front of a fire until his body had burnt brown, he wanted to lash out. But Tony wanted an excuse to torture him, too. Mc Queen wasn't going to give him one. He forced himself to stay calm. To make it worse, he was not used to arrogance such as this. As Chief Earth Officer, for years, he had been respected. To have a guard that wasn't fit to wear any uniform act and talk to him like this was irritating.

He cocked his head to the left and looked at Tony. "You have no idea of what is right or wrong."

Tony laughed a mocking tee-hee laugh. "We know what's right. We're always right."

"If I ever get out of here" — McQueen clinched his fist — "I'll show you what's right and what's wrong."

Sproat leaned back in the chair and exhaled a great whoosh of air. "Look, McQueen—" The chair shifted. As if he and the chair were about to tip over, Sproat jerked.

McQueen was amazed that the plastic legs on the chair were holding Sproat's enormous weight. The legs were bending but they hadn't broken, yet.

Sproat leaned forward and continued. "Why don't you wise up, McQueen? Quit fighting for nothing. We only live once. This is it. There is no heaven or hell."

Sproat was going against everything McQueen's father had taught him. McQueen wanted Sproat to understand how life really was; but in case the chair legs broke, he wanted to be far enough away that Sproat wouldn't fall on him. He turned, sat on the tiny bunk, and looked up at Sproat. "But the stones of life tell us different."

"There is no such thing," Sproat said with a definite finality in his voice. "This is it. One shot at life is all you get. Just give us the key. Then you'll be able to enjoy every bit of the rest of your life."

McQueen placed his head in his hands. Now he knew why Sproat was the way he was. He didn't care about the world. He was a 'right now' person.

He lived for today and the future be damned. He would be a hard man to reason with.

McQueen dropped his hands from his face and looked up. "Captain Sproat. Do you know that if the pig people go off the blue grass we will all die?"

A big smile spread across Sproat's fat face. "You know the virus is a farce. While you've been enjoying an easy life in your corporation-protected home and taking pleasure trips to your secret Orangeville resort, we've been out there swimming in the water and running around in the green forest."

Tony stepped forward and pointed to himself. "Look at us. We're as healthy as ever."

McQueen stared at Tony's belly. It stuck out like a huge overinflated balloon about to burst. "I wouldn't say you're healthy. However, it isn't about a single person's health. It's about the future health of the world."

Sproat waved his hand down. "So what if we're not around for the future, we'll live for today."

"If you want a future for our children, you must give the earth a chance to recover."

Sproat's voice gained a mocking tone. "I wasn't privileged like you. I was never granted the right to reproduce."

"When I captured my five hundredth Dinky, I earned the right to select a mate and marry."

Tony placed his hands on his knees and giggled in Sproat's direction. "Not having the right to reproduce never stopped you."

In a defensive manner, Sproat waved his hands in front of himself. "They're not my kids."

"Whose are they, then?" McQueen asked.

As if he were uncomfortable, Sproat squirmed in the chair. "Those kids belong to the people who had them."

"Don't you care about your own flesh and blood?"

Sproat quit squirming. "I don't have time to care about other people's kids."

"Don't be a worry wart," Tony said. "The earth has recovered. Anybody can have as many kids as they want."

Sproat nodded his fat head in agreement. "Very soon, things will be like they used to be."

McQueen objected with a violent pitch to his voice. "Things can't be like they used to be. The canals are the last link to an inhabitable planet. When the pig people destroy the canals we'll all die."

Sproat stood up and placed his heavy foot on the edge McQueen's bunk. "The only things that are going to die are the liars in the Friends of the Earth Corporation who think they are saving the earth. And when they die, the world will be a better place."

"Maybe for a few wild months," McQueen said and edged away from Sproat's stinking foot. "But as the years pass, a community has to have fixed laws and patterns." He waved at Sproat's foot. "Laws, like keeping one's stinking feet off a person's bed."

An amused expression formed on Sproat's face. "My feet don't stink. And anyway, what do we need laws like that for?"

"Those laws and patterns put people into their appointed places. Without those laws, people fear what others may do to them."

"Nobody will be afraid of anything," Sproat said with a triumphant smile. "It will be a new world." He lifted his foot from the bed and kicked the plastic chair. It flew against the wall. He raised his voice. "Just like I'm free to put my foot anywhere I want, and kick anything I want, people will be free to do what they want, too."

McQueen glanced at the plastic chair. "The people *were* free." He waved his hand around in the air. "And what did they do with that freedom? They exploded atomic bombs and spread radiation over the world."

"So what?" Sproat said with a careless flick of his wrist. "That doesn't mean it will happen again."

McQueen whirled around and talked directly into Sproat's face. "Don't bet on it. History has shown that we can't change the human condition of wanting more. In the name of progress, the *free* people cut down most of the trees. For a few dollars, they polluted everything they touched. In your new world, they'll do it again. Laws will be more necessary than ever before."

As Sproat goggled with amazement, Tony said, "We'll have laws." He smiled a full-toothed exaggerated smile. "We'll make it illegal for the pig people to go off the blue grass without paying us."

"The pig people don't know it," McQueen said. "But they need to stay on the blue grass."

Backing away from McQueen, Sproat grunted. "What for?"

"People need to be organized within established levels. Laws must be equal for all. If they are *not*, life will be no good."

Sproat nudged Tony's elbow and gave him a conspiratorial wink. "Laws are equal if I say they're equal."

Tony giggled and his lard-balloon stomach quivered.

"It might be funny now," McQueen said, "but if you let everyone do what they please, food and water will become scarce. Every drop of water and every scrap of food will have to be protected People will form mobs and eat all the food and drink all the safe water. There will be no freedom at all, only fear and starvation."

Wagging his head like an arrogant cartoon clown, Sproat replied, "I always get a big hoo-hah out of that starvation story you keep feeding the stupid people. The buffet for the wheelbarrow people will never run out of food." He stopped wagging his head. "Face it, McQueen. Money is power. With enough power we can have all the freedom we want." He held out his hand. "When you give us that key we'll have enough money to buy the world."

McQueen placed his hands into his pockets and leaned back. "There is no key."

Shaking his head in denial, Sproat pulled his hand back. "But we know there *is* a key, and we know you have it. We want that key and the money in that treasure chest."

"I'm telling you three is no treasure. And if there were, it wouldn't fix the earth. No one can spend money when they're dead."

"How do you know?" Tony said. "Have you ever died?"

McQueen could have told him about the time he had died from the poison antidote and had been brought back to life by the Patagonia Dinkies' serum. And he could have told him about the recent water reports about the coral in the warm waters. It was worse than the year before. The recovering coral was not the vibrant colors found in healthy reefs of years ago. Poisons being returned to the waterways no longer caused the coral to become the warning colors of brown or discolored. Now, it was dead. He could have told them that the coral was like the canary in a coal mine. If it died, others were not far behind. He could have told Sproat this and more, but he knew it was all useless. Sproat and his friends were acting like the ignorant pig people they were. He didn't answer.

Tony repeated the question. "Have you ever died?"

McQueen turned his head away from Sproat.

Sproat stepped to the doorway and turned toward McQueen. "If you're not going to answer, I'm leaving."

McQueen kept his head turned.

Sproat turned to go, but stopped in the doorway. "We'll see how good you can talk when you're starving to death."

He turned and left the doorway.

Tony grinned without humor. "When we forget to let you out, you'll find out what it's like to die"

McQueen stood up and took one step toward the door. "You can't let me in here to die."

Standing in the doorway, Tony formed circles with his fingers and placed them over his eyes. "Watch me."

Whomp! He slammed the thick iron door.

Clank! He locked it.

McQueen sat on the bunk and looked around the room. He knew he was locked in the most secure room ever built. It was built that way to convince the pig people that the Chief Earth Officer would always be safe from the virus. The virus fallout shelter always contained enough food and water to last for months. If they locked him in, he could survive long enough to find out where they were holding his son. He could escape, rescue him, get the key, and take him to Orangeville.

He went to the stack of emergency ration boxes and opened one. It was empty. He tried another. It was empty, too. He tried them all. They were all empty. He shook the translucent water jugs. They contained nothing but air. Sproat and his men had cleaned the place out. They were actually going to starve him to death.

He studied the walls of stone blocks. If he could find the right block, then it wouldn't matter what Sproat did. When the Dinkies were going to overthrow the Friends of the Earth Corporation, they had dug an escape tunnel that traveled more than two hundred meters under the safety of the blue grass and came out at the beginning of a path that traveled through the green grass and into the forbidden forest. No guard would go there without a protective white suit and a facemask. The guards were ordered to fill that tunnel in, but they didn't want to go the rigmaroles of suiting up and pretending to be afraid of the green-grass virus. So they ran over the outside entrance with the big wheel of a steam car and crushed it closed. If it hadn't caved in, part of the tunnel would still be there. If McQueen lived long enough, he might be able to dig his way out. All he had to do was find the right block.

He put his ear to the iron door and listened. Tony was already snoring. McQueen went to the opposite wall and began feeling the stone blocks. They were all solid. He hoped a few of Sproat's men hadn't become ambitious and filled the tunnel in. He squatted down and leaned the small of his back against the corner of the room. A block moved. He turned around and pushed on the block. It moved easily. He pushed more. Steel rails appeared under the block. The little Dinkies had put the rails down for the block to move easily. He pushed the block more. It moved with a loud grating sound. He stopped pushing, stood silent, and listened for Tony. Nothing. He went back to the iron door and put his ear against it. Tony's snoring was slow and easy. He was in a deep sleep.

McQueen went back to the block, sat on the floor, and pushed the block in until he could see inside. Light from the room shone a few meters into the dark recess. Beyond the movable stone, a tunnel with yellow dirt walls and a yellow-dirt floor was a welcome sight.

He knew if he crawled into the tunnel and couldn't dig his way out on the first try, he would have yellow dirt all over his uniform. Tony would see it. He would know he was digging his way out.

He stood up, kicked his boots off, and stripped to his underwear. Then he dropped to his hands and knees and crawled into the tunnel. Spider webs laced across his face and tugged at his eyelids. He reached up, brushed them away, and continued crawling. When the floor began to slant upward, he knew he was crawling toward the surface. Now it was pitch black. Twenty meters later, Klunk! His head ran into the caved-in section of the tunnel. He could go no farther. He had hit a dead end. Here was where he would have to start to dig his way out. If he remembered right, the steam car only caved in a few meters of the entrance, but he had never checked. He would be able to dig a few meters out with his bare hands, but if the more of the tunnel had been caved in, it could take him weeks to dig himself out.

He shrugged and asked himself, "What else do I have to do?"

He began to dig.

Gravel and chunks of concrete cut into his fingertips.

He quit digging.

He would have to find or make something to dig with. His knife would have been nice. But Sproat had taken that. He decided to crawl back to the room. There might be something there.

Back in the room, he rummaged through the thin plastic food and water jugs, but he didn't find anything to dig with. Sitting on the plastic chair, he surveyed the room for something he could use for a shovel. He studied the metal legs of the bed. They could be used like a pick and loosen the dirt, but they were riveted to the frame. He leaned over.

73

Apparently Sproat's weight had weakened one of the chair's legs. Now it was bending under McQueen's weight.

That was it.

He tipped the chair until all his weight was supported on one plastic leg. Then he jerked downward.

Crack! The leg broke.

Thump! He fell on the floor.

Bam! Bam! Tony banged on the iron door. "Keep it down in there. I'm trying to sleep."

McQueen jumped up off the floor and yelled through the door. "Yes, sir."

He waited a few minutes and checked the door again. Tony was asleep. With the broken chair leg in his hand, he crawled back into the tunnel.

Digging with the chair leg was easier and faster, but the dirt piled up underneath his body. Before he realized it, he was stretched out digging while lying on his stomach.

The tunnel ceiling was getting too low. He would have to do something with the dirt. He decided to spread it out on the floor. The tunnel ceiling would be close, but the entrance couldn't be that much further. When he got to it, he could crawl on his stomach.

He pecked at the dirt with the chair leg until so much dirt piled up under his body that he couldn't use his arms anymore. He stopped, breathed in a few breaths of musty air, and crawled back out of the tunnel.

He had to find a place for the dirt. He decided to put it in the empty food boxes. Tony or Sproat would never look in them.

Dragging the empty plastic food boxes behind him, he crawled back into the tunnel. After a short rest, he filled the boxes with dirt and pulled them back out. Stacking them in the room, he saw that the yellow dirt had stained the sides and bottoms of the boxes. He would have to hide them on the bottom of the stack of clean empty ones. He did that and walked toward the tunnel. He was too tired to continue. He pushed the block back in place, put his uniform back on, and fell asleep on the hard floor.

***

The iron door clanked open.

Tony yelled, "Hey! Git up!"

McQueen opened his sleep-filled eyes and looked up. Tony stood over him with his hands on his hips. "You're still alive? I thought maybe you kicked the bucket."

McQueen sat up. "Did you bring me anything to eat?"

"Why? Are you hungry?"

"I haven't eaten for two days."

Another guard stood in the doorway. He tilted a jug of wine to his purple lips and happily gurgled wine down his throat. Grinning a wet-wine smile, he said, "Don't worry about it." Laughing, he wiped his mouth on the sleeve of his shirt. "Food still tastes the same."

Tony broke into a loud horselaugh. "Food still tastes the same. Har, har, har. That's a really good one." His jovial demeanor changed. He held out his hand. "Give me the key and I'll feed you."

McQueen cocked his head at an insolent tilt. "I keep telling you, I don't have the key. Don't you have any compassion for a fellow warrior?"

"You're not a warrior. You're an ex-chief earth officer."

Giggling, a guard in the doorway butted in, "We're not room service. Where do you think you are, in a hotel or something?"

In-between his guffaws, Tony managed to say, "We just come in to see if you were still alive."

The guard in the doorway silently mouthed the words ha, ha, ha, and said, "If you hurry up and kick the bucket, we can get out of here."

Tony looked toward the broken chair. McQueen realized the chair leg, he had broken off, was still in the tunnel. If Tony noticed it was gone, he might find the tunnel.

McQueen stood up and blocked Tony's view of the broken chair. "If you're going to let me die, why don't you tell me what you did with my son?"

Tony's face took on a look of seriousness. "Your son will be just fine. They'll train him right."

"Did they put him in a youth camp?"

"He could be anywhere."

"You just said, 'They'll train him.' He has to be in a youth camp. Which one is it?"

Vigorously shaking his head, Tony said, "I never said he was in a youth camp. Don't worry about it. Even if we let you go free, you'll never find him."

The guard in the doorway waved his hand signaling for Tony to come out. "Come on, Tony, let's get out of here. If the old geezer won't give us the key, we'll just let him die."

Tony walked out the door and slammed it behind him.

After he made sure Tony wasn't coming back, McQueen took off his uniform, moved the stone, and crawled back into the tunnel.

As he crawled through the dark tunnel, more spider webs stuck across his face. He batted them off and kept on crawling. At the end of the tunnel, he banged his head into loose dirt. He figured three more meters and he would be out. With the broken chair leg, and in the darkness of the skinny tunnel, he picked at the dirt. When he couldn't pick anymore, he used his hands to scoop the dirt and push it behind him.

Three meters later, he was not out. Hoping the steam car hadn't caved in more of the tunnel than he could dig out before he died, he rested for a few minutes and dug some more.

After he had dug one more meter, a beam of yellow light flowed into the darkness. He paused and breathed in the fresh outside air. He continued to dig; but not wanting to open an opening right at the feet of a guard, he dug slower and carefully.

When the hole was big enough, he poked his head through the opening and breathed a sigh of relief. Tall blue grass surrounded his head, and no guard was there to greet him. Extra bright light shone between the blades of grass. It hurt his dark-adjusted eyes. He cussed under his breath. The pig people had messed up the sky again. Pretty soon the ozone layer would be so thin everybody would have to wear sunglasses.

Mechanical whiffering and wheezing came from his left. Squinting through the spangled sunshine beaming through the grass, McQueen looked toward the road. Three of Sproat's men, in a steam car, were coming his way. He pulled his head back into the hole.

He figured he should wait for dark. But if he did, Sproat's men might see the opening.

He eased his head out of the hole and watched. The steam car was closer now. Three pig people were standing at the edge of the blue grass. While one man steered the steam car, the other two men held illegal squirt guns. Laughing, they squirted the pig people. Believing they would mutate into Dinkies, the pig people gasp in horror.

Sproat's men let out roaring belly laughs.

Being too fat to run, the pig people took off at a brisk pace. Between labored breaths, one of them managed to huff out, "We've been shot with virus water. Get us to the decontamination chamber."

As the steam car puffed past, leaving a trail of black coal smoke, Sproat's men continued squirting water into the air and laughing.

McQueen figured the smoke would be a good smoke screen and would cover his escape; but after he crawled back through the tunnel and put on his uniform, the smoke screen could be gone.

As fast as he could, he crawled back to the room, put on his uniform and boots, took one last look around the room, and crawled into the tunnel. On the other side of the wall, he put his hands on the block and had a pleasant thought: After I pull this block back, Sproat's idiots will think I vanished into midair.

He pulled on the block. It didn't move.

Like a sick joke, laughter exploded from the other side of the wall and was interrupted with, "Where do you think you're going?"

McQueen craned his neck around and looked back.

It was Tony.

He had his fat foot on the block.

"Grab him!" the other guard shouted.

McQueen whipped his head around to start down the tunnel. . On his hands and knees, he took one step with his hand, moved forward, and fell flat on his face. Tony had grabbed his feet.

Tony giggled like a sick kid picking the wings off a fly.

McQueen pulled and strained. One of his feet gained a few inches, but Tony's hands came forward. They held tight. McQueen dug his hands into the yellow dirt sides of the tunnel and pulled. As his body stretched, dirt fell from the sides of the tunnel. He lost his grip. Tony was pulling him out. McQueen re-gripped and kicked one foot hard and fast. It broke loose. Kicking his free leg as fast and as hard as he could, he pulled again. No forward movement. Tony still had his other foot.

"He's kicking my hands off," Tony yelled to the other guard, "Get in here and help."

"I'm not going in. It's caving in."

McQueen kicked both feet harder and faster. He felt the dirt from the ceiling of the tunnel falling on his back. Salump! The ceiling behind him caved in. His other foot broke free, but his back and legs were buried in dirt. He quit pulling and gasped for air. Loose dirt, in front of him, fell in his face and covered his eyes. He jerked his head. The dirt flew away. Far down the tunnel, the pinpoint of light from the tiny hole at the end beckoned. The whole damn tunnel was caving in. As if they were powerful steel claws, he dug his fingers into the dirt floor and pulled. As he dragged his body forward, more loose dirt in front of him fell. He pulled again and again, until, at last, he was free and crawling as fast as he could. Stray spider webs no longer draped over his face, but crumbling dirt fell from the ceiling and continued to pepper the back of his head. Ignoring it, he rushed forward until he rammed his head into the dirt surrounding the tiny exit hole.

Digging with his bare hands, dark topsoil flew behind him. The tiny hole grew. Within seconds, he crashed through.

Outside, in the bright of day, he stood up and broke into a trot. When he looked back over his shoulder, the steam car was gone, but one of Sproat's guards pointed at him. The guard knew he was escaping.

The sirens of Blue Town whined with warning. Amazed by the sudden mass movement of pig people, McQueen froze in place. The sirens were drawing them outside. They would enjoy the intermission from their usual routines. McQueen jerked himself out of his amazement and took off running. He sprinted past the orange danger signs and into the green grass. Increasing speed, he jumped over a stream. Running with great laboring strides, he jumped into a stand of thick brush. Whoosh! He came out the other side. If he could make it to the Grotto, Tommy and the Dinkies would hide him.

Racing across a stretch of gray sand, sharp pains erupted in his side. He ignored them and rushed on. After he quickly wound his way around the doomed land that held a scattering of still and empty wooden houses, he was out of breath. He bent over, placed his hands on his knees, and looked up. Like a cold breath, white vapor hung over the surface on the brine-filled lake. Walking on bare brown land and working his way through a milky mist, he circled around the lake and stopped at the stone foundation of his father's old burnt out farmhouse. He needed to rest, but he had to get the key. He tromped down the old cellar cement steps. Although it had been over twenty years since the house had burnt down, the smell of burnt wood still hung in the air. He went to the iron latch that was hid up under the steps and pulled. It didn't move. He put both hands on it and pulled again. It moved, but rust crunched and fell from the lever. The stone slid just a few inches. He turned his hand sideways and reached in. With his little finger, he managed to press down and drag out the orange turn key. The key was encased in a chip made of lead. The lead protected the key from magnetic field interruptions caused by the space junk, magnetic pulses, and earth shifts. He slid the key into the secret sewn in flap around the waistband of his underwear and ran halfway up the stairs and stopped.

Two of Sproat's men were at the top of the steps; but their backs were turned to him. Both men raised their arms and pointed down the road.

Without thinking and without warning, McQueen ran up the stairs, held his hands in front of himself, and shoved both men. They tumbled into tall weeds and onto the ground. Before they could get up and see what had happened, McQueen had run past them.

Just below a yellow and black sign warning, 'VIRUS STAY AWAY', McQueen was so exhausted he was unable to do anything more than breathe. Beyond the sign, a thin blanked of white grime, from a dust storm, covered the ground and coated the bare branches of dead trees. He stopped, placed his hands on his knees, bent over, and took three deep breaths. If he went to the Grotto the guards would follow his footprints and find the entrance. He couldn't let them find Tommy and his Dinky friends. Even though exhausted, he cut around the Grotto and fled into the forbidden forest. Sproat and his men didn't follow. But he spotted a band of border guards from Patagonia.

The whole force was after him. He wouldn't be able to double back and make it to the Grotto today. Up ahead, something he hadn't seen before blocked his way. Parched brambles baked brown with heat, surrounded young, withered birch and spruce trees. An odor of burnt plastic seemed to hover over a crumbling blanket of dry black moss. A once recovering showcase of what nature could do, if given a chance, was now an ugly plot of dead, fetid land. Wondering what could have caused such a disaster, McQueen circled around the sad place, detoured around a vast field of poison-soaked soil, and headed toward the river below Niagara Falls. Border guards never followed anyone through that river. But he would have to find a place where might be able to cross.

CHAPTER 4

With the sun struggling to throw its gray light through the semi-permanent, dirty-orange haze of a sky that was partially covered with black smoke from the steam cars, Tommy held his little shovel in his hand and surreptitiously slinked around the border of Blue Town.

When he came to the edge of the blue asphalt road, he crouched down and looked at the field of blue grass that surrounded McQueen's home. Although the ruts from the steam car wheels had carved deep impressions into the ground they could not be seen from the road.

Tommy angled toward the house and continued along the rutted dirt track until a stretch of broken glass crunched under his feet. Then he waded into the grass and toward the caved-in escape tunnel. Most of it was covered with tall blue grass.

Off to the left, Sproat's men, dressed in rumpled, tan uniforms were walking around like they were pretending to be guards. They marched a few steps and stopped. Then, like dogs, they walked in a circle, mashed down the grass, and formed a bed. Sitting on the thick blue grass, they opened lunch bags, and snacked on sandwiches piled high with fat-riddled meats and slimy sausages. As fat dripped down their chins and dribbled onto the front of their shirts, some poked their heads into the cover of the tall blue grass and snuck swigs from bottles of beer or other alcoholic drinks. A man with three chins, tilted a bottle of wine to his lips; and in one great swiddle, he drained the bottle. He exhaled a long satisfied hiss of air and threw the bottle. It crashed and fragmented into the broken glass that Tommy had walked around. Now that McQueen was no longer in control, these men seemed to be celebrating his imprisonment with lazy guard duty.

Tommy liked this. It would make it easier for him to sneak into the house and get to the shelter. He crouched low and duck-walked through the tall blue grass. When he was at the library window of the house, he tried to push it open. It was solid. He wouldn't get in there. He crawled under the blue shrubbery and stopped a few meters from the backdoor. As if he were standing for an inspection, a skinny guard with a bowl-over-the-head haircut stood at attention.

This guard was not goofing off. That meant Sproat would be near. Tommy wouldn't get past him. Tommy turned around, crawled to another window, and stood up.

Klink! It didn't break, but someone had thrown an empty beer bottle at the side of the house.

Tommy dropped down onto the ground, crawled back under the shrubbery, and lay perfectly still.

The big idiot of a guard from the front of the house tromped past.

Tommy figured the place was too busy. When the big idiot went past again, Tommy would go back to the caved-in tunnel and try to dig out McQueen.

The idiot guard walked to the back door of the house. While he chatted with the skinny guard there, Tommy dropped to his hands and knees and weaved his way through the tall blue grass until he was at the entrance of the tunnel. In the fresh dirt, hand and knee prints, of a single person, led away from the entrance. The guards hadn't found the prints, and McQueen was nowhere to be seen.

Like a disturbing baby's cry in the night, warning sirens wailed.

From the back door of McQueen's house, the guard with the bowl-over-the-head haircut bellowed through a greasy mouth, "McQueen's escaped! Search the grounds."

In a panic, Tommy studied the area around the tunnel. Mashed-down grass led away from it. It had to be McQueen's trail. To suggest that McQueen had taken off in another direction, Tommy mashed down grass so it would indicate another trail. Then he scrambled over the original broken-down grass trail. Behind him, the feet of guards, swishing through the tall grass, filled the air.

A guard yelled out, "The tunnel's right here."

Tommy scrambled off to the side, lay on his stomach, and looked through the tall blades of grass. A guard's foot, with a thick warrior boot, swished right past his head. He froze. Moving his eyes upward, he watched. The guard pointed at the grass McQueen had tramped down. "Look! He went this way."

Another guard pointed to the fake trail. "No! He went this way."

A herd of Sproat's men stampeded over McQueen's grass trail and obliterated it. Swishing toward the fake trail, their feet whispered past Tommy's head so quickly he thought he would surely get kicked. But he was glad they had rushed to the fake trail. Now, McQueen would have a head start.

Tommy sat concealed in the grass, waited, and watched. Pig people came out of their blue apartment buildings and gawked at Sproat's men. These men were not wearing their white protective suits. They were not wearing their virus-blocking facemasks. They were in plain sight, tramping through green virus grass.

"Hey everybody," a pig person with a yellow baseball cap shouted. "The guards are not afraid of the green grass."

An excited pig person wearing a red and blue cape, jumped from the balcony of his apartment. Like a flag of freedom, the cape fluttered behind him. Thump! His feet hit the hard, blue cement. He fell to his hands and knees and looked to be in pain. Ignoring the pain, he jumped up, swinging his hands in the air and shouting, "The scientists found the cure. We're going to be free."

Another pig person, wearing pink shorts, ran toward the edge of the green grass. As if it were poison, he stopped. More pig people flowed toward the green grass and stopped at its edge. The person in the pink shorts became brave. He slipped off his shoes and wiggled his toes in the green grass. With an excited squeal he squeaked out, "Look! Nothing's happening."

With the loose fat on his butt sagging, another pig person stepped next to him and jumped onto the green grass. As his loose butt jiggled up and down, he jogged around in a little circle once and stopped. Then, he pulled a red squirt gun out of his pocket and squirted himself in the face. Like some kind of happy half-wit, he sang, "Nothing is happening to Sproat's men. Nothing is happening to me. I told you McQueen was a liar."

A puke-covered, drunken blue grass guard staggered to an orange warning sign at the edge of the blue field and held on to its post. He tried to unzip his pants, but did not have the coordination to do it. Giving up, he sighed and urinated in his pants. A pig person walked up to him and asked, "Is it safe to go off the blue grass?"

The guard wobbled his head, opened his bloodshot eyes, and looked down at his urine-soaked crotch. "It has always been safe. McQueen lied to keep you people on the blue grass."

The pig person's eyes goggled with amazement. "What do you mean, he lied?"

"There was never a virus. He claims that you people are too stupid to go on the green grass."

Another guard came up to the drunken guard. "Shut your mouth!"

Pointing to pig people running onto the green grass, the drunken guard tipped back his head and shouted into the sky. "It doesn't matter anymore. People are going off everywhere. We can't stop them."

The other guard grabbed him by the shoulders and looked into his face. "We must keep them on the blue grass. Sober up. It's our job."

The drunken guard lowered his head and put his hand over his tear-filled eyes. "McQueen's escaped," he whimpered. "He'll find out we have taken money to let pig people go off the blue grass. We're going to be recycled."

The other guard opened his mouth to order the pig people to get off the green grass, but the scene before him was unnerving. Hundreds of pig people began massing in a huge group, chanting shouting, waving their hands, and pumping their fists into the air. Some looked nervously over their shoulders and watched other pig people whooping it up, dancing, and rolling in the green grass. They paid no attention to the guard's order. He knew it was useless. The act of going off the blue grass was spreading like an out of control, raging fire. Soon it would engulf the whole town.

The guard closed his mouth.

Another mass of pig people streamed across the field of blue grass and stood beyond the orange warning signs. At first, they bent over and wiggled their fingers into the green grass. Then they joined the celebrating mob and whooped it up, too. More and more pig people rushed over the field of blue grass and herded onto the green grass. Orange warning signs were grabbed, shook, and pulled to the ground. The people cheered and rejoiced. Like drunks rushing to a free booze party, they streamed into the green grass, rolled in it, pulled it out, and tossed it into the air. They jumped into the small stream. Smiling and laughing, they splashed each other with forbidden water until they were out of breath. Others grabbed tree limbs and shook them. Lush green leaves fell to the ground, and a branch was broken off. Like a trophy, the formerly feared, wood-virus-carrying branch was carried above a pig person's head. Top-hatted and wearing a cloak flapping like useless wings, he led a parade of jovial celebrators walking on the green grass in a wide circle next to the field of blue grass.

A hairless pig person, with a crooked eye, jumped into the air. "We're free at last." He pulled an antique cell phone from his pocket. "They fixed the virus. Maybe they fixed the cell phones, too."

Another pig person tugged at the drunken guard's arm. "Turn on the cell phone towers. I want to call someone."

Tommy turned from the celebration, stood up, and walked toward the forbidden forest. Walking along the path Sproat's men had mashed down, he sensed that McQueen was headed for the falls.

CHAPTER 5

McQueen rushed along the river toward the falls. With his heart pounding in his chest and his lungs gasping for air, he forced his legs to run beyond their limits. Just when he thought he could stop and rest, up ahead, menacing masses of black smoke hovered over the tops of the trees. On the other side of the trees, Sproat's men waited in their steam cars. That escape route was blocked.

With his breath coming in ragged gasps, he stopped running.

Watching the approaching smoke, he bent over, put his knees, and sucked in much needed air. Between breaths, he looked back over his shoulder. Downriver, shelf-like rocks jutted out from the cliffs that ran alongside the mighty rushing water. He scanned the banks of the river. Nobody was coming that way.

His breathing slowed. The sound of his heart pounding in his head, faded. Faint voices filtered through the thunder of the water. People were coming upriver. If they were the Patagonia Patrol, they would be afraid of the water virus. The threat of rain would scare them under those shelf-like rocks. He looked up. Not a single cloud obstructed the view of the dirty-blue sky. There would be no help from heaven today.

He thought to make a stand, but there would be too many of them for him to fight. He turned and ran away from the river. After fifty meters, he stopped and stared at a potholed road that encircled a pond that had an unusual shiny surface. Goo on the water, from tree fungus spores, with an iron base that had begun to rust, caused the pond water to glow sour orange. He looked beyond the pond and searched the forest for movement. The glimmer of a luminous gold feather of a mega-mutant blinked once and merged mysteriously into the mist.

Before he had become the Chief Earth Officer, he had been a warrior. He was still strong, and he was still fast; but he was no match for the triple strength of the mega-mutant Indigo people. He knew what he had to do. He had to swim across the rapids and whirlpools on a ghastly stretch of water that would surely pull him down to his death. And, he had to swim across before the mega-mutants chased him to the bottom of Niagara Falls.

When the lakes began to dry up, the river above the falls had been dredged deep. Although it was a failed attempt to keep the hydroelectric turbines running, the river was still as treacherous and unforgiving as before. And he had to find a safe place to swim across.

He had thought about swimming across before, but he was younger then. At that time, he had had enough to eat; and his body was in top physical shape. Years ago, his friend Webb wanted to show off, wanted it to be a "most memorable swim." And it was. He drowned.

McQueen needed to remember the details of that day, and he had to remember them right now. No one had been chasing Webb. People were just beginning to be herded onto the blue grass. All the way to the falls, Webb had taken bets with border guards. He said he needed the money for his family, which was foolish. No one in Blue Town knew how to swim. They were all afraid of the fake virus water. Even if Web had made it, no one would have believed he had went into any water; and even though McQueen had taught him how to swim, the pig people believed that swimming in water was just something that couldn't be done. Just as he was doing now, McQueen and Webb had probed along the high cliffs of the gloomy river and had tried to find a way down. Now the same noise of the crashing water soaked his thoughts with fear. To his right, like throbs of a painful headache, the sound of Sproat's high-pitched voice, screeching orders to his men, cut through the trees and bounced off the boulders. They were getting closer.

McQueen worriedly looked back. Behind a huge black rock, stench from a faint green-yellow fog hovered over a man with his wrists tightly bound with wraps of cord, and his feet were tied together with a wire. Raving like a booze-addled alcoholic, the man hobbled toward McQueen.

When he was a few meters from McQueen, wind whipped up a lone dust devil. With fear in his eyes, the man tried to quickly hop away from the little whirlwind, but he lost his balance and fell to the ground. Squirming like a snake, the man covered his head with his hands for protection, and cried, "Get it away from me. Get it away from me!"

As quickly as it had come, the whirlwind danced away. The man took his hands from the top of his head and looked up at McQueen. As misery clouded his eyes, he spoke. "Did you see them?"

"See who?" McQueen questioned.

The man began to speak, but it seemed that whatever he was going to say fell from his mind. He just lay there with his mouth agape.

Fearing the Indio people were close and may tie him up, too, McQueen asked the man, "Did the Indigo people tie you up?"

Babbling unintelligible, the man sat up. His fat-swaddled green eyes stared straight ahead. His dilated pupils matched the outline of his round pumpkin face, and burst capillaries webbed the surface of his red bulbous nose. At first, McQueen figured the man was drunk, but when he opened his babbling mouth, took a breath, and exhaled, an odor of sour milk crawled from deep in the dark cavity of his throat. The man wasn't drunk. Apparently he had wallowed in self-pity, taken drugs, and believed to be victimized for such a long period of time that his mind had become too flawed to be of use to anyone, including himself. It would hard to say that this babbling idiot could contribute anything to human civilization.

McQueen reached down and untied the man's hands and feet. The man quit babbling, drew his knees up to his chest, and hung his head between his knees.

Looking around the area searching for Indigo people, McQueen tried to communicate again. "Did the Indigos do this to you?"

As if he were in another world, the man didn't acknowledge McQueen's presence. McQueen turned to leave but noticed 'Dim Wit' had been crudely painted with a stick or something onto the back of the man's shirt. The accurately descriptive sobriquet was some one's sick joke. Being on drugs, a long time, and being called the humorous name, surely had diminished the man's self-esteem and adequately dehumanized him.

McQueen decided to help him anyway. He bent over and grabbed the man's hand. To help him to his feet, he pulled. But before he could pull the man upright, the flash of many gold feathers caught his immediate attention. If he stayed, the Indigos would not only tie him up, they would throw him into the raging river. Shaking his head, he took one last look at the man.

"Sorry," McQueen said. "Sproat's men will be by in a few seconds. You look like one of them They'll help you."

The man continued to stare straight ahead.

It was a terrible waste of life, but the man would be a fitting addition to Sproat's band of idiots.

McQueen let the man's hand go free and took off running.

With the Indigos close behind, McQueen rushed farther upriver and searched for an opening, searched for a walkable or climbable path, searched for a place where he could get down to the river and cross.

Breathing with much labored breaths, he stopped, placed his hands on his knees, and tried to remember what was up ahead. He knew that beyond the foot of the falls, the river surged green, but it had dirty-gray veins of scum and white foam that resembled a heaving marble floor. If he tried to cross there, he would never be able to stay afloat in the airy foam. Down from that, the river slid quiet and slowed. He wanted to swim across there, but the steep cliffs blocked his way. Faint voices of his pursuers coming upriver picked in his ears. He glanced to his right. Curling smoke from a steam car diffused the light from a weak sun. Sproat's men were there, waiting. He couldn't go that way.

With his eyes focused on the water, he started running upriver, again. To his left, the water turned into a dull jade green, and sped up, swift, smooth and ominous. Where the walls of the ravine ran close to the rocky shore, the water boiled, eddies threatened, and the river turned into terrifying rapids. He could not cross there.

He kept running. The taste of coal smoke from the approaching steam cars invaded his mouth, flowed into his throat, and stung his lungs. He tried to spit the carcinogenic threat from his mouth. It didn't work. He kept searching for a place to cross. Where big black rotten-tooth-looking rocks lined the shore, the water slashed forward, faster and faster. Like a hungry demon from the deep, the slashing water leaped and leaped. It would surely swallow anyone brave enough to get close. He could not cross here. He kept running.

When he finally saw a place where he might be able to cross, he sauntered along the brink of the rapids and worked his way down a long spiral staircase of jagged stones until he was at the edge of the river. Here, he walked to a solitary hollow and looked to his right. He was a kilometer from the bottom of the falls.

He looked to his left. He was two kilometers up from the whirlpool. Now that he was close to the river, he felt the unsympathetic aura of its surroundings. On his side of the river, as if they were drinking, dark limestone rocks slanted down into the turbulent water that continually mined the banks and broadened the riverbed. On either side of the river, the cliffs rose straight up, three hundred meters; and even though the bottom of the falls was a kilometer away, the hungry-looking waters in mid channel boiled and bubbled; and streams of foam raged along and spread across the water in all directions. He wasn't in the safety of the blue grass anymore. He was in a strange world.

He picked up a piece of driftwood and threw it into the current. It spun around in circles until it was trapped in a little whirlpool, where it turned and twisted against the sharp rocks. When it escaped, it looked like a splintered wooden soldier; and just as Webb had done, the wood floated into the main stream and rushed on down to the rapids. There, it was sucked into a dangerous whirlpool where it spun until it was suddenly swallowed with one effortless sip.

In desperation, McQueen looked around for some kind of help. There was none. For a moment, he couldn't breathe. He felt trapped. His body tensed. He sucked in a quick stream of air. Letting it out, he prayed that the great river would not swallow him, too.

He knew the flow through this deep ravine of rocks, even at the edges, would be over one hundred meters deep. There would be no wading in. There would be no way to check the strength of the current. He would have to dive in. He would have to hit the water swimming.

He looked up at the top of the cliff. Like some monstrous offspring that had gone mad because of an unnatural mating, the Indigo people started making their way down the long spiral staircase of jagged stones.

He figured he was doomed, until, at the top of the staircase, Sproat's men stood with stones in their hands. As if they were afraid to be the first to cast a stone, they stood there watching each other. A man, not as round as the others, stepped to the edge of the staircase, and rolled his stone down it. As it bumped harmlessly down the rocks, the other men raised their rocks above their heads and roared in approval. Then, as if taking turns, they began throwing rocks at the Indio people. In unison, the Indigo people turned toward Sproat's men.

McQueen figured the Indigos would run back up the staircase and give chase. When they did, he would follow, run up the staircase, and find a better place to cross the river. But when a stone came close, the Indigos effortlessly tilted to the side and avoided it. They made a game of dodging the stones, until, one Indigo caught a stone and threw it back at Sproat's men. With fear flashing from their lard-like faces they dropped the stones. As fast as their chubby legs could carry their ballooned bodies, they ran away. That diversion was gone. McQueen wouldn't be going up the staircase.

With a fixed and reckless stare, he turned his attention back to the water. The roar of the distant falls traveled downriver like a preliminary drum roll signaling the debut of some great life or death event. The power manifested from the rapids hypnotized him. It moved him with a sense of awe and terror. The gigantic power of the place would make any man feel helpless. He looked to the staircase. Sproat's men were gone. The Indigos had thrown all their stones. They were coming down after him.

Trapped and outnumbered, McQueen needed another diversion. He didn't know if it would work, but sometimes in battle when a man acted as if he were possessed the enemy would quit advancing. Like watching a circus sideshow freak they would stand in awe.

As if he were going take on the whole tribe, he let lose a vicious war cry and advanced. Amazed at his actions, the Indigos stopped on the staircase and stood still, watching with great interest. McQueen thought he may be able to act crazy enough to walk right past them. But the Indigos only laughed and began jumping down steps three at a time. They were halfway down those spiral rocks.

McQueen flexed his legs for the dive, but didn't dive. He remembered his clothes would weigh him down. He needed every advantage he could get.

Keeping an eye on the advancing Indigos, he kicked off his boots, ripped off his uniform, and tossed it aside. Clad in only his underwear, his nerves throbbed and his heart thudded in his chest. Breathing in deep long breaths, he stepped to a ledge of rock that jutted over a clear and deep, glassy-green pool. Above the roar of the crashing water, the shouting voices of the Indigo people sputtered in his ear. From the sound of their voices, he knew they were close, too close.

Although he could feel the wind from their grasping hands at his back, he didn't look back. He sprang from the rock, headfirst. The cold current yanked at his senses, immediately swiped at his elongated body, thrust him sideways, and pulled him under. Using overhand strokes, he powered himself to the surface. The sudden shock of the cold water caused his lungs to feel constricted. He sucked in short gasps of air and felt his muscles tire from the effort. If he were going to live long enough to swim across, he would have to conserve his strength and energy. He switched to the breaststroke, threw his head back, and thrust his chest forward. His breathing came easier.

This isn't so bad, he thought, but his confidence overcame his common sense. He switched to dog-paddling, and the current swept him towards the whirling water of a huge whirlpool. Convinced he could steer himself around the whirlpool, he paddled with ease, almost enjoying the thrill ride. Right next to his ear, Ker-plop! Something plunged into the water. Then, a dark round shadow of something falling caught his eye. It zinged past his body, and Ker-plop! It plunked into the water, too. He looked up. From the high cliff, Sproat and his men were hurling rocks. He stroked toward the side of the cliff, smiled inwardly, and relaxed. Now he was out range of the raining rocks.

But his safety was short lived. Just ahead, and to his left, like broken teeth in a dark giant mouth, razor sharp rocks stuck out. And the current was towing him toward them.

"What are you doing?" he shouted to himself. "This is no place to take it easy."

He went back to the breaststroke and barely powered past the sharp rocks. It was all he could do to keep his body from being torn to shreds.

With labored breaths, he swam along the fringes of the whirling whirlpool. More rocks rained from above. Sproat's men had moved. One rock thunked in the center of his back. His breath rushed from his lungs and sent a hollow crying pain over the water. Pain was replaced with anger. With powerful overhand pulls, he cut through the whirls for a few brave strokes; but then, the whirling water swept him down and across the river. There was no bank on the far side. It was a smooth sheer cliff. There were no jutting rocks. There were no overhanging trees. There was nothing to grab onto. Fighting the pull of the whirlpool, he looked downriver. The high jumping rapids loomed close. No boat could float or anything could live in that water. The swirling current sucked him closer to the center of the whirlpool. He felt cold cramps in his toes and fingers. His body tossed and skittered around the whirlpool, faster and faster. He needed to slow down, not panic. He scissored his legs and tried the long powerful sidestrokes. The whirling whirlpool held him in its watery spin. It pulled him, more and more, to its center. On top of the cliff, dark outlines that resembled big black eggs with sticks for arms and legs, jumped up and down cheering. It was Sproat's men.

More rocks fell.

The terrible center of the whirlpool of death was right before McQueen. He stroked harder, but made no progress. He kicked his legs with extreme force. Still, the river was conquering him. To get a fraction of a second of a rest, he switched back to the dog paddle position. The current grabbed his legs and sucked him downwards. He stroked his arms and fought to the surface. Spinning water broke over his head and blinded him. He began to breathe in water. Spiraling in a tighter and tighter circle, he searched for a way out. The white and green foam-filled water raged all around him. He wished he had surrendered to the Indigo people. No one had ever crossed this part of the river before. It felt like he wasn't going to either.

Losing strength, each stroke became more and more difficult. His will to go on waned. Voices of the dead, who had tried to cross but failed, called to him. Their weeping invaded his mind, and their ghostly hands tugged at his feet. As if taunting him, the raging and hissing waters of the whirlpool seemed to be laughing in his ears. If he got through the whirlpool, he would have to contend with the rapids. He kicked at the thick current of the whirlpool and searched for a rock, anything to help him. Even if it was only the toe of his foot on a little stone, he could rest, even if it was for only a second. Then he could suck in one gulp of waterless air. But there was nothing below, only deeper water. And now, that water was in his throat.

He felt that this might be a fitting end to his life. He had finally found something that he could not change or defeat. But it was nature, not man. He wasn't prepared to go where his friend Webb had gone. He wasn't prepared to drown.

He slipped below the surface, but refused to give up. He held his breath and struggled against the waters that hurled his dying body deeper and deeper. A life or death, fight or flight sensation, controlled his mind, took over his body. In a last desperate attempt to live, from deep inside, he found new strength. He forced his arms to make powerful strokes. Finally his head was above the whirling water.

He took in deep needed breaths of life saving air. When he turned on his side and switched to the slower but less exerting sidestroke, he looked up. Sproat's egg-shaped men ran along the high ridge above him. At first, he figured they were running from the Indigos, until, Kerpluk! A stone hit the water right next to his ear. Again, Sproat's men were gathering and throwing stones down at him. Kerplunk! Kerplunk! The stones bombed into the water. He switched to the over hand strokes, made two strokes and, Klunk! A rock hit him in the back of the head. The current sucked him into the center of the whirlpool. Everything went black.

Dizziness invaded his mind, bobbing, turning, and twisting his thoughts. In a dreamlike state, he felt an arm around his neck and the sun on his face. The surface became smoother. Someone had towed him from the vortex and was pulling him towards the rocky shore; and that person's other hand was feeling all over his body, searching. He heard the boiling commotion of the tremendous rapids. When he opened his eyes, all he could see was spume flying into the air. He felt the rocky shore plow up his back and stop. Waves of water lapped at his feet. He looked up. Everything still whirled round and round. Like cymbals, the sound of the water crashed in his ears.

He wondered what kind of man could have pulled him through that death spiral. Whoever it was, he had to have tremendous power. McQueen rolled to his stomach and lifted himself to his hands and knees. Shaking his head, he looked down. The last rays of the setting sun reflected his shadow. It trembled on the gray rock.   Another shadow appeared next to his. He turned and looked up.

CHAPTER 6

McQueen leaned back on his elbows, and tilted his head back. The silhouette of a face hung above him. He tried to make it out; but looming light from the tangerine sun flared around the dark face; and the brightness of the light stung his eyes. He slammed them shut and turned his head away. Water lapped at his bare legs. When he opened his eyes, scum and littered water frothed around his feet and streamed along the shore. With each wave, like a devil's black tongue, patches of tar and oil laved his rock-beaten legs. Beyond that, many fish of different shapes filled the water. Some had two heads, some had three. Irregular blotches of colors amidst predominant rusty-orange scales covered their bodies; and a white film clouded their wide lidless eyes, a sure sign of death. The sand between the rocks was blackened with poison oil. But a single crayfish, stained oil-black, moved its pinchers in a defensive mode. McQueen jerked his feet out of the water.

He looked to his right. A rusting pipe jutted out from under a huge rock and gushed oil into the water. *Even in the harshest conditions, the will of the crayfish to survive continued.* He hoped his son could survive, too. When he found him they would get away from all this. They would go to Orangeville.

McQueen had reached the limits of his ability to save the world. He was exhausted. His hand was covered with blood, but there were no cuts. He put his hand to his head. A lump was forming where the rock had hit him. Holding his head, he looked off into the distance. The sun dipped behind the cliff. The dark face that had been hovering above him was gone.

He turned to his right. Just beyond his reach, his boots sat on a rock. Next to his boots, his uniform had been folded neatly and it was dry. He didn't know how that had happened. Feeling where the waistband of his underwear should have been, panic struck his chest. The chip wasn't there. If the chip had fallen into the river he'd never get it back. If the person who had towed him to shore had found it, the future of a new world could be lost. He felt for the chip again, only lower. The swift water had almost ripped off his underwear. The chip was still there. He exhaled a sigh of relief. Wagging his groggy head, he tried to get his bearings.

The sun was down, but like the ropes of an opened Dinky capture net hovering from a tree, it sent secret shrouds of evening light into the gray air. He looked around. A rush of some impending charging frenzy was in the misty air. Now that he was on the other side of the river, and Sproat's men and the Indigos were not, there was no reason for him to be afraid. There was no reason to be on the defensive, but he was. He felt the need to run, but he did not know why.

He donned his uniform and sat on a rock to slip on his boots. In the heel was a secret compartment that contained a tiny first aid kit. Antibiotic salve and needles with thread for stitching wounds was in there, too. If he needed stitches, he could sew the wound closed; and to avoid infection, he could smear the antibiotic salve on the cut.

When he tried the trick combination to the lock in the heel of his boot, he couldn't remember the numbers. He felt the lump on his head. The bleeding had stopped, and he felt the familiar sting of the antibiotic salve. He didn't remember putting that on. He felt the wound again. Tiny knots from his stitched-up wound indented the tips of his fingers. He couldn't have seen the back of his head to do that; and he didn't remember trying to blindly stitch up his head; but he remembered that with a head injury, number sequence was one of the first things to go; and because he couldn't remember the combination, he knew he had a concussion.

He felt thankful to be alive. But he wanted to know who had pulled him to shore and nursed his wound. If his memory loss was temporary, eventually he would remember who took care of his head; and he might remember who had pulled him from the river.

Again, he tried to unlock the heel in his boot. Again, he couldn't. He pulled his boots on, stood up, and looked for a way to get away from the river. Except for a tiny dark opening that ran through a solid rock cliff, un-climbable rocks lined the shore. Off to the left of the opening, a bluish-purple baby whirlwind of filth danced on a pool of stagnant black water. He had never seen one of those before. It was something else the polluted world had produced.

He looked at the raging river and then at the cave-like opening. It was the only way out. Still shaky on his feet, he took a deep breath and walked into the dark hole.

Inside, except for one tiny shaft of yellow light that came from deep inside the cave, it was pitch black. He slapped his hands on his thighs. "Where's there's light, there's life. I hope it's the right kind."

In the dark, he took three steps forward. Sounding like a thousand miniature fans buzzing, a slew of black bats raced over his head. When he reached up to cover his head, his legs crumpled under him. His head hit the side of the cave and everything went black, again.

When he awoke, he was lying in a bed of straw, and he was away from the river. Twinkling arcs of gray-sky-light peeped through the dark green leaves of the tree he was under. Somehow he had gotten out of the cave and had slept through the night. He turned to his side, bent to rise, and studied his boot. He wanted to do something with it, but he couldn't remember what.

He looked at the nametag on his uniform. It read, McQueen. At least he knew who he was and remembered something about blue grass, but his head hurt. He sat up and lowered his head into his hands.

He remembered Sproat's men chasing him and swimming across the river, but he couldn't remember why. The haze in his head cleared a little. He remembered that he had a concussion from the rock Sproat's men hit him with. On the verge of crying, he said out loud, "Stay on the blue grass. I couldn't do it. The great Chief Earth Officer just couldn't keep the pig people on the blue grass."

He wondered if it had been Tommy or the wise old Dinky who had said, "Pig people don't walk forward into the future of a better life, they run backwards, and as fast as they can."

Rubbing his sore head, McQueen stood up. Dizziness took a hold of him. He sat back down. All he needed was a little rest. Then he would be okay. But that was what he had thought just before that rock hit him in the head. He was amazed he wasn't dead.

Suddenly afraid, he looked around. The silver sun sent warming beams to long yellow grass and a gentle wind prodded the tops, making them sway like little friends welcoming him back into the world of the living. Now he realized why the Egyptians build pyramids and worshiped a sun God.

There had to be a decent person somewhere close. Someone had saved him and stitched the cut in his head. Maybe that little Dinky, Tommy, had tossed a rope out, lassoed him, and pulled him to shore. When they were kids, they always played jokes on each other. That little trickster could be hiding in the grass, playing a joke on him right now. McQueen could almost see him trying to make him laugh. He would be walking in a curious way. Not a walk and not a run. He would be walking in a series of little leaps. They were exactly the same length; and as if he were rowing an invisible boat in midair, he would be swinging those short arms. And that smile: Even on a cloudy day, McQueen could see his magnificent teeth gleaming in the gray light.

McQueen stood up and moved his arms like Tommy's rowing motion. His head hurt but not as bad. He cupped his hand to his mouth and shouted, "Tommy, are you out there?" Pain, from shouting, shot to his brain. He quit rowing his arms, grabbed his head, sat back down on the straw bed, lay back, and closed his eyes.

The next time McQueen opened his eyes, a little bird was twittering amongst the branches above his head; and a canteen of water sat on a covered metal food plate. Little brown ants were crawling around the plate looking for an opening.

"Go ahead, little ones," he said. "We'll search together. I'll search for my past, and you can search for food."

He sat up and felt the wound on his head. This time, he didn't feel the stitches. He felt a bandage. From the feel of it, he knew it was the kind of bandage that dissolved with time. Whoever bandaged his head wasn't coming back.

Most likely, it would be the last of the help he would get. There was a time when it wouldn't have mattered. He could have swum the river with no problem. He wouldn't be here watching tiny ants searching for a scrap of food. He would have fought his way, forced his way through ten times anything Sproat's men or the Indigos could throw at him. He looked at his scraped hands. His strength had dwindled. He had lived on the blue grass too long. Before he could stop himself, he called out, "Danielle, where are you?"

A sudden realization of remorse dawned in his mind. Sproat's men had killed her. He wondered if they had killed his son, Miles. Sharp pain flooded his head. Sproat's scabs had taken him. He wasn't sure, but they could be holding his son in a youth camp.

He grabbed his head and held it until the pain subsided. He couldn't stay where he was. Sproat and his men had time to cross the river. They would be coming anytime now. Unless Sproat and his band of idiots stoned them to death, the Indigo people would be coming, too.

He brushed the ants off the covered plate and opened it. Inside, strange brown and green chunks of food that resembled sawdust and salad waited to be eaten. At first he thought it may be poison, but the person that saved him hadn't tried to kill him, so the food had to be okay.

He ate all the squares of food except for a few little pieces. Then, he tilted the plate and dumped the pieces in front of the searching ants. "Everybody eats today." Watching the ants scramble for the food, he picked up the canteen and took a few swigs of water.

From behind him, a jovial voice rang out. "Hey, rich guy, you have so much food you can dump it on the ground?"

McQueen jerked his head in the direction of where the voice had come from. A smiling faced Dinky walked out of the tall golden grass. It was Tommy. He had his floppy hat pulled down over his big ears, and his big round eyes shone with happiness.

McQueen stood up and walked toward him. They embraced and tears fell from McQueen's eyes. "Tommy, I'm really glad to see you," he said. "I was losing my mind.

"Tommy looked up at McQueen's stitched head. "Yes, I can see that. It was coming out the back of your head. Good thing you stitched it closed to hold it in."

McQueen laughed. It made his head hurt, but Tommy's foolishness made him feel better.

Tilting his head, Tommy jerked it as if he were going into spasms. Making a distorted face and pointing to his crossed eyes, he said, "It's easy to get knocked senseless. Sproat and his half-wits learned how to throw rocks." He gestured to McQueen's head. "Good thing they hit you in the head, instead of someplace important."

To keep his head from hurting, McQueen smiled a faint smile.

Tommy stopped jerking his head and looked at the ants on the plate. "I'm starved. You got any more food?"

McQueen pointed to the plate. "Didn't you bring this?"

"Are you kidding? I just found you."

"How did you know where to look?"

"Don't you remember? You said that if something ever happens, meet you at the falls."

As if he were trying to shift memories back into his brain, McQueen moved his head from side to side. "Now that you mentioned it, I vaguely remember telling you that, but I got hit pretty hard."

"Tommy smiled big. Maybe you just got a big hangover."

"I wish I did. I got to get my head straight. I have to find Miles."

"Ahh ha!" Tommy said and his voice ratcheted up a little. "I almost found him."

With hope and anticipation, McQueen asked, "Where?"

"I went to see if they were keeping him at the Blue Town youth camp."

"Was he there?"

Tommy's shoulders sagged and his voice lowered. "I don't know. Sproat and his gang had the place surrounded. I couldn't get in."

McQueen shifted his weight and leaned back against the tree. "Sproat doesn't want another McQueen running around the world disrupting the unnatural flow of things. Wherever Miles is, they'll keep him there until he's propagandized. I have to find out which camp they're keeping him in and get him out."

With a patronizing tone to his voice, Tommy said, "In the old days you would have never let them brainwash anybody. You would just go in and take him."

"These aren't the old days. Now, I have to plead geriatric exhaustion. I couldn't even swim across that river."

With an expression that he had no intention of believing McQueen was over the hill, Tommy smiled. "You still got it. You're a prince of peace. No one ever beat your five hundred mutant Dinky capture record."

McQueen smiled at his victorious memories, but he knew his best days were gone. "Thanks for the confidence, Tommy, but I know what my limitations are."

"You mean you're giving up?"

McQueen jerked his head up with a start. "I never gave up in my life."

113

"That's right," Tommy said with a look of delight. "There's no use starting now."

"I might not be able to flaunt my power, but I can still use my mind." McQueen reached up and rubbed his aching head. "That is, if I ever get it back."

"What do you mean, if you ever get it back? You seem just as sharp as ever."

"I'm still fuzzy on some things."

"Like what?"

"I don't know why, but the image of an oil-soaked crayfish keeps clouding my thoughts."

"Oh that," Tommy said. "That's what happened to the crayfish when they dumped oil and sludge into the river. It's the start of a refuse for the refuse."

A pang of sadness entered McQueen's mind. He gave Tommy a sidelong glance. "Refuse for the refuse?"

Tommy placed his right foot on a rock, rested his elbow on his knee, and stared into space. "That's what the old Dinky said."

"If someone doesn't do something; and soon, Sproat and his men will make the whole world a refuse for the refuse."

Concern filled Tommy's voice. "That will be a sad place for your son to grown up."

A sense of urgency filled McQueen's chest. "I've got to get back to the Grotto. The Dinkies will help."

"I don't mean to throw cold water on your hopes," Tommy said, and a wounded look appeared in his eyes, "but they've changed."

"Don't they know they must help or perish?"

"They don't care. They say they can live underground and let the pig people die in their own filth. They won't help."

"What made them change?"

"Yellow Ring convinced them that you have the key to the Orangeville treasure, and that you use Orangeville for a vacation resort. But the clincher was when Sproat's men dumped dead animals in the Grotto's entrance."

McQueen looked down at the ant-covered plate. "I should have stopped that whole treasure deal before it got started."

"Why didn't you?"

Leaning away from the tree, McQueen threw up his hands in despair. "Everyone has to have a dream. They have to have a goal or a belief that something will change their lives for the better. I thought the promise of a treasure would keep the people's hopes for a better future alive."

"It couldn't have been all bad," Tommy said. "It worked for seventeen years."

McQueen felt his face grimace with disgust. "That may be so, but the pig people can't or won't accept the complications of protecting the earth. They prefer to have others think for them. As Chief Earth Officer, I should have known greed would take over."

"Sproat and his scabs are a sneaky bunch. There wasn't much you could do."

"I took it easy, too long. When atomic bomb tests were stopped, that was a great beginning. But when hydrogen from water replaced natural gas and the gas companies no longer sucked crack water out of rivers and streams, poisoned it, and dumped it down thousand-meter deep wells, I believed the pig people were really changing."

"You had that all wrong," Tommy said and took his foot off the rock. "The gas companies claimed they replaced natural gas with hydrogen, but they didn't. After Sproat's men and certain selected pig people started going back on the blue grass, they weren't afraid of the water or green-grass virus. Then they went into the fields. They went into the creeks. They went into the lakes, and they went any place there was water. Using chemical soaps, they bathed in it. They crapped in it. They even drank it."

"That's why a lot of rivers and streams never ran clear and why water and dry washing clay sales see-sawed."

"You got it," Tommy said. "When the pig people found clean water in some of the canals and lakes was safe to drink, the water sales went way down."

"That cut into the profits of the water and clay companies. Sproat couldn't have that, so he polluted every drop of drinkable water he could find."

"That would explain what is killing the animals they have been throwing into our tunnel entrance."

"That's a shame," McQueen said. "I don't mean to sound heartless and project that I have no feelings for the Dinkies in the Grotto, but right now, Miles is more important."

"The Dinkies will be all right," Tommy said and a look of despair filled his face. "But there are a lot of camps to search. And we can't go back the way we came. We'll have to take the long way around, and there's no telling what we'll find."

Somewhere, a bird of some sort sang a pleasing melody, but the blast of a sick air horn blasted it away.

McQueen leaped up from his sitting position. Tensing for a fight, he turned toward the sound.

"That's probably one of Sproat's drunken men," Tommy said. "He's playing with the horn on the steam car. They're on the move. We better get out of here."

McQueen held up his hand in a halting motion. "Wait! With Sproat's men are after me, it will be a lot of walking, hiding, and sneaking around. On top of that, we'll be going down an unknown path to an unknown world. Are you sure you want to go with me?"

Tommy flashed McQueen a look of delight "Sure I'll go." He shrugged. "What else do I have to do?"

McQueen remembered how they had been on the run years ago when they were wanted dead or alive. "You may not want to live like that again."

Tommy turned toward the golden grass. "It might be easier this time. They don't have our pictures on wanted posters."

The earth shifted. Like seasoned sailors of a rolling ship, McQueen and Tommy swayed with the movement and didn't fall down. One hundred meters away, a streaming liquid, laced with putrid chemicals, rocketed upward, forming a geyser thirty meters wide and shooting five hundred meters toward the sky. Other sections of forest were dying because their roots were being cooked by heat or poisoned.   Usually after a geyser spewed toxic vapors into the air, within five minutes, people close by were killed on the spot.   Estimates predicted the toxic geysers would cause two thirds of the world's land masses to become sterile and uninhabitable.

Backing away, McQueen stared at the nauseating sight.   The wind was blowing the dangerous liquid away from them, but at any moment, it could change direction.

"It may be easier now, but before we didn't have to contend with crack water flying out of the ground." With determination, he tightened his lips. "There are not too many livable places left to search, but if we have to check out every youth camp in the world, we will."

With the wind direction changing, they took off running.

CHAPTER 7

Tommy could see McQueen wasn't in a very good frame of mind. His eyes were haunted with inner pain and his face was drawn. Tommy wanted to do something to change it. He ran ahead of McQueen and stopped at the top of a gully. Trying to encourage him to follow, he looked back and waved his little hand. "Hey, old man, I'll race you to the bottom."

McQueen broke into a trot. Tommy put his feet together; and like a runaway jack-in-the box, he hopped down the steep grassy hill. Like he had done when they had been boys, McQueen jumped off the crest of the hill. Clomp! With both feet placed together, he landed in the soft dirt. He flexed his knees and jumped again. Clomp Clomp! Clomp! He took big leaps and loped past Tommy.

Using his little springing steps, Tommy kept hopping. When he hopped next to McQueen and stopped, he was at the bottom of the gully. McQueen smiled and patted him on the back. "Ha! You never could beat me downhill."

"I could have beaten you in the old days. All I had to do was throw a little water in your face."

McQueen laughed with a deep laugh. "You got me there. It's hard to believe how afraid everyone was of water."

"And don't forget the green grass and the wood."

"Ahh, the wood," McQueen said, and chuckled. "That was funny when your Dinky friends used those wood two-by-fours against the warriors."

"I'll never forget the look on their faces." In his mind Tommy could see Sludge holding a two-by-four and the warriors jumping back like it was radioactive. "When Sludge told them it was wood virus, I thought you were going to bust out laughing."

"I didn't have time," McQueen said. "I was too busy fighting Nelson."

"He wasn't a bad Chief Earth Officer." Tommy bent over and adjusted the one-size-fits-all Dinky moccasin on his tiny foot. "It's too bad he sacrificed his life to make the pig people believe the fake virus was real."

A look of regret ranged over McQueen's face. "Looks like he died for nothing. Sometimes I wish I had never found out it was safe to go off the blue grass." His eyes grew wide with fright. He placed a handkerchief over his mouth, and pointed behind Tommy.

A huge dust cloud drifted out of nowhere and engulfed the area.

With McQueen by his side, Tommy placed a handkerchief over his mouth and started walking up a dusty yellow hill. When the land leveled out, they shook and batted most of the dust off their bodies and clothes, then dropped the handkerchiefs from their faces, breathed cleaner air, and walked along a worn walkway.

While moving his little hands, Tommy talked to McQueen. "The first time people started to go off the blue grass, I tried to tell you."

"Why didn't you?"

"I tried, even came close a few times. But I could never get past all the guards."

McQueen rubbed the bandage on his head. "If you would have been able to tell me, maybe I wouldn't have lived in that corporation house so long."

"Why not? You had it made."

"I felt guilty most of the time."

"What was there to feel guilty about? You exposed the virus farce and then for the good of the world, you kept it secret."

"I know," McQueen said with regret in his voice. "But I knew a few people were going off."

"There was no way you could have known how many were going off. With the money Sproat made letting pig people off the grass, he paid off every one on the Board."

"I never dreamed the pig people could do such damage, and in so little time."

Tommy shrugged. "Well, the damage is done now."

McQueen sadly nodded in agreement. "Real Augur knew what the radiation, the chemicals, and the wide array of pollutants were doing to the reproductive cells of life on the earth."

"But you knew that, too."

"But I didn't know if one pig person was permitted to go off the blue grass, eventually they would all go off and that the destructive cycles of pollution would start anew."

"Do you mean you regret being appointed Chief Earth Officer?"

A spasm crossed McQueen's face. "Sometimes. It's was always difficult to lie and make the pig people believe in a fake virus that turns them into mutant Dinkies." He looked off into the distance. "The radium levels were one thousand times greater in samples when compared to those collected upstream of the water plant. Cracking flow-back water is highly saline and radioactive." He felt his face contort. "For cryin' out loud, oil and gas producers were producing over a hundred billion gallons of wastewater at day. The scientists on the Board said it was okay." He disgustedly jerked his head. "But it was just junk science. I should have figured out that the high readings were the result of flow-back fluid that had returned to the surface and was being pumped into the river." He lowered his head in shame. "I think the real Augur would have made a much better Chief Earth Officer."

The sight of the real Augur burned in Tommy's mind. Although a mutant with three heads, the real Augur was powerful in mind and body; and he was the legend no one thought was real. When Tommy had first seen him, he had been surprised. But when he had seen a three-headed bass and a three-headed frog at Hidden Lake, he should have suspected human life had mutated or would soon. The real Augur had sat under a haze of a green light in a motorized wheelchair. When he wheeled out of his OvalCar and into the blue light, the light had affected the color of his frog like skin; but the change in light hadn't affected his rat-tailed Pygmy assistant, who stood tall and spoke like a machine. He had said, "Augur's brains have mutated. His one functioning head is a combination of the three brains. He has mutated into a Godlike intelligence."

When McQueen had asked, "Can we talk to him?"

The little Pigmy said, "You may be able to get through today. Augur has changed since we rescued him from the sideshow. His mutation has advanced past an intellectual level. Some of my fellow Pygmies say he evolves in and out of the future."

At first McQueen told Tommy that he thought the Real Augur must be some kind of a nut who belonged in a carnival, but when he asked the Pigmy if the real Augur was a mutant, the Pigmy said, "You can ask him, but Augur has trouble talking to common people."

McQueen asked, "What language does he speak?"

The Pigmy told him, "Augur speaks all languages known to man and more. We mere humans are not on the same communicating level as he is. It is difficult for him to lower his intelligence level long enough to communicate with people."

Tommy remembered looking at the real Augur's three heads. The one on the left hung off to the side and rested on the head support. Clear mucus streamed from its weak opened mouth. The head on the right sat solid on the support. Like lifeless wet stones, its eyes stared straight ahead and blinked as if they were on a timer; and its mouth was small and shut tight, but with whimsical abandonment that head would spring to life like some kind of knuckleheaded idiot. The center head resembled a frog's head. The skin had a light green cast to it, and hints of yellow lines crisscrossed his face like a child's scribbling.

When the head on the left, had slobbered out of its mouth, the Pigmy had walked up and wiped that head's mouth. The head on the right had constantly irritated the real Augur with its comical antics. But before the real Augur had gone, he had made McQueen and Tommy realize that if the earth was to recover, the pig people had to stay on the blue grass.

Tommy had no doubt that the real Augur had super intelligence, but he still shuddered at the thought of him.

He shook his head and looked toward McQueen. "When that three-headed genius showed up, were you afraid?"

"Not really," McQueen said. "I suspected more mutations would be found."

"Why didn't you tell me? You know his three heads scared me."

McQueen kicked at the dry dirt beneath his feet. A little dust cloud streamed from the toe of his warrior boot. "I don't know," he said, and kicked up another little dust cloud. "Maybe I thought you would grow three heads, too."

As if it weren't there, Tommy walked through the little cloud of dust. "I don't think I would have minded thee heads if I were as smart at the real Augur."

McQueen turned his palm up and waved it around. "Actually," he said and smiled in Tommy's direction. "The real reason I didn't tell you was because I didn't want to put up with three heads like yours."

Tommy waved off the friendly harassment. "If two extra bodies came with them, three heads wouldn't be a bad idea. I could put the two other Tommys to work while I take it easy."

Nodding, McQueen chuckled. "Always looking for the easy way out."

"Too bad the real Augur can't come and get us and the world out of this mess."

"Even if he wanted to, he couldn't. The way the electricity is messed up, his OvalCar no longer works. His motorized wheelchair is probably useless, too."

Tommy waved dust away from his face and coughed. "It looks like we're on our own. The first thing we have to do is find an easy way out of this dead dust."

As they walked through the dust, it gradually tapered off into a field of dead black grass. At the end of the field the black grass merged with brown grass that merged with green grass that grew under trees thick with lush leaves.

Standing under the coolness of the first tree, McQueen swished his hand in front of his face. "Whew! What's that smell?"

"It's sewage sludge," Tommy said and pointed to a gray-black mountain of filth.

McQueen wrinkled his forehead. "I know the Friends of the Earth Corporation don't treat sewage anymore, but they said they always spread it out on barren land."

"Breath in," Tommy said with a mischievous grin. "The fragrance of truth will enhance your awareness."

"How could I have gone on living in that corporation house so long without checking?"

"You had no reason to doubt the system."

"They claimed that there wasn't any money to repair the systems and reported that the sewage would be dumped on wastelands only. It would fertilize the land and speed up the earth's recovery."

"That's not what happened," Tommy said. "And to make it worse, the Friends of the Earth deliberately let the sewage plants deteriorate until they could no longer operate."

Covering up his sour expression, McQueen pulled the front of his shirt up over his mouth. "But they were only going to dump sewage until there was money to repair the systems."

Tommy pulled the front of his shirt up over his mouth. "Common sense tells us that there was more than enough money to repair them. Someone had to have taken that money."

McQueen's face pinched with disgust. "The credit system was abolished and replaced with untraceable money. There is no way to tell where it went."

Tommy pointed to another mountain of sewage sludge. "We both know Sproat and his scabs took the money and never repaired the systems. Not only is it cheaper to dump it into the country, they dump it next to water and make it unfit to drink."

Shaking his head, McQueen said, "And even if the pig people know the virus is not real, when they go off the blue grass to get water, it's contaminated."

"That's right," Tommy said and hopped over a diseased tree branch. "It keeps them buying bottled water."

"Because I trusted the Friends of the Earth Corporation" — McQueen looked at the stinking mountain of sludge — "that's what I have let the world become."

"A leader is only as good as the people he leads. It wasn't all your fault."

McQueen stopped walking and looked at the ground. A sad depressed look came over his face and radiated over his entire body. "I should have picked better people to lead, and I never should have told the people what the corporation told me to tell them."

Tommy placed a comforting hand on the small of McQueen's back. "The corporation used you. They let you believed Blue Town was doing just fine."

"By keeping the pig people on the blue grass, I thought I was saving the planet. But I was only telling them lies. Anything I told them was used by men like Sproat to produce a profit." McQueen lifted his head and continued walking. "Makes you wonder where it will end."

Walking by his side Tommy said, "They're even raising kids for profit."

"How can they do that?"

"The mandatory five-year airborne virus shots that were only glucose now contain birth control. When people are granted the right to reproduce, they can't."

"So the people who want a family have to buy children."

"That's right. And if they propagandize your son, they'll use him to produce children. With your name, he'll be a money maker."

A strong look of determination spread across McQueen's face. "Not if we have anything to do about it."

Slosh! Tommy's foot sunk into a soft spot under a high growth of grass and weeds. He reached down, grabbed his leg, and pulled. With a sickening suck, it came out. He had just stepped into a hidden black ditch of filth. The smell of black, aged sewage crawled into his little wrinkled nose. In anger, he jerked his head. "Those people are worse than pigs. They should be forced back onto the blue grass."

McQueen jumped over the ditch. "It would keep the earth safe from sludge like this.

"Tommy stomped his stinking black foot on the grass. "And it would keep it off my shoes."

McQueen let his shirt drop from his mouth and hastened his step. "Come on, Tommy, let's get outa' here. I can't breathe."

Tommy swung his little arms and moved his little feet faster. "They keep dumping this stink and there won't be any good air left to breathe."

"It smells like future death all around us." Realization shone in McQueen's eyes. "That's probably just what they have planned, Tommy. Just think of how much money they'll make selling air."

Tommy breathed in shallow breaths. "I wouldn't mind buying some fresh air right now."

Trying to get away from the smell, McQueen walked, swinging his arms, as if he were rushing to a fight. "You'd think the money they make selling water and letting people off the blue grass would be enough for any person. I wouldn't be surprised if they *do* try and sell air."

"They don't have to try." Tommy forced a long breath of air out of his mouth and fanned the stinking smell away from his face. "During the last heat wave, I saw them setting up air stations down from Patagonia. Sproat hooked a big fan to a steam engine and ran it until he had stirred up enough dust to stage a pollution alert. People came to the air stations in droves. They actually paid to breath air that Sproat's scabs ran through a filter."

"Damn," McQueen said and violently shook his head. "This air still stinks."

Tommy laughed. "You look like a dog that stuck his nose in hot pepper. You keep shaking your head, the next thing you'll be scratchin' for fleas."

McQueen blew out and tried to force the bad air from his lungs. "It feels like sewer fleas are crawling down my throat. Did the filters work?"

"They may have helped a little, but the people got scared. They caused such a demand that the filters clogged."

"Did they shut the stations down?"

"No way. They just took the filters out and ran regular air. The people breathed into breathing masks and were charged to breathe the same air everyone else was breathing."

"I can't believe people are so stupid."

"They fell for the blue grass didn't they?"

"But that was for their own good and the good of the planet."

"So . . . they believe that the air they bought was for their own good, too."

"I heard Sproat say, 'There are still a lot of sheep out there to shear.'"

Off to the right, a flash of a gold feather whisked through the trees. McQueen stopped walking and put his hand on Tommy's shoulder. "Did you see that?"

"What?"

"It looked like an Indigo person's gold feather."

"I didn't see anything."

They continued walking.

Keeping a wary eye out for the feather, McQueen said, "I never could figure out what those Indigo people do."

Tommy turned to McQueen. "Living on that blue grass must have made you stupid.

"Why do you say that?"

"Most everyone knows Indigo people are three times as strong as other people."

"I know that, but are they mutants?"

"Maybe. Word is that they have a genic defect."

"Are some short like you?"

"No, they're regular size, only the myostatin in their bodies is nonexistent."

"With no myostatin, there is nothing to stop muscle growth."

"Have you seen what an Indigo girl can do?'

"Not really."

"I have."

A look of immediate concern froze on McQueen's face. "What can an Indio girl do?"

"I saw one swim across the whirlpool below the falls. When she got to the other side, she wasn't even breathing hard."

McQueen swung his hand down and snapped his fingers. "That's it. One of those super strong Indigo people must have pulled me from the river."

"But didn't you say the Indigo people were chasing you toward the falls?"

"Maybe they were. Now I'm not sure. Sproat and his scabs had me hedged in. The Indigo people were coming upriver. Maybe they just wanted to talk."

"Sproat's men usually stone people until they are dead. Something had to stop them from stoning you to death."

"You think the Indigo people stopped them?"

"Sproat and his men are afraid of them, probably scared them away."

McQueen stared into the forest ahead. "I'm glad someone did something."

"Maybe the Indigos stitched up your head."

McQueen smoothed the stitches on his head with his hand. "I wonder why they didn't stick around."

"Probably didn't want to get near Sproat's scabs. They say Sproat's men are disease carriers. They infect everything they touch."

"But if the Indigos are so super strong why don't they fight to get their earth back?"

Tommy shrugged. "I don't know. They seem to want to keep Sproat and his scabs away from something. If we really want to know, I suppose we'll have to ask an Indigo."

"Let me know when you see one."

Tommy knew the Indigo were reclusive people and only showed themselves when they wanted to be seen. He smiled and shook his head as if it were possible. "Yeah, right."

They walked deep into the forest and stopped at the edge of a circular pit. Even though they were five meters above the stinking black water in the pit, the smell hovered in the air and a cloud of sewer fleas swarmed in it. All around, except for little swords of light that sliced its way through the leaves and twinkled like tiny diamonds dancing on the forest floor, the trees were dark and damp.

Tommy held his nose and swatted at fleas that swarmed around his head. "This is a really bad pit."

Waving his hand in front of his face, McQueen grimaced and hastened his step. "More stink. No sooner do we get away from one stinkin' mess, we run into another one."

"More, fresh air, just for you" — Tommy grinned a sarcastic grin — "compliments of the Friends of the Earth Corporation."

McQueen placed his hand on Tommy's back. "Hey, old buddy, there's plenty of fresh air to go around. I'll share. Don't be shy. Breathe in deep."

As they walked away from the pit, another sewage ditch appeared in front of them.

Walking along the side of the ditch, Tommy slouched down to make himself look even shorter than he actually was. He looked up at McQueen. "I'd breath in deep, but the closer I get to it, the much better is smells."

"You short guys get all the breaks."

Finally Tommy realized that all the joking in the world wouldn't take the smell away. They looked at each other, made ugly faces, jogged away from the sewer-scented air; and didn't stop until they were out of the forest and standing in an open field dotted with rocks and patches of tall golden grass.

Between breathing in deep breaths of fresh air, Tommy said, "I'm glad we're out of there."

McQueen gestured with a twitch of his eyebrow. "I think we're about to have some unwanted company."

Sproat and his crew were fifty meters in front of them."

Tommy balled his fists and puffed up his chest. "Do you think we can fight them?"

"My head hasn't recovered from the last rock storm."

Tommy pointed to McQueen's legs. "I hope those things still work."

They turned around and ran back toward where they had come from.

From out of the sewer-odor-filled-forest, a line of Sproat's men jumped in front of them.

Tommy tugged at McQueen's sleeve. "Every one of them has a rock. Why don't they use their antidote guns?"

"They believe that if they kill us they'll never find out where I hid the Orangeville key."

"Whatever you do, don't tell them there is such thing." Tommy raised his arms in anticipation of being stoned.

Unafraid, McQueen stood tall and proud.

"Hey wait a minute," Tommy said. "Sproat's men didn't care if they stoned you to death when you were in the river."

"That's right," McQueen said and quickly crouched down. "I hope it's because Sproat didn't tell them about the key."

Behind them, Sproat made himself known. With his men following, he advanced. Like a heavy windstorm, their feet mashed the straw grass down into a wide path. Sproat marched like he had a sense of urgency, but his large form was not accustomed to walking at such a rapid pace. He wheezed with the effort, his face glowed pink, and his forehead beaded with sweat. Many of the stones in his men's hands were hard granite, and heavy. Evidently, he planned to do away with Tommy and McQueen once and for all.

One of Sproat's men, a rare skinny one, toted a triangle red banner. It flapped near Sproat's face. He lifted his hand and signaled for his men to stop. Then he grabbed the banner and wiped his sweaty forehead. Almost whinnying like a horse, he shouted high-pitched unintelligible commands and pointed to the skinny man carrying the banner. The man handed Sproat the pole with the banner and fell to the ground. Being skinny, the man probably had cancer and was too weak to continue. Flaunting their rotten uncaring personalities, not one of Sproat's men offered to help the fallen man.

Being the coward he was, Sproat slowed and let another man take the point. Although the man looked like a candidate for a wheelbarrow person, his gait was fast. Remarkably agile for a man of his girth, he had a mean and hungry look; and it seemed he was mad because he had had been away from food too long. Sproat was letting his eager blubber-bellied friend charge first.

Tommy studied the blubber-bellied man. The man opened his mouth to scream. No sound came out. Like it was stuck, his mouth just gaped open.

As if they were infected and full of puss, the encased rolls of loose fat in the man's face and neck puffed up and looked like they were glued on pieces of clay. In the dark of his mouth, five teeth in a black sunken cavity stood out, dirty white against dark filth. Three teeth were in the lower jaw and two were in the upper. His closed eyes were shaped like swollen hog's testicles and had such heavy fat on the lids that they looked like infected boils. He had no eyelashes or eyebrows. His dirty-brown hair hung straight, but was uneven and ragged at his shoulders. In front of his face he wore straight-cut bangs to his hairless eyebrows.

Tommy wondered if this was the man was a mutant defect or the results of being a slave to his apparent veracious appetite.

The man's voice cracked. He screamed a painful scream. "Charge!" He took one step, tripped over his big feet, and as if his round stomach had just fallen out of a wheelbarrow, he rolled onto the grass.

Tommy turned to McQueen. "Too bad we're not on a hill. He would roll away."

The wind picked up and blew toward McQueen and Tommy. Sproat's men had a strong sweet-sour odor, like urine. One of them opened his mouth and squeaked like a mouse. Next to Tommy's foot, a stone thunked on the straw grass.

In the distance and from behind the trees, the cry of a bird shrieked. Sproat's head snapped around. His men turned toward the sound.

It wasn't a bird.

Tommy caught a glimpse of a gold feather. "Just what we need, if Sproat doesn't get us, the Indigo people will."

Volleys of fiery arrows hissed overhead. At the apex of their smooth arcs, the fire went out; and the arrows streaked trails of smoke until they stuck in the ground.

"Must be bad shots," Tommy said. "Not one came near us."

"Just warnings," McQueen said. "But watch out for the rocks."

Sproat pointed the end of the banner at the forest from where the arrows had come. About fifty meters from Sproat, secret shadows of the Indigo people could be seen. Sproat's men charged toward them. The Indigo people didn't move. They came out of the shady fringes of the forest and stood at its edge, defiantly waiting.

This was the first time Tommy and McQueen had seen this many Indigo people for a long time. Their hard sun-cured muscles accented their stocky bodies. They looked more like perfect man-made machines than people. Each had a huge dagger stuck in his belt that warped around slim waists. When Tommy had caught glimpses of them before, they had worn uniforms with jackets. Now, loin cloths covered their mid sections, but their thighs, legs, and feet were bare. In their hair, they wore a single gold feather.

Off to the right, an Indigo person ran out of the forest and threw something. Before Tommy could duck, a rock hit him on the side of the head. A bright, four-pointed white star appeared in front of his eyes. At first he enjoyed the beauty of it. It was like fabulous fireworks making spiders across a purple sky. The light of the star went out, Tommy's mind went blank.

CHAPTER 8

The Indigo person on McQueen's right threw another rock. McQueen jerked his hand up and batted it aside. With hostile intentions, he directed a threatening stare at the advancing Indigo people. At his feet, on the mashed yellow grass, Tommy lay lifeless.

"Damn it, Tommy," McQueen said. "It looks like the Indigos are not on our side."

Sproat yelled at his men. "Draw you weapons. Take care of those savages." He turned his back to the Indigo people and threw another rock.

It sailed toward McQueen.

He ducked.

The rock fell to the ground.

Sproat pointed at McQueen and laughed a squeaky, tee-hee mouse laugh. "Dodge this one."

He hurled another rock in McQueen's direction.

McQueen jumped out of the path of that rock, too.

At the forest line, an Indigo lifted a trumpet to his lips and played "Taps".

The other Indigo people stopped advancing, stepped back, and stood at the edge of the forest.

Sproat turned toward the sound of the trumpet.

The skinny cancer riddled man stood up, weakly pointed one finger, and yelled, "Goin' to Canady!"

As if someone had pulled a switch, all action ceased.

Mesmerized, everyone stared at the man.

The man slowly walked off the field and into the forest.

McQueen stopped watching, dropped down to one knee, and shook Tommy's shoulder. "Tommy, are you okay?"

Tommy didn't answer.

McQueen watched Sproat's men.

They formed a crooked line, dropped their rocks, and tensed their fat bodies into unbalanced standing positions. With no order of shot sequence, they drew their antidote guns and fired at the Indigo people. The trumpet player stopped playing. The perfect line of Indigo people, stood tall and proud. They didn't move. They didn't run. When they were hit with the poison antidote bullets they simply brushed them from their bodies. The poison had no effect.

"They've taken the antitoxin," Sproat yelled in his excited squeaky voice. "Stone them to death."

Staying in a small area, his men scrambled around the field searching for and picking up rocks. After they had gathered two rocks each, they stood in a crooked line.

"Sproat lifted his arm and squeaked out, "Fire!"

All at once, his men threw the rocks. When the rocks were in the air and sailing toward them, the Indigo people relaxed as if it were a game. Lackadaisically, they held out their hands; and with their gold feathers flashing into the day, they caught the stones like small children catching harmless rubber balls. Another volley of stones was thrown. Again, the Indigo people plucked them out of the air.

Sproat shook the banner. His squeaky voice rose with childlike anger. "Charge!"

His men charged blindly into the waiting Indigo people and Sproat followed. When they were within reach, the Indigo people simply dropped to their knees, grabbed Sproat and his men around their legs, and picked them up over their heads. While they carried them into the dark forest, other Indigo people took the antidote guns; and as if they were searching for something, they felt all over Sproat's men's bodies.

McQueen shook Tommy again. "Come on, Tommy. They're gone. Wake up."

Tommy didn't move. McQueen bent down to pick him up. Tommy opened his eyes and rubbed his head where the rock had hit him.

"You'll have a good goose egg there." McQueen offered him his hand. "Come on. We got to get out of here."

Tommy grabbed McQueen's hand and stood up. "But won't the Indigo people protect us?"

Searching for more rocks flying their way, McQueen looked toward the forest. "No way. One of them hit you with that rock."

"You said they might only want to talk."

"I think the only talk they are speaking is rock language."

From in the forest, shrieks of a terrified man cutting the air were followed by a splash.

Tommy jerked his head around and looked to where the shrieks had come from. "What was that?"

"I'm not sure." McQueen gestured toward the forest. "The Indigo people carried Sproat and his idiots over there."

Another shriek that sounded like painful whinnying of a horse filled the air. Then the sound of a huge splash crashed through the trees.

Like he was laughing a silent laugh, Tommy nodded in a downward motion. "I know why the Indigos are wearing those loincloths." He chuckled. "They just threw Sproat into that sewer pit."

McQueen and Tommy exchanged amused glances.

Tommy laughed out loud. "So, that's why."

"That's why what?" McQueen asked.

Tommy grinned like a sly three-headed fox. "Sproat and his men are so fat, that when they throw them in the pit they splash tidal waves of sewer water. The Indigos wear the loin cloths because they don't want the sewer water to splash on their clothes."

Shaking his head, McQueen smiled. "Let's get out of here before they throw us in, too."

They dashed around the golden patches of golden grass and started walking on a deep-worn path lined with thick brambly bushes.

A ways down the trail, McQueen noticed Tommy was getting tired. He stopped. "Let's take a break."

Tommy sat down on the dead-leaf-covered ground. "It's about time," he said and exhaled a whoosh of air. "I feel like I'm wearing the bottom of my legs off. I'll end up shorter than I already am."

Chirrup! An unfamiliar sound came from deep in the forest.

Tommy jerked his head toward the sound. "Now what?"

Searching, the forest for signs of someone sneaking up on them, McQueen turned his head from left to right. "I don't see anything."

Tommy stood up. "Maybe not, but those Indigo people could be right next to us, and we would never know it."

"It looks like you're going to wear your legs down a little more."

"Here we go again." Tommy reluctantly got up, and they scrambled up the side of a ridge.

On the other side of the ridge, where water lilies and large green leaves stuck to the black muc, a faint brown smudge filled the air above a mud pond. Here they followed along the edge of the bank.

Tommy stumbled.

"Be careful," McQueen said. "That stuff's like greasy quicksand. If you slip and fall in, you'll never be able to climb out."

A soft, fluttering cracking came from the brush on the other side of the pond.

Tommy jerked his head in the direction of the sound. "What's that?

Before McQueen could answer, an enormous black boar with tusks as long as Tommy's arm came barreling toward them.

"That water's shallow," McQueen said and pointed to the center of the pond. "He's coming across."

Tommy turned to run but slipped in the mud.

McQueen reached down to pull him up, but slipped and fell to his knees.

The boar let out an aggressive grunt.

Tensing to defend themselves, Tommy and McQueen turned toward the boar. Charging in a straight line, it charged right into the shore of the pond. For a few steps its hoofs plopped into the mud. Then as it struggled, it slowly sunk up to its neck. After one desperate whine, the boar's head went below the surface.

Now that the threat was gone and he didn't have to be in a rush, Tommy easily got to his feet and turned to McQueen. "I wish everything was that easy."

Brushing the mud off his knees, McQueen breathed a sigh of relief. "I think it caught us both off guard." He paused and looked to where the boar had sunk into the mud. "We should have picked up something, a rock, a stick, anything, to defend ourselves."

"We didn't have time."

"Anything can happen out here. Wild boars made that path we were walking on."

Tommy nodded. "I know that now. We have to be ready to react."

McQueen held one finger in the air. "Remember, the main thing is, don't get excited."

About a hundred meters in front of them, a tiny log cabin came into view. Except for a patch of close-knit vines, the ground around the cabin resembled dirty-salt. Not a single blade of grass or a scraggly weed grew in that area. Off to the left of the cabin, three ten-meter-high corroded pipes had been planted into the ground. In the center of the wood-shingled roof of the cabin, a wisp of dusky smoke rose from a tin cooling chimney and stretched out to a thin thread.

"Tommy rubbed his pudgy belly. "I'm hungry. Maybe they're cooking something."

McQueen flashed him an animated grin. "The whole world could be falling down around you, and you would still think of food."

Tommy smiled back. "Even if the does fall down, I'd still be hungry."

When they were close to the cabin, McQueen noticed that it had been built with ax cut logs. "Who ever built this did a lot of physical work."

"And look at that roof." Tommy said and jerked his head upward. "They had to split each log into shingles to make a roof like that."

"Whoever's in there, is a rough individual."

Tommy knocked on the rough-sawed wood door. "And this person was never afraid of the wood virus. Maybe he's an Indigo."

No one answered the door.

Tommy knocked again. The force of his little knuckles on the door caused it to sway open. Inside, a black dirt floor led to a filth-caked wooden table. Light from cracks in a wood-burning stove, chase away some of the bleak darkness of the room. Sitting at the table, a dried-up little man, with yellow skin and almost black teeth, looked at them through watery eyes. He had the look of death. Struggling to his feet, he extended his hand. "You friend?"

McQueen reached out to shake the old man's hand but drew back. The old man's hand was covered with ulcerated open sores, and many boils were growing on his forearms.

"Tommy stepped in front of McQueen and grabbed the old man's hand. "Yes, we're friends."

"Good," the old man said. "You can go to hell." His ragged voice sounded hoarse and weary. The air around him seemed to be filled with exhaustion drained of all physical and mental reserves.

Tommy's face turned to one of confusion. "What are you saying?"

The old man coughed and spit up blood. "I'm dying. I need an enemy to kill me."

Tommy released the old man's hand and sarcastically said, "That's just what I needed. Thanks."

McQueen stepped toward the man. "No need to die, we'll get you back to Blue Town. They'll help you there."

"The old man stepped back. Holding one hand on his stomach, he moved his other opened hand in front of himself like a shield and vehemently said, "No! No Blue Town, they kill people that look old."

"You may be old," Tommy said. "But I don't think they'll kill you."

"The man forced a feeble smile. "I'm not old. I only look old. The gas and oil companies came and offered us a lot of money to drill on our land. We knew the companies had a reputation for chemically and genetically damaging people's children. We knew it could turn into a poison from profit situation."

"Then why did you let them do it?"

They threatened us with eviction and all kinds of legal stuff. In the end, we figured we'd get our money; and if something happened, we'd move away." His face grimaced with pain. He grabbed his stomach and bent over. After taking a deep breath, he straightened up and pointed to a shelf stacked high with yellowed sheets of paper. "There are the test results. When they indicated that our well contain high levels of arsenic, manganese, selenium, radiation, and barium, the gas company said it was at a levels too low to hurt anyone, and that it could actually be healthful." He bent over, gasp for breath, and tilted to one side.

McQueen stepped toward the man to catch him "Are you all right?"

The man held up his hand in a halting gesture. I'm not all right. After we couldn't take a deep breath without gasping for good air, and we couldn't see fifty feet in front of ourselves, then we knew we couldn't believe the gas companies. We wanted to move, but we couldn't find any safe place to move to."

"So you stayed?"

"We didn't have a choice." The man lifted his feeble arm and pointed to the window and the three pipes outside. "Whatever they put around my home poisoned the water. It has made me sick."

"It can't be that bad," Tommy said."

The man cocked his head in tortured wonder. "Did you see my garden?"

"I didn't see a garden."

"It's those vines. It's the only thing that will grow. Whatever is in the ground kills everything I try to grow. It has already killed my son and my wife."

"How old were they?" McQueen asked.

"My son was only three. My wife was six years younger than me." He held up his boil-covered forearm like it was a trophy. "They got the boils. We went to Blue Town for help. Sproat's men gave them the antidote."

McQueen grimaced at the thought of more murders in the name of stopping a fake virus, but he held out hope that the people of Blue Town may have done something to help. "Did it work?"

A tear formed in the man's eye. "It didn't do anything but kill them."

"Did they give you the antidote?"

"Since I lived off the blue grass, they were going to give me the antidote on TV."

McQueen nodded with an-it-figures gesture. "They do that to show people what will happen if they go off the blue grass."

Tommy tilted his head to one side. "How did you get away?"

"The TV signal went black." He leaned on the edge of the table and supported himself with his hands." While they were waiting for it to come back, they got drunk. I snuck out of the station and ran out of that town. Been here ever since."

Figuring the Dinkies would never turn away a sick man, McQueen said, "There *is* someone who will help."

The man coughed a loud hacking cough that seemed to start from ragged lungs deep inside his chest. He leaned away from the table, placed his hands on his feeble, bony knees, bent over, and opened his mouth. Although it didn't seem possible, he coughed harder.

When McQueen reached out to help the man, a sour stench wafted out of the man's mouth. He held up his hand in a halting gesture. With his watery eyes blinking and splashing like puddles, he coughed one long painful cough. A huge clot of dark-red blood flew from his opened mouth. With a sickening splat, it landed on the dirt floor. As the man moaned, an acrid odor floated from his mouth. He stumbled backwards, fell to the floor, and lay still.

Fanning the odor from his face, Tommy looked to McQueen. "Can't you revive him?"

Holding his breath, McQueen shook his head and pointed to the clot. White ribbon-like worms, with long spiral pointed hooks, curled and slithered away from the clot.

Alarmed, Tommy jumped back.

McQueen shook his head in wonderment. "I can't believe it. Echinococcosis!"

Tommy's face filled with confusion. What's echinococcosis?"

"Tape worms called echinocodde. I've seen them before. They cause big cysts in the liver and lungs. If not treated, they're fatal."

"Tommy winced and stepped back. "Can we get it?"

"Not likely. The worms used to come from sheep but mutated. Now the creepy things thrive in sewage. Sewage gave him worms. They're crawling through his body, probably ate right into his brain. He didn't have much to live for."

Tommy tried to keep a positive outlook. "But where there's life there's hope."

"Except for those worms there is no longer life in this young man. Those worms and the Friends of the Earth Corporation have seen to that."

Tommy stared at the man lying on the floor. "We should have never let any of the people go off the blue grass."

"It's too late now, McQueen said with muted anguish. "I don't think we can fix the earth in our lifetimes.

Making a face, Tommy wiggled his rear end with excruciating discomfort. "We can't just sit back like idiots and watch ugly sewage worms crawl up our butts. We have to do something, and your son can help."

McQueen paused. The thought of his son continuing the quest seemed almost possible. "Maybe you're right," he said but changed his mind. "We can't save the earth in our lifetimes, and we should at least help someone who can, but it's impossible." He whipped his head around and stared out the window.

A buck-toothed Pigmy was peeping in. With eyes filled with sadness, he stared down at the dead man. As mysteriously as he had appeared, the Pigmy vanished.

Tommy stared at the window. "I hope there are a few decent people left on this earth that deserve a future." He reached up, pulled a ragged towel from the back of a chair, and mercifully covered the man's face.

Outside, the wind sighed sadly.

The sight of the sad Pigmy and Tommy covering the man's face made McQueen's mind search for answers. During his first few years as Chief Earth Officer, he had never wavered. He had never forgotten who he was or why he had been given the supreme opportunity to keep the pig people on the blue grass. It had been a meaningful and necessary cause and was necessary for the dying world to recover. But now a few tyrannized the many. He wondered how many more people lived on the edge of despair or in hopeless poverty, just so Sproat and his manic manipulators could live in the comfort of their alcohol induced stupors, while men, woman, and children in faraway lands, ended up like the man on the floor. He wondered, but he didn't really want to know. He just wanted to leave it all behind. He wanted to do the orange turn.

He turned to Tommy. "Maybe we could colonize another planet."

A disgruntled look came over Tommy's face. "That's far-fetched. You know we can't get a space vehicle out of the earth's atmosphere. There's still too much space junk."

McQueen held his hand over the waistband that hid the secret chip. "Maybe they have designed a ship that could repel the junk, something like a bullet proof vest."

"I doubt it."

McQueen took his hand off his waist. He still had the chip. If he used it, he could forget about the pig people and Blue Town. He could go to Orangeville with Tommy and his son. He could do the turn. He could let the pig people and Sproat's scabs die in their own squalor. But an inborn feeling in his chest kept gnawing at his insides. Even though he was no longer considered the Chief Earth Officer, he still felt that he had a duty to mankind. He had to get the pig people back on the blue grass. He forced the conflicting thoughts out

149

of his mind. But now he wasn't sure he wanted to go to Orangeville and do the turn. And, if he told Tommy about the chip, he would want to use it.

"You're right," McQueen said. "I think I'm just looking for an easy way out this mess. That space junk blasts right through the strongest alloy metals known to man."

"We might be stuck in this stink hole of Earth," Tommy said. "But with your popularity as former chief earth officer, we still have the power to change it."

"I don't have any power." McQueen helplessly dropped his arms to his sides. "Now that the pig people know the virus is fake, they won't believe a thing I say."

"But you were the most powerful man on earth."

A weary, McQueen placed his hands on the table, bent over, and lowered his head. "If it hadn't been for Danielle, I would be the most deadest man on earth."

"The Friends of the Earth Corporation reported that she strayed off the blue grass, caught the green grass and water virus and died. What really happened?"

With a tear forming his eye, McQueen lifted his hands from the table and turned toward Tommy. "She jumped in front of an antidote bullet that was meant for me. She died and they took my son."

"Sorry to hear that," Tommy said with disappointment. "She was a good person. What did they hope to gain?"

McQueen started to tell Tommy about the chip and the turn, but he didn't. "What do all greedy people want? They want wealth and the power that goes with it."

"But they have all that."

"They always want more. They still think I have a key to a treasure in Orangeville."

Staring at the body, Tommy placed his hand on the small of McQueen's back. "Maybe they ran out of towns that they could destroy in the name of democracy and freedom. It looks like they have decided to use or kill anyone who can turn them a profit."

McQueen raised his voice. "What is the matter with those people?" He turned from the body. "The planet's natural resources are greatly stressed. The social order of the world is about to collapse back to the Stone Age."

Tommy gave McQueen a blank look. "Maybe the people need to be thrown back to the Stone Age."

"They act like they have a pre-Stone Age intelligence, but there are not enough Stone Age environments to support even primitive life."

"The earth needs you," Tommy insisted. "A few of the Dinkies asked me to get you to help."

McQueen looked at the long white worms inching along the floor toward the dead man's body. "I would like to help, but what kind of people would let something like this happen?" He grabbed an earthen clay water pitcher from the edge of the table and threw it at the worms. It crashed down. The worms stopped wiggling for a brief moment then continued on toward the body. "What right do those pig people have to even think to ask us to go to all that trouble when they don't give a damn about us?"

"Take it easy," Tommy said referring to getting too excited to think during the boar incident. "Remember, the main thing is, don't get excited."

McQueen pushed a broken piece of the clay pitcher with the toe of his boot. "It's my fault, too." He felt his face tightened as if he were going to cry. "If I had gotten off that blue grass more often, none of this would have happened."

"But you just don't know that."

McQueen turned toward the body. "Maybe not, but before we do anything we have to give this man a decent burial."

After they dragged the body outside, McQueen lifted a pickax and crashed it down onto the salt-like soil. It twanged; and like a blow from a steel hammer, the handle stung his hands. Thinking he had hit a rock, he looked at the spot where the end of the pickax had hit. It had only made a tiny dent.

He looked to Tommy. "This stuff's like cement. We'll have to try another spot."

Tommy and McQueen bent over to lift the body. The sound of grunting came from the thicket of vines. They looked toward the sound. Five wild boars with long sharp tusks came charging toward them.

Preparing to defend the attack, McQueen lifted the pickax high.

"There's too many," Tommy cried. "If we don't get in the cabin those tusks will cut us to ribbons."

Rushing toward the cabin, McQueen threw the pickax in the direction of the advancing boars.

Looking back over his shoulder, he couldn't see if the pickax had delayed the boars; but he and Tommy made it back inside the cabin, where they barred the door and looked out the window. The boars had not chased them. Instead, they had run right to the body. Now they were ripping it to pieces and carrying it into the thicket of vines.

McQueen looked to the barred door. "We'll have to get out of here while they're eating."

With an upbeat tone in his voice Tommy said, "And then we'll search the youth camps. Miles has to be in one of them."

McQueen pulled bar from the door. "Yes, it would be nice to see Miles again. But which camp?"

CHAPTER 9

Samara, meaning from God, watched the other Indigo people throw the last of Sproat's men into the sewage pit. As the others were doing, the last man joined them and tried to climb up vines that snaked into the pit, but he only managed to get tangled in the clinging vines. Watching the filth-covered-men disentangled themselves and winced in exaggerated pain, Samara's brother, Hack, stood next to her. Towering over her petite body, he threw a rock into the pit. Kerplop! It splashed black sewer water into Sproat's face.

Sproat wiped his face with the sleeve of his sewer-soaked shirt and jerked his finger at Hack. With his squeaky voice, he cried out, "You're going to be sorry you did that."

Hack reared back to throw another rock. "Don't worry, Sproat, there's no soap in the water. You won't get clean."

Samara tugged at Hack's elbow. "I don't mean to interrupt your fun, Hack, but why did you throw rocks at that little Dinky who was standing in the field?"

As Hack held the rock in the ready to throw position, a mischievous smile formed on his lips. "If he doesn't have the other key," he said, "then he's like all the rest of the scum." He lowered the rock and pointed to Sproat. "All they do is interfere with our state of being and try to stop our movement."

"But we didn't see that tall person or that little Dinky do anything that would harm us or do anything that would interfere with our stop the pig people movement"

Hack reared back to throw. "You don't have to see them do it." Sling! He threw the rock. "What they leave behind is proof enough." Kerplunk! The rock hit and splashed more sewer water into Sproat's face. This time Sproat didn't talk back.

"That's it, Sproat," Hack jeered. "Don't talk. I know you're suspicious of anything over three syllables."

Anticipating another rock, Sproat turned his back and cringed.

Shaking his head in a ha-ha taunting gesture, Hack pointed to Sproat. "Too bad that Dinky and that tall pig person aren't in there with you. I'd make you and your paltry playmates stay in there all day. Then you could all go back to your fruitcake farm and stay there."

The thought of McQueen getting thrown into the pit made a coldness rush up Samara's spine. She looked into her brother's devilish eyes. "But that tall one's McQueen. He has been trying to serve the planet."

Hack picked up another rock, threw it up into a little arc, and caught it in his hand. "I haven't received any input showing that to be true."

Samara defied him with a cold stare. "Just give him a chance."

"Nope! I'm going to throw all the rocks at him he deserves. When we get done here, we'll find him. If we hit him with enough rocks, he'll go down. Then we'll search him." Sling! He threw another rock.

Samara didn't watch the rock land in the water. "Instead of stoning him couldn't we just ask him if he has the other key?"

Hack's voice took on a teasing tone. "After he's down on the ground, maybe we'll ask him if we can search him."

"I wish you wouldn't stone him"

"Why not?"

Samara didn't want her brother to know she cared about McQueen. "I don't know," she lied. "Do you think he has the key?"

A smile quivered across Hack's lips. "He's not the type of person who would have the other key, and I'm not going out of my way to stone and search him."

Samara smiled in his direction. "Oh thank you, brother Hack."

Hack turned away from her. "Don't thank me for something I might not do." He turned back. "Wait a second. You aren't going sweet on that ex-warrior, are you?"

Samara felt her face flush. She knew her brother knew the answer. "There's no law against it, is there?"

"There's no law. But you know what those kinds of people do when they are allowed the freedom to choose a mate or anything else for that matter."

"I know." She patted the key that was sewn in the belt that wrapped around her hourglass figure, and remembered the first time she had seen McQueen. She had let her gaze slide down his body. He was uniquely attractive, and his confident walk gave him a look of controlled power. Maybe that was why she had saved him.

"I think this one is different," she said. "He may be the one I will have to do the turn with."

Hack sighed. "I keep trying to tell you. McQueen's not the type of man who would be entrusted with that kind of power." He looked at her through narrowed eyes. "You'll save yourself a lot of trouble if you just forget about that one."

Samara didn't want to disagree with her brother, but a strong sense of impending sadness overwhelmed her. Before she could stop herself, she said, "I don't think I can do that."

Hack glared at her. His voice had an awful arrogant air to it. "If he's not already a pig person, he'll turn into one."

Samara placed both hands on Hack's shoulders and talked directly into his face. "Listen to me, Hack. You can't judge everyone the same. I think he's different."

"They all change," Hack said, and Samara felt his body flinch under her hands. He shuddered. "And when he does change, we'll have another situation to correct."

Samara thought about how much strength McQueen had shown when he had almost swam across the rapids and whirlpools below the falls. "Maybe he's an Indigo person and he doesn't know it."

Hack eased away from Samara's hands. "If he were, he would have three times the strength of a normal man."

"I hope you haven't forgotten that strength isn't the only thing Indigo people have."

This time, Hack put his hands on her shoulders and talked directly into her face. "Don't be stupid, Sis. McQueen allowed himself to be ambushed in the middle of an open field. That shows he isn't very bright."

Samara searched her mind for a reason to make Hack accept McQueen. "If he isn't intelligent," she said, "maybe he has a super immune system."

Sproat's men had climbed out of the pit and were running away. Gasping for air, others clung to the vines on the sides of the pit. Hack dropped his hands from Samara's shoulders and turned toward the action. "Sorry, Sis, I got work to do." Signaling to the other Indigo people, he waved his arms in the air and shouted, "Keep those pigs in there. Let them wallow in what they have done to this land."

Up on the hill, above the pit, Indigo people with wooden poles pried at the bottom of a pile of skinny logs. The logs broke loose, rolled down the hill, and bowled into Sproat's escaping men. They tumbled backward and splashed back into the stinking sewage pit.

Sproat had dodged the logs and now he stood at the edge of the pit. Knee deep in a stagnant pool filled with slimy algae, he squeaked at the top of his lungs, "You'll pay for this." We'll hunt you down. No one disrespects a man of the Friends of the Earth Corporation."

Hack shouted down at Sproat, "Tell it like it is. It's the Pigs of the Earth Corporation."

CHAPTER 10

Tommy woke in the dark of night. McQueen was still lying in the same position he had been in when he had passed out from exhaustion.

Tommy cupped his hand to his ear and listened. In the distance, the sound of Sproat and his men grew. Tommy figured that they must be in one of their alcoholic conditions or under the influence of the full moon. He didn't know why a full moon agitated lunatics, but he had seen it happen many times.

He looked at the twisted trail ahead and thought about what tomorrow would bring. When the sun came up, if they could get far enough away, McQueen would want to hunt bugs and butterflies, or snakes to eat. Tommy was hungry, but he wasn't ready to do that.

He felt his empty stomach. If Sproat's men were drunk, maybe he could sneak into their camp and get some food. But first, he would tell McQueen he was leaving. He bent over and shook him. He didn't move.

"Sorry, old buddy," Tommy whispered. "I gotta get something to eat. I'll be back in a jiffy." He snaked his way through the thick underbrush, crawled out the other side, and set out toward the sound of Sproat's men.

Near the camp, the sound of Sproat's men died down, but the crap and urine they had deposited along the fringes of the camp reeked to the point of suffocation. It told Tommy they were too damn lazy to cover their own crap. He didn't want to get sick. Any food he stole would have to be boiled.

In the shadows away from the emerging moon, he tiptoed over a fallen log and stopped. A bright spotlight beamed into his eyes. He dropped to the ground, but his night vision had been lost. To readjust his eyes to the dark, he closed them seven times for five seconds. Lying in silence, he waited for the spotlight to beam past again.

It did not.

He listened to the yammering of the drunken men. Their slurred speech indicated they were well past a state of keen alertness. Even if the light beamed on him again, he figured the person using it wasn't watching what it was illuminating. He rose to his feet and stepped closer.

In the center of the moon-dazzled camp, a fire smoldered and flicked occasional flashes of orange light. Underneath, a tripod made of iron rods, a blur of steam lingered over a big black iron kettle. He knew by the dying fire that Sproat's men had not taken any food from the kettle for a long time. They had already eaten their fill. Whatever they had cooked, had cooked so long that all the disease and parasites had to be cooked out; and even though it was in the center of the concentrated stink of the camp, it would be okay to eat.

Rubbing his little belly, Tommy goggled at the kettle of food. Then he shifted his focus around the camp. No guards were posted. But one guard sat on an upturned log and leaned against a tree. As Tommy walked close to him, a strong, take-your-breath-away, obnoxious odor wafted into his face. He never knew anyone could smell so bad, and apparently this man couldn't stand his own odor. He had a plastic clamp holding his nostrils closed.

160

With each breath he took, his belly rose and fell. The enormity of his belly was amplified by great mounds of blubber loosely adhering to his huge frame. Other than that, he was sitting motionless with his hand wrapped around a tall silver tankard. It was upside-down and the handle pointed away from his hand. Holding his breath, Tommy walked past him. The man didn't wake. Scattered around the camp, bodies of men lay in various positions, most curled up with their hands clutched over their huge stomachs. Except for occasionally waving their hands at buzzing mosquitoes, not one moved.

They were all dead drunk, passed out or dying from food poisoning, or the awful smelling guard had gassed them to death. Tommy stepped up to the kettle over the fire, lifted the lid, and looked inside. Just as he recognized there was soup in the kettle, the sound of a snore, the kind that would injure a common man's throat, belched from a heap of dirty blankets. Tommy looked toward the sound. The strong odor of alcohol wafted into his face. Whoever or whatever was under the blankets seemed to be on the brink of spontaneous combustion, but it was alive. Tommy looked into the kettle again. There was not much soup left.

He checked the camp for movement. Except for a few drunken voices on the far side of a big tree, the camp was in a state of lethargy. He reached down, grabbed his shirttail, wrapped it around the hot kettle handle, and lifted. His little arms quivered and his feet felt like they were going to sink into the ground. The iron kettle was too heavy. He could not lift it off its hook. He went to the sleeping guard, held his breath, and reached for the tall silver tankard. But just as his fingertips touched it, it fell, hit the ground, and let out muffled clunk. The guard grumbled, turned over, and folded his chubby hands together. Like he was praying, he placed his hands on the side of his face and went back to sleep. Tommy picked up the tall tankard. Breathing again, and keeping an eye on the guard while walking backwards, he made his way to the kettle. Once there, he stopped and turned around. For fear of getting an incurable disease, he didn't want to eat or drink from the smelly guard's tankard. He pressed the tankard's hinged cover open with his thumb and held it over the hot coals of the fire. After he felt it had been sterilized and cooled, he dipped it into the soup. Looking around, he lifted the tankard out, put it to his mouth, and took a small sip. Except for a slight charcoal taste from the hot coals, the soup went down smooth and fast, but he was so hungry he couldn't really taste it. He lifted the tankard to his lips again. This time, it didn't taste bad. His ravenous hunger took over. He took big gulps until the tankard was empty, and then dipped into the kettle for more. This time he drank slower.

He figured he would have to have to drink three tankards. The first one was for hunger. The second one would be for taste. And the last one would be for pleasure.

He drank his fill, filled the tankard to the brim, and backed into the forest. Just over the fallen log, he waded into a huge mud puddle.

It was the same path he had used when he had come into the camp. He figured that if he didn't have to carry the full tankard of soup he wouldn't sink in so far into the mud. For a moment he figured that if he drank all the soup the tankard would be empty, then it wouldn't be as heavy, and he wouldn't sink into the mud. He pounded his head with his little hand and laughed at himself. If he drank all the soup, he would still weigh the same. The extra weight would be in his stomach. It would be much better to carry the tankard to McQueen. That way they wouldn't be stopping all day tomorrow searching for insects to eat.

When Tommy got back to where McQueen was sleeping, McQueen had changed positions but he was still asleep. Tommy tapped him on the shoulder. "McQueen, wake up. Breakfast in bed."

McQueen opened his eyes. As if he were shooing a fly, he waved his hand. With a groggy voice he said, "I don't want anything to drink. It'll dull our senses."

"No, you big dummy. It's soup."

McQueen sat up. "What?"

Tommy held the tankard out to him. "It's still warm."

McQueen rubbed his eyes. "You must have been busy."

"Drink up."

McQueen grabbed the tankard flipped open the hinged lid and drank. When he was done, he held the tankard upside-down and let every bit drip into his mouth. After he placed the empty tankard on the ground, he looked at Tommy. "Where did you get this?"

"Stole it from Sproat's camp."

McQueen's eyes opened wide with alarm. "You could have been killed."

"I couldn't help it. I was hungry."

"You shouldn't take chances like that."

"Nodding in agreement, Tommy said, "Anyway, they're all passed out." He patted his round stomach. "And, we have something in our bellies."

McQueen looked around. "How long was I out?'

"A few hours, I guess. Before I got the soup, I passed out, too."

A sense of urgency filled McQueen's voice. "If we want to get a head start on those guys, we better get going."

"Okay," Tommy said and lay down on a bed of leaves. "Just let me take a little break."

McQueen put his hands behind his head and leaned back against a log. "Okay, but just for a few minutes. The Indigos will be chasing Sproat and his scabs as soon as the sun comes up."

The night had turned chilly, but Tommy's stomach was warm from the soup he had just eaten. It comforted him. He fell asleep.

CHAPTER 11

McQueen woke up to the sick cries of a lone dog and one lonely bird greeting the morning. But the sound of Sproat and his men crashing through the trees and brush hushed that sound. Beyond that, platinum reflections of the Indigo people glinted through the deep dark recess of the forest.

McQueen shook Tommy. "Get up. The Indigos are headed our way."

Tommy jerked to a sitting position and shook his sleepy head. "They're after Sproat. Why can't we get out of their path and just let them pass."

"I wish we could. But they're everywhere. It's like they're physic or something."

Tommy fixed his eyes on the silver tankard lying on the ground. "I thought we could circle back. That big kettle might have some soup left in it."

"Sorry," McQueen said with a small repentant laugh. "If we stay here much longer, we'll be in a soup of hurt."

Tommy got up. Like a wet dog shaking off water, he shook his head. "Let's get moving." He started walk-running with those little rowing strides.

Trying to make Tommy laugh, McQueen swung his arms the same as Tommy, and followed. After a few meters, McQueen noticed why Tommy's way of walking seemed easier. Each time he thrust his hands forward he was taking a step forward. The momentum of his arms going forward pulled his body and made each step smoother. He watched Tommy in front of him swing his little

165

arms and thrust his little legs forward. "That's a stupid way to walk."

"So what?" Tommy said, and thrust his arms forward with an exaggerated swing. "We're ahead of them now."

McQueen stopped and looked ahead. "We may be ahead of them, but it looks like we have to climb that thing."

Ahead, a steep slope leading to a mountain top blocked their way. On each side of the slope, dry powdery soil that would swallow a man up to his waist, eliminated those ways around. Tommy stepped to the bottom of the slope and looked up. "When we get to the top we'll have a good view of everything."

With labored breaths and sluggish footfalls, they trudged up the steep slope. Every step stirred up yellow dust and amplified the harsh lifeless dryness of the slope. At the top of the mountain they sat on an ancient tree stump. As if on cue, a filthy cloud covered the sun and stretched from horizon to horizon.

Gasping for breath, Tommy turned to McQueen. "Are you enjoying the view?"

"Oh just great," McQueen replied, and a bone-chilling wind whipped out of the north. He peered off into the distance. In near darkness, anemic beams of weak sunlight caused the surroundings to be bathed in shadow. At various places on the other side of the steep slopping mountain, patches of exotic underbrush bathed in the shade of a few scattered trees.

Tommy rubbed his little arms. "Let's go down there. It should be warmer."

After they descended halfway down the slope, an unusual sun came out bright, harsh, and humid. It reminded McQueen of his past childhood days. But in this liquid-thick heat there was no scent of newly-mowed blue grass. There was no intoxicating essence of summer.

To the right, leaves of a few trees drooped wearily under the scorching sun, and three other trees appeared to be ravaged beyond recovery. Almost hidden by overgrown brush, the crumbling ruins of an old brick power plant found their eyes. They walked into the cool, purple shadow of the plant, and carefully descended stone steps, slick with some kind of maroon goo.

At the bottom, they circled around a stand of dead trees, avoided a pool of churned up filth, thick with something mustard colored, and stopped at the edge of a dust-caked clearing.

Here, they looked out at a deserted town. Various colors of dust-covered OvalCars looked to have been resurrected from some junk yard and placed along the streets to make the town look inhabited and friendly, but something tapping an uneven metallic rhythm disturbed the air.

Tommy tilted his head to the side and listened. "What's that sound?"

"I don't know," McQueen said. "But somebody must be here."

Searching for the source of the tapping, they continued walking.

Beyond the clearing, broken-down dump shacks with half rusted corrugated metal roofs and wooden doors, held shut by old rusted latches, tilted as if they were going to fall over. Walking through what once was Main Street that connected to acres of crumbling blue concrete side streets, McQueen stopped at a shack with no door.

The tapping grew.

He looked up. Hidden behind a tall tower, a gentle wind was causing the torn and tattered Friends of the Earth flag to flap restlessly. Its metal grommets were tapping an uneven rhythm against the metal flagpole.

"I guess nobody's here," McQueen said and looked into the shack. Inside, an ancient cast-iron cook stove sat covered with dust. Pots with dry mummified food gave the impression that the occupants had left in a hurry.

Tommy peeked around the door opening and pointed to something in the corner. "What's that?"

"Let's go see." McQueen nudged him on the shoulder.

They entered the shack, stepped to the object, and stopped. The purple-and-black-speckled, shriveled remains of the occupants lay in fetal positions. Horrified expressions on their dehydrated, skin-shrunken faces revealed they had died a horrible and painful death. And a faint unmistakable odor of burning flesh, amplified with an overpowering metallic taste, filled the air.

With his face twisted in utter disbelief, Tommy backed away. "I don't know what killed them, but let's get out of here."

With his eyes twitching left and right, McQueen scanned the room. "I think we're safe. Whatever killed these people has come and gone a long time ago." He bent over and examined the bodies. "It looks like an intense heat killed them where they stood." Trying to get the sight of the bodies out of his mind, he shook his head, backed away, and studied the inside of the shack. Wood widow frames, wood tables, wood chairs, and the door frame, showed no signs of being scorched by heat.

Outside, wondering what could have caused so much heat and not damaged any of the wood in the shack, they walked out of the desolated village.

Walking down the faded-blue, pot-holed street they passed broken-down fences that surrounded what used to be gardens, but were now filled with scraggly trees and waist-high weeds. A ways from the gardens, perfect shells of unfinished plastic houses that had been printed on a 3-D printer and linked together like a jigsaw puzzle, stood as a reminder of just how advanced computers had become before a virus wipe out the process. A little further down the road, the remains of a front lawn that had been neglected, was now bare dirt and a base for dead clumps of grass. Beyond that, McQueen noticed some things he hadn't seen in years. He pointed to them.

Looking to where McQueen had pointed, Tommy said, "I haven't seen one of those in a long time."

They walked off the street, past a blighted grove of skeletal trees, over a clearing that had been dyed black with used motor oil, and stepped onto an unpaved service apron in front of a deteriorating cement block building.

Once nestled on a lonely stretch of highway, the building had offered everything a weary traveler needed. A warm diner, a service station, and maybe there had been rooms to rent. As McQueen and Tommy neared the building, gravel scraped under their feet until they stopped at three gasoline pumps. Big red letters ran diagonally down the front of the seamlessly-plasticized, purple pumps and spelled out 'E.COLI'.

E. coli, in human gastrointestinal tracts and responsible for diarrheal diseases, had been genetically engineered to produce gasoline for these pumps. Standing like stubborn soldiers rusting away, but believing they would once again be the returned to the glamour and importance of their ancient past they had enjoyed before the much more efficient electric OvalCars shut them down, the ancient pumps stubbornly refused to fall over.

As if it were celebrating the death of gas and oil cartels that once controlled the legislation that tilted laws in their profitable favor and permitted them to ruin sixty percent of the oxygen of the earth, add nerve agents to the fuel that chemically killed and genetically damaged children's chromosomes, an orange butterfly, bright as a fluttering flame, delicately flew over a stretch of rare succulent grass and an even rarer smattering of milkweed plants.

Remembering the oil cartel's shambolic behaviors and how their profits from poison had disfigured and killed thousands of people, McQueen and Tommy took one last look at the butterfly before it flew behind the moldering building that was next to the pumps that had contributed to the earth's ongoing tragedy.

Standing next to the pump, McQueen stared off into the distance. Under a sky streaked with long, purple clouds, lines of dust-covered, dilapidated

170

houses stretched for kilometers. Little blue, glowing lights decorated ten houses on the shore of a small lake. Off to the left of the houses, little dried-up dirt paths wound around parched and yellowing trees and led to broken-down boat docks that slanted their rotten boards into the crystal clear water that not only reflected the beautiful blue color of the lights, but also gave off an aqua glow. The houses had been built and jammed so close together they were almost touching, but they seemed to be empty. In the darkened spaces between the houses, more tiny lights, the size of grains of rice gave off more blue glows.

"Oh no!" McQueen moaned and felt sick. He pointed to the blue lights. "I don't believe they did that."

Tommy shrugged. "What's the big deal? Someone put up lights and tried to make the place look like a new Blue Town." He stepped toward the houses. "There has to be something generating the electricity, and it's going to those lights. I'm going to take a closer look."

McQueen reached out and jerked Tommy back onto the center of the road. "Don't even think about going over there."

Confused, Tommy turned and faced McQueen.

McQueen held him tight.

"Take it easy," Tommy said. "Somebody may have found a new source of electricity. We may be able to find out what it is."

"It's not that. It's not that at all," McQueen said almost crying. "Those are not lights on those houses. They're Colbalt-60." He let Tommy free of his grip. "It's a radioactive material that used to be used in radio therapy. Instead of hauling it to a proper disposal point, a radiation disposal team must have found they could save a lot of money by dumping it into the lake. The water stops the gamma rays, but some poor misguided souls have taken the Colbalt-60 out of the lake." He pointed to the ten houses with the blue lights. "Those blue grains of Colbalt-60 have contaminated all those houses. Anyone inside has to be dead."

Tommy turned and stepped toward the road. "Let's get out of here."

As they rounded a bend, as if he had been hit with a speeding OvalCar, Tommy jerked back.

McQueen looked down the road. What appeared to be dark mounds of dirt scattered on the roadway turned out to be leather-covered skeletons in various positions. Some curled up with noting on but bathing suits. Business suites covered the few that were splayed out, and other bodies were nude. The ones who had kept crawling had fingers that stuck out like spidery legs, and long lines of dried blood trailed behind. They seemed to be clawing their way down a road of death. All along the sides of the road, mummified corpses, in various stages of deterioration had been stacked in overlapping layers.

"What happened?" Tommy asked.

"Take a close look," McQueen said and stepped off the road.

Tommy studied the corpse off to his left. Around its neck, a necklace of tiny Colbalt-60 beads glowed with a bright blue color. He looked to his right. A glowing band of blue beads curled around a man's arm.

Tommy turned to McQueen. "These people must have been exposed to a large amount of radiation. All their hair is gone and the Colbalt-60 is still glowing." He stepped off the road and stood next to McQueen. "What should we do?"

"We can't do anything. These people have been dead for months or more." McQueen shuddered. "Just keep walking around them."

Keeping a wary eye on the dead people on the road, they walked through a field of just as dead, brown grass. As they avoided the tiny blue beads glowing from the bodies, McQueen could almost hear ghosts of the hurrying feet of the now mummified people. They had been in terrible pain, panting and calling out with horse and strained voices from their radiation-induced sore throats, rushing away from the effects of the Colbalt-60, but dying on the road. Rigid bodies of men and women carrying children, who couldn't walk, seemed to be frozen in place. On down the road, more men carrying old men and old women trying to flee an invisible enemy had also died. Every few meters, the bodies of the old people, who couldn't keep up anymore, had died sitting, lying down, and crawling along. All had their hair-less heads directed straight ahead as if they were calling to the others up ahead to help them. The few bodies of people up ahead seemed to have been young and strong, but not one had stopped. From the positions of their heads, not one had even looked back. The Colbalt-60 had been an awful thing to try to flee from.

For a moment, Tommy stood motionless. "It's a wonder wild animals didn't eat the bodies and rats didn't gnaw the bodies away."

173

McQueen pointed to the last corpse on the road. Mummified remains of a rat had its mouth clamped on the finger on a corpse. "Even the animals and rats couldn't survive long enough to do any major damage."

"The way I see it," Tommy said and stepped back onto the road, "is that the earth could not tolerate people slamming a little piece of land full of houses. The people that built those crowded houses back there, forgot that the land does not belong to people. People belong to the land. The earth only lets people use it when they do not harm it. When the people harm the earth, the earth shakes them off just like a dog shakes off fleas."

They continued on down the road.

With the horrible sight still burning in their brains and a few kilometers later, McQueen and Tommy entered an oppressively dark tunnel created by long, curved, thorny branches that were interlaced with winding vines of poison ivy that led to a swampy bug-infested stretch of trees and pools of stagnant water. They didn't want to go through the tunnel. They wanted to turn around and go back. But the threat of Indigos trapping them was worse than going through the tunnel. So... they entered.

Except for a few stray mosquitoes buzzing around, nothing happened. After they came out of the tunnel, they made a few twists and turns around ragged piles of splintered trees and bright-red muck pools, with shiny surfaces, and happily leaped to solid ground.

Then, as if someone had thrown a switch, the air became dead quiet. Not a single tweet of a bird or a small movement of an animal of any kind disturbed the air.

With his mouth hanging open, Tommy looked around. Beams of pink light hammered through the gloom of an old world. McQueen couldn't help to look up. Tall slender towers, made of some sort of metal unknown to him, reached into a steamy sky. At the tower tops, huge propellers, to catch the wind, and run generators, sat motionless. Below the propellers at various points, irregular shapes hung over the sides of cauldron-like platforms. Next to the cauldrons, spiral escalators curled around the spherical towers. A few meters from the towers, trunks of trees climbed four stories high. At their tops, sparsely leafed branches fanned off from the trunks and looked like they were trying to escape the poison below by clawing toward the heavens. To the right, huge gray-white sculptures that resembled stretched bathtubs, turned on end, pyramided upward but were only half the height of the trees.

In the distance, spherical tops on chalky-white buildings climbed high into the sky and pierced the jagged clouds. Along the buildings, skinny pools filled with liquid, the color of pale dried blood, spread outward like spooky fingers. Next to the pools, mummified bodies lay in awkward positions. Beyond the buildings, arranged like spokes on a wheel, rows of pointed shapes that resembled rockets, aimed toward to the sky. For a hundred meters in front of McQueen and Tommy, patches of land that once were gardens were now havens of weeds, vines, and anything that could grow in the contaminated soil. Here and there, walkways made of queried stone wrapped around the edges of rectangular pools that held various colors of putrid liquids.

McQueen studied the closest pool. As if it were fighting the poison fouling its once pure water, the yellow-gray mud boiled angrily. Randomly popping, it spewed a sulfurous steam that burned McQueen's nostrils. To his left, a ballpark that once had a sand infield, now had an infield, heat had turned to glass. Fed power, from the tiny remains of a solar panel, a small green light staved off the full embrace of the darkness that filled a dark dugout, partially sunk into the ground. A sudden wind caused a ragged plastic flag on a tall flagpole to weakly ripple. Below the flag, a small propeller spun. It apparently generated electricity to a string of Christmas lights, hanging over the railing of the dugout. They lit up, dull and dirty-white. When the wind ceased, all the lights except the little green light in the dugout blinked to black.

McQueen imagined how all of this must have once looked. He pictured the propellers turning slowly enough not to harm any birds, but turning fast enough to generate free electricity that lit stadium lights that brightened the darkness and beamed on baseball players and amplified the beauty of the colorful flowers and plants growing in the spaces next to the pools. Then, the escalators had been running, transferring hundreds of working people up and down the spiral towers and depositing them onto the cauldron-like platforms, where after a satisfying day of work, they sat under shaded porches and enjoyed views of the vast distance. It had been a picturesque spot. Even though the experiment had failed, and hundreds of thousands of people no longer worked in the city, it had been an amazing feat of engineering. Except for the mummified bodies, and the occasional out-of-season Christmas lights, the place looked deserted.

Off in the distance, grand structures, build by captains of industry were in complete collapse. The dreams of the dead had been left to rot.

McQueen had believed keeping people on the blue grass had stopped this spectacular mismanagement and corruption. But it had not. Even though he could not see a reason why these ancient people had been eliminated, he figured that they weren't driven out. They were killed where they had stood. The irregular shapes hanging on the cauldron-like platforms were nothing special; they were only more blackened mummified bodies. At the time of death, no blood had been splashed, and no screams of children or women had echoed throughout the city. Some powerful force had come. Without warning, it had frozen all the people in the exact positions they were in at the time of death. Mummified bodies, with black leather-like skin stretched tight over bones and recessed eye sockets in hairless skulls, was something only a greed-driven Godless society would have created. McQueen stared at the shadowed bodies and the deeper gloom beyond. He wanted to look up and offer a silent prayer toward heaven, but Tommy tugged at his sleeve and pointed to a grime-covered sign that had fallen next to the rectangular pool in front of them.

McQueen took a few steps toward the sign. With the toe of his boot, he cleared enough of the grime off to read the sign. 'Welcome to Retirement Community of One Thousand REMS. Have no Fear. Roentgen equivalent in man is friendly. Courtesy of the Friends of the Earth Corporation'.

McQueen felt his face twist in anguish. "So that's where the old people went."

Mesmerized by the sign, Tommy froze in place. "Greed won again," he said with a voice tightly tethered with sorrow. "Way before the earth's shifts disrupted the earth and caused generators to bird nest, the Friends of the Earth turned off the propellers so they could charge the old people for electricity generated from radioactive materials."

McQueen felt his skin crawl. "These old people were played." He remembered the overpowering metallic taste of the town they had just left. "Tommy, you know those pots with the dry mummified food we saw in that town we just left?"

"What about them?"

"Those pots weren't left there because the people had left in a hurry. They were there because the manganisn people couldn't remember what they were doing."

Tommy reached up and scratched his head. "That's where the manganism people went. But why were they called manganism people?"

"That's one story I remember well," McQueen said and continued. "That metallic taste we had in our mouths was from high concentrations of manganism."

"I don't remember anything about manganism."

"It's something the Friends of the Earth were going to use to control the pig people, but I thought I had convinced them not to use it.

Tommy impatiently waved his little hand. "Yeah, but what is it?"

"It is a byproduct from the high production of methamphetamine drugs. Sproat must have had pig people manufacture it in a powder form. He probably sold the drugs to pig people, who snorted the powder to suppress their veracious appetites and acquire the euphoric release of dopamine into their brains."

"That sounds like they died happy."

"I wouldn't bet on it. Even though the effects lasted four to six hours, afterward, those people had slurred speech, their heart rates increased, and they couldn't stop talking."

"Is that all it did?"

"I wish," McQueen said getting fired up. "It decreased and increased sexual function. It made people sleep long periods of time. It made them hungry. It caused nosebleeds and depression. And they couldn't understand the importance of simple matters." He stopped to catch his breath.

Tommy threw his hands into the air. "In short, Sproat had people make dope that caused an entire town to become a bunch of bumbling idiots." Whew! He let out a disgusted breath of air. "I wonder if any moved away before they lost the ability to feed themselves."

"Not many," McQueen said shaking his head. "Drug users make their own misery. Even when they want to change, they won't. This place and that town was something they knew, something they

179

were used to. Like an old shoe, it made them feel comfortable. Many consumed so much methamphetamine that its byproduct, phenyl-2-propanone, accumulated in their brain tissue. Eventually they experienced toxic psychosis which always caused them to become uncontrollably violent and use more. So they stayed. When they became meth-wrecked people who could no longer function and produce the methamphetamine, they were considered useless. In the end, some unctuous bastard set off a neutron wave and killed them all. It was genocide."

Surveying the still intact buildings and towers, Tommy seemed puzzled. "How could a blast kill everyone and not damage anything else?"

"If I remember correctly," McQueen said. The paper books back at my library say that a neutron bomb produces a great numbers of neutrons but hardly any blast. The radiation destroys life but spares property."

A look of discomfort filled Tommy's face. "It looks like there aren't too many livable places left on the earth."

As McQueen nodded, the pool in front of them gurgled. Yellowish clouds of toxins hissed upward, forming clouds of steam that burned the skin on his hands and face. He coughed out the bad air. "This place is nothing but a death trap."

Tommy shuddered and turned away. "Everything the Friends of the Earth Corporation touches turns to crap. This place gives me the creeps."

McQueen's mouth took on an intense burning metallic taste. It felt as if bugs were crawling all over his body. "This must have been what the Friends of the Earth claimed was one of their so-called harmless radiation experiments."

Bending at the waist, Tommy gestured toward the devastation. "Just another inconvenience with warm regards from the Friends of the Earth."

McQueen looked to Tommy. He had a slight glaze to his eyes. Whatever was in the air was having a toxic effect on him. A new mouth-fouling alkaline taste erupted in McQueen's mouth. Moving his tong around, he tried, but was unable to work up enough saliva to spit out this new taste. He reached over and shook Tommy's shoulder. "Are you all right?"

With his eyes watering like puddles, Tommy blinked excessively. "I don't know," he said as if in a daze. "My eyes and mouth are burning."

He jerked away from the odor and took off running.

Trying to spit the alkaline taste from his mouth, McQueen took off after him.

Racing for water, and with the odor and taste huffing out of their nostrils and mouths, they ran across hard-packed earth and fields of loose shale left over from surface mining. Hoping to find an unpolluted flowing spring, they zigged and zagged among masses of dry dead bushes that had died next to weather-sculpted pillars of rock.

No water was found.

Up ahead, under one hundred fifty meter tall Hemlock trees, there should have been a dense evergreen branches that created a shaded environment like a forest cathedral, but there was not. McQueen and Tommy slowed and walked

181

under the ruined cathedral. For ten years the trees had battled the slow deadly spread of a tiny creature. Global boiling changed the extremely cold winters to warm weather. Cold being the only thing that killed the tree's only natural predator, the Hemlock wooly adagios, they thrived and laid their eggs on the underside and fed on sap. The great Hemlock trees lost needles and died. There was no shaded rest stop here. McQueen and Tommy trudged on.

Kilometers away, at the bottom of a huge hill, they stopped in a clearing and stared at the horizon. The light of the sun dimmed. A sudden cloak of cold covered them. Big heavy drops of rain fell from the sky. It spattered on the tops of their heads and exploded like miniature bombs. .Expecting to have the rain wash the alkaline from his mouth, McQueen held his palms up, lifted his face to the sky, and opened his mouth. As if it were being shot with buckshot, lead-gray rain pelted his face, entered his mouth, and brought on a taste of coal soot. Enraged, he cussed under his breath and talked out loud. "Pig people have polluted the air so bad that the rain can't even fall without picking up filth."

Tommy lifted his arm and wiped his wet forehead on the back of his hand. When he looked at his hand, a gray streak ran across it. He lifted his hand to McQueen. "Look, the sky's crying gray tears."

"That's not all it's crying," McQueen said and looked up into the sky. An ugly black ominous cloud surged toward them. The sound of a violent wind filled the air. When it arrived, it bent the tops of the trees as if they were fragile green feathers.

McQueen hoped it wasn't the beginning of a tornado or the tail end of a hurricane. World wind currents disrupted with global boiling had produced hurricanes one hundred kilometers wide with winds of three hundred kilometers an hour. If that hadn't been bad enough, gargantuan storms had lifted waves five hundred feet into the air and more. Not one person lived near any ocean.

McQueen searched the landscape for shelter. He saw none. The filthy rain increased and fell like vomit from the sky.

Wind grew stronger.

Then it roared.

Tommy shouted something.

The howling spray of the storm whipped his words away.

McQueen couldn't hear him.

Leaning forward, he searched for a protective place. The only thing that seemed to hold a little bit of promise loomed a hundred meters in front of them. It was a narrow trench. If McQueen didn't block the wind from getting to Tommy, it would lift his little body high into the air and sling him into eternity. McQueen turned his back to the wind, waved his arm, and signaled for Tommy to get in front of him.

Tommy did.

As they ran for the scant protection of the trench, wind whipped their clothing tight to their skin, and torrents of rain pounded their bodies. For a full minute McQueen couldn't see a thing. Trying to see if Tommy had been blown away, he put his hand in front of his eyes. But still, the wind-driven rain peppered his face and stabbed the back of his hands, stinging them like dull needles. A sudden gust of wind puffed the rain away for a brief moment. It allowed him to see ahead. Tommy had made it. He was lying in the little trench.

McQueen looked above his head. The broken branch of a tree twirled like a piece of dancing straw. He dove into the trench. Lying flat, the wind sucked the air out of his lungs and continued like a bad dream. The ground shook with a sudden hard thump, followed by a deep bass drumbeat that pounded deep in McQueen's chest cavity. Then, like an unwanted extra added attraction, flying branches swatted across his back.

After a long horrifying time, McQueen peeked over the top of the trench. The wind slowed; and as if it were leaving a few violent sparks in farewell, the lightening quivered in the distant sky; flashing parting zigzags of white veins across a purple horizon.

Rain fell harder.

Hunching their shoulders against the rain, it flowed off the backs of their heads, ran into their mouths, and washed the alkaline taste away.

In a few minutes it was over. Although blocked by a dirty-yellow sky, the sun came out, and the wind went back to normal.

McQueen and Tommy stood up and surveyed the damage. The feather-like leaves on the tops of the trees had been blown away. The resulting bare branches looked defeated and weary.

Tommy pointed to a meat-cleaver-shaped end of a broken-off treetop. It was just in front of them. "That's what that thud was."

McQueen reached up with the back of his hand and wiped the rain from his forehead. "That was close. The sharp part of that tree stuck right into the ground. If it would have hit us, it would have chopped us right in half."

"That was close, but we finally got rid of that that alkaline taste."

Off to their left was something they hadn't noticed. A big husky fellow, wearing a torn black and red plaid jacket, had been lying next to them.

He stood up.

Tommy and McQueen back away.

The strong rain had washed the back of the man's jacket. Except for his face, the entire front of his body was covered with black sewer filth. His long stringy hair hung down; and where it rested on his neck and temples, it was matted as if it had been pasted on with sticky tree sap. His hands were covered with semi-healed cuts and gashes that he must have gotten when the Indigo people threw him into the sewage pit. It looked like a purple worm was stuck on his face. It stretched from under his chin to the left side of his face and all the way to his right ear lobe. When McQueen took a closer look, he saw that it wasn't a worm. It was an ugly scar that had formed into a thick purple welt. Looking for a sign of compassion, McQueen stared into the man's eyes. All he saw were blank, iron-gray eyes that resembled the lifeless eyes of a corpse.

McQueen squared his shoulders and assumed a defensive posture. "Are you one of Sproat's men?"

The man cringed and drew his shoulders forward. "I'm supposed to be, but I got lost last night."

Just for spite, Tommy asked, "Did you enjoy it?"

"No." The man's mouth twisted into a leery smile. "Sproat made me drink too much. He always does. He thinks it's funny. I'm always the laughingstock of the night."

"How did you get this far?" McQueen asked.

The man's face beamed like he had just won one of Sproat's drinking contests. "I ran and walked all night." His beaming face dulled to disappointment, and he gestured to the ground. "I tripped and fell in this trench here. I was going to get up, but that wind came."

Tommy eyeballed the husky man as if he were studying a fossil in a museum. "You sound like you don't like Sproat. Why do you stay with him?"

The man drooped with helplessness. "I have no talent. I can do nothing else."

"Living with those half-wits is no bed of roses," McQueen said. "But everyone has some kind of talent."

"A look of confusion flushed the man's face. "What's a bed of roses?"

McQueen hadn't notice it before, but the man had a scorched smell. Maybe he had been hit with lightning. He was acting like his brain had been shot with enough electricity to fry eggs on his forehead.

With a weary look, Tommy shook his head. "Remind us to tell you sometime. Can't you find something to do besides run with Sproat?"

186

"All I need is one great capture." He turned to McQueen. "And then, just like the other man who captured McQueen's son, I could get promoted." A spark of happiness filled his eyes. "Just one capture, then I could live like the rich."

McQueen's heart raced with anticipation. There were a lot of youth camps. It could take him weeks to find the one where Miles was being held, but this idiot should know which camp Miles was in. McQueen wanted to put his fingers around the scab's neck. He wanted to put him in temporary discomfort. He wanted to choke it out of him. He raised his hand to grab the man by the throat.

Tommy stepped between the two and talked fast. "I thought all Sproat's men were rich."

McQueen remembered Sproat's men never responded to violence with an honest answer. He almost had lost the chance to find out where his son was. He would have to catch this man off guard. He would have to set a word trap. He dropped his hands.

"We make a decent wage," the man said and waved his hand in the air. "I have a couple a money credits on record. But they treat me like a piece of garbage. They always ask me, 'Who do you think you are?'"

"You look like a very talented man," McQueen said with phony compassion. "What do you tell them?"

"Tell them? All I can tell them is that I'm one of Sproat's men."

McQueen knew there was no sense trying to make this man feel better with flattery or praise.

His mind was too far gone. Tommy and he would have to try something else.

As if in thought, McQueen placed his hand on his chin. "Maybe you should tell them what your special talents are."

As if he were about to cry, the man curled his lower lip down. "I already told you," he whined. "I have no talent. I only know that I'm supposed to help those half-assed idiots catch you two, and I can't tell them that's my special talent."

"If you really want to show them you have talent," Tommy said and held out his hands. "Go ahead tie us up."

A dumbfound look filled the man's face. "What For?"

Tommy tilted his heat toward McQueen. "He's McQueen and I'm Tommy."

The man gasped and his hands began to shake. "I ain't never seen McQueen up close. Are you sure you're McQueen?"

McQueen followed Tommy's lead and held out his hands, too. "Who else could I be?" He jerked his hands with encouragement. "Here, tie us up."

With shaking hands, the man reached for Tommy's hands but drew them back. "This is too easy. What will happen if I tie you up?"

"I'm not sure, McQueen said and intentionally glanced toward the forest. "Maybe when you tie us up it will be a signal to our Indigo friends." He pointed to a tree. "Maybe they'll come out from behind a tree and carry you back to the pit and throw you in again."

Warily looking at the tree, the man stepped back. "I can't capture both of you."

Still offering his hands, McQueen jerked his head toward the forest. "Go ahead. Tie me up."

The man's eyes teared up. "Please don't give them the signal."

"Why not?"

As if he were searching of an answer in his empty mind, the man shook his head. "Because, I, I, I," he began but stumbled over the words. Fear showed in his eyes. "Because I can tell you where your son's at."

"We already know where he's *at*," Tommy said, emphasizing at.

The man turned toward McQueen. "Sproat said you would never go back to Blue Town. How did you know your son was at the Blue Town Youth Camp?"

"The Indigo people told us," McQueen lied and shook his hands in front of the man's ugly face. "Here tie me up. Just do it."

The man looked into the forest and then looked back at McQueen. "I'm afraid to tie you up. I'll just let you go."

"You can't," McQueen protested. "It wouldn't be right. Good men of Sproat don't run off and neglect their duty."

With a look of defiance, the man stared into the forest. "I don't care. I won't do it." He slapped his pockets. "I don't have any rope." A look of relief came over him. "If I show Sproat the way you went, he will respect me."

McQueen surmised that Sproat and his men probably got blown away in the storm. Or at least it slowed them down enough that they would never catch up. He lowered his hands. "Go ahead tell them what you want. We just don't care."

Like a dog wagging its tail about to be tossed a treat, the husky man smiled and nodded with quick little jerks. Then he waved his dirty hand in a shooing motion. "Be on your way. I'm still tired, been up all night." His eyes traveled to the trench. "I'll lie down and wait right here." He smiled with delight. "Sproat will come."

Tommy and McQueen tromped off into the dying forest, but this time they walked at a leisurely pace.

At the base of a tall hill, Tommy stopped. "Do you smell that?"

"Smell what?"

"Water."

"You think it's going to rain again?"

"No, this is different water. We could be close to the river."

"Are you thirsty?"

"No, I'm tired. I'd like to get into that river. If I had to, I would float all the way back to Blue Town on a piece of kindling wood."

They walked up over the hill. The metallic orange sun was setting to black. Now, there was a flicker of hope on the horizon.

CHAPTER 12

For protection from falling debris, Samara kept face buried in the dirt and held her hands on her head. After the wind had died down, keeping her face down, she peeked out from behind the tree roots. The wind had blown a huge oak tree down, and it had landed right in front of her. After the roots of the tree had groaned and heaved up out of the ground, it had created a big hole in the earth. She had dived into the hole. Hack and a few of his friends had dived in, too.

Samara lifted her face from the dirt. Hack stood on the big trunk of the downed tree and surveyed the area. Looking down at her, he asked, "Are you all right, Sis?"

"I'm okay," she said, and although she didn't mean to do it, her voice took on a pleading almost begging tone. "Do you think McQueen lived through the storm?"

As if he didn't want to answer and was just being polite, Hack smiled. "I doubt it. You know how weak those pig people are."

Samara's voice took a serious tone. "But I keep telling you, McQueen's different."

Hack waved off her seriousness. "For your sake, I hope he's dead. Later on, it will save you a lot of grief."

Samara looked at him with a sly grin. "Back at the pit, you didn't say grief. You said it would save me a lot of trouble. Have you changed your mind about McQueen?"

Like two children playing a game, they exchanged amused glances.

Hack asked, "Why would you think I have changed my mind?"

"Because in my heart, I feel McQueen is the man for me. And like you have said many times, 'Risk nothing, gain nothing.'"

Hack cocked his head in puzzlement. "Why would you say things like that?"

"I believe in things like that. It doesn't matter why."

A defeated look came into Hack's eyes. "Whatever." He waved his hand in the air and signaled to the other Indigos. "The little rainstorm's over," he shouted. "Let's get on with the task at hand."

From little indentations in the earth, a few Indigo people appeared. Then, from behind stumps, along fallen trees, and from the tangle of splintered branches, more Indigos materialized. All were unharmed.

In the distance, moans of Sproat and his injured men riddled the calm air above the storm-broken trees.

Hack picked up a long stick and jerked it toward the sky. "Drive Sproat's pig people back to where they came from."

Samara stood up. "Wouldn't it be more civilized if you gave them a chance to regroup and carry their dead and injured away?"

Hack snarled. "Anyone can tell they're not civilized. They have no feelings for others. Why should we have feelings for them?"

Samara cast Hack a cold knowing look. "Because we're better than they are."

Leaning on the stick, Hack sat down on the tree trunk. "You just might have something there?" He stood back up. The gathering group of Indigos gathered around him. He raised both arms. "Okay, listen up."

The indigos listened.

"Sproat and his men may be injured or dead," he said. "We don't want dead bodies lying around stinking up the countryside. So, we'll come up on Sproat's men, slow and easy. We'll give them time to pick up their dead and disabled. Then we'll scare them a little."

An Indigo in the group lifted his sinewy arm and spoke up. "What if they're too stupid to carry their injured?"

"Then we'll show them how to make litters. Sproat's men carry a lot of diseases. We should do all we can to persuade them to get *their* dead away from this place."

The Indigo spoke again. "We all know many of Sproat's men are infected with boils and have many other communicable diseases. Do we all help?"

Nodding, Hack turned toward the Indigo. "Good point." He turned to the group. "Only those of you who have the super immune systems will come into contact with Sproat's men. But just to be on the safe side, don't touch the bodies."

When the Indigos got to where Sproat's men were, Samara stopped and regretted that she had felt sorry for them. They were in a big gully, unharmed, drunk on their feet, and laughing about the storm they had managed to duck. One man lay on his back, waving his arms, moaning as if he were in pain, and yelling, "Help me! Help me!"

Samara turned toward Hack. "The devil must take care of its own."

Hack lifted his stick and shouted, "All new orders are off. Push these pig people back."

Slowly walking toward Sproat and his men, a swarm of Indigo's began chanting a low base chant. The vibrations from their combined efforts entered the atmosphere and created an unfriendly, spooky sound.

When Hack and the other Indigos had lined the top of the gully, Sproat and his men looked up in horror, turned, and ran into the forest. The chase was on, again.

CHAPTER 13

The evening shadows of dark trees shivered and the spooky chant of the Indigo people pounded through the forest. McQueen looked straight ahead. No movement met his eyes.

"Those Indigos sound healthy," he said. "I guess the storm didn't faze them. I wonder if the storm got Sproat and his men"

"I don't think it did," Tommy said and shifted on the log he was sitting on. "Sproat's men are some tough buggers."

McQueen feigned a smile. "If the storm didn't kill them, I hoped it washed their stink off."

A glimmer of mischief flashed in Tommy's face. "They smell so bad, the rain probably slanted away from their stinking bodies."

McQueen began to laugh, but grimaced from the stiffness from sleeping on the ground. He was still tired. He looked on the ground for a nice place to lie down for a few moments, but Tommy had his little arms poised, ready to start that rowing motion.

"Here we go again," McQueen said, swung his arms, and walked with that efficient arm rowing, half-walk half-run technique.

Over a steep hill and halfway down the other side, a mass of metallic bugs swarmed down from the sky and covered McQueen's and Tommy's bodies.

Whapping at the biting bugs, McQueen looked to Tommy.

Wildly swatting bugs from his head, Tommy slipped and fell to his back. But instead of trying to stop his momentum, he folded his arms across his chest and lay back. As if he were on a sled, on the slippery, rain-soaked grass, he started sliding on down the steep slope.

Wiping bugs from his face, McQueen managed an amused tone. "If you can do it, so can I." He dropped down onto the steep grassy hill. Then he lay on his back, pushed off with his arms, and slid down behind Tommy. Almost at the bottom, a line of trees seemed to pop up right in front of them. Tommy didn't slow. He pushed with his little arms and went faster. McQueen reached down to slow his slide, but when he saw what Tommy had done, he lifted his arms and gained more speed. Together, they steered toward the only opening between the trees. That narrow opening led to a wide green river.

Tommy flew over a yellow mud embankment. Suspended in midair, little droplets of mud flew from underneath his rear end, until, Splash! He dropped into the water.

McQueen skimmed right through the mud, flew into the air, and skidded on top of the water until he came to a slow stop, where he sank up to his waist in the cool water.

Paddling with his little arms and legs, Tommy swam up to McQueen. "We got most of the bugs off. The water should get Sproat's men off our trail."

"How do you figure that?"

"Those filthy scabs won't come in after us. The water's too clean."

McQueen wiped the bugs from the back of his neck and smiled a big water-rinsed-face smile.

"You got that right." Trying to get all the bugs off, he wiggled around in the water.

"What are you doing?" Tommy asked.

"Trying to shake these bugs off."

"Stand still for a minute. The fish will eat them off."

With wrinkled brow, McQueen stood still. Small fish nibbled at his back, arms, and legs, until every bug was gone.

'See," Tommy said. "Nothing to it." He rolled to his back and paddled toward shore. "Blue Town is a ways downriver. Maybe we can hitch a ride."

McQueen scanned the banks of the river for something that would float. He saw nothing. "On what? I don't even see a piece of kindling wood?"

Tommy lifted his head and pointed behind McQueen. A big log with one branch sticking out of it was floating down the river. "How about that?"

McQueen turned around. "All right." With water up to his waist, he walked toward the approaching log. "It's about time things started going our way."

Tommy swam out to the log and hooked his arm around the branch. McQueen stepped to the log, swung his foot over the biggest part, and sat like he was riding a horse. "This sure beats walking."

Holding onto the log with one hand and making those little rowing motions with his arm, Tommy smiled back at McQueen.

"Don't tell me you have some way of swimming with that stupid stroke."

"Not this time." Tommy climbed up on the log, lay face down with his belly resting on the log, and let his arms and legs hang in the moving water. "This trip, I'm taking it easy. The current is going to do all the work."

As they leisurely floated down the river, from heavily wooded banks, great sycamore trees stretched their giant white limbs across the water. Dimmed in flickering shadows, trunks of hickory and walnut trees supported branches that rose to touch the heavens. Next to the shore, long thin branches of pale-yellow willow branches drooped to the surface of the calm water. This was one of the very few places untouched by Sproat and the Pig People.

But the serene sight didn't last. A few kilometers downriver, the first one appeared: A pipe, with an opening the size of a man's head, was gushing some sort of dirty-white, chalky brine into the clean river.

Tommy sniffed. "Smell that chemical smell?"

"How can you not smell it?"

Tommy lifted his hands from the water and placed them on the log. "That's the stuff the gas companies said would stay under ground forever."

"Do you think they lied?"

"When poor people say something that isn't true, it's a lie. When rich people tell a lie, it's good business."

Nodding in agreement, McQueen glanced under the pipe. Whatever was in the chalky water had covered a muskrat. It lay on the edge of the water, its eyes bulging and stomach swollen. Tommy turned away from the site. "When people

198

sneak off the blue grass, they do anything they want. And they don't care who or what it hurts." He studied the pipe. Rust and corrosion ran along its entire length. "That thing's been here a while." He sighed. "Sproat and his men make money off polluting anything they can."

Floating past the pipe, McQueen turned his attention downriver. Another pipe jutted out into the water. "Are those pipes everywhere?"

"Looks like it."

McQueen shook his head in amazement. "I never thought anyone would drain unknown chemicals into the river. How can anyone be so stupid? Don't they know they have to drink this water?"

"Sproat and his cronies don't drink water, only booze."

After they drifted past the second pipe, McQueen looked around the bend. A glimpse of another pipe, vomiting a mix of mustard and gray water, flashed.

"There's another on," he said. "And we're headed right for it."

Tommy's face pinched with disgust. He kicked his little feet in the water and tried to steer the log away from the fetid flow. He maneuvered the log to the opposite side of the river and stopped kicking. To his right, another pipe flowed black, oily liquid, and a sour sewer odor rushed into the air. Tommy lifted his feet from the water and sat on the log with his knees up and his hands folded around them. "I give up."

In a friendly mocking tone McQueen said, "Relax, after a while you'll get used to it."

Breathing is shallow breaths, Tommy violently shook his head. "I'll never get used to anything like this."

"You might have to," McQueen said. "If we can't get over the stone wall at the youth camp, we'll have to crawl through a big sewer pipe to get inside."

Tommy winced and wrinkled his little nose. "I hate that smell. I hope we can find a way over the wall."

McQueen jerked his thumb toward the left side of the riverbank. Like a black mechanical monster, another big pipe, held up with metal beams, craned out into the middle of the dark river, but nothing came out of the end of it. This time the discharge came from a break in the pipe a meter from shore. Plants and leaves all around the broken pipe were brown, and others were a dying yellow color. Hypodermic needles and medical waste held back a thin tar-like liquid and created a marinade of filth. McQueen had no idea what the liquid was.

"If we have to crawl through a pipe," Tommy said, "I hope it's not as bad as this one. That stuff reeks. His nose wrinkled until his eyes squinted. "Look at it. You can see the stink rising in the air."

Shaking his head, McQueen fanned his face with his hand. "Those smells stick in your lungs like glue."

Tommy let his feet slip into the water. "The water's a little cleaner on the other side of the river. Let's kick this log over there."

McQueen took one strong kick and stopped. He slapped at a mosquito on his arm. "It's almost dark. The mosquitoes are coming out in droves."

He swatted another mosquito. "The current's getting stronger. I don't want to be running into those discharge pipes in the dark."

Tommy smacked a mosquito that had landed on his forehead and pointed to a little sand bar at the end of a stream that ran into the river. "Push the log into that little stream outlet."

McQueen kicked harder. "Good idea. We'll camp there till morning."

They pushed the log halfway onto the sand bar, made a fire to repel the mosquitoes, and had a good night's sleep.

Roused from sleep by the howl of the distant wind, McQueen jerked up in a cold sweat. He tilted his head to the side, sat motionless, and intently listened. The drunken voices of Sproat and his men had vanished; and as usual, the Indigo people could not be seen.

Rubbing the tiredness from his eyes, Tommy glanced at the remains of their fire and turned to McQueen. "Do you smell fresh smoke?"

McQueen wiped the sweat from his forehead with the back of his hand, sagged back, and rested his back against a tree. "The wind is probably blowing smoke from the campfires Sproat's men abandoned.

Tommy gazed into the forest. "It doesn't smell like wood smoke."

McQueen jumped up and faced upriver. "I don't believe it."

Tommy whipped his head around. "Believe what?"

McQueen thrust his hand to the left and pointed. "Right there."

Oily black smoke from an oil and fuel fire was crawling downriver.

Tommy gasped. "I've always heard the Mahoning River caught fire, but I didn't believe it." His mouth dropped open with awe. "The water's on fire. It's coming right at us."

Fed by a pipe gushing black oil, the fire was advancing at an alarming rate. McQueen looked toward the little stream. "We won't be able to go downriver until that thing burns off. Maybe we can go upstream and get away from it."

Without warning, the earth shifted. Tommy and McQueen tumbled to the ground. Something in the river exploded. The log they had been riding on whipped around, left the sand bar, and stopped on the other side of the river. Blue and white flames shot down the river and ignited a pool of oil that sent raging flames of the fire right at them.

McQueen turned his face away from the intense heat and screamed at Tommy, "Run upstream."

With the fire's heat causing steam to rise from their damp clothes Tommy and McQueen ran up the shallow streambed. The earth shifted again. The water upstream burst into flames. On each side, a thick thicket of trees blocked that escape. Tommy and McQueen ran back toward the river. A tree fell right in front of them. They hurdled over it, sprinted to the river, and dove beneath the fiery mess. Under water, and beneath the burning surface, they swam downriver. When they surfaced, the fire was twenty meters behind them, but it was racing forward. McQueen looked right and then left. A high wall of huge stones lined both sides of the river. There was no escape there, and the fire was approaching too fast to swim away from. He looked at the floating log. It was close to the wall and would offer no protection.

Treading water and breathing hard, Tommy lifted his little hand and pointed behind the log. Wedged between a fallen tree and the wall, the shiny side of a tin garbage can reflected the orange fire light.

McQueen nodded to Tommy. With the advancing fire chasing them, they swam to the can. When they stopped at the can, McQueen grabbed it. Its hot metal burned his hands. He released his grip and splashed water onto the can. The can cooled. He grabbed the can again and pulled. It was stuck in the muck.

Tommy hopped up onto the fallen tree, placed his feet on it, and took a hold of the edge of the can.

Standing in water up to his waist McQueen grabbed the can again. "Okay, Tommy, on one. Three, two, one."

They pulled in unison.

The can broke free.

The creeping fire was five meters away.

To McQueen's left, a wave of black smoke spewed into his eyes. .With his eyes stinging and his throat burning from the heat, he turned the can upside down and held its opening just under the water.

The fire was a meter away.

With his wet clothes steaming from the heat, Tommy jumped into the water. Holding on the edge of the can, he ducked his head under the water. McQueen did the same and popped his head up inside the can.

While the fire raged around the can, inside, McQueen blinked the water from his stinging eyes. In the darkness, he reached over and touched Tommy.

"I'm alive," Tommy said and his voice resonated in the can. "Are you okay?"

"I'm a little toasty but not burnt."

"Tommy breathed a sigh of relief. "That's just great. For a while there I thought we were in trouble."

***

After the fire, McQueen and Tommy pushed a charred log out into the main current and continued downriver. Under a smoky-gray sky, they passed open sewers that ran down black and gray ditches that oozed into the river like open wounds bleeding dark diseased blood. Beyond those, more chemical and oil pipes stuck out over the water; and like some grotesque long-throated monster, the pipes heaved sludge from their openings, letting it plop into the water. As they continued to float, the ruined river widened. In places, where it flowed slow, the water took on the consistency of some kind of sickening soup.

At a wide pool of shallow, blue-gray, fetid water, McQueen and Tommy slid off the log and stood up. They were at the outskirts of Blue Town. In the distance, black edifices of concrete and steel windmill factories, stood idle. Higher than their heads, coils of razor wire topped a tall stone wall. Trash on the shore and plastic bags caught in bushes and in trees were a quiet reminder they were in the squalid section of Blue Town.

Somewhere close, the whining of a noisy chainsaw smothered the peace and tranquility of the shoreline. It was another one of the far-reaching effects of no electricity. Without electricity there were no air compressors to run the quiet air chainsaws.

A school of fish, with three heads, swirled around the center of the pool. On their backs they struggled to force enough water into their gills to keep them alive."

With a look of hope, Tommy turned toward McQueen. "Do you think any of them will live?"

McQueen lowered his head and turned away from the struggling fish. "It's a losing battle. There's not enough oxygen in the water to keep them alive."

"They look like they were good healthy fish."

McQueen took a few steps toward the fish, but backed away. "Evil or good, Mother Nature treats all creatures the same."

Trying to keep their wet feet from sloshing, McQueen and Tommy waded through an opening under the razor-wire-topped wall, snuck up over the riverbank, and walked along a blue concrete road until they were on the outside of the high, stone walls of the youth camp. Here, McQueen bent over, walked along the wall, and felt the big square stones at its base.

"What are you doing?" Tommy asked."

"I'm looking for a secret block. I used to use it when I was here." He straightened up, put his hand on the small of his back, and surveyed the wall. To his right, a deep sewage pit that hadn't been there before blocked their way.

Tommy pulled at a square stone. It moved a little. "Is this it?"

McQueen bent over. "Everything's changed. "Let me see."

He took one tug at the stone.

Tommy tapped him on the shoulder.

McQueen looked up.

In the distance, a band of warriors marched toward them.

McQueen pointed to his right. "We have to jump in the pit."

Tommy's forehead lined with disgust. "A dirty cloud is covering the sun. Maybe they won't see us."

"Don't kid yourself. They're looking for us. When they get close, they'll see us."

They jumped in the stinking pit.

Standing up to their knees in the filth, at the bottom of the pit, they looked to their right. Only a few feet away, an open sewer pipe loomed like a gigantic open mouth full of sores.

McQueen jerked his hand toward the opening. "Let's go in."

Balancing on odd shaped stones, they walked in, stood in the black sewer crap and other slow moving stuff, and waited.

On the gray-clay, sewage-stained wall of the pit, the shadows of thirty warriors flowed past.

"How long do we have to stay in here," Tommy whispered and held his breath. "It's awful."

McQueen took a deep breath. The air was fetid with the stench of human waste. "I don't know about you," he said and placed the front of his shirt over his mouth. "But just as soon as they pass, I'm getting out of here."

The warriors passed. Tommy took a step toward the pit and fresh air. Another shadow of a figure appeared. It carried something in its hand.

"Damn." Tommy stepped back into the stink.

"I hope he isn't going to get water from this stinking pit," McQueen said.

"No, that's a bucket of burn-off fuel. This place stinks so bad, he's going to dump fuel in the pit and light it."

"What for?"

"Sometimes it burns off the stink, replaces it with a burnt smell."

McQueen looked into the darkness of the pipe they were standing in. He knew what was going to happen. He edged further into the pipe. "I don't see any light at the other end, but we can't get out of here the way we came."

A spasm crossed Tommy's face. "Are you sure we have to go through the pipe? It smells like it's full of half the crap in Blue Town."

"Maybe we can hold our breaths.

Tommy stiffened with resentment. "It's dark and I don't know what else is in there." Stress lines formed on his little brows. "Maybe we can find another garbage can."

"Come on, Tommy." McQueen tried to smile a mischievous smile, but the smell stopped him. He huffed out a fast breath of air. "We won't be in the pipe forever. We'll come out somewhere." He breathed in shallow breaths.

207

Tommy pointed to the shadow on the yellow dirt side of the pit. "Let's wait and make sure he's going to light it."

Splash! The shadow threw the bucket of fuel into the pit. Then another, then another. A bright, orange, slow rivulet of fire, inched its way along the top of the sewer water until the whole pit was ablaze. Smoke and fuel fumes swirled into the pipe.

Squinting from the smoke, McQueen looked to Tommy. "You want to wait some more?"

Trying to clear his throat of the smoke and fumes he had breathed in, Tommy managed to say, "Funny." He started making those little rowing motions with his arms. "Let's get going."

McQueen held out his right arm; and with the front of his shirt drooping from his mouth, he felt his way. Sidestepping around moiling trash and scaring out rodents that ran around his feet, he walked blindly into the darkness of the pipe. The smell intensified. He put his left forearm over his mouth and used his shirtsleeve for a filter. Tommy did the same, and they waded through trash that was alive with rats.

A few feet into the dark, McQueen felt a curve in the pipe. "We'll have to turn here."

He turned.

Bam! His head ran into the top of the pipe.

The pipe had gotten smaller.

He crouched down. "Watch you don't hit your head on this pipe."

Tommy talked through the sleeve on his shirt. "I'm not as tall as you are."

When Tommy talked, his voice echoed back from the sides of the pipe. The shape of the galvanized steel pipe was acting like a megaphone.

McQueen dropped to a crouching position and duck-walked like he had walked in the old hand and knee mines of the old tunnels of the Dinky complex. Forcing a smile, he turned toward Tommy. "Just like home, isn't it?"

Tommy's voice megaphoned into the dark air. "My home never smelled like this. Seems like every time you breathe in, you get invisible crap rammed into your mouth."

McQueen giggled into his shirtsleeve and kept inching forward.

"Damn it's dark in here," Tommy complained. "Light a match or something."

"Just keep moving. With all this crap gas, if we light a match, we'll get blown up."

"Maybe it'll blow us clean outside, and we'll be able to breathe."

A few feet after the curve, searching for an end to the stench, McQueen squinted into the darkness. Like a dot at the end of the long skinny black tunnel, a little light-blue circle of light blinked.

Tommy cried out, "The end's in sight."

"It's about time."

When they stepped into the light, a black and white dog saw them first. It charged out of its secret pen, running with a limp, yapping, growling, snarling, and the hair on its back stood up, stiff and menacing.

Tommy's mouth gaped open. The dog was big enough that he could ride it like a horse. He turned and ran back into the sewer pipe.

As if he were at a rickshaw stop waiting for a ride, McQueen leaned back and nonchalantly stood at the pipe's entrance.

The huge dog rushed toward him.

"Get out of the way!" Tommy yelled. "He'll rip your throat out."

McQueen stood his ground and smiled back at Tommy. "What's the matter? Can't you stand a little fresh air?"

Tommy didn't answer.

The dog ran faster.

When the dog was three meters from McQueen, it leaped into the air, mouth open, snarling. McQueen braced his body and stood erect, waiting. The big dog landed in McQueen's arms and began licking his face.

Other dogs came out of the bushes, wagged their tails, and rubbed their sides against McQueen's legs.

"Come on out, Tommy. These dogs have a good judge of character."

Tommy cautiously crept out of the pipe. The dogs quit wagging their tails and sniffed the back of his hand. He reached out and patted one on the top of its head. It wagged its tail, walked away; and as if it were guarding them, it stood a few meters away.

"McQueen ruffed up the dog in his arms and set it on the ground. It whined a gleeful whine and turned in submissive circles. It was glad to see him.

Look at this," McQueen said. "This dog's old, but he still rules the pack. When I first came to this crummy place, his father was just a puppy."

Tommy patted the dog on the head. "And lucky for you, he's a nice puppy now."

McQueen knelt on one knee and rubbed the dog's neck. "His father never did like Burke."

"You should have taken a hint from that dog. Maybe if you hadn't helped Burke, he would have flunk out of warrior school."

McQueen realized that Burke had been one greedy man, and for years he acted like he was his friend. Burke wasn't a smart man, but because McQueen treasured their friendship, he had helped him struggle through warrior school; but in the end, Burke used him to gain favor from the old Chief Earth Officer and tied to have McQueen killed. McQueen still felt guilty about helping an inferior person become a warrior. Continuing to rub the dog's neck, he looked at Tommy. "If he would have flunked out, it would have made things a whole lot easier."

Tommy shrugged.

McQueen stepped next to a huge blue spruce tree and peeked through an opening in the spiny branches. Long rows of brown plastic barracks sat in a straight military line. "Finding Miles isn't going to be easy."

"That's right," Tommy said and stepped next to McQueen. "If Sproat told these kids that you're wanted, we might have to run for our lives."

"I think we'll be okay. We're current events. The students are shielded from all new news."

"I hope you're right." Tommy looked at the barracks and then looked at the dog. "I don't see any guards. If that dog's so smart why don't you tell him to lead us to Miles?"

McQueen looked down at the dog. "You know, that might just work." He bent over, held the old dog's head, and looked into its bloodshot eyes. "Take me to Miles."

The dog looked at him as if it were confused.

"He doesn't understand you," Tommy said. "He's just a dog."

McQueen held the back of his hand in front of the dog's black nose. "Find, Miles, find!"

The dog sniffed McQueen's hand, let out a small yelp of recognition, and hobbled toward the second plastic barracks. There were no guards outside.

McQueen and Tommy followed.

The other dogs stayed a few yards from the sewer pipe, watching.

At the entrance to the barracks, Tommy tugged on McQueen's sleeve. "You think he's in there?"

"I don't know." McQueen stared at the door to the barracks. "The dog stopped here for a reason. Let's go in and see."

Tommy waved his hands in a sideway motion. "I can't go in. They don't allow Dinkies on the grounds."

"You'll be okay. I'll say your here for Dinky show and tell."

Tommy's big eyes grew wide. "Show and tell? Are you nuts?"

"That's what we used to call it. The boys have to know what a Dinky looks like up close."

"Why don't they just go for a ride in a rickshaw, or have someone show them a picture?"

"That would be too easy, and it would show them the truth. The corporation wants future warriors to believe Dinkies are inferior."

Tommy stared at McQueen for a moment. A trace of a smile formed on his face. "So you're going to present me like a free sample?"

"No, I'll present you like a big lie."

"You think it'll work?"

"These boys are very susceptible to suggestion. They call it propagandizing."

Making a crazy sign, Tommy spun his hand in a circle next to his floppy ear. "Everybody knows that. It's just another name for brain washing."

The old dog crawled under the cool shade of the barracks and turned around in the dark. His eyes glowed until they shut.

Tommy stepped on the first concrete step to go into the barracks.

McQueen put his hand on his shoulder. "Wait, Tommy. What I have to do might get you angry. Are you sure you want to go inside?"

"You can't do anything to get me mad at you."

"I hope not, but I'll have to treat you like they treat all Dinkies in here. Remember it's nothing personal. It's only a way to find Miles."

"Give it your best shot. I can take anything you can dish out."

McQueen put his hand on his chin. "I sure hope so. I don't like you to be mad at me. You're the only person I can trust."

Tommy flashed McQueen a big exaggerated smile. "What do you think I am, a baby?"

"I guess we're about to find out."

They went into the barracks. It was just as it was when McQueen had left years ago. The bunks were lined in perfect rows with perfect hospital corners and the blankets were stretched tight enough for a gold medal to bounce off them.

McQueen and Tommy walked down the center of a snow-white, high-gloss, polished floor. A blond-haired student with a buzz haircut and wearing a white T-shirt sat on his footlocker with his head down, buffing his brass belt buckle. When McQueen stopped with his feet under the boy's line of vision, the boy jumped to attention.

At the top of his lungs he shouted, "Attention!"

All along the left side of the barracks, half-dressed students bounced off their footlockers and jerked to attention.

McQueen stood extra erect and scanned the students for signs of panic. No one sounded an alarm or ran to alert the commandant that he was in the barracks. Apparently they hadn't been told that he was wanted. He relaxed his erect stance. "At ease!"

With twisted faces brought on from the sewer odor coming from McQueen and Tommy, the students changed from attention positions to parade rest. Even though some of them were in their underwear and some had only parts of their uniforms on, they did not relax.

McQueen began, "Gentleman." He talked loud and pronounced each word with clarity. "I apologize for the inconvenient odor.. Today, I have the pleasure of presenting a Dinky that you may or may not have seen before." As if he were a piece of

214

unwanted garbage: Spack! McQueen slapped his hand on Tommy's back and pushed him.

Tommy grimaced and for a brief second his face filled with anger, but he stepped forward.

McQueen looked at him with a threatening stare that would scare an ordinary Dinky.

Tommy regained his composure.

McQueen continued. "Using this specimen, my job is to point out flaws and genetic defects that you may not be aware of." He turned to his right. An older black-headed boy with sergeant stripes on his sleeves and a white name tag with black block lettering that read. 'MYERS', stood extra erect. Myers had to be the sergeant of the barracks.

"Sergeant of the barracks, Myers!" McQueen barked. "Pass me your instructional pointer."

"Yes Chief Earth Officer McQueen." Myers raced to his locker, reached in, and pulled out a metal stick as big as a pool cue. He rushed back and stood at attention in front of McQueen. With the stick at a present arms position, he said loud and clear, "Chief Earth Officer McQueen, instructional pointer." He jerked the stick. "Sir!"

McQueen took the stick. "At ease, Myers."

Myers rigidly stepped to parade rest.

McQueen turned toward the others. "Gentleman, this fifteen minute block of instruction will cover the Dinky." Tapping the big end of the stick in the palm of his hand and flashing Tommy a better-than-thou look, he began the demonstration. "You will note discrepancies that set Dinkies apart from all other forms of life. First!" He pointed with the pointer to Tommy's head. "You will notice that all Dinkies are short." He pointed to

Tommy's eyes. "Their eyes are larger than normal. A result of the mutant causing virus and some can't see without glasses." He pointed to Tommy's big ears. "Dinkies ears are extra-large to make up for their lack of sight. This trait makes it very difficult for anyone to sneak up on them." He pointed to Tommy's hands. "Note the hands. They are little hands. They cannot compare to a pig person's hands. This is another effect of the virus. However, these small hands are just right for the planting and growing of crops. They can get into smaller rows and weed out weeds more easily than a pig person's hands."

Tommy's face tensed and formed into a serious frown. McQueen was afraid he was about to say something and ruin the whole act. As a threatening gesture, Mc Queen cleared his throat.

Tommy's face relaxed.

McQueen pointed to Tommy's head. "Because of brain damage, a Dinky's head is bigger than a normal head. As if it has an infected cut inside that hasn't had a chance to heal, the brain has swollen. However, the mutated brain can still function and provide the Dinky with a limited intelligence that enables them to farm the green lands where they contacted the virus in the first place." He pointed to Tommy's feet. "And see these little feet? Dinkies cannot run fast. But they can make sharp, quick turns. Although Dinkies are not easy to catch, their feet and strong legs enable them to pull the heavy rickshaws with ease."

McQueen let his hand with the pointer fall to his side. "Gentleman, you can see that if you go off the blue grass, come into contact with wood, water, or green grass, this will be your future. You will be reduced to this specimen. You will be condemned to live your remaining miserable life as Dinky mutants. You will become agricultural slaves, rickshaw pullers, and perform other demeaning work." He nudged Tommy's shoulder.

Tommy stepped back.

McQueen looked off to his right. Painted lettering on two footlockers spelled out the names McQueen and Burke. "I was scheduled to address a full barracks," he said. "Where are McQueen and Burke?"

No one answered.

McQueen cast an icy glare at Sergeant Myers. "Sergeant Myers, do they have guard duty?"

Myers snapped to attention. "I don't think so, Chief Earth Officer McQueen."

"Then where are they? Isn't it your duty to be responsible for each other?"

Myers stood at attention, but quivered. "Yes, it is, Chief Earth Officer McQueen, but he *is* your son."

The blond-haired kid with the buzz haircut clicked to attention and spoke up. "Chief Earth Officer McQueen, they were on guard duty. They should have been back by now."

McQueen realized that's why there were no guards around the barracks. His son and Burke were on guard duty when they escaped. If this Burke was anything like his two-faced father, he may have set a trap for Miles just to get promoted. A Burke just couldn't be trusted. McQueen needed to know where they were going and find them before Burke had a chance to use his son for evil gain.

He looked at Sergeant Myers. "Do you know where they have gone?"

"Chief Earth Officer McQueen," Myers said and relaxed his tense military stance. "We tried to get the dogs to find them. No one has seen them go out the gate. They are still within the confines of the camp."

McQueen stared at his son's footlocker. Maybe it contained a clue as to where he went. He had to get in that locker, but he couldn't let the boys in the barracks know he had escaped. He reached up; and rubbing his forehead, he covered his eyes with his hand. He turned toward Tommy and flashed him a secret wink.

Tommy understood.

McQueen dropped his hand and pointed to Tommy. "Pay attention, men. Today, with the help of my son and Burke, this little Dinky may be able to show you something new. Somehow this Dinky may have acquired an Indigo trait. Regardless of the odor around him, he can pick up the scent of a person and lead us to them. Drenched in the stench of sewer water, he will sniff their footlockers. He may be able to recognize the scent of a place they may have been and of one of where they are now."

"Chief Earth Officer McQueen," Sergeant Myers said. "We have never heard of a Dinky that can pick up a scent."

"This is one of the reasons I brought this one today. Mutating into a Dinky is a brain damaging process, but sometimes the genetic defects produce amazing traits." He pointed to Tommy. "This one has a dog-like intelligence no one has ever managed to train. We have been working with him for a while. It will be a good test for him."

McQueen patted his thigh as if he were encouraging a dog. "Come here, Dinky."

Tommy obediently stepped to his side. McQueen opened his son's footlocker and looked for a clue as to where he may have gone. Arranged neat and orderly, the locker would pass any inspection.

Tommy lowered his face to the locker and sniffed the various items: socks, soap, a toothbrush, a razor, but he passed on the underwear. Everything in the locker was youth camp issue. Everything was what and where it should be. It was just like any other youth camp footlocker. It had no clues.

Burke's footlocker was the same. No clues.

McQueen glanced up. A small scratch in a movable ceiling tile caught his attention. Just as he had done, his son had kept his locker ready for inspection at all times; and he had actually lived out of the small space in the ceiling where he stashed ordinary living things like extra razors, soap, shoe polish, dirty towels, plastic writing paper, cards, and anything that was not permitted in the barracks.

With his back turned toward Sergeant Myers and looking at Tommy, McQueen nonchalantly pointed two fingers on his eyes, and looked up.

Tommy interrupted the signal and looked up at the tile in the ceiling. McQueen looked up, too. "Ahh, ha, he sees something."

McQueen closed the footlocker and stood on it. He reached up, moved the tile, reached in, and found nothing. When he pulled his hand across the tile, one small piece of paper raked between his fingers. He palmed it and put it in his pocket.

Whatever was up here, his son had taken it with him. He wasn't coming back, and since he had been gone only a short time, he couldn't be very far away. Before his escaping son got further away, McQueen needed to get out of the barracks as fast as he could. But he couldn't make it obvious that he was in a hurry. It would arouse suspicion. He couldn't give the boys in the barracks a reason to report that his escaping son had gone AWOL.

As if he were expecting McQueen to say something to him, Sergeant Myers tilted his black-headed head.

McQueen peered down at the sergeant. "Nothing up there," he said. "But I'm sure the commandant is testing this Dinky. Just like we planned, my son and Burke are hold up somewhere in this camp waiting for this Dinky to sniff them out."

Acting as if he were anxious to search for McQueen's son, Tommy looked out the window of the barracks and howled like a dog on the scent of a rabbit.

McQueen turned toward the boys. "Gentleman, it looks like the mutant has sensed something. We'll check the grounds. That is the conclusion of your block of instruction for today. We'll be back tomorrow and report the results of our exercise."

Sergeant Myers snapped to attention, held his hand in salute, and shouted, "Attention!"

With immediate precision, the other boys snapped to attention.

As if he were evaluating the boys McQueen studied then. "Gentleman, you're doing a fine job here. I must *again* apologize for the sewer odor." He returned the sergeant's salute, did a snappy about face, and walked down the white-tiled aisle. Tommy danced down the aisle at his side.

McQueen knew Tommy wanted to know what was on that piece of paper.

CHAPTER 14

Outside the barracks, Tommy struggled to keep up with McQueen, but he didn't mind. He knew McQueen was in a hurry to find his son, and that piece of paper could show where he was. He tugged at McQueen's elbow. "Does that piece of paper show where Miles is?"

McQueen slowed to a brisk walk. "I'm not sure."

Tommy skipped beside him. "If you don't know where he is, why are you walking so fast?

Searching, McQueen jerked his head right and then left. "About this time all the students and all the instructors come outside for physical training. They'll be everywhere."

"Do we have to go back through that stinking sewer pipe?"

"That's another reason to hurry. If we get to the secret block before they come out." He broke into a trot. "We'll be able to slip through."

At the wall, a thick thicket of berry bushes covered the lower blocks. The meter-high jagged canes swept to the ground like bent bows. McQueen examined the thicket. "Looks like no one has been using this."

Tommy stepped to the edge of the thicket. "I don't want to crawl through that stinking pipe again. Where's that block?"

McQueen tramped the long jagged canes down with the side of his warrior boots. At the wall, he bent over and pulled on a big square block. It didn't move. He pulled again. Nothing.

"Now what?" Tommy tilted his head toward the sewer pipe and grimaced.

McQueen straightened up. "Years ago, I put steel runners on the bottom of the block to make it easier to move. Maybe it's rusted in place. I used to keep them oiled." He bent over and grabbed the block. "It should move."

Tommy stepped to McQueen and put his little hands around the edges of the block. "Let me help."

Together, they pulled. The block moved, but let out a loud tooth-hurting screech. As if he had just bit into a lemon, McQueen clinched his teeth but kept on pulling until there was a space big enough to crawl through. Then he took a much-needed breath of air and looked at Tommy. "I'm glad that's open."

Tommy playfully shoved McQueen to the side. "Let me through there." He crouched down, and duck-walked through the wall. McQueen dropped to his hands and knees and followed. On the other side, they reached through the opening and pulled the stone back in place. It squeaked but this time not as loud.

Behind a bush that concealed the block, they stumbled awkwardly to their feet, but Tommy pulled McQueen back down. "Wait."

"What for?"

Holding his finger to his lips in a shushing gesture, Tommy whispered, "I think someone's coming."

Tommy eyes scanned up and down the blue concrete road. He saw nothing. But in the far distance, a pleasing shimmering sound, like that of a songbird's lullaby, filled the morning with a barely audible but soothing ambiance.

Tommy stretched his neck to see further down the road. "I hope it's them."

"Who?"

"Don't you remember?"

"No."

"If it's them, you will."

The sound got closer. It was bicycle bells. Excitement filled Tommy's face. "It's them!"

As if he had just realized who they were, McQueen leaned back with anticipation. "It sounds like those girls, but it can't be."

"It has to be them," Tommy said, "but didn't the Friends of the Earth outlaw that protest years ago."

For a better look, McQueen leaned toward the road. "They did, but the public outcry was so great they brought them back, claimed it was a new right of freedom." With a wave of his arm, he motioned to Tommy. "They are beautiful, but I have to wash this sewer smell off my clothes. Let's get out of here."

Tommy dug his heels in and tugged at McQueen's shirtsleeve. "You can hold your breath for a little while. Let's watch."

McQueen leaned back, and they settled into the bushes.

While they waited, Tommy remembered how the girls had looked the last time he had seen them. He had been out of his agriculture boundaries. McQueen and any warrior had the right to shoot him with the antidote or captured him. But he had climbed to the center of a blue spruce tree and was concealed behind its thick branches. He didn't know what all the commotion was about, but he had a clear view of what was about to happen.

In the distance, a group of girls came down an extremely narrow lane, ringing their bicycle bells, making a kind of fairyland music. Cherry trees in full blossom lined the path ahead of them and formed a canopy of sweet scents. Tommy had never seen trees as beautiful as this. The blossoms were profuse, rich pink, and delicate. Laden branches dipped down over the path and a rare blue sky showed through.

The cherry trees had no green leaves, and it was considered safe to go near them; but the wood in the branches and trunks were supposed to contained wood-virus. McQueen and other warriors guarded the lane and warned the people of the wood-virus dangers. At all other times the people would have stayed well away from trees, but for this event they were willing to take a chance. They hurried beneath the blossoms, filled the walkway, and waited. Tommy had wondered why they were waiting.

Standing in the walkway, McQueen had given him an answer when he had turned to the warrior on his right and said, "Those are the famous girls of Blue Town: The Blue Bottomed Girls."

And then, with golden grins on their exquisitely charming faces, the delicate girls gracefully pedaled close. They wore powdery blue shorts that showed off their long slender legs. At their necks, little gold necklaces, with tiny twinkling pink stones, accented their full breasts and framed their fabulous faces. Their silken hair flowed nearly to their shoulders and formed the rest of the frame for their sunny

225

eloquence. They were graceful works of art. They were all gorgeous.

When the loveliest one wobbled, McQueen had reached out to catch her, but she didn't fall. She had barely touched his hand with hers, and Tommy could tell McQueen had been amazed at how elegant and pleasing she was. After she had passed, with a sensual twist to her shoulders, she had peddled on down the lane.

"Why do they call them Blue Bottomed Girls?" the warrior on the right had asked. "They don't have blue bottoms. They're stunning."

"It was just a joke," McQueen said. "They started the rides to protest not being allowed to reproduce."

"That doesn't make sense."

"The girls claimed that if they didn't have a family to raise, they would sit around all day and their bottoms would not get enough circulation and turn blue."

As if his breath had been taken away, the warrior let his head fall to one side. "I don't care what they said." He lifted his head. His face brightened and his tone became enthusiastic. "They can sit around my place any day, and all day."

No matter where or when it happened, in the past, the Blue Bottomed Girls were a special spectacle. Flaunting their clear skins and firm healthy bodies, they would ride their bicycles in a subdued protest. While their long hair flowed behind, they would smile and show straight white teeth and pink kissable lips.

They carried water bottles in plastic containers that hooked to the bicycle's crossbars. When they

226

would stop to drink, warriors would hold their breaths and watch. Their attempt to bring back the right to reproduce had almost caused the Friends of the Earth Corporation to change the law.

Now, the bicycle bells rang closer. With his heart jumping with anticipation, once again, Tommy craned his neck to see the beautiful sight.

And then they came, pedaling, with a to and fro motion and nothing on but painted on pink panties and skimpy bras.

As if he had just experienced a sudden extreme headache, McQueen gasped and his brows furrowed. An instant ugly moment of silence filled the air.

Tommy couldn't believe what he was seeing. Not wanting to look, he covered his eyes with his hands but peeked thought his fingers. Like a deflated balloon, he leaned back against the wall. "The sewer pipe has better scenery than that."

Pedaling below a cloud of hovering flies, the girls all had huge fat bottoms. Like flabby rubber, their butts hung over the small bicycle seats. As if they had been created by a drunken painter, boils and broken skin, with red splotches adorned the girl's bodies. Their stomachs and breasts sagged and hung down, some to the crossbars. And their hair was fuzzy, all short and various shades of gray-green with split ends. When they stopped to drink, they drank from a horde of plastic pouches that they carried in corroded wire baskets on the front of the handlebars of the bicycles.

It was hard for Tommy to believe that if those pouches were on the crossbars, the girls huge stomachs wouldn't allow them to bend over far

227

enough to reach them. And although their stomachs were not as gigantic as the wheelbarrow people's, one drink would never be enough to satisfy those huge stomachs.

This new barrage of Blue Bottomed Girls stopped just a few meters from Tommy and McQueen. The smell of urine and sweat blew back at them. It was worse than a combination of the sewer pipe smell and the breath of a rotten-toothed person. After the girls had tilted the pouches to their mouths and drunk their fill, they wiped their thin tight lips with the backs of their sweaty hands and didn't smile. As if they were hiding years of rot, they held their lips over their teeth.

Like the pig people they were, they threw the empty water pouches on the road, turned sideways, and prepared to mount. Now, a new angle of ugly appeared. Frenched in with fat, their noses, eyes, and mouths, set back into their fluffy faces.

The fattest girl burped a loud discussing belch. It must have been the signal to get back on the bicycles. As the marshmallow faced, overblown bottomed girls, stutter-stepped, their loose hanging butts shook like thick fluttering flags. When they strained and swung their heavy legs they only managed to lift them halfway over the bicycle seats. When they all had one foot on the blue road and the other foot hanging over the bicycle seat, the leader burped again. They took deep breaths; and with great effort, they plopped their elephantine bottoms on the tiny bicycle seats. With faces that sat on narrow round shoulders that broadcasted meanness and greed, they began pedaling.

Tommy was thankful they were riding away. He was even more thankful that they weren't allowed to reproduce. After they were out of sight, he noticed that what was once a clean road, with shrubs and a few flowers along its former garden-like path, had been changed to a stretch of filth for the idiocy of the pig people. There was junk along the side of the road, paper boxes, cans, more plastic foil pouches, and all kinds of paper with fat grease and writing on it.

"Must be Sproat's sweethearts," McQueen said.

"And he probably thinks they're beautiful."

"I don't really care what they are," McQueen said. "This place reeks of disease. Let's get away from here."

Tommy felt his eyes growing watery. "What a waste of beauty."

"They look like they take baths in that sewer pit."

"If they were in a beauty contest with that sewage pit, I think the pit would win."

McQueen reached into his pocket and took out the piece paper he had found in the ceiling of the barracks.

Tommy leaned next to him and tried to read what was on it.

McQueen turned the palm of his hand over and let Tommy read it. "Hant, what is Hant?"

CHAPTER 15

Although Samara had the Indigo's triple strength of an ordinary person, she felt a weak pain sag in her chest, but it wasn't physical. When she was just a child and didn't know the value of an appropriate diet, without the proper preparation, she had run sixty kilometers. A terrible pain had erupted in her chest. It had only happened once; and she had learned from it; but this pain was nothing like that pain. But still, it was a deep hurt, a yearning to be with another person. Maybe that person was McQueen. She had to find out.

Sproat and his men were doing terrible things to the earth, and the pig people weren't much better. She felt throwing Sproat and his men into the pit was a small price to pay for the evil they were spreading, but she didn't like it when they stoned McQueen and the little mutant Dinky. She didn't want to argue with her brother about it, but after she had seen McQueen, a strange curiosity had awakened: She felt a need to follow him. With intentions of tracking him, she had simply walked away from her tribe.

After the storm, she had lost McQueen's trail, but she knew he had risen from the warrior ranks in a way no other had ever tried to do. He held the five hundredth Dinky capture record; and he had done it without killing a single Dinky. He had been proclaimed a Prince of Peace, with the privilege to choose a mate, reproduce, and raise his family in the safety of an ocean of blue grass. As if this were not enough fame and good fortune, when the Real Augur had appeared, the then Sergeant John

McQueen had been appointed the highest position in the land: Chief Earth Officer. She knew his accomplishments and fame would be a lot for him to walk away from. She hoped he would return to his roots. She hoped he had returned to Blue Town to rule it the way she knew he could.

She didn't have the physic abilities of the intellectual Indigos. But if McQueen wasn't in Blue Town, she could at least feel his vibrations in the aura of the town; and maybe, just maybe, she could pick up a direction and follow it to where he was.

In the suburbs of Blue Town, just a few meters from the blue road, she sat on a branch in the center of a cluster of spruce trees. Stumbling feet rumbling on the pavement caught her immediate attention. A swish that sounded like a plastic bag being swooped away cut the night air. She parted the branches and looked out. Someone, about the size of McQueen was walking down the road. The person had the same gait as McQueen. Her heart jumped. *Could this be him?*

He drew near. It wasn't McQueen, but this person could pass for a miniature McQueen, except his eyes were wide with fright. Even when she had pulled McQueen out of the rapids, fright had never been in his eyes. And this person wasn't a man. He was a boy with scared searching eyes. If McQueen had the ability to be afraid, those eyes were the kind of eyes he would have. She wondered if the boy was the person she would have to do the turn with. She waited until he was far enough away that he wouldn't see her. Then she followed him. The boy walked past a line of dead black trees and kept looking up into a rare luminous sky.

The Big Dipper was there, tilted way up; and off its two front stars, Polaris was there, too. The boy kept walking and looking toward the Pole Star. He was heading north. This kid was good. Now that the pig people were allowed off the blue grass, he knew that a compass was useless. When the pig people stayed on the blue grass and the atomic test had stopped, the atmosphere had begun to clear up. A few magnetic motors would run sometimes. Now, each day, more and more pollution was pumped into the earth's fragile air. When tall towers of factories released metallic fluff into the air and intertwined with the space junk, it disrupted the earth's magnetic fields. Electrical motors in the great OvalCars would not run. They continued to sit idle.

Before the boy vanished into the moonlit night, Samara eased down out of the tree. She had a feeling the boy was walking toward McQueen. To be sure, she would follow him; but just before she stepped onto the blue road, a dark figure trotted toward the boy. When the boy turned to look back, the figure veered off and hid in the shadows of a line of broken fences that lined the road. Whoever it was that person was following the boy. Under the celestial sky, Samara followed them both.

The boy walked on toward the hills. On his right, just where the road started to climb, a little bunch of houses were setting in the dark. As if they had been built by cross-eyed carpenters, the little houses looked crooked. Bare dirt yards, with poison soil, struggled to support a few yellowing weeds and even fewer skinny blades of light-green scrub grass. The green grass was evidence that

Sproat's spraying teams were not spraying all the people's yards with the contaminant dioxin that defoliated yards and areas of forest.

A vicious Clunk! Ruptured the silence of the night. Then again, Clunk! At the side of a wrecked OvalCar, a shirtless young boy, with a tattoo on his back, was chunking a rubber ball at the plastic dome of the OvalCar. A man's voice yelled from inside the house, "Quit throwing that ball."

The kid stopped throwing the ball, but didn't answer. Clunk! He threw the ball again, only this time faster and harder.

The earth shifted. The boy had difficulty keeping his feet under him. Then the wind sprang up and spewed dirt everywhere. Staggering sideways, the boy covered his face with his hands. The earth stopped rocking and the wind died down.

A woman's voice from inside the house screeched into the night. "Percy, don't come into this house with dirt all over you. And stop throwing that ball! You know it attracts fire-tornados."

Samara quickly scanned the area around the house for a trail of charred earth. If she was in a fire-tornado alley, a tornado could come at any moment and without warning. Tornados that had reached down and sucked methane from lines of abandoned gas wells were highly charged with oxygen, but they were no more dangerous than a regular tornado, until they caused a spark or came into contact with anything that would ignite them. Then, they became a magnificent sight. But their majestic whirling rainbow of blue, yellow, and orange, fire was deceiving. Racing along the earth, these fire-filled funnels, produced heat so intense it

233

turned water to steam, melted metal, and fried every living thing in its searing path. Samara didn't think that throwing a ball against a house would attract a fire tornado, but evidently the boy's mother wanted to scare the boy so he would quit throwing the ball.

Clunk! Percy threw the ball again.

The man's voice had a pleading, almost begging tone to it. It sliced through the air. "Quit clunking that ball, Percy. Why can't you stop doing what I tell you to stop doing?"

Clunk!

"That's no way to treat your father." The boy's mother whined. "Instead of breaking party equipment, you should try to help us out."

Percy didn't answer. For a moment, stunned silence filled the air. Then, Clunk!

The man raised his horse voice to a threatening pitch. "Did you hear me?"

In a horse, mocking tone, Percy mimicked his father. "Did you hear me?"

No answer.

With a calm defeated voice, his father threatened again, "You want me to come out there?"

"Aw, come on out," Percy said in a cartoon voice. "I'll throw this ball right between your eyes, you dried-up old goat." He slammed the ball against the side of the OvalCar dome so hard that it cracked.

Percy's father stood in the mildew-riddled doorway with a plastic bottle of beer in his hand and his fat hairy belly hanging over his belt-clinched waist. He belched and shook his fist at Percy. "Ain't you gonna listen to me?"

Percy reached into the OvalCar, pulled out a plastic stick with a rubber ball on the end, and pounded the side of the OvalCar. Boom! Boom! Boom! Loud bass pounding blasted the night.

Percy's father yelled over the pounding. "Percy! You wanna go deaf? Stop that."

Samara wanted to get away from this incident. She walked faster, but slowed down when she could read the tattoo on the boy's back. Beneath a crooked purple arrow that pointed toward Percy's head were the words 'NO BRAINS'.

As if he were confirming the message tattooed on his back, Percy yelled into the house, "It ain't my fault dat I got deef."

Samara ran from the scene. It was hard to believe that the kids of Blue Town had no discipline, and that they didn't care what kind of image they projected. Getting off the blue grass was an excuse for everyone to do just what they wanted to do, and kids were no exceptions. When people started going off the blue grass, everything had changed, and changed fast.

Samara didn't know if the boy would spend a lifetime living a wasted life or if things would change and he could be helped. When McQueen had first become the Chief Earth Officer, he knew how to save the people from themselves. If he knew what was happening now, he would try to change it. Sproat's men weren't chasing him for just any reason. They wanted him because he could force the pig people back on the blue grass where they belonged.

Slowing to a walk, Samara stepped on down the steam-car-rutted asphalt road. In the driveways of every three of four houses, broken down OvalCars, rusted with age, were dented or turned over on their sides, most with their plastic domes gone. These clear plastic domes made great containers for Saki burns. The pig people turned the domes upside-down and used them as if they were gigantic punch bowls. When the atmosphere allowed TV signals to be received, in a prelude to watching the most popular event of Blue Town: 'The Wheelbarrow People at the Moving Buffet', the bowls would be filled with anything that contained alcohol, which was mostly Saki, a cheap rice wine. The Saki had such a high alcohol content that if ignited it would burn blue.

When these huge bowls were full and the wheelbarrow people event was over, there was no end to the alcohol induced good times. And the pig people loved them.

In a state of suspended sensibility, the men would sit there in their dirt and scrub-grass-littered yards; and the women would carry on, singing and dancing. Their lard bellies and loose flabby butts would wriggle, sometimes rippling like fat rags in the wind. Samara's brother, Hack, claimed that if you watched them long enough it would make you wish dancing had never been invented. Most drank a lot and tried to get everyone else to do it, claimed there was not any other way to stand the lives they lived.

The morning after, if people were lying in the street and the level of alcohol in the makeshift bowl was low, it was considered a good party. The success or failure of a party was measured by how much alcohol was consumed. It was rare that a bowl was ever emptied. But when it was, there were usually a few deaths; and that was the sign of a really good time.

Drinking themselves to death was a goal most of the partying pig people tried to achieve. They believed that when a person died sober, they would go to heaven or hell, but if they were drunk when they died, they would eliminate the possibility of going to hell: They would immediately go through the neon lighted gates and enter the great drunken party in the sky.

In their years of drinking they had learned that a drunken person hates a sober one and a sober one hates a drunken one. To be admitted to a party, the person had to show up drunk. That way there would be no negativity or talk about the dangers of drink. No matter how much they danced or sang, Samara didn't believe any of it. To her, the parties were cruel useless events. When the Friends of the Earth had begun to torture her father they had tried to take away his optimism and self-esteem. It would be difficult for anyone to torture that out of these pig people. They had no optimism or self-esteem. They were worse than dumb animals. They were un-trainable. But when one did die, Samara figured the intellectual level of the pig people's gene pool had slightly increased.

Walking on down the road, she passed more dark houses; and she was glad the pig people inside were not having parties this night.

A few kilometers up the long hill, she stopped and stood perfectly still. The boy cut off into a slanted field of tall green grass. He wasn't afraid of catching a virus and mutating into a Dinky. If he wasn't someone special, he was a pig person who didn't care about going off the blue grass.

When he got to a line of rocks and trees, he stopped and surveyed the area. Using her incredible speed and stealth that was close to invisible, Samara slipped along the tree line and watched. The boy started walking again, but he didn't cut through the tall gray grass. It would have made a clear path to wherever he was going. It would be easy for anyone to follow. He stayed along the rocks and did not disturb the tall grass. In a clump of trees, at the center of the hill, he stopped under an overhanging rock.

Samara was amazed at the boy's knowledge. If he were going to bed down there for the night, he had chosen a place that was dark and quiet. It was a smart move. If Sproat and his men came for him, he wouldn't be hemmed in. He would have some cover and would be able to scramble out either way.

She watched the person that was following the boy. Bending low, the person turned, headed out of the field, blended into the tree shadows, and was gone.

Maybe he was going to get Sproat's scabs. If he were, the boy should be safe. He had a way out; and if he had to fight, he would have something at his back. Sproat's scabs liked to gang up on a person. And the boy would be sleeping where he could get away from whatever wanted to chase him.

As she watched, the boy checked behind the three tall bushes that were in front of the ledge. The three bushes reminded her of the shell game where a pea is placed under one of the shells and moved around, and the person being fooled has to decide which shell is hiding the pea. If Sproat's men thought the boy might be behind one of the three bushes they wouldn't know which one to attack, and that short burst of confusion would be a chance for the boy to escape.

This boy didn't act like a pig person. Maybe he was part Indigo. He picked a good color to hide under: dark. Sproat's men probably didn't know a fleeing person didn't need a camouflage suit or special hiding devices. From his actions, the boy knew he needed to be just one thing, and that was to be the same color as the place he was hiding in. If that place was high, like that rock ledge he was climbing onto, he could fall on an intruder's back; and like a blaze of light out of the dark, he could scare them long enough to dash away; and if he got cornered, he could bash them right in their face. Too bad he didn't know the odds were against him. Impressed with the boy, Samara waited and watched.

A while later, the aroma of sweaty socks and booze wafted across her face. Sproat's men were near. Her rapid eye movements enabled her to search the dark. Six shadows of Sproat's men skipped across a line of low bushes. Then, they were right in front of the boy. He kept perfectly still.

The first man shook the tall bush on the right. "Come on out, Miles."

The other men shook the other two bushes. "There's no way out, Miles. We got your old man. Come on out and watch us give him the antidote."

Samara had an idea who the boy's father could be, but she wasn't sure. Sproat's men wanted to make an example of him. He had to be someone important to have them want to do that.

"Come on out, Miles McQueen," The first man pleaded. "We know you're in there."

Samara gasped with surprise. Her suspicions were right. Miles was McQueen's son. She figured he would dodge the threats by running away.

But he didn't.

Like a young hawk after prey, Miles swooped down from the ledge and pounced on the first man's back. The man heaved his body from side to side and tried to jerk Miles off. Miles hung on. With his uncoordinated chubby arms, the man tried to reached back and get Miles, but his arms were too short. He couldn't get a grip.

Samara let out a little giggle, but she knew Miles would be no match for six of Sproat's men. They could sit on him. Under their fat rear ends, he could be squashed to death. Depending on how drunk they were, just for laughs, they might castrate him, cut his head off, and spill his guts all over the rock, or tie him up against a tree, and use him for head butt practice. They were always under orders. They were permitted to put fleeing people in temporary discomfort and bring them in alive. But they didn't always follow orders. It was a compliment to call them unreliable drunken swine.

As if he were riding a spinning bull, Miles hung onto the man's back. Three men waddled up to Miles and the man. The man quit spinning. One of the men grabbed Miles's arm and pulled. "Come on, Miles. Let go."

Miles jerked his arm free and wrapped it around the man's neck; and with the heels of his feet, he kicked the man in the ribs."

A painful pleading whimper escaped the man's trembling lips. "Get him off, get him off."

The two men struggled to free the man of Miles's grip. As they pulled, Miles placed his feet on the man's back. At the same time he took his arm from around the man's fat neck, straightened his legs, and pushed off. The unexpected push and the pulling of the two men caused them to stumble to the ground. Miles landed on his feet and turned to run. But he was no match for the other two heavyweights. They pulled him down to the ground and held him with his back flat against the ground. The fattest one squatted over Miles and wiggled his big butt. "Here's a treat for you." He sat on Miles's chest.

Samara wondered why Miles didn't scream. But she realized he couldn't breathe. The weight of the man sitting on him must have made him feel like his chest was in a gigantic vice, and someone was screwing the handle in.

A rush of air left Miles's lungs.

The man, who had gotten Miles off his back, rolled to his stomach, struggled, and got up off the ground. Almost losing his balance, he huffed over to Miles. "Let me sit on that little creep, Puff, Puff, we'll show his old man who's in charge around here."

The other heavy man stayed on Miles's chest and motioned to the other man. "Come on, Henry, he's not going anywhere."

Samara crept closer. When she looked back, the dark figure of the person that had left, had emerged from the murk; but that person didn't seem to be a threat. He was just watching. She looked toward Miles. In the moonlight, his face was pale blue.

Henry squatted above Miles's face. "Let me sit right on that face." He lowered his rear end down towards Miles's face.

Samara got ready to jump.

Henry's fat rear end touched Miles's face.

Miles opened his mouth and bit into the flabby butt.

Henry tried to jump up; but like a stingy dog on the end of a bone, Miles hung on. Trying to pull away, Heavy Henry screamed in pain. Miles still kept his teeth clamped on Henry's butt. The sound of cloth tearing cut the night. Miles had bitten right through Henry's pants.

Samara looked back at the dark figure to see if it was going to join the attack. It didn't. It was still watching.

She turned and leaped toward the man sitting on Miles's chest. With one foot, she kicked him off.

As Miles rolled free, Henry's butt broke free from his mouth.

Contorting his face into a scowl, Henry grabbed his behind and whimpered into his chubby hands.

The other five men surrounded Samara. "Get that bitch!" one ordered; and they closed in. Samara simply kicked them, one by one, with not much effort at all, right in their ballooned stomachs. They fell to the ground, puffing and gasping for air.

She picked up Miles's lifeless form and took off running. Bounding over a stretch of rocks, she glanced down at Mile's face. He had a piece of Henry's pants in his mouth. She hoped it wasn't a death grip. If it was, he could be dead. She didn't know who was watching. It could be more of Sproat's men waiting to ambush her, but she couldn't stop to find out. She kept running.

Miles was no baby, but she ran with him in her arms as if he were. She raced over the hill and down into the next valley. Miles wasn't moving She would have to find a place to give him the kiss of life, and fast.

CHAPTER 16

Even though Tommy was his best friend, McQueen wasn't sure he wanted him to know he had the chip to the orange turn. He leaned his back against the stone wall that ran around the Blue Town youth camp and put the note he had found in the barracks back into his pocket.

"What is Hant?" Tommy asked again.

"Hant isn't a place we can go."

"Do you know where it is?"

McQueen knew they could get to Orangeville if they headed north, but he wasn't sure he was ready to go there. "I think the note means, head always north, true. The true means true north, not magnetic north."

Tommy stepped away from the wall and swung his little arms. "We going?"

"We should," McQueen said. "But I feel like I would be like running away from my duties." Standing away from the wall and staring at the rubbish on the blue road, he remembered how it used to be when the people had to stay on the blue grass. Clean electric OvalCars would hum past with their clear bubble tops, and the drivers inside were all women. Nice women, like his wife, Danielle. These women weren't like the Blue Bottomed girls. They didn't have boils or scars dotting their bodies. They didn't have cigarettes hanging from mean tight lips. Their uniforms were crisp and clean. Their bodies were slender and graceful. But those wonderful OvalCars and the professional women, who drove them, were gone, replaced with rickshaws pulled by unwilling Dinkies. Back then,

Dinkies had planted lines of flowers along the roads and cared for them as if they were beautiful children. Now, black soot from the coal fired steam cars that only Sproat and his men could ride on, caked the roadside. Here and there, only scrub grass and a few nameless weeds sagged with death. What was once lovely was now a sickening sight.

Tommy quit swinging his arms, put his hands in his pockets, and hunched his back. "It's hard to believe you were once in charge of this place. I bet you hate it now"

"I don't hate the place," McQueen said. "Living in the field of blue grass, I became too complacent."

"Didn't you ever go off the blue grass?"

"Sure I went off, but I now can see that I was tricked into only going to places they wanted me to go." He placed his hand on his chin and looked at the road. "I hate what the system has done to Blue Town."

"Too bad we can't fix it."

They quit talking and stood at the wall. Tears formed on Tommy's face. He lowered his head to hide them.

McQueen suddenly realized that the blue world he had known and loved had been torn apart. He broke into a dull panic. "I thought I was fixing it," he said. "I talked and reasoned with everybody."

"What about Patagonia?" Tommy lifted his head. "Did you go there?"

"I did, but the people in power treated me like I was a stinking man who had just gotten off garbage duty."

"It couldn't have been that bad," Tommy said. "Someone must have a little common sense."

"If they did, they didn't show it. When I told them about possible breaches in security and the canals, they said it was only a temporary setback. And I believed them." As if a hidden nerve had been pierced, pain filled McQueen's face. "And when I asked them if they were absolutely sure, they laughed with formal indifference." His face hardened into a frown. "They tipped their wine glasses at me, said, 'So what if a few people going off the blue grass, a little poop in the canals won't hurt a thing. Everything is just dandy.'"

"Look, McQueen," Tommy said. "You have fought all your life for the good of the people. Maybe they just don't deserve to be saved."

"I must be out of my mind to try and fix this place just so Sproat's men can ruin it."

A mischievous grin formed on Tommy's face. Referring to the Blue Bottomed girls, he joked, "Won't you save it for Sproat's women?"

McQueen smiled a slight smile, but his face turned back to a frown. "I can't save people who are given the chance and refuse to save themselves."

"But you always have a plan."

"It's hard to make any plan when people no longer care what is right or wrong."

Tommy dropped to one knee. As if he were going to draw a plan, he pointed to a patch of lifeless sand on the ground. "If you don't have a plan, we can make one."

McQueen tapped the palm of his hand and looked off into the dirty-gray sky. "I think my plan making times are over." He paused and discovered that he was suddenly surprised to hear himself talk in a negative way. He quit tapping his palm. He wanted to know what was the matter with himself. If he kept thinking negative, negative things would happen. He watched Tommy.

Tommy's shoulders sank down, and he buried his little chin into his chest.

Waving his hand in an irritating gesture, McQueen said, "My father was right when he said, 'Look for the negative things and you'll surely find them.'"

With a look of appeal, Tommy turned toward McQueen. "You never quit anything in your life."

Nodding his head, McQueen leaned against the wall and thought about how he almost quit in the rapids. Someone else had not given up. Someone or something had saved him for a reason. His eyes ached and a terrible rotten feeling invaded his chest. Then a sick feeling crawled over his whole body. He had just made up his mind to just quit trying to save the town, and now indecision wrenched his entire being. His instincts were going off in all kinds of directions. Cobwebs of conflicting thoughts and suspicions invaded his mind.

"You ready to go?" Tommy asked.

McQueen put his hands on his knees and lowered his head. "I don't feel so good."

"Maybe you picked up something from that sewer pipe. There's enough disease in there to kill an army."

"It's not that," McQueen said shaking his head. "Nothing makes sense anymore."

Tommy looked questionably at McQueen. "Tell me about it."

"Sometimes I believe it's useless to save people from themselves."

Running his hand over a clump of blue grass that was growing next to the wall, Tommy said, "Sometimes they don't know they need to be saved."

McQueen bent over and pulled a handful of blue grass away from the wall. "That's why this blue grass worked. Maybe we could get the pig people back on it."

"Maybe we can't," Tommy said. "Maybe our hopes for the future are only demons in our heads. If we ignored them, they might go away."

"But I can't ignore anything." McQueen threw the blue grass onto the ground. "It's like I'm being pushed and guided by something greater than anything I have ever known."

Tommy's face pinched with disgust. "The very people we are trying to help betray us."

McQueen kicked at the blue grass he had thrown on the ground. "We would have to be crazy to continue to fight."

Pacing in a little circle, Tommy threw his hands up. "What else can we do?"

"I don't mean to sound like a spoiled little kid," McQueen said. "But if we were playing ball. And it were my ball, I'd take my ball and go home."

"Then, no one would play."

"That's right. We're the ball they're kicking around. If we quit, we'll take the ball out of the game."

Tommy stopped pacing. "Let's quit."

McQueen stood away from the wall and ran his hand through his long black hair. "Maybe that would be the best thing to do."

A look of indecision filled Tommy's eyes. "I don't know if it really is the best thing."

"Maybe not, but it would be the smartest."

"You're not going to quit on your son, are you?"

"I wouldn't do that," McQueen said, and his body shuddered.

"What's the matter?"

"I feel weird, like a man who just swam through rough water and finally grabbed onto a life preserver, but as soon as he grabbed it, someone let the air out."

"Letting the air out of a lifesaver is something Sproat would do."

"You may have something there. The Friends of the Earth Corporation are constantly making things worse for people."

With a bored tone to his voice, Tommy said, "Tell me something new."

"They'll never expect us to just quit."

Tommy's voice showed some excitement. "We'll take our ball and go home."

"We'll quit, but we won't go home. We'll make a new home in Orangeville."

"Orangeville's a myth," Tommy said. "And even if it isn't, how will we get there? The Indigo's chase everybody back to the filth they try to escape from."

McQueen knew it might be time for the orange turn, but he couldn't tell Tommy, yet. "Orangeville is an experiment," he said, "a place where no ignorant pig person has ever gone and stayed."

Tommy cast a look of disbelief. "Is Orangeville just a fairy tale, like Atlantis or The Land of Mu?"

McQueen placed his hand on the chip sewn in the waistband of his underwear and began. "Officially Orangeville doesn't exist. It is something like the land of Mu, but it's a secret place, a hideaway. It has a group of buildings that have been private experiments and have been converted into earth friendly homes. And it is confined to an area almost like the protective cages used for hawks when they shed part or all of their feathers and are replaced by a new growth. In Orangeville, a select group of Pigmies beyond the upper confidence limit of most people, have cast off the ignorance of the pig people's world and created a new way to live."

McQueen wanted to tell Tommy about the chip and the Orange turn, too. But if he did, and Tommy was caught and tortured by Sproat, he might give away the secret. Then, after he did, Sproat would kill him. McQueen loved Tommy. He didn't want to place him in unnecessary danger. As long as Sproat thought Tommy knew about the turn, and he thought that Tommy just wasn't telling him about it, he would not kill him. Telling Tommy about the Orange turn would have to be a last and only resort. McQueen didn't tell him.

He shook his finger at Tommy. "I'm telling you, Tommy, Orangeville exists. We'll find Miles. He must be going there."

"As we speak," Tommy added.

McQueen continued. "We'll go to Orangeville, build an army of good warriors, and maybe get some of the old ones back. We'll come back to Blue Town. We'll take our town back."

Tommy face distorted with confusion. "Now let me get this straight," he said. "We have no idea where Miles is, but we're going to find him. We don't know how to get to this great Orangeville, but were going to go there."

McQueen smiled a big ear-to-ear smile. "That's right."

Tommy smiled back. "And we're not giving up?"

"We're not? "

"And we'll come back to Blue Town?"

"Yes, we will, "McQueen said and satisfaction filled his heart. "But for now, we'll be taking one toy out of their game: Us."

Tommy jumped up. "What are we waiting on?"

McQueen looked down the blue concrete road. In the distance, a filthy pillar of black coal-smoke seethed into the air.

Tommy saw it, too. As if frozen in astonishment, he stood motionless.

McQueen grabbed Tommy's arm. "We're leaving right now. Sproat's gang of half-wits are coming in one of their great steam cars."

Clank! The thick bottom of an empty wine bottle hit the road, but didn't break.

"They're throwing things at us," Tommy said. Let's get out of here." He stepped toward a stretch of jaggers that ran along the stone wall.

McQueen put his arm in front of Tommy. "Wait."

The steam car with Sproat's men chugged closer.

Tommy tensed his face muscles and pulled on McQueen's elbow. "Let's go. I don't want them to shoot us with those antidote bullets. Those things hurt."

McQueen chuckled. "They couldn't shoot us if they wanted to. The shape they're in, they could fall over and miss the ground."

Tommy relaxed and turned toward the approaching steam car. Its huge rubber tires, with iron spokes, supported a round, cylindrical, black iron riveted boiler with a firebox on the front. The firebox was topped off with a long sooty chimney that flared at the top. Up front, coupling rods connected to egg-shaped lobs on the rotating driving wheels. The rods went to the pistons that went to the steam cylinder that drove the rods back and forth. It was a crude machine, but it was the only form of transportation that could operate efficiently in the earth's interrupted electrical environment.

Like broken windup toys, Sproat's men stumbled on the platform and tried taking turns steering the great steam car. The car weaved and zigzagged from one side of the road to the other. One man, wearing dirty, baggy pants, leaned on a flat shovel in front of the opened firebox door. Flames shot out and burned his hands. He did not move them. As if he were trying to decide whether to close the firebox door or shovel in one more shovel full of coal, he just stood there. The steam car jerked to the right and the door to the firebox clanked closed. The man stumbled, caught his balance, and jammed the shovel into the little pile of coal on the back of the steam car. The car smoothed out. He tried to lean on the shovel. But just as he was about to put his weight on the end of the handle, he staggered backwards and fell off the steam car. He hit the road, big butt first. It sounded with a terrible plop.

"Get George!" one of the drunken men shouted.

The man trying to steer the car, let go of the wheel, jumped off the steam car, and ran back to George. The steam car puffed straight down the road. Without the driver, it ran true. The driver lifted George's head and tipped a bottle of whiskey to his lips. He waved at the moving steam car and yelled. "He won't take a drink. He must be dying. Go get help."

The last man on the steam car jumped off and ran toward the entrance to the youth camp.

The passenger-less steam car continued on down the road.

Tommy looked at McQueen.

McQueen looked at Tommy.

They both shrugged and sprinted to catch the steam car.

When they were close, McQueen grabbed Tommy and tossed him up onto the car. Tommy stepped to the steering wheel, sat on the tractor-like metal seat, and steered. McQueen hopped on. Tommy teased the throttle and coaxed more speed out of the engine.

When the driver of the steam car realized he had jumped off the car and there was no one to steer it, he let out a sudden shriek. As if in shock, his outstretched arm pointed at the escaping car.

Leaving a filthy fog of thick black smoke, and a tailwind of sewer odor, McQueen and Tommy chugged on down a road hemmed in on both sides by parched desert soil.

CHAPTER 17

With Miles in her arms, Samara ran into the woods. With one arm she held Miles. With her other arm, she fended off branches in front of her and never let them slap back onto Miles.

When she came to a thicket of thorny vines that had taken over the branches of a waist-high tree branch, she assumed a semi-crouch; and stepping balletic, she avoided the sharp thorns and carried him to the other side. Then, she took ten steps into a boulder-strewn area and stopped. Under a dead twisted tree, a small spring flowed and sent a little trail of water into the lifeless land. She laid Miles on the ground and tilted his head back. A light shade of blue filled his face, and fresh red blood surrounded his mouth. She jerked the suggestion that he could be dead out of her head. She wished she had jumped on Sproat's scum-buckets sooner. She looked at Miles' chest. It wasn't moving. She didn't have time to think about it. She had to give him the kiss of life.

She reached into the little pool of spring water; cupped her hand, scooped up a handful, and rinsed the blood from his mouth. Holding his jaw open, she pinched his nostrils closed and lowered her mouth to his. She took a deep breath, placed her mouth over his mouth, and blew. She watched for his chest to rise. It did not. His airway was blocked. She looked into his mouth. A glob of fat from the fat man's butt blocked his airway. With two fingers, she reached into his mouth. Being careful not to jam the ugly piece of flesh down further, she pinched it with her fingernails, pulled it

255

out, and cast it onto the stones. Miles's airway was clear.

She put her mouth to his again and blew. This time his chest rose. She repeated this six times. Then she turned his face to one side, slid her fingers from his Adam's apple, and pressed into the groove alongside it. There was no pulse. She rolled him over onto his stomach; and with the heel of her hand, she slapped him in the back. He didn't move. She whacked him again, looked at his chest. She thought she saw a slight movement. She flipped him onto his back and tried the kiss of life again. No movement. She knelt alongside him, placed her hand on his chest, but didn't push.

She couldn't remember where she should place her hand. Was it the lower half of his breastbone? Mimicking the ancient voice of her Indigo teacher, she spoke to herself, "About an inch above where the ribs meet. Not on the end of the breastbone or below it."

She wiped her brow. She wasn't sure of what to do next. To give herself a chance to think, she took a deep breath. Slow and easy, she let it out. She searched her mind for an answer. The ancient teacher's words came clearer now. She said them out loud, "In cardiac compression, place the heel of your hand on the lower half of the breastbone, about the width of two fingers, above where the ribs meet."

She did that and continued to mimic the Indigo teacher's instructions. "And place the heel of your other hand on top." She was ready.

She straightened her arms, rocked forward, and pressed down about four centimeters. If she had someone helping her, she would have to give five compressions, followed by one deep inflation on the upstroke of the fifth compression, but she was alone. She would have to give compressions at least fifteen times and then two lung inflations. She pressed three times. Miles coughed and weakly lifted his hand to his mouth.

As if he were protecting himself from being beaten, he curled up and retracted his knees until they touched his chest. In an almost fetal position, he coughed as if he were coughing up his stomach.

Patting him on the back, Samara whispered softly, "You'll be all right."

But he wasn't all right. He quit breathing and pointed to his throat. With the heel of her fist, she whapped him on the back. His head jerked backward. A piece of cloth flew from his mouth. He sucked in much needed air. When his breathing slowed, like she was massaging him, Samara ran her hands over his body. Now that she knew he would live, she was searching for the key.

With his eyes wide with fright, Miles sat up and held his hands in front of his face in a defensive position. "Stay away!"

Samara jerked back, hesitated, and then put a gentle hand on his shoulder. He batted it away. She stared at him for a moment. "Why are you acting like this? I just saved your life."

Miles snarled angrily.

She spoke curtly. "I usually don't save pig people."

"I'm not a pig person," he barked back.

"You were in the pig people's neighborhood."

His shoulders sagged. "I have a lousy sense of direction."

"I don't believe you."

With a dejected look and as if he just made it up, he said, "I got lost."

"You were following Polaris. Is there something I should know?"

With a blank look on his face, Miles stared straight ahead. Like a barrier between them, the question hung in the air. After a few moments, Miles looked straight into her face. "I don't tell Sproat's people anything."

Samara didn't like his attitude. She could have left him with Sproat's men. Now she wondered why he was being so difficult. She suppressed her anger and forced a slight smile.

"You ought to get some rest," she said. "Your eyes are playing tricks on you."

"I can see just fine."

"Then you can see I'm an Indigo person."

"You should ease up on the booze." He raised his hand to fend off an expected slap in the face. Nothing happened. He looked down. "A lot of pig people claim their Indigos when they're drunk."

"I'm not drunk."

Miles raised his head in an arrogant gesture. "Let's be fair about this. Prove it."

Samara was puzzled. She had just saved this kid's life by knocking away six of Sproat's men, and he didn't trust her. She wondered if the pig people's ignorance had spread to everyone. She decided to find out.

As if she were surrendering, she held her hands above her head. "This is fair, isn't it?"

Looking up at her, Miles's eyes widened.

She jumped up higher than Mile's head, snapped off the end of a branch from the dead twisted tree, came down, and held the broken branch high in the air like a knife. "Why don't we just have a stabbing match?"

Miles jumped to his feet and tried to break off a branch. But he couldn't jump high enough to reach one. He searched the ground for something to use to defend himself.

"You don't need another stick," she said, and offered him the pointed stick, dull side first.

He didn't take it.

Trying to encourage him, she waved the stick in front of his face. "Go ahead. Take it."

As if he were going to grab the stick, he held his hand open. "You want me to just grab it and stab you?"

"Wait a minute," she said and lowered the stick. "I think you should stick it in my stomach. She moved closer and held the pointed end of the stick in front of her stomach. "As long as we're going to do it, I think this way will be better. You can push the stick through my stomach. That way you won't hit any bones. It will be very easy to push it right into my heart."

Miles placed his hand on the stick but did not take it. Samara insisted, "Go ahead. Take it. If you believe I'm one of Sproat's people, stab me." She motioned with her hand toward her stomach. "Come on. Stab me!"

Miles took the stick. As if she were his prisoner, Samara raised her arms above her head, left her stomach unprotected, and moved closer. "Do it!"

Miles held the stick, but slowly let it drop down.

"Hold it tight," Samara said. "Or it will slip through your fingers. Human flesh is tough to break through."

Rage filled Miles's face. He gripped the stick. His knuckles turned white in the night.

"Yes, that's better," Samara said. "See, then when you bring it up, you will have a clear swing, and there's a better chance of getting it into my heart."

Miles relaxed the grip on the stick. "Come on, lady, cut the crap."

Samara lowered her hands and lowered herself to the ground.

As if he had just realized that only an Indigo could jump as high as Samara had jumped, Miles let the stick slip from his hand. It slid down the side of his leg and fell next to his foot.

Samara turned her head from him and sat in silence. Through the corner of her eye, she watched Miles drop to the ground, lay back, and relax. She leaned back on her elbows and watched a mist fall over the rock field to their left.

After a long silence, Miles spoke. "Without watching someone jump as high as you did, how can I be sure a person is an Indigo?"

"You can't. All people are the same."

"There are a lot of ignorant people on this earth. I'm not the same as they are."

"Don't be surprised, but you are the same."

A questioning expression flashed in Miles's face. "You think I'm ignorant?"

"I didn't mean to imply that you're ignorant," she said. "Everyone is the same inside, but the real truth is that everyone is ignorant, only in different things."

Miles sat up with a jolt of revelation. "I never thought of it like that."

"I'm glad you agree." She paused. "Common sense must run in your family."

"What do you know about my family? Do you know where my father is?"

Samara flashed a confident grin. "I thought you could lead me to him."

Miles backed away. "You're not trying to use me to find him, are you?"

"Yes, I am."

"Is there another reward? Is he wanted dead or alive, again?"

"I don't know."

"Then what do you want with him?"

"I'm not sure."

"Are you crazy?"

"I must be." She warily looked around. "Sproat's men are coming, and I'm sitting here with you."

Miles whipped his head around and looked directly at Samara. "Are they getting close?"

"I hope not, but don't get excited." She turned and peered into the distance. "That should help."

Moving his head from side to side, Miles searched where Samara was looking. Apparently not seeing anything significant, he asked, "What should help?"

With her hand, Samara motioned to the fog that was looming down on the field. "That should slow them down."

Miles tensed to run. "Do you see them coming?"

"When your name's McQueen, they'll always be coming."

Miles stood up and stepped toward the field. "Let's get going."

Samara nodded in agreement. Together, they tramped around the broad stone field, crossed a valley full of black, bony trees, and the odor of dead animals wafted through the gnarled and broken branches.

On a dusty dirt road they came across an abandoned OvalCar. Miles stopped next to it. "This is what my mother used to drive."

Samara smiled. "She must have been a great lady."

"They killed her."

"Sorry to hear that," she said and frowned. "They would have killed a lot more people if it weren't for your father."

"So... you not only know his name, you know him?"

"I know of him."

The wind kicked up and sent a dry swirl of red dust into the air. Miles waved it away from his face and tried to lift the oval dome. "It's locked."

Samara reached over and pried at the dome lever. Clunk! The lock snapped off inside the door.

A look of amazement came over Miles's face. "You are one strong Indigo."

She lifted the dome and motioned with her hand. "Have a seat."

Miles stepped into the Oval Car and sat down "Feels like old times."

"Old times are gone."

"If it weren't for you, I wouldn't be alive."

"I should have never let that fat pig sit on you that long."

"What are you saying?"

"I didn't fight off the Sproat's men soon enough."

"You saved my life."

"But I was afraid."

"With your strength, how could you be afraid of anything?"

Samara wrung her hands and looked at her slender but powerful arms. "This super strength is such a responsibility. Sometimes I wish I never had it."

Miles held out his hand. "If you don't want it, give to me."

She eyed him from head to foot. He had the same black hair and the same strong graceful build as his father. "My strength would be better on your body. The great weight of Sproat's men is too heavy for my small bones. I can pick up their heavy bodies and throw them, but if I do, my bones could snap."

Miles looked at the broken gauges on the dashboard of the OvalCar. "I never thought about that."

Samara paced next to the car. "I shouldn't have waited to see what that person watching was going to do."

"What person?"

"I don't know. At first I thought it might be your father."

"Why didn't you go to him, instead of saving me?"

Samara thought about the whirlpool rapids below the falls. "I don't know. I found your father once, but I set him free."

"Where did you find him before?' His face lit up with excitement. "Maybe he's there now."

A hint of exasperation entered Samara's chest. "No one but Indigos can live where I found him. If he went back there, he would be dead. He won't be there."

Miles's face fell. "Could your Indigo friends help?"

"Until I find your father, I will not seek refuge amongst my people. They believe: Once a pig person always a pig person."

"But my father was never a pig person. We're still the fair people of the old order."

Samara shrugged. "What's in a name? I believe people are people, some are bad, some are good, and some just don't know they are bad."

Miles nodded toward the dashboard of the OvalCar and rubbed his sleepy eyes. "The ones that don't know they're bad are the ones to watch out for."

"I'd say Sproat's men have a monopoly on that."

"Youth camp teaches that Indigos are just savages."

Samara felt like Miles had just insulted the dignity of her proud race. "It's better to be a savage Indigo than a pig person with all their honors."

As if her reply went right over his head, Miles leaned back in the dusty seat, and looked up at the stars. He talked in a semi-dream state. "My father raised me in an idyllic place. I went into the green many times, and he taught me many things."

Samara felt a spark of interest. "What things?"

Things the pig people would never think of learning. Things they would not want to learn."

"I can't understand why anyone would not want to learn anything new."

"Have you seen the OvalCar domes the pig people use for parties?"

Samara thought about the alcohol-filled domes and the drink-till-you-die Saki burns. "Yes I have seen them. Does it go on all the time?"

"Just about." Miles took a deep breath and slowly let it out. "A good party and as much free time as can be had is all most of the pig people live for."

"That sounds pretty shallow."

"It is, and they don't care who or what they hurt to get it." Miles smiled a faint smile. "Look what they do to the wheelbarrow people."

Samara had watched the wheelbarrow people, and even though they were amusing, the amusement came at a terrible price. Without cracking a smile, she said, "The clown show that poses as the Friends of the Earth Corporation allows wheelbarrow people to have more and more stomachs surgically connected. It causes them to die from heart attacks, and when many lose the ability to take a simple breath of air they die, too."

The wind howled and a whirlwind of dust danced toward the OvalCar. Samara stepped into the car, closed the dome, and lay back in the body-forming seat. She bowed her head and felt a tear well up in the corner of her eye. "God must be gone from the pig peoples' world."

CHAPTER 18

Pup-up! Pup-up! The steam engine sputtered and jerked. Pup-a-ooh-mowl-mowl! It jerked one more time. An ear-piercing squeal came from where the driving rods connected to the wheels Tommy reached up and pulled the disengaging lever into the neutral notch. The wheels quit turning The squealing stopped. The steam rolled to a stop Steam hissed out the top of the safety valve at the top of the boiler.

Over the sound of the hissing steam, Tommy yelled, "Those idiots never oiled the coupling rods."

Shaking his head, McQueen reached down into the toolbox and picked up the oilcan.

Tommy leaned over the side of the car and pointed to the coupling rods where they connected to the big wheels. "I'll run it slow. You walk alongside and pump oil to the driver bearings."

McQueen jumped down onto the ground and held the oil spout over the first bearing. He motioned for Tommy to go ahead. The car crawled along. As he pumped oil into the bearing, it squeaked once and then ran with smooth quiet strokes. He oiled the other bearings and swung back up onto the thick plastic steam car platform. "Those should be oiled every day."

"I wouldn't get excited about it," Tommy said. "If Sproat's men can get away with not doing something, they will."

"I guess you're right. I just can't understand why they can't do a simple task."

Tommy pulled the throttle. The car picked up speed. Over the horizon, with its last rays struggling through a blue haze, a watery sun nipped the bottom of the sky.

Steering the car with one hand, Tommy pointed up ahead. At a bend in the road, a short metal-ribbed bridge stretched across a little stream. "You want to pull next to that crick and sleep for the night?"

"Not really," McQueen said. "If we travel at night and the space junk clears, we can follow the north star. And better yet, Sproat and his band of idiots won't see the smoke from the steam car in the dark."

Waving his hand in front of his face, Tommy gestured toward the coal. "We have enough coal to travel all night. But I got to wash this sewer stink off, and the boiler needs water."

McQueen made a face and expelled an exaggerated breath of air. "Facing into the wind, I almost forgot about that sewer smell. Pull over."

At the edge of the bridge, Tommy steered the steam car off to the side of the road and stopped. Next to the bridge, jumbled piles old red bricks, damp and smoke-stained, were the remains of what had once been a building. McQueen grabbed a bucket, jumped down to the edge of the stream, and began filling the bucket.

Tommy zipped past and jumped into the water. Waving his little arm, he said," Come on get the stink washed off."

McQueen jumped in. After they were finally free of the sewer odor, with wet clothes sticking to their skins, McQueen filled the bucket with water, and Tommy climbed up onto the car. McQueen handed him buckets of water until the boiler was full.

After they took off their clothes, wrung out them out until they were almost dry, and put them back on, McQueen looked down the road where they had come from. The shadows from the last rays of the sun were long and about to vanish in the coming darkness.

"I never thought of it before," he said. "But maybe the reason some pig people aren't afraid of the water virus is because Sproat's men are so lazy they probably filled the boilers with stream or river water right in front of them."

"That's something they would do," Tommy said. "A lot of pig people probably realized a long time ago that there was no virus."

McQueen jumped onto the steam car's plastic platform. "Half of Sproat's men probably didn't even know there was supposed to be a virus."

"If they did, they didn't care."

"I don't know everything they did," McQueen said, and gazed at the devastation of the darkening countryside, "but from what I've seen so far, the people have been going off the blue grass for a long time."

As the evening light began to fade to gray, Tommy pushed his floppy hat back on his big round head. "You know about it now."

In silent agreement, McQueen nodded.

Tommy reached up and put his hand on the engaging lever. McQueen watched him, but Tommy didn't pull the lever.

Rolling his hand with encouragement, McQueen said, "Pull it. Let's get this thing moving."

"I would, but it'll be dark soon. I won't be able to see."

McQueen jumped off the steam car platform and walked to the front of the car.

"What are you going to do?" Tommy asked. "Lead the way on foot?"

McQueen reached up and checked the oil level in the oil lamp that was on the front of the car. He smiled back over his shoulder. "At least they kept the oil in the headlight filled."

Tommy tapped his head. "I forgot about that. They probably keep it filled because they're afraid of the dark."

McQueen turned the igniter wheel. Sparks flew onto the oil soaked wick. It glowed orange, burst into a yellow flame, and sent a strip of weak light on the road ahead. He jumped back on the platform. "Let's go."

Tommy jerked his head toward the bend in the road.

McQueen glanced back over his shoulder. In the distance, black smoke from a steam car flow toward them. He turned toward Tommy and grinned. "I wonder who that could be."

"It's Sproat and his merry band of idiots." Tommy pulled the engaging lever. The steam car puffed and the coupling rods groaned. The car gradually picked up speed.

McQueen looked back. From beneath the black smoke from the stack of Sproat's steam car, orange oil light from its headlight bounced, and white spotlights flashed at their backs. "Do you think they'll catch us?"

Turning his little body toward the edge of the steam car, Tommy said, "It looks like they have a faster steam car. You want to jump off?"

McQueen looked out at the fields. Although it was almost dark, a chemical-filled fog and a methane gas odor signaled the fields were the byproduct of gas injection wells. To get natural gas trapped deep underground, drillers pumped a high-pressure mix of water, fine sand and chemicals deep into the ground. This caused cracks in rocks and other voids to be filled with jelly-like goo called crack-water. The crack-water forced the gas out of the voids and up to the surface where it was collected and sold. Although the drilling companies and hydrologist had guaranteed the crack water would never work its way to the surface, after only a few hundred years it had. And it had brought with it, bacteria and diseases never heard of before. The water that the gas companies guaranteed would be treated never was. Instead, it was dumped down holes. Years later, similar to the gushing water in an artesian well, the crack water came spewing up from the depths and poisoned the land far from where it had been produced.

When the odor of the methane changed to a new odor, it caused McQueen's lips to feel as if they were coated with a soapy wax and his eyes burned. He groaned. "If we jump off now, we'll have to breathe methane and slosh thorough all that stinking crack-water in the dark." He turned and looked from where they had come. Now that it was closer, the carbide-gas lights from steam car behind

271

them burned brighter. "And, they have carbide spotlights. We don't."

With his eyes watering from the fumes, Tommy gave a resigned shrug, squinted, and continued to steer the steam car.

McQueen grabbed the shovel, scooped up a shovel full of coal, and kicked the firebox door open. Light from the fire inside radiated and made the top of the steam car glow to a warm orange. He slung the coal into the fire and kicked the door closed. After five times of doing this, he stopped. Wiping the sweat from his head, he said, "Every time I open the door we become a brighter target."

"That's true, "Tommy said. "But if we make more steam, maybe we can generate enough speed and get away." He pulled the throttle wide open and secured it with a piece of wire. "Let the race begin."

Sproat's steam car was now one hundred meters behind them and gaining. The fire in the firebox roared bright yellow-orange and illuminated the steam gauge. It pegged past the white safe zone and into the red lines of danger.

McQueen threw in more coal.

Tommy waved his hands in front of McQueen's face. "That safety valve doesn't always work. If you don't quit shoveling in more coal, the boiler's going to blow."

"So what?" McQueen said. "If they catch up, we're as good as dead anyway."

Tommy wagged his head in defeat. "Well, shovel on a little more coal."

McQueen threw in another shovel full. The steam pressure gauge stayed in the red. The car went faster. But Sproat's steam car was now fifty meters behind them. Spotlights blazed across the tops of McQueen's and Tommy's heads.

Each time coal was fed to the fire box of the approaching steam car, flashes of orange light illuminated two huge beer-bellied men. Used to intense bursts of physical exertion rewarded by celebratory excess, even though they were sweating profusely, they continued to shovel coal. Others had antidote guns draw, and pointed them in McQueen's and Tommy's direction.

A loud squealing filled the air.

"What's that?" McQueen asked.

Tommy shook his head in disappointment. "It sounds like our driver is going. You sure you don't want to jump."

McQueen frantically rolled his hand in encouragement. "Just keep steering."

Sproat's steam car was twenty meters behind them. The earsplitting squealing pierced McQueen's brain like the pointed end of an ice pick.

A voice from a mechanical megaphone blared at them. "Pull over! Pull over! Or we'll shoot."

The steam car was ten meters from them. The first poison antidote bullet zinged past Tommy's head.

McQueen screamed, "Duck down,"

Tommy ducked down.

The wire came off the steering wheel.

The car swerved to the left.

Tommy reached his hands over his head, held the steering wheel, and blindly steered the steam car.

McQueen dove behind the toolbox.

Sproat's men were five meters from crashing into them.

A volley of antidote bullets zinged over McQueen's head, and some thudded into the back of the toolbox.

The megaphone blared again, "Stop! You can't get away."

Bam! Sproat's steam car humped into the rear end of their car. Tommy jerked sideways. His hands slipped off the steering wheel. McQueen reached over and pulled him back under the steering wheel. Antidote bullets whizzed. The megaphone blared. Now the squealing was bare metal against bare metal. The driver couldn't last much longer.

Another bump, from behind, sent McQueen rolling backwards. Just in time, he grabbed the grab iron at the edge of the car. His foot hit the road once. The sudden shock to his foot caused him to jerk himself back onto the steam car. Now Sproat's men were laughing.

McQueen's lips curled with disgust. "They think it's a game."

"Wait until you feel this one," One of Sproat's men said, and the steam car rushed toward them again. High-pitched squealing wildly penetrated the air and caused McQueen's head to throb with pain. The driver would break at any second. He braced himself for the wild rush and deadly crash.

All of a sudden Sproat's steam car let out one long squeal, slowed, and screeched to a halt.

Tommy and McQueen pulled away.

Surprised, McQueen looked at Tommy. "What happened?"

Tommy smiled big and bright. "Sounds like *their* driver broke."

With a smile on his face and sarcasm in his voice McQueen said, "I wonder what caused that."

With a confident grin, Tommy replied, "Maybe they didn't oil it."

McQueen let out a breath of relief and sat on the toolbox.

Sitting on the steering seat on top of a box, Tommy looked back over his shoulder and smiled at McQueen. "You want to go for a midnight drive?"

"Might as well. We oiled our drivers."

CHAPTER 19

Samara opened her eyes and looked through the clear dome of the OvalCar. Before her, a barren mountain created a backdrop for a lifeless beige landscape that spread toward the horizon. Being one of the many areas where fierce winds continually scoured the land, young trees and plants didn't have a struggling chance to grow to any size. Wind had ripped them out, roots and all.

As Samara studied the desolate site, the sun crawled out from behind the mountain, punctured a yellow mist, and backlit the sky with a harsh green hue. Off to her left, wind whistled through a huge heap of sharp rocks, and thunder rumbled like a thousand steam cars running wide open. Coming up the hill, red sand boiled in a great cloud. Hot wind had created another storm. If Samara and Miles got out of the OvalCar now, the sand could blast the skin off their bodies. The wind increased in force and whistled through the space beneath the dome.

Miles sat up in the seat. "What's that?"

"Don't get excited. It's only another one of the pig people's great creations."

Miles's eyes opened wide with amazement. "They taught us at youth camp that there was no such thing as global boiling, and that only ignorant pig people believed that global boiling caused hot wind to carry sand for kilometers."

Samara flashed him a quick grin. "You think they may have lied?"

Before he could answer, the storm boiled closer. Fine particles of sand seeped into the dome. Samara and Miles bent their heads down and covered their noses and mouths with the fronts of their shirts.

Samara turned to Miles. "You still believe there is no global boiling?"

With his face covered against the sand, Miles shook his head. "I never did."

The force of the blowing sand hit the dome. As incredible heat blasted into Samar's face, the dome lifted for a moment and settled back down.

Miles gasped in horror, closed his eyes against the sand, slouched down in the seat, and placed his hands over his face.

Samar placed a comforting hand on his arm. "It's only the angry breath of mother nature. She's trying to cure the sickness the pig people have caused. We'll be all right."

The intensity of the storm subsided; and as quickly as it had come, it was gone; but it had sand blasted the dome. Now Samara could barely see through a dull-white, rough surface. She lifted the dome and looked out. In the far away sky and behind a canyon of red and brown crumbling cliffs, smoke from a steam car sent big black clouds of smoke into the dry morning air.

Samara shook Miles's shoulder.

He opened one eye and jerked away from her touch.

She pointed to the smoke.

Squinting through sand-covered eyes, Miles shook his head. "Who do you think it is?"

"Sproat's men are the only ones authorized to run steam cars. It can't be anybody but them."

With sand falling from his body, Miles sat up in the body-forming seat. "They're after me?"

"That's obvious," Samara said, stood up, shook the sand from herself, and stepped from the OvalCar.

Miles stepped out and placed his foot on the sand-blasted, shiny metal fender of the OvalCar. "What are we going to do? Stand here and wait for them?"

Samara hooded her hand over eyes and studied the approaching smoke. In a taunting but playful voice, she said, "Only if you want to."

"Are you out of your mind," Miles whined. "They have antidote guns."

"Don't worry," she said with unwavering confidence. "They'll probably miss."

Miles's voice thickened with fear. "I don't want to stick around and find out."

"I'm sorry," Samara softly said. "I keep forgetting that you can't run as fast as I can."

"Look at that." Miles pointed toward the big zigzagging clouds of black smoke. "The way that smoke is pouring out they must be drunk."

"Either that or they're pushing the steam engine to the limit. Which means they really want you, and badly."

Miles's eyes flamed with hate. "The Godless scabs want to use me to control my father."

Samara knew with her strength and speed she could do something to stop them. "Maybe we can control *them* instead."

Miles looked into the OvalCar. A metal turn-signal rod stuck up from the dashboard. "Maybe we could break that off, stick it in the road, and give them a flat tire."

"I don't think it would pierce that thick rubber But those big tires are hard to steer when they hit something."

"Do you have something in mind?"

"I think so." She stepped toward the approaching smoke. "Come on. I need your help."

Samara ran up ahead of Miles. He tried his best to keep up, but he didn't have the speed and strength of an Indigo person. He lagged behind.

Samara slowed.

Miles caught up.

Trotting with the smooth efficient effort of a welled tuned machine, Samara looked over at him. "I'll be up ahead. Keep coming. I'll have things ready when you get there."

Samara pulled ahead. Behind her, Miles became a dot in the dust.

When she stopped at the edge of the dirt road, she had to find something to dig with. A flat rock would work, but it would be difficult to dig through the hard packed gravel and yellow dirt. If she could find a sturdy piece of scrap metal, it would make a better shovel than a flat rock. She searched the edge of the road. Tailings from an old coal mine, mostly fine shale dust and small rocks, ran along the shoulder; but a single flat rock or a piece of scrap metal could not be seen. She had nothing to dig with. Maybe there would be something up ahead. She ran down the road and stopped at a dried-up canal. At the side of the canal, an orange virus warning sign bent to the ground. From months in the polluted air, it was faded and the plastic had deteriorated. The plastic couldn't be used for a shovel, but the metal signpost could. She shook the signpost. It wiggled but wouldn't break free. She reached down, grabbed the top of the bent over signpost and pulled. It bent sideways, but still did not come out of the ground. She pulled it down until it was waist high. Then, like a Dinky pushing a grain wheel, she held the signpost in front of her and pushed the sign around in a circle. Its base stayed in the ground, solid. She reversed her circling movement and stopped to look back. The steam car smoke was getting closer. She held the signpost in front of herself and ran around in a circle. The sign post broke off at its base. Now she had something to dig with. She ran back to where Miles could see her and thrust the end of the metal signpost into the wheel ruts in the road. It hit with a solid clunk.

Gasping in ragged breaths, Miles came up to her, bent over, and placed his hands on his knees. "Now What?"

"We need something to cover this hole I'm digging. Find it."

Miles tramped off of the road, into the barren dust, and stopped at a little dead tree.

Samara lifted the signpost and whacked its sharp end into the dirt road. This time a big chunk of the hard-packed road broke loose; she continued to slam the signpost into the road. When she had enough loose chunks of dirt, she scooped them out with her hands and continued digging until the hole was big enough for the steam car's wheel to plop into and jam solid.

Miles struggled, but walked out of the dust carrying a stack of black tree branches that were higher than his head. He dropped them on the road.

"Quickly," Samara said, "that car's almost here. Cover the hole."

They covered the hole with branches and threw dirt on top of them. The dry dirt sifted through the branches and fell into the hole.

"Stop," Samara said. "It isn't working. We'll only fill the hole back up."

Miles reached up, unzipped the zipper on the front of his jacket, took it off, and handed it to Samara. "Put this over the sticks and cover it with dirt."

In her mind Samara could see Miles shivering in the cold dark. "It gets cold at night," she said. "You'll need that jacket."

Miles shook his jacket offering it to her. "Here take it. I'd rather be cold than lead them to my father."

Samara nodded.

Miles threw the coat onto the sticks.

Now when the dirt was thrown onto the coat, it did not fall through. They covered the hole so fast that dust filled the air.

Miles studied the trap. "The dirt is a different color," he said. "They'll see it and stop before they drop into it."

"In their inebriated state, I doubt it, but just to be sure, we'll keep their attention off the road."

"How?"

Samara walked a few meters beyond the hole and stopped. "You lay at the side of the road. I'll stand here and yell for help."

"Miles cringed with fear. "They tried to kill me before. This time they'll run over me."

281

Samara placed a comforting arm around his shoulder. "No they won't."

Miles looked into Samara's eyes. "How do you know that?"

"After you got away, one of the men, no doubt, told what had happened. When word got to Sproat that man received a reward. They may not care about keeping you alive to find your father, but they'll keep you alive for a reward."

"Are you sure?" he said and backed away from the road.

"You got to have a little faith."

The steam car loomed closer. Samara reached out, grabbed Miles by the shoulder, and ushered him toward the ground. "Get down. If they try to run over you, I'll run out and pull you away."

Miles breathed a sigh of relief. "Okay," he said, and lay on the side of the road. "But Sproat's men never stop for anyone."

"They'll stop when their wheel falls into that hole."

Black smoke filled the sky and the steam car rounded the bend. Samara and Miles waited.

CHAPTER 20

After taking turns steering all night, McQueen was at the wheel. As the chugging steam car and rounded another bend in the zigzagging road, Tommy sat on the floor, and McQueen made another sharp turn. Tommy tilted to one side. He began to fall over. He put out his hand. It hit the floor. He stayed upright

"What are we on? An obstacle course?"

McQueen steered into another turn. "It sure looks like it. This road must have been designed by a highway engineer strung out on dope."

"I guess we only have two options," Tommy said, rolled over sideways, and came up on one knee. "As our progress is measured in millimeters, we can watch years of our life slip away and cry about it." He raided one finger. "Or, we can go down the road twisting and turning and laughing about it."

Feeling himself shake with a muffled spasm of amusement, McQueen steered around a bend.

As if threatening rain, a morning wind picked up and came in taunting dust-filled gusts. Ignoring the gusts, Tommy fanned the dust away from his face and looked to McQueen. "We should pull over and get some sleep."

McQueen rubbed the sleep from his left eye and scanned the dusty road ahead. "Just as soon as we get away from this dust and find a place to hide this steam car, we will."

"After we get out of this dust, how are we going to hide all the black smoke from the steam car?"

"I don't know," McQueen said. "But we need a few minutes rest. Let's find a good place to pull over."

Searching the countryside, McQueen looked to his right. The crack water swamp was gone and so was the smell. Now the dry wind rushed over the red fields of dust and bent the branches of a few sun-sicken trees. Trying to stay awake, he glanced periodically to his left. The steam car rounded another bend. His body begged for sleep. His weary head drooped, and his eyes closed.

From somewhere ahead, a cry of, "Help!" came.

McQueen's eyes flew open. He jerked his head to the front. Before his wide, open eyes, a beautiful girl stood waving her hands. As she seemed to glow with an ethereal lightness, he wondered if he were dreaming. He rubbed his eyes and shook his head. In the harshness of the bright morning sun, the girl still stood out like a precious jewel. Her hair flowed to her shoulders like purple-black silk. Long lashes fringed her large jade-green eyes. The top of her opened jacket exposed part of her elegant breasts.

Next to her, a body lay on the road. In his sleepy state, the poetic swaying of the woman's long legs and the lithe hidden movements of her body captivated McQueen. The body on the road didn't immediately register in his mind.

As a wind began to blow, Tommy frantically waved his hands at the girl and shouted, "Look out!"

As if she had internal injuries, the girl wrapped her arms around herself and didn't move.

McQueen jerked to reality, and shouted, "Get out of the way!"

Tommy pulled the disengaging lever, but the steam car continued to move. When he stretched his little foot to jump on the brake:

Thud! The steam car's right front end dropped down.

Snap! The heavy wheel cracked.

Then it broke off the axle, crashed through the floor, smashed into the boiler, hit the firebox door, and gouged into the steam pipe's safety valve. Steam spewed from the top of the broken valve and formed a cloud. Hot red coals from the fire box spewed into the air. The sudden stop threw Tommy out of the seat and toward the front of the steam car. In midair, he grabbed the steering wheel. It bent, but it stopped him from slamming into the steaming valve.

McQueen felt himself flying through the steam and hot-coal-filled air. He sailed over Tommy's head and landed hands first on the hard-packed dirt road. He jumped up and turned around. "Tommy!" he shouted, and ran back to the steam engulfed car. He searched the hot steam cloud. Tommy's little hand appeared waving for help. McQueen reached into the steam and pulled.

Tommy didn't move. Urgency filled his voice. "I'm stuck," he cried.

McQueen jumped into the steam. For a moment, the wind increased to a fierce force. It blew the steam back for a second. McQueen could see the steering column. It was jammed against Tommy's leg. The firebox door was broken off. The pile of coal had been jerked into the fire. The wind blew harder. Like a miniature blast furnace, it fed oxygen to the red coals, turning them white hot. The heat was melting the plastic platform. Soon it would be burning.

McQueen pulled the steering column.

It wouldn't budge.

"Come on McQueen," Tommy joked. "Quit fooling around. Get me out of here before I become a steam cleaned shish kebob.

Quit making jokes, Tommy," McQueen barked at him.

Again, he tried pulling the steering column away from Tommy's leg. The column still didn't budge. Now the plastic was on fire, adding more heat to the boiler, and sending black toxic smoke into their faces. In the midst of the hot white steam, like an ethereal vision, a small hand appeared.

"Pull with me!" a stern, but beautiful voice commanded.

McQueen grabbed the steering column and pulled. The other hand pulled at the same time. As if it were soft clay, the steering column bent back. Tommy was free. He sprang away from the column, and dove out of the steam. Away from the crawling fire, he jumped onto the ground.

The steam from the pipe hissed slower and slower. Suddenly it stopped. McQueen looked at the steam gauge. It pegged past the red. He looked at the person who had helped bend back the column. It was the girl who had been on the road

She looked at the steam gauge. Then she looked at McQueen.

No words were spoken.

They both knew they had to get off the platform.

They jumped from the steam car.

When they landed on the ground, McQueen grabbed the girl and Tommy by the hand. McQueen looked at another person, but through the increasing black smoke, he didn't recognize him. "Come on," he said. "That safety valve is jammed. That boiler's going to blow."

They all raced from the pressure-building boiler and ducked down into a gully at the side of the road. For the first time McQueen noticed who was at his side. "Miles!" he said and tears of joy erupted from his eyes.

Miles kept his head down. "Pop, you think it'll blow?"

"I don't know, but if it does, the shrapnel will fly into the air and land on our heads. Let's get out of here."

With the wind fanning the fire and blowing smoke their way, they all jumped up and ran down the road. Tommy's little legs couldn't keep up. As if he were a light bundle of air, Samara effortlessly picked him up and sprinted ahead of them all.

A half a kilometer down the road, and beyond a hill, McQueen and Miles slowed to a walk. Up ahead, as if they had just returned from a picnic and were waiting on a rickshaw to pick them up, Samara and Tommy stood alongside the road, calm and unruffled.

Kabloom! In the distance, the explosion of boiler of the steam car echoed over the land. Seconds later, the sound of the heavy metal boiler crashing to the hard ground clunked into the air.

287

The percussion of the explosion caused McQueen's shoulders to move with an unexpected jolt.

"Man," he said and shook the sudden scared feeling from his spine. "That thing will jerk you right out of your boots."

Miles shuddered and put his hand over his heart. "That felt like I had a bass drum in my chest."

Samara turned toward Miles. "You first explosion?"

"Yes, and I hope it's my last."

McQueen stepped back and appraised Samara. Cocked slightly to one side, her clean, hard face gave him the impression she was waiting for something to happen, and if nothing did, she would make it happen. She didn't have a single wrinkle on her face. On the verge of a cocky smile, the corner of her mouth was turned up on one side and gave McQueen a glimpse of her straight, white teeth. She gave off a healthy glow. From the way she was talking to Tommy, McQueen could tell she wasn't as tense as he was.

He stepped forward and extended his hand. "Thank you for your help. I'm John McQueen."

Samara turned her cute head and grasped his hand. "I know who you are. Everyone knows Chief Earth Officer McQueen."

McQueen shook his head. "I think it's ex-officer."

As if she were shy, Samara turned her head to one side. "I've been wanting to meet you."

Miles stepped forward. "Samara, you already know this is my father." He turned toward his father. "Father, this is Samara."

Samara extended her hand in friendship.

McQueen grasp her hand and felt crushing strength. He pulled his shoulders back and held back a painful grimace. "Are you Indigo?"

With her mouth forming an O, she pulled her hand away from McQueen's. "I'm sorry. Sometimes I forget how strong I am."

"It doesn't matter how strong you are," Tommy said. "You shouldn't have dug that hole in the road."

"We thought you were Sproat's men," Miles broke in. "They ambushed me. A fat one sat on my chest until I couldn't breathe. I would be dead if Samara hadn't rescued me."

For a moment the thought of Miles being killed caused McQueen's chest to fill with rage. He exhaled a calming breath and looked into Samara's face. "Thank you. Thank you so much."

Samara tilted her head. "No problem."

"You look familiar," McQueen said. "Have we met before?"

Samara blushed. "We haven't exactly met."

Searching for an answer she didn't give, McQueen stared into her green eyes. "Can you swim?"

She put her thumb behind her long black hair and gathered it until it was behind her ear. "I can swim better than you can."

McQueen felt his eyebrows shoot up in surprise. "You're the one who saved me in the rapids. Why did you run away?"

Shyness shone in her eyes. "Indigo people are not allowed to save pig people."

McQueen figured she had tied up the man with the red bulbous nose. "Is that why you tied up that helpless man at the falls?"

"I tied the man up for his own protection. He was going to jump into the river. I knew Sproat and his men would find him. I hope my brother never finds out I saved a pig person."

Tommy grunted in disapproval.

She looked toward Tommy.

"We're not pig people," Tommy objected.

"It doesn't matter," she said. "My brother says all people who are not Indigos are pig people."

"But that's not true," Tommy said with a wounded voice.

As if she didn't have a care, Samara put her hands together and tapped her fingers. "I know that, but sometimes I wonder."

A feeling of concern spread in McQueen's chest. He stepped close to Samara. "Then you know that there are good and bad people in all things and in every race."

Samara pointed her toe and toyed with the dirt on the ground. She looked up. "I hope I do?"

"Sure you do," Miles said. "There are good dogs, bad dogs, good cats, and bad cats. Good pig people and bad pig people, and I'm sure you have good Indigo people and bad Indigo people."

Playing with the fingers on her hand, Samara looked at Miles. "Maybe that's why I saved you."

"You may have saved him," Tommy said, "but you almost ended my life in that steam car trap."

Samara flashed Tommy a slight grin. "You have to admit that was a good crash."

"What do you mean a good crash? I could have been killed."

"We got you out in plenty of time. And besides, it added a little excitement to your life."

Tommy's face took on a pitiful look. "I don't need any more excitement."

"It keeps your heart pumping, keeps your young."

McQueen smiled at Samara's banter. "What are you going to do now?"

I'm not sure," Samara said. "There is supposed to be a land up north where things are like they used to be."

"Are you talking about Orangeville?"

"Yes, I am. I would like to go there."

"What would you do if you went there?"

Samara placed her hand on her belt. "I have what's left of family here. I'll probably just stay for a few days and come back."

"It's not an easy trip to Orangeville," Tommy said. "Why would you go through all that trouble?"

"It's better than setting in my brother's house doing paperwork."

Tommy looked at the dwindling smoke that was rising from the steam car explosion and looked back at Samara. "Nobody in their right mind would go all the way to Orangeville just to stay a couple of days. Are you sure you don't have brain damage?"

"Maybe I do." Samara smiled a knowing smile. "We all have brain damage, only in different parts."

"Enough talk, "McQueen said. "Let's get going."

"What's the rush?" Miles wanted to know.

"We don't know what happened to Burke. If he's like his father, he'll lead Sproat's men right to us for an extra stripe."

"I don't think he'd do that," Miles said. "We're good friends."

"If you are, then where is he?"

Miles's face scrunched up with confusion. "I don't know."

"Even if you're right about Burke," McQueen said. "The explosion and smoke from the steam car will attract Sproat's men right to us."

McQueen, Tommy, and Miles started walking. Samara stood with her arms across her chest and tapped her foot. "Where are we going?"

McQueen and Tommy both turned and smiled back at her. In unison they said, "Orangeville."

CHAPTER 21

Three days later, McQueen watched Samara sitting next to the fire. Its soft orange glow illuminated and outlined the soft features of her body. She had the profile of a Blue Bottomed girl before they turned foul and flabby. Parted in the middle, her hair flowed down until it barely touched her shoulders. When she turned her head and looked at McQueen, it reflected the firelight and shone like it was orange-black.

"It's getting warm." She unbuttoned the top buttons of her jacket.

McQueen didn't know if she wanted him to see the cleavage of her breasts, but he didn't look away.

She smiled and put her hand on his. "Did you ever fool around with an Indigo girl?"

McQueen felt his heart thump, but it faded. "I was always true to my wife."

Gently, she squeezed his hand. "But she's not here."

"She might be. I watched her die, but I still feel she is alive."

Samara pulled her hand back. "I'm sorry. It must be difficult for you."

McQueen's wife's murder flashed in his mind. "It is." He wiped a tear from his eye. "Especially when Sproat and his scabs killed her."

"I know how you feel. Before he let my father die, Sproat tortured him."

"I'm sorry that had to happen," McQueen said sincerely. "I feel like it's my fault."

"You can't be everywhere. My father was the one who started the push back the pig people movement. The Indigos wear the gold feather to honor him and as a symbol to keep the movement alive."

McQueen bent toward her. "When that movement started, the Indigos never hurt anyone."

"Sproat didn't care that they didn't hurt anyone." She settled back on her elbows. "He wanted it stopped. He claimed that if he cut the head off the snake, the body would soon follow."

McQueen bent forward, put his hands between his knees, and looked into the fire. "I should have never let anything shut down the OvalCars. OvalCar transportation could have caused unrest. Instead of watching lies and wheelbarrow people on TV, people could have traveled from place to place. They could have found out what was really happening and gotten mad enough to do something about it. They would have gotten my attention, and maybe we'd still have the OvalCars today."

Tommy gave McQueen a knowing smile. "I miss those OvalCars, too,"

"I was supposed to be an intelligent Chief Earth Officer." McQueen jabbed an angry finger at himself. "But I lost my leadership. We needed a leader who could blow people away with intelligence, a leader with a working knowledge of the real world, a leader with dignity, a leader who could inspire people, a leader the world would respect. We needed a man who could make us proud, a man who had vision."

"We still have one, "Tommy interjected.

McQueen shook his head. "Nothing was the way it was reported. I should have known everything was appearance. I became a complacent man in the system. Before all this happened, I should have gotten off the blue grass."

"You're off now." Tommy said with a questioning look. "Are you going to take back command? Are you going to herd the people back onto the blue grass?"

"It's too late for that."

Samara seethed quietly." You *are* the Chief Earth Officer. More is expected of you than of an ordinary person."

McQueen nodded to himself, his feelings grim. "That may be so, but the pig people have gotten a taste of freedom. They'll never stay on the blue grass."

"But you should fight to put them back on. I think my brother, Hack, will help."

McQueen wearily shook his head. "It's too late. All the fight went out of me when they killed my wife." He looked at Miles. He was sleeping next to the fire. "All the family I have is right here."

"But don't you miss the thrill of the fight? Don't you miss the satisfaction of making things right?"

"I don't," McQueen said but uncertain. "Maybe I should. But right now, I am simply going to better world."

Samara lay back and laced her hands behind her head. "Of course you know we can't go past the global boiling damage."

"We could go past it, but most people don't know there is radiation there."

"So what?" Samara said. "That radiation happened years ago. It should be harmless by now."

"You sound like Sproat," McQueen snapped back.

Samara glared at him.

McQueen shot her a pitiful look of appeal. "I'm sorry, I didn't intend to sound mean, but most people just don't know how long the killing effects of radiation last."

"It couldn't be that long."

"If a half-life of over seven billion years isn't long, then it isn't."

Samara's face shone with serious concern. "In seven billion years that land will still be radioactive but only half as much. It will never recover."

McQueen sighed. "There are a lot of places that will never recover."

Samara's face had a glimmer of hope. "But isn't the land around the canals still safe?"

"The last time I read a report, it read that many places were recovering and had an abundance of life and ample water, but now I can see that was just a lie."

"If the pig people have their way," Samara said, staring into the fire." Then the whole planet will be void of life."

"It's sad," McQueen said and poked a stick into the fire. "Years ago, when I became Chief Earth Officer, the blue grass farce was just starting to have an effect on the pollution that caused global boiling that has caused wind changes."

Samara talked with encouragement and hope in her voice. "But there are still a few scattered bands of land that are livable."

"Not as many as there should be. It didn't take Sproat and people like him long to reverse years of progress."

Samara persisted. "But maybe we could still get the pig people back on the blue grass."

McQueen thought for a moment that maybe he could. He felt the chip in his waistband and thought about telling her about the orange turn. The thought faded.

"Maybe the Dinkies are right," he said. "If we do nothing, before the pig people destroy the earth, they'll just die in their own filth."

Samara stared at McQueen.

He stared back.

Her eyes glowed with a soft love glow.

"I would love to start a new life in a new place" she said and looked into the fire. "If I find a good man in Orangeville, maybe I won't come back."

McQueen thought about how life would be with her, but it only caused his heart to fill with sorrow. He pushed the thought out of his mind. "Without my wife, I can't even think of starting another family.

"With Sproat controlling Blue Town," Samara said, lay on her side, and bowed her body into a fetal position. "Anything has to be better."

With sleep overtaking him, McQueen nodded, curled up next to the fire, and thought about the orange turn. Watching the gentle flicker from the orange fire, he murmured, "When we get to

Orangeville everything will be better." And he closed his eyes.

CHAPTER 22

Bursts of drunken laughter cut the crisp morning air. Samara's ears twitched toward the sound. She opened her eyes with a start. She was ready to fight.

"What's that?" Miles said from his warm spot next to the dwindling fire.

Samara looked toward the sound. Beyond the dry stretch of lifeless ground and above yellow scrawny treetops, white wood smoke from a steam car puffed into the air. "It's Sproat's men." She looked to McQueen for advice.

McQueen lifted his back from the rock he was leaning against. "How can anyone be drunk this early in the morning?"

They probably stayed up all night," Tommy said and sat up. "That's how they avoid hangovers. They stay drunk."

Samara jumped up. "If they're drunk, they'll be easy prey." With her hand, she motioned toward the smoke. "Let's go over there and disable them."

"We can't," McQueen said. "If we go over there and disable them, there will be a good chance the others will know where we're going."

Samara didn't like waiting for things to happen or letting things she could change left to luck or some other uncontrollable circumstance.

"I think you're wrong," she said, and paced around the fire like she warming up for a foot race. "The minute your steam car blew up, they all knew where we were."

"Maybe not," McQueen said. "They don't know if the steam car we were on was the one that blew up."

Miles nodded in agreement. "That's right. "Why give them another clue as to which direction we are going?"

Samara stopped pacing and turned toward the direction of the drunken laughter.

"Whoopie! Ahh! Hah!" Came from beyond the stand of trees.

"They're ready to fall over," Samara said with a hint of anger in her voice. "We don't have to walk all the way to Orangeville. We can go down there and just take that steam car."

Miles grabbed a dry stick and threw it into the smoldering fire. "That steam car won't get us to where we want to go," he said and lay back down.

"Why not?"

"Orangeville's not at the end of a road." Miles laced his hands behind his head for a pillow. "Those steam cars are too heavy to run off-road."

Samara's face brightened with encouragement. "It'll get us close."

"Not close enough." Miles closed his eyes.

Samara didn't want to argue. "I'll go get it myself." She bolted toward the trees.

"Wait!" McQueen said, but she had trotted off toward the sound of the Sproat's drunken men.

When Samara came to the side of the road, she crouched in a clump of tall dead yellow weeds and watched the steam car chug past. It didn't have the coal pile on the back. It had been replaced with a woodpile. The six men on the platform weren't afraid of any fake wood virus, and they didn't care who knew it. White smoke and wood sparks puffed out the tall smokestack. The driving levers to the wheels pushed back and forth and put power to the huge tires. This steam car was different. Because of the wood virus farce, other steam cars had plastic platforms. This steam car had a platform made of ax-cut wooden logs, some with the bark still on them. Three men were passed out, just barely hanging onto the platform. The driver was bent over the toolbox trying to throw up between the control levers. He had the dry heaves, but was holding a steady course. He seemed to be almost sober. He was the only one that would give Samara trouble.

Quietly, and with the swiftness of an eagle diving for prey, she sprinted alongside the steam car and took a hold of the first drunken man's hand.

She pulled.

The man slid off the steam car platform.

Thud! He hit the road.

With her head up and watching, Samara bent over and kept running alongside the car. The driver winced as if he had heard something, but he didn't turn back to look. She grabbed another man and pulled. He flew off, hit the road rolling, and ended up at the side of the road. The driver looked back. For a moment his scraggly, bearded face flashed in Samara's direction. She kept running and ducked down. The driver still didn't see her.

She pulled a third lard-like man off.

Plop! He hit the ground and lay still.

The driver turned toward the sound. "Drunken half-wits," he yelled and tobacco juice splashed from his mouth and onto his beard. He slammed the engaging lever into neutral. Cussing, he tromped on the brake. The steam car stopped.

Samara kept low and watched the driver.

He shook the other two sleeping men. "Wake up!"

They opened their groggy eyes. "Whoopie!" one said, and twirled his finger around in little circles.

"Come on, wake up," the driver repeated. "Your drunken friends fell off. We got to pick them up."

One of the men rolled off the platform. His feet hit the ground. He fell, got back up, and started walking. The other man rolled over and went back to sleep. The driver sat on the platform and watched the other man staggering down the road.

Samara jumped up on the steam car, turned toward the driver, and politely said, "Get off."

As if he were seeing things, the driver grabbed his forehead.

Samara told him again, "Get off."

Staring at her, with his tobacco stained beard trembling and more tobacco running out of his mouth, the driver defiantly hung onto the steering wheel. "I'm not walking," he stated. "I have gland trouble. I'm too fat to walk."

Samara braced herself against the steering wheel; and using one hand, she pushed him. The heavy man dug his heels into a space between the logs of the platform floor. His powerful lungs huffed out streams of breath that sprayed vomit particles away from his nostrils and into his moustache and beard. He resisted. With a set concentrated stare, Samara pushed harder.

Suddenly the bone in her arm cracked. She quit pushing. In pain, she grabbed her arm.

The driver lunged toward her. Holding her cracked arm securely against the side of her body, she stepped to the side and kicked him in the rear end. The momentum of his lunge and her kick caused him to stumbled and fall off the steam car.

Keeping an eye on the sleeping man, she lifted her foot, placed it on the engaging lever, and pushed it into forward. As the steam car chugged on down the road, the driver plodded after it. He caught up with it and placed his chubby hand on the rear grab iron. He tried to swing on, but after a few meters he was huffing and puffing. His chubby feet couldn't keep up with the slow pace of the steam car. Sweating profusely, he pulled himself up and tried to place his foot on the bottom rung. The man sleeping on the platform woke up, but he didn't move or offer to help the driver.

The driver yelled at him, "Wake up! She's stealing the steam car!"

The man still didn't move.

The steam car picked up speed. The driver hung on. His flabby legs hopped on the dirt and kicked back, sending clouds of dust into the air and into his sweating face. He couldn't control his legs. He took a deep breath, and it seemed that he was using every ounce of his dwindling strength just to hang on. With great determination and effort, he swung one of his feet up onto the platform. Just before he was about to pull his body on, too, Samara ran over to the sleeping man and pushed him with her foot. He rolled toward the struggling driver, woke up, reached for the driver's foot, grabbed it, and rolled over. But hanging onto the driver's foot to keep from falling off, proved to be too much weight for the driver. His hand slipped off the grab iron. Both men whirled around and fell to the ground. Like two baby elephants with stubs for legs, on their backs, they rolled along the dry yellow road, twirling circles of dust around their round bodies.

On down the road, McQueen and the others stood at the side of the road. From behind the steering wheel, with her good arm waving, Samara ecstatically shouted, "See, I told you."

When she stopped the steam car, with ashamed faces, McQueen and the others hopped up onto the log platform. Samara didn't talk. She only smiled at them. She was happy. They were riding again.

McQueen stared at her arm. "What's the matter with your arm?"

"Samara glanced at her arm. "I cracked it when I tried to push that elephant away from the steering wheel."

Tommy smiled a big smile. "What did you do? Highjack a circus wagon."°

"I thought elephants were extinct, but he was big enough to be a baby one."

McQueen cast her look of concern. "Will you be all right?"

"I've cracked it before." She waved her hand as if the cracked bone in her arm was an everyday occurrence. "It'll heal."

"Let me put a sling on it," McQueen offered.

"It will be all right," she insisted.

Affectionately, McQueen put his hand on her shoulder. "Come on, Samara, don't be so brave. It'll heal faster if you don't move it."

Samara thought it would be nice to have McQueen put a sling on her arm. Maybe she could convince him to do something else. "Okay." She stepped away from the steering wheel. "Here, Miles, take the wheel."

One of the logs on the platform had a branch sticking up out of it. Like a waving flag, a clean shirt hung from it. She watched McQueen. He took the shirt from the branch, tore it, folded it into a triangular sling, and stepped close.

She felt goose bumps all over her body.

He bent forward. His face was next to hers. He put one corner of the sling over her neck and draped the straight side down over her breasts. He leaned back. "Put your arm against your stomach."

Cautiously, she placed her arm in the sling. McQueen grabbed the opposite corner of the sling and pulled it around her neck until it touched the other end. Again his face was next to hers. Her mind drifted to what they could do together. For a moment, she felt strange delicious warmth in her heart. McQueen had an effect on her, and she knew she wasn't going to get over it.

After McQueen had tied the sling, he looked into her eyes. She closed them and waited for his lips to touch hers.

Nothing.

She opened her eyes.

He drew back.

She suppressed her feelings. Maybe McQueen would like her better if she didn't act so tough.

"Thank you, McQueen," she said. "You remind me of my mother. She was always putting slings on my arms and fixing my cuts and bruises."

"Where is she now?"

"She died from the polluted water, didn't even know what was in it. It was clear and cool. But it killed her."

"Was that before the blue grass farce?"

"That's the bad part. It was after. Pig people were going off the blue grass and polluting the water for years, said it was for the progress of man."

"I'm sorry that had to happen," McQueen said with a shamefaced, hopeless look. "I thought I was making a difference."

"You were," Samara said compassionately.

"Not enough difference, your mother didn't have to die."

Although Samara had the key to do the orange turn, she still wanted to push the pig people back onto the blue grass. She was beginning to think McQueen was going in the right direction. Maybe the orange turn was the only way to do it.

She sighed and looked into his eyes. "Maybe the only way to defeat the pig people is to let them defeat themselves."

McQueen replied with a lame smile. "You may be right."

"She is right," Tommy said with a triumphant whoop. "Let them pollute the water and drink themselves into extinction. We're going to a better place. We're going to Orangeville."

Nodding in agreement, Miles sat in the metal tractor-like seat and steered the steam car. Smoke, from the smokestack, whirled down and puffed into his face. He turned around. With pleading eyes, he looked at Tommy. "You want to take the wheel for a while?"

"Sure," Tommy said and stretched. "I'm so short, that smoke will go right over my head."

Miles stepped down. Tommy stepped up and sat in the seat behind the steering wheel, and the smoke puffed just over his head.

Breathing smokeless air, Miles sat down on the log platform, leaned back, and put his hands behind his head. "It's nice riding. But I'm telling you, we can't get to Orangeville on a steam car."

"Why not?" Samara blatantly placed her hand on her hip and waited for an answer.

Slouching down, with his back against the toolbox, Miles folded his hands across his chest. "You'll find out."

Trying to make the steam car increase speed, Tommy put his hand on the engaging lever and pulled. "Doesn't this thing go any faster?"

Miles ran his foot along the bark of a thick platform log. "It might if they wouldn't have made this platform out of logs. They're too heavy."

"Oh well," Tommy said with a satisfied smile. "It's better than walking." He turned the steering wheel, and the steam car chugged around the bend. Then, he turned it to the right again, then to the left. "This road has so many bends and turns. It looks like a drunk built it."

"Hey," Samara said and pointed toward the sun. "The sun's at our backs we're heading west."

"We won't be for long," Miles said.

After Tommy had steered the car around many turns, he asked, "Doesn't this road ever straighten out?"

"Hey," Samara said, and spun around facing away from the sun. "The sun's at my face. We're heading east. We're going back where we came from."

Miles squinted. "No foolin'."

"Don't you care that we're going the wrong way?"

"Sure we do," Miles assured her. "But this road will never go true north. Sproat's men built it with a compass."

"Ahh, come on," Tommy said. "No one is that stupid."

Miles offered his hand to Tommy. "Do you want to bet?"

McQueen nodded. "That's right. Sproat's men are too stupid to know the compass doesn't work because of the magnetic fields being messed up with magnetic pulses and God knows whatever else."

As a faint breeze stirred the brown canopy of dead trees above the moving steam car, Miles spoke seriously. "The magnetic pulses didn't mess the poles up as bad as the underground nuclear explosions."

Like an inquisitive pupil, Tommy looked at Miles with questions in his eyes. "You mean those nuclear explosions did more that spread radiation?"

"They set them off so deep in the ground that they disrupted the earth's molten core. Magnetic north moves hundreds of kilometers every month."

Tommy cocked his head with suspicion. "Why didn't they stop?"

"They did, but only after they discovered that if they destroyed the magnetic fields the solar winds would scour away all life on the planet."

"I don't care why it happened," Samara said and took her hand off her hip. "The road's still crooked."

Showing no emotion that he had been right, Miles sat and stared at the floor. "They built this road with a different reading each time they began the workday." He crossed his eyes and wagged his head around as if he were intoxicated. "And those beer and wine barrels they tow around with them didn't help their sense of direction either."

Tommy turned the wheel again, stood up, and stretched his neck to see as far ahead as he could. "Look up ahead," he said. "There's another turn. We could be going around in a big gigantic circle."

"And the sun's on your face," Miles said. "We're still heading east."

McQueen looked to Samara. "Orangeville is a long way off."

"We don't need to make it longer," Tommy said. "You want to get off?"

McQueen reached up and put the engaging lever into neutral. The steam car stopped. "Let's get off this thing."

Samara stood up and leaned off to the side. Beyond a line of dead trees with yellow frothy sap oozing from trunks and branches covered with scabs of deformed purple bark, she could see around the next bend in the road. It straightened out.

"Wait," she said. "We have a clear road ahead. Let's see where it goes."

CHAPTER 23

As the steam car chugged down a long stretch of straight road, the air was reasonably clear until a cloud of bluish-gray, muggy haze, reeking of disease and decay, smothered it.

"Don't breathe," Tommy said. "I'll get us out of this." He hunched over the steering wheel and guided the car over a series of bumps and potholes and out of the haze, where they entered a land of a blue-feted swampland. Here, thick steamy air invaded McQueen's mouth, crawled into his lungs, and hung there like an implanted chamber of gas. He tried not to breathe.

Samara closed her hands into small fists and held her breath.

Miles covered his mouth with the sleeve on his shirt.

As if the steamy air didn't faze him, Tommy drove on.

A ways down the road, the air cleared, and the land smoothed out; but dead gray fields of lifeless land lined the road.

As the steam car chugged on, its passengers watched the gray land change. Through a dry, cracked yellow earth, little sprigs of green life began to appear. A few straggly trees with only a few branches on spindly trunks began to grace the edges of the road. Beyond that, trees became bushy, and the land became a little greener; but the curves began again.

"Now, what's going on," McQueen wanted to know. "One minute the sun's at our backs and then

311

the next minute it's right in front of our faces, shinning right in our eyes."

Miles rolled over, put his elbow on the steam car's log floor, and rested his head on his hand. "How many times do I have to tell you? We're going in circles."

"No we're not," Samara shot back. "Wait until dark. If the space junk clears up, we'll see the north star."

Tommy reached up and pulled the engaging lever into neutral. The steam car stopped. "We'll find out which direction we're going, and right now."

McQueen looked a few meters off to the side of the road. Half buried in fine dust, a fallen tree that had been sawed into firewood for steam car fuel, was piled next to a big tree stump.

"We need wood for the firebox," Tommy said and jerked his little head toward the stump. "While we're here, that stump will tell us which way we're going."

He jumped off the steam car and motioned for Samara to come to the stump.

Even though her arm was cracked and in a sling, with little effort, she hoped off the steam car walked to the stump, and stopped.

"Look here," Tommy said and pointed at the growth rings of the fallen tree. "The pattern of the rings is more widely spaced on the side toward the equator. So...we're headed north."

"That may be true," Samara said. "But moss on the side of the tree, grows on the north side."

"Not here," Tommy said shaking his head. "Pollution has caused mutated moss to grow on all sides of the trees. Moss is no longer a true source of direction."

McQueen studied the rings and looked at the hazy outline of the sun. "It's like we were tacking on a sailboat, we've been going north east and north-west, but still headed north."

Samara tilted her head and smiled a big smile. "See, I told you we weren't going in circles."

"Maybe not," McQueen said, "but even if the road eventually heads north, at this rate, it'll take us weeks to get to Orangeville."

Samara put her hand on her shapely hip and tilted to the side. "So what?" She tapped her foot. "We'll still get there, and we won't have to walk."

For a moment, Tommy studied the rings in the stump. Then he looked at Samara. "It could take longer than weeks. I would like to get there before I'm too old to enjoy the place."

"Let's keep riding," Samara said. "If the road doesn't start to head north, then we'll go on foot."

Tommy gestured to the wood lying on the ground. "After we throw on some of this wood, we can do that."

While they tossed chunks of wood up onto the platform Miles laid on his side watching.

Samara stopped pitching wood and snapped at Miles. "Aren't you going to help your father?"

"You can pile all the wood on you want," Miles said with a defiant voice. "It isn't going to do any good. We'll still just be going around in circles."

McQueen gave Miles one stern glance.

Miles jumped down off the steam car and began loading wood.

After a big pile of wood was on the platform, Tommy and Miles climbed back onto the steam car.

McQueen grabbed the grab iron and swung on."

Samara stood next to the steam car and flexed her legs. With one powerful bound, she jumped higher than the platform and landed on it, standing up.

McQueen was amazed at her agility and strength. "You shouldn't be jerking around like that. Your arm won't have a chance to heal."

Samara flashed him a playful smile. "Thanks for the concern, but I'll be all right."

Miles lazily rolled to his back and looked up at the sky. "I still say, we're going around in circles."

No one replied.

Tommy put the engaging lever into drive. "We're off again."

The car chugged and puffed around three bends.

Samara pointed straight ahead. "Look, the road's going north, and as far as we can see."

Miles jumped up and looked ahead. "The road was smooth and straight and had no turns for a long way. "How did Sproat's men do something right?"

"They probably didn't," Tommy said and peered at the road from under his floppy hat. "It looks like the work of Dinkies."

Samara reached under her sling and scratched her cracked arm. "I don't care who did it. But does this mean we're going to ride all the way to Orangeville?"

"I'll go where you want me to go," Miles said. "But, like I told you before, no road goes to

Orangeville. We'll still have to go a long way on foot."

Now that sun wasn't in his eyes, Tommy tilted his head back and steered the steam car straight down the long road. "Look out Orangeville! Here we come."

An hour later the road turned and turned again. Miles unlaced his hands from behind his head and sat up from his lounging position. "I don't think we're going north anymore."

"You're crazy," Samara said. "It may be in a roundabout way, but we're still going north."

McQueen knew which direction they were going, but wanted to see if his son remembered what he had taught him. He didn't say a thing.

Miles stood up and turned toward Samara. "I'm going to settle this directing thing once and for all." He reached into his pocket, took out the antique carbon fiber watch his father had given him, and jerked his open hand toward Samara. "Come here, look."

Imitating Miles's voice, Samara said, "We're not going north anymore." But she stepped next to Miles.

Ignoring Samara's mimic, Miles held the watch in one hand and pointed the hour hand toward the sun. With his other hand, he pointed his finger and bisected the angle between the hour hand and twelve mark. "See... this gets us the north-south line. So, we're going north."

"Maybe we aren't." Samara said. "That north-south line isn't always true."

Miles grimaced and a hurt feeling appeared in his eyes. He let his hand with the watch fall to his side and paused as if he were thinking. "If we were in the southern hemisphere," he said, "that would be true. Then we would put the *twelve* toward the sun and bisect the angle between twelve and the hour."

Samara arched an eyebrow, but didn't reply."

McQueen smiled inwardly. He was proud that his son had remembered what he had taught him, but he didn't want to start an argument with Samara. He kept silent.

Steering the steam car, Tommy looked back over his shoulder. "Hey, Miles, instead of doing all those magic tricks with that watch, why don't you just tell us if we're going north?"

As if he had just tasted something he didn't like and was trying to shake the unwanted taste from his mouth, Miles violently shook his head. "It's not that hard to understand. It's the hour hand on the sun in the northern hemisphere and it's twelve on the sun in the southern hemisphere."

McQueen knew Tommy was only kidding Miles. He tried to suppress it, but he let out a little laugh. He tried to cover it with a fake cough, but Samara heard the laugh.

"What are you trying to pull off?" She glared at McQueen. "You two can't tell me, I don't know which direction I am going."

"Nobody has to tell you where you're going," Miles said. "You can read a book and find out yourself."

Samara's face contorted grotesquely. "I never liked book learning or sitting at a desk." She paced from one end of the steam car to the other. "I have always been where the action is."

As if he were searching for help from above to stop the impending chaos, Tommy looked up in the air.

McQueen gently patted Samara's shoulder. "Calm down, Samara. We'll get there. Miles knows what he's talking about."

Samara sat down and didn't say another word.

McQueen knew she was simmering like a hot piece of steel thrown into a puddle of virus water. He looked toward Miles.

Miles knew he wanted him to let her cool off.

Tommy tapped his foot to the beat of the steam engine and steered the steam car around a sharp bend. "It doesn't matter where the road goes," he said and pointed ahead. "Look!"

McQueen and the others jerked their heads around and gaped in surprise.

The front wheels of the steam car were rolling over the top of a steep hill.

McQueen shrieked, "Hit the brakes!"

Tommy jumped on the brake pedal and stood on it. The car slowed. The brake pedal slammed to the floor. Tommy's body violently jerked and knocked the engaging lever into the wide open speed. The stem car lunged forward.

Tommy turned to McQueen. "The brake broke."

McQueen jumped up and pulled the throttle back. But it was too late. With no breaks, the steam car ran free. They were halfway down the steep hill and gaining speed. At the bottom, a raging river had washed out a bridge.

Tommy reached up and grabbed the steering wheel. "That river is too wild to swim across." He glanced at McQueen. Maybe I can drive across."

McQueen glanced at the river, and then looked at the height of the steam car. "Those wheels are pretty tall. If the bottom clears, you might make it."

"Less weight will give us more clearance," Miles said; and kicking off the pile of wood, he looked to Samara. "Throw off that rope and that toolbox. "Then we'll all get off."

Samara snarled at Miles, but she threw off the rope and toolbox. Then everybody, except lightweight Tommy, jumped off the steam car. McQueen and Miles thumped onto the ground and rolled in the dust. But when Samara left the platform, it was as if she had just stepped off the bottom step of a staircase. Her feet gently touched the ground.

When McQueen got to his feet the steam car was the length of a blue grass field away from the edge of the broken bridge. Tommy turned up the boiler and watched the steam pressure gauge. The pointing needle jumped into the danger zone. To keep the steam car traveling toward the river, he wrapped a wire around the steering wheel and the steering post. Then he jammed the engaging lever into forward. The steam car chugged fast and powerful. It picked up speed. Smoke raced from its stack. The car went faster. The wire wasn't holding the steering wheel steady. Tommy stood at the side of the steering wheel; and with one hand, he held it steady. He flexed his knees to jump. The steam car was ten meters away from the river.

"Jump!" Samara shouted.

Tommy held the wobbling wheel and didn't move.

"Jump!" Samara yelled, again.

Just before the car was at the river's edge, Tommy jumped. He landed on the soft sand next to the riverbank; and like he was doing a circus trick, he somersaulted and stopped in a sitting position with his legs spread apart. The front wheels of the heavy steam car rolled over the edge of the broken road. Like a tired wheelbarrow person's stomach, it plopped down into the water. Underneath the steam car, control rods jammed against the edge of the broken road. The car stopped with a sudden jerk, sending the log platform off the frame and sliding forward into the water. The platform started downriver, but one end caught on the sharp edge of a piece of the broken bridge. It swung around and bobbed in the current. As if it were an afterthought, the hot smokestack, still attached to the steam car's frame, snapped off and sizzled into the water. As the steam engine kept chugging, the back wheels on the bare frame spun slow and powerful. Without a platform or a smokestack, the steam car did not move forward. It stayed in one place: The tires turned and ground into the pavement, sending rolling smoke into a blue circle. As water rushed into the firebox, the engine gave one last final chug and went silent. Like a final breath of death, steam hissed out the release valve of the boiler.

Samara looked at Miles. "Okay, bright boy, how do we get across, now?"

Miles looked back over his shoulder and looked toward the river. "I don't know, but we better get moving."

McQueen turned to look down the road, but a long rattail snaked into the tall grass at the side of the river. It was one of the elusive Pigmies. McQueen knew they wouldn't hurt them. He looked down the road. In the distant sky, three plumes of steam car smoke swirled in the air. Sproat and his men were coming with reinforcements.

Tommy sat on the ground, held the palms of his little hands up, and moved them in a begging manner. "Which way do we go?"

McQueen looked at the raging water. He didn't remember the water being so wide and so deep. It had been a canal, and it usually had slow moving water that permitted the recovering plant growth to thrive. Hoping he was at the wrong place, he searched the sides of the canal for signs of familiarity. Water raced along the banks scouring away the fragile aquatic life. Down river, the furious water undercut sand, removed the aggregate underneath, and caused a landslide that collapsed the slopping land that led to the river. Further down, the water surged up over the banks and cut away the roots of trees and bushes. The trees tumbled into the water, and the bushes were sucked down until they vanished with a heartbreaking sip.

Holding back tears, McQueen turned toward Tommy. "This isn't a canal anymore. It's a river."

Tommy threw his hands up. "Maybe we *are* going the wrong way. The way we've been twisting and turning would confuse anyone."

"We're on the right road," McQueen said. "But the water shouldn't be so high." He didn't want to tell the others, but he hoped the high water didn't mean what he thought it meant.

"Okay," Tommy said, still sitting on the ground. "We're on the right road. Now how do we get across?"

Samara stuck out her beautiful chest; and like a superhero, she said, "I can do it. I can tow you all across on the log platform."

McQueen looked at the sling on her arm. "You might be able to, but you might break that arm completely."

Holding up one finger, Miles suggested, "Why don't we just walk upriver until the water is shallow enough to walk across?"

With suspicion in her eyes, Samara looked at Miles. "Now what are you trying to show us? Another stupid thing you learned in those books of yours?"

"It's not book learning," Miles said. "It's just common sense." He knelt at the edge of the river, cupped water in his hand, and lifted it to his mouth."

Samara grabbed his arm and jerked it.

His cupped hand flew away from his mouth. Shocked, he looked up at Samara. "What are you trying to do?"

"Giardia and other intestinal parasites are in that water."

"But when the water runs it is usually okay to drink."

"That's not true anymore. Sproat and his money-making schemes have polluted just about every drop of water they can find."

McQueen placed his hand on Miles's shoulder. "She's right. Don't drink it. They'll have clean clear water at Orangeville."

Shaking the water from his hands, Miles raised to his feet, turned toward Samara, and mumbled, "Thanks."

McQueen surveyed the banks of the river. Where there should have been healthy cattails and reeds, stunted grass struggled to survive. He looked into the sky. The sun was hidden in hazy polluted smog. He felt that the river led to Orangeville, but it had changed so much he wasn't sure.

"What are we going to do," Tommy said; and waiting for an answer, he stared up at McQueen.

McQueen watched the raging water rush down river. "Most rivers run south." He swung his arm over his head and pointed to his right. "We're going upriver."

CHAPTER 24

Beginning the trek upriver, Tommy took three steps into tall grass, tripped over a hidden rock, fell to his hands and knees, and stood up. When he put his weight on his right foot, it felt like a piece of broken glass had cut into his big toe. He fell to the ground.

Samara looked down at him with disapproving eyes. "Now what's the matter?"

In an almost crying voice, Tommy said, "Don't get excited." He felt tears of pain flood his eyes. "I think my toe's out of place."

Samara knelt down and placed her hand on Tommy's foot.

He jerked it away.

"Don't get excited," she said, mimicking his crying voice. "Let me take off your shoe."

Tommy didn't want her to think he was a little crybaby, but with caution, he inched his foot forward until it was in front of her. She took off his little shoe and ran her fingers over his foot, but she didn't touch the toe. "It's out of place," she said. "But I don't think it's broken." She jerked her head toward where Sproat's men were advancing. "Are they already here?"

Tommy turned his head to look.

Kalunk! She manipulated his toe joint back in place.

"Ahh! Tommy moaned. "Why didn't you tell me you were going to do that?"

"I know what a big baby you are. I didn't want you to know it was coming. Anyway it's fixed."

"You sure?"

"It better be," McQueen said. "We got to get out of here."

Tommy stood up. The pain was still there but not as bad. "I'll just hold you up," he said. "I'll can stay here and hide. I'll catch up later."

McQueen patted Tommy on the back. "Nice try, old buddy, but there's a big problem with your idea."

Tommy looked up at McQueen. "What's that?"

"You don't know the way to Orangeville."

"And, they'll find you," Samara added.

Tommy was surprised Samara was showing concern for him. It made him think of his Dinky friends living in the underground tunnel complex. Suddenly he missed them. If he were in the tunnel complex, he wouldn't have to constantly watch out for Sproat's men. If he were back there, he could sleep in peace. In the tunnel system, he could be with his own people. He would be safe. He was tired of this complicated life. He wanted to go back. He wanted to go home.

"They won't find me," he said. "When they're gone, I'll go back to the Grotto."

"What?" McQueen questioned.

"I hate to be a glorious pain in your butts, but I'm tired. My little legs have to make twice as many moves as you big people do." He let out an exhausted breath of air. "I just need a rest."

"You never complained about it before," McQueen said. "And besides, you've been riding on the steam car most of the way." He looked toward smoke of the threatening steam cars. They were getting closer. "Let's get going."

Tommy didn't move.

McQueen pondered in silence for a few moments

Tommy felt McQueen wanted to tell him something, something important.

McQueen turned.

The feeling faded. Now Tommy not only felt pain in his toe, he felt pain in his little legs. He dreaded going upriver on foot. It had been nice riding on the steam car. Maybe if he refused to go, Samara could use her super strength and fight off Sproat's men. "Can't we just stay here and fight?"

"No way," McQueen said. "Where one goes, we all go." He started upriver, stopped, and turned back. "Don't act so crazy. You may be the only sane one of us left."

Managing to hold in a smile, Tommy said, "If we start upriver, Sproat's men will follow."

"We can stay ahead of them." McQueen turned and started walking again. "They'll never believe we went off the road."

"Think again," Samara said and pointed to the steam car. "With that thing blocking the road and the bridge out, they'll know the only way we could go would be upriver or downriver."

Tommy got up, ran until he was next to McQueen, and struggled to keep up. "With my bad toe and short feet, it will only be a matter of time before they catch up. Then, we'll have to turn and fight. Why don't we do it here? Samara can fight them off. If we win, we can go upriver at a leisurely pace."

Keeping a steady pace, McQueen turned his head toward to Tommy. "What's the matter with you, Tommy? You know she has a cracked arm."

Tommy didn't want Samara to get hurt any more than she was. He lowered his head in shame. "You're right."

Samara ran ahead of McQueen and turned around. Waking backwards and facing him, she said, "No, he's not. I can whip those fat pigs with one hand."

McQueen stopped walking. "That's how you'd have to do it."

Samara stood in front of McQueen, blocking him. Her whole body took on a defiant aura. "I have to fight for Tommy. He's too little to fight."

"I'm not too little." Tommy balled up his little fists. "I fought before, and I've won before."

A sudden look of recognition gleamed in McQueen's eyes. "That's right, but you always used your mind. Why do you want to get physical now?"

"Now that you have brought it up, I really don't want to get physical." Tommy jokingly hunched his back as if he were an old crippled man. "I must bet getting old. "We can beat them at their own game." He straightened up. "But how?"

Samara opened her palm and gestured to Miles. "What does book boy have to offer?"

Miles stared into Samara's jade green eyes. "Why don't we combine our strengths?"

CHAPTER 25

The mental gears in McQueen's mind meshed and spun. They searched like a slot machine looking for a jackpot. Miles's suggestion seemed the way to go. If they combined all their talents, they could get away; and somehow they could lead Sproat and his men down a wrong path. Then they wouldn't have to keep looking back over their shoulders. And they would be on their own terms. Tommy would be happy. They would be making their way to Orangeville at their own leisurely pace.

"Miles is right," he said. "If we combine all our strengths, we'll be rid of Sproat once and for all."

Samara looked at him with doubt in her eyes and said one word. "How?"

Let's put all our cards on the table." McQueen pointed to Tommy. "You're short and tricky. You can hide in places other can't. He nodded toward Samara. "You have triple strength but a broken arm."

Like a volunteer, Miles stepped forward. "What can I do?"

You have the speed and stamina of youth and a good mind." McQueen put his hand to his own forehead. "But what card can I play?"

"They want you more than anything else," Tommy said. "You'll make good bait."

Miles stepped forward with a worried look on his face. "Don't risk your life for us, Dad. We need you."

"There'll be more risk if I don't."

With a look of reluctance on his face, Miles nodded in agreement. "What kind of a trap can we set?"

Like a bird with a broken wing, Samara held her slinged arm away from her body and paced around in a circle. "What are we standing around trying to build a mousetrap for? Let's just fight them and get it over with."

McQueen looked back over his shoulder. Smoke from the puffing steam cars was creeping closer. "If we can't figure out what to do, and pretty quick, we'll have to fight."

Samara pursed her lips in a businesslike manner. "If we have to fight, we have to fight."

McQueen was afraid a huge number of Sproat's men would unexpectedly bunch up like a pack of gloating beast of prey. With the mentality of an uncontrolled mob, it wouldn't matter that Sproat wanted them alive to find the orange turn key. His men would brutally pounce on them the moment they saw an opening. It wouldn't matter how strong Samara was or how agile Miles could be, or how clever Tommy was, or how long they fought. They would all die. McQueen had to get everyone to work together and start upriver.

"The big problem," he said and paused, "is that we don't know how many of them there are."

"Don't get excited," Tommy said, and looked at the threatening steam car smoke. "We'll think of something."

Samara leaped up on the end of the tilted steam car frame and pointed in the direction of the approaching steam cars. Great clouds of gray smoke puffed into the air; and like evil supernatural beings, they reached into the sky and darkened the sun's light. She balanced on the edge of the steam car frame and stepped onto the moving log platform. Her weight lifted the end of the platform. It turned into the current. Then it lifted off the broken cement and almost broke free. She jumped off the platform. The raft-like platform dropped down, snagged on the jagged end of the broken cement, and bobbed in the water.

"Hey," Tommy said with excitement. "We could use that platform for a raft."

The jackpot, McQueen had been searching for in his mind, paid off. "It's too heavy to pull across the water. "But Sproat won't know that."

Samara pointed to the wooden toolbox lying on the ground. "We could use that for a boat."

"We could," Miles said. "But if the rope breaks that current will sweep us fifteen kilometers downriver. We'll be fifteen kilometers further away from Orangeville"

A look of amusement spread across Samara's face. "If Sproat was on it, he would float right into the dry lands. Without his beer wagon next to his side he might just die of thirst."

Tommy flashed a mischievous look. "Without that wagon and nothing to drink, he would have a hangover that would last a week."

"The toolbox is too small for him and his men," McQueen said with a shake of his head.

"That's right," Miles agreed. "But it isn't too small for us to go across one at a time."

McQueen felt his confidence rising. "If Sproat thinks we're using that platform to go across, he'll be dumb enough to jump on."

Miles stared at the platform and then looked to his father. "And you'll be the bait?"

"Yes," McQueen said. "After you're all across, I'll stand on the platform like I'm waiting for you to pull me across. When Sproat gets close, I'll dive in and swim to the other side."

A look of concern came over Miles's face. "That current's strong, Dad, can you make it?"

McQueen remembered how Samara had pulled him to safety below Niagara Falls. He flashed a knowing smile in her direction. "If I can't, I think this lady can give me a helping hand."

Samara stared at McQueen; and for a brief moment, her face took on an unexpected bashful look. She turned her head away, picked up the end of the rope, and tied it around her waist." She stepped to the shore and pointed across the river. "When I get to the other side, I'll throw the rope around that steel pillar and tow the rope back here."

"Good idea," Miles said. "Then we can pull the toolbox from both sides."

Samara snarled at Miles. "No kidding, Finestein."

Miles smiled back. "History tells us that it was Einstein."

Shaking her head, Samara said, "Whatever." She threw off the sling that was on her arm and dove into the rushing current. The current immediately pulled her downriver. She side-stroked; and although she couldn't swim in a straight line, ten meters downriver, she managed to get across. She stepped onto shore, walked to the steel pillar, looped the rope around it, and waved.

On the other side, McQueen jerked his arm sideways and pointed upriver. So Samara could hear him over the roar of the water, he shouted, "Start upriver or the rope will be too short."

Samara rotated her hand next to her ear, signaling that she couldn't hear him. She stepped closer to the shore and shook her head again. She still couldn't hear him.

While Miles and Tommy pulled the toolbox to the edge of the water, McQueen shouted, jerked his arm, and pointed upriver; this time with more immediacy.

Samara nodded and tied the end of the rope around her waist. Then she walked upriver, dove in, and swam across, coming to shore right in front of the wooden platform. Dripping with water, she untied the rope from her waist and handed the end to McQueen. He looped a section of the rope around the toolbox, pulled it tight, and tied it. Then he looped the end around the frame of the steam car and tied it to the other end of the rope. "Okay, Tommy, get in."

Tommy got in the toolbox and looked up at the double strung rope. "This will be just like hanging out the wash."

Miles stepped to the rope and put his hand on it. "It might not work."

"Hey," Samara said and flicked her wet hair away from her face. "Cut the negative talk. Have a little faith."

The fresh smell of smoke from the approaching steam cars entered McQueen's nose. He looked down the road. Like some enormous black cotton blanket, the white clouds of smoke began to invade the treetops. He yelled, "Let's get moving!" and rolled his arm with encouragement. "Those steam cars are just around the bend."

Miles yanked the rope once. The box moved toward the water and stopped. "The rope pulls pretty easy," he said. "What if the box sinks?"

"Don't worry," McQueen said and patted Miles on the back. "If we pull the rope fast enough, the box will skim the top of the water." He reached up and grabbed the rope.

Like a man about to go over Niagara Falls in a wooden barrel, Tommy stared at them from in the box.

"You ready?" McQueen asked.

Tommy jerked his finger toward the other side of the river and gave them a thumbs-up. "Start pulling."

As fast as they could, they pulled the rope. The wooden box slipped into the water. Tommy and the box skimmed across the surface of the swift current. All was going smooth until he was a few meters from other side. A sunken log or something rushed downriver and hit the side of the box. It tipped to the side. Water gushed into it.

McQueen shouted, "Keep pulling"

With furious water pulling at his waist, Tommy hung onto the rope.

The others all pulled, faster. The power of the water rushing into the box was a tremendous force. Tommy hung on. The water gushed over his head and all over his little body, making him look like a toy doll in a curtain of silver. Finally the box plowed into shallow water and up onto the shore.

Tommy got out and signaled that he was okay. The others pulled the empty box back.

After Miles was skimmed across with no problem, McQueen lowered himself to his haunches, held the box, and motioned to Samara. "You're next."

Samara smiled a superior smile. "I don't need a baby box to go across a little crick."

"I guess not," McQueen said. "But we have to let it go downstream. Last chance for a thrill ride."

"If you can't swim across, you'll have all the thrills you want." She swept her arm over the box. Why don't you go across in the box? I can stay here and taunt Sproat?"

McQueen gave her a helpless smile. "I would like to do that, but Sproat wants me so bad that he won't take time to realize it's a trap. He's afraid to come after me alone, so he'll have his men get on the platform, too."

He untied the box and let it get sucked into the current. It spun once, turned on its side, and a whirlpool swallowed it with one gulp. Then he tied the rope around the branch on the log platform and then back around the steam car's frame. While smoke from the steam cars hovered over his head like a cloud, just around the bend, three steam cars puffed into view. He turned toward Samara. "They're here. Get moving."

Samara dove into the water; and now, without the heavy rope to weigh her down, she swam across the swift current as if she were swimming across a calm pond.

McQueen stood on the platform and held onto the rope. He excitedly waved his arm and yelled loud enough for Sproat and his approaching men to hear. "Pull me across! Pull me across!"

On the other side or the rapid water, Samara and the others put their hands on the rope but didn't pull.

Sproat's men stopped their steam cars, jumped off, and ran toward McQueen. McQueen waved his arms maniacally and shouted across the water. "Hurry up! Pull me across."

Sproat was the first to arrive at the riverbank. He pulled his poison antidote gun and aimed it at McQueen. Before he could fire, McQueen dove into the water. Underwater, it was like when he had tried to swim the rapids below Niagara Falls, he felt the familiar strength of the water and its terrible undertow. He could swim further underwater but feared for his life. He surfaced and began side-stroking. The fast water swished him downriver. He kept stroking and looked back at Tommy and Miles. To give Sproat the impression that they were not going upriver they ran away from the rope on the steel pillar and headed down the center of the road. McQueen didn't know where Samara was. He kept on stroking. He kept on being swept downriver.

In the middle of the river and far from the washed out road, he stroked as hard as he could. He made it through an angry eruption of spray, but he could not escape the pull of a whirlpool. The horrible thought of being washed downriver past the dry lands and into the netherworld of radioactivity flashed in his mind. Suddenly he was grabbed from behind. "Come on, big boy," Samara said. "I'll tow you in."

Holding him with her good arm and scissor-kicking her legs, Samara towed McQueen to shore, and they walked toward the road.

At the road, they stood next to the rope, waved to Sproat, and watched. Sproat and one of his men were gathered around the platform, talking and excitedly gesticulating. The river still raged and roared, and it made it impossible for McQueen to hear what they were saying. Shaking their heads, pointing to the McQueen, and then to the rope, showed that they were arguing about using the platform. Sproat stepped onto the platform and pointed to the rope. Six of his men jumped onto the platform and rushed to the rope. They put their hands on it, but did not pull. Shaking his head as if he weren't sure he wanted to cross, Sproat stepped off the platform.

With his mouth opening and closing like he was yelling, he shook his fist at the six men standing on the platform. They stepped off the platform.

Sproat wasn't falling for the trap.

After he took a few steps away from the platform, five Pigmies walked out of the tall grass. Their rattails stuck up in a threatening S curve. In the center of fiendish smiles, their white buck teeth stuck out as if they were ready to bite. As if on cue, the earth shifted. Like experienced sailors on a ship, the Pigmies gracefully bent their knees and went with the shift.

While the bulk of his men backed away from the pigmies, Sproat and the six men tumbled sideways. Sproat regained his balance and jumped onto the platform. The six men rushed onto the platform so fast they almost bowled Sproat over. Sproat didn't have to tell them what to do. With eyes wide with fright and looking back at the Pigmies, they pulled.

The heavy log platform tipped up and off the sharp edge of the piece of broken bridge and swung into the current. The rope held the end of the platform up and water sailed under the heavy logs as if it were a huge surfboard.

"They're going across," McQueen said. "I never thought that rope would hold all that weight."

Sproat's face beamed with happiness and delight. He signaled to the rope pullers. They pulled faster. Now he was in the center of the river.

Miles and Tommy walked up behind McQueen. Tommy pointed to the taut rope. "That thing's not going to break."

Samara gasped. "They're going to get across. Then they'll pull the others across."

Miles smiled at her and reached into his pocket. "No they're not." He walked to the steel pillar, placed the blade of his knife on the moving rope, and looked at Sproat.

Snapping his head to the right and to the left, Sproat's expression changed from one of happiness and delight to fear and horror.

Miles took the knife blade off the rope. "Who wants the honors?"

Tommy held out his hand.

Miles handed him the knife.

Jumping up and down, Tommy got Sproat's absolute attention. As Sproat watched, Tommy waved the knife over the rope.

Sproat shrieked and recoiled in shock.

Tommy cut the rope.

Sproat shook his fists at Tommy; and over the roar of the water, his voice squeaked in a high pitch. "I'll get you for this."

Tommy yelled back, "There's never a dull moment with a sharp knife."

As the Pigmies' tails snaked back into the tall grass, the platform spun and rushed downriver.

McQueen was happy with the thought that if the platform ever stopped it would take Sproat a long time to work his way back upriver; and while he was doing that, his men would do nothing but sit on the riverbank and drink until he came back.

McQueen and the others walked down the road as if they were going west. After they were are out of Sproat's men's sight they cut off the road and headed upriver.

The paradise of Orangeville lay ahead.

Miles stared at Samara. "I hope we don't run into any Indigo people."

CHAPTER 26

Walking upriver, Miles turned to his father. "Do you think Orangeville has changed since we were there?"

McQueen thought about the rushing high water that had transformed the peaceful canal into a raging beast. "I hope not. But if it has, we can stay there until the other person shows up with the other chip."

Tommy struggled to keep up and apparently only caught fragments of the conversation. "I'm glad we gave Sproat the slip," he said. "It's nice to be getting away from death-by-stupidity without someone chasing us."

Samara put out her arm. "Stop! Just stop, right here."

McQueen realized he had let the secret about the chip slip. He hoped Samara hadn't heard it. If she did, she was going to be angry. He stopped walking and tensed for a verbal fight. He tried to control his voice, wanted it to be calm and nonchalant; but the words came out strained, almost whining. "What is it?"

"What's this chip you're talking about?"

McQueen felt his face flush with embarrassment. She was Indigo and he didn't know if they were people users. If he told her about the chip and she used her super strength and somehow managed to get it from him, she might use it against him. She could be a spy. He just wasn't sure he could tell her about the chip.

"I'm sorry, he lied. Did I say chip. I meant tip. "There is supposed to be another person like the real

Augur. When he shows up, he'll give us a tip on how to put the pig people back on the blue grass."

Samara reached down and placed her hand on her belt. Her face brightened and she smiled big, but her eyes confessed confusion and caution.

Shaking his head, Miles pointed across the river. "Look at that."

The others turned and looked across the river. Burke, Miles's roommate from the youth camp, was leading a band of Sproat's men up the other side of the river.

McQueen turned toward Miles. "I'm sorry you thought he was your friend."

Miles smiled a half disappointed smile. "It's okay. At least he's on the other side of the river.

"That's the kid that was following you," Samara said. "I wondered why he didn't try to help when Sproat's men jumped you."

Like the betrayal by his best friend had just registered in his mind, Miles slumped; and a wounded look covered his face.

McQueen placed his hand on his son's shoulder. "Don't feel so bad, Miles. "It's not your fault. It happened to me, too."

"But I should have figured it out. He was the one who wanted to escape, practically planned the whole thing. Then, when we were outside the wall, he disappeared."

Samara stepped close and placed her hand on Mile's back. "He probably couldn't wait to tell Sproat that you had escaped and collect a reward."

"It's nothing new for that family," McQueen said. "His father would have done the same thing."

"But why?" Miles asked with a slight almost crying quiver to his voice.

"Simple," McQueen said. "Burk knew I would be looking for you. And he knew you would go to a place where I could find you. He made you think you were escaping and he followed you."

"If that's true, then why did Sproat's men beat me up, almost smothered me?"

McQueen thought about it for a moment. "Following you on foot" — he cupped his hands in front of his stomach — "with their fat stomachs weighing them down, it would have been a tiring job."

"But I wasn't traveling that fast."

"Maybe not, Sproat's men like to drink and they are lazy. My guess is that they would have killed you just to get back to their beer barrels."

"That's no lie," Tommy said. "If they hadn't beaten you up and they had to keep on following you, they could have died of alcoholic thirst, got the dry heaves, and sweated to death."

McQueen looked back from where they had just come. "By now, Sproat should have floated downriver far enough to be in the dry lands."

"Yeah," Tommy said with sardonic amusement. "He's probably dying for a drink."

"So what do we do now?" Samara asked in a voice quivering with exasperation. "This river's getting narrower and narrower. It won't be long before they can cross."

"They're headed in the right direction," McQueen said. "But they're on the wrong side."

"We know that," Tommy said with a twinge of alarm. "But you know as well as I do that they will come across. Then what?"

"We're going to let them," McQueen said and smiled a sly smile. "We might even have to encourage them a little."

A battle roar thundered from downriver. McQueen squinted into the distance. "It sounds like there's a whole army of Sproat's men coming upriver."

Miles cringed and looked upriver. "They're probably after a big reward."

McQueen's face flushed with discomfort. "Greed is a mighty motivator."

"Pain is a better one." Samara picked up a rock and threw it across the vast expanse of the wide river. It landed a few feet from Burke. He jerked around and yelled something back, but the roar of the water drowned out his voice.

McQueen smiled with satisfaction.

"What are you smiling about?" Samara asked. "I didn't hit him."

"If you can get them mad enough, they'll all cross the river, and that's just what we need."

"What?"

"McQueen smiled a coy smile. "Orangeville is on *their* side of the river."

Tommy threw his hands up in the air. "Oh just great. I damn near get drown in that wooden coffin. You said that they were on the wrong side of the river, and now you tell us we've been going up the wrong side of the river. Now I suppose you're going to tell us that we have to go back across, and

341

a whole army of Sproat's men will be there to greet us."

"What did you expect?' McQueen joked. "A welcoming party of Dinky clowns making toy animals out of balloons and Sproat spreading his arms welcoming the lunacy around him?"

Tommy conceded the point and smiled a faint smile.

McQueen turned serious. "If Samara can go downriver and throw enough rocks at them, she might get them to try to cross over to this side."

Miles stepped forward. "They won't follow one person. I'll go with her."

McQueen studied his son's face. Even though he saw no fear and only determination, he didn't want him to be captured.

I don't know," he said. "I wouldn't want them to catch you."

Miles crouched down. "I could alternate duck-walking with Tommy's hat on my head. They'll think there are at least three of us."

Tommy protectively placed his hand on his hat. "I don't like that idea."

"I just don't know," McQueen said.

"Don't worry about it," Samara said with an air of superiority. "If they even start to get close, I'll pick up Miles and run with him."

"McQueen remembered her pulling him from the rapids and the river. He felt a little better about the idea. "I believe you can do that." He held up one finger. "Remember, a slow-moving person is not as perceptible as a fast-moving person. When you don't want them to see you, slow down."

Tommy pulled his floppy hat down over his head and held it there. "Do I have to give Miles my hat?"

"Sorry, old buddy," McQueen said. "We all have to make little sacrifices."

Tommy took his hands from his hat. "Okay, but let's wait until we're out of sight."

McQueen's jaw hardened. "You can keep your precious hat until we go a few meters past the Y in the river. We'll have to cross two smaller rivers, but they shouldn't be as swift."

They continued up the side of the roaring river.

***

Dodging an occasional rock, Samara threw, Sproat's men staggered and tromped up the other side of the river. When a rock hit one of them, they shook their fists, aimed their antidote guns, and shouted profanities that McQueen and the others could not hear.

McQueen and his entourage increased their pace, and the sickening sight of Sproat's merry men was left behind.

Upriver, the water branched off into two rivers. About a kilometer up from the left side of the Y, the water slowed and became shallow.

McQueen held up his arm in a halting gesture. "After we cross this river, we'll have to go upriver a ways to cross over the other river." He turned toward Samara. "Samara, you and Miles can go back downriver. When you see Burke and Sproat's half-wits, throw rocks and do whatever you can to get them to cross the river. Once they're on the wrong side they'll probably keep going upriver until it ends."

Tommy took off his hat and handed it to Miles. "Don't lose it. It's like an old friend."

Miles placed the hat on his head. It drooped down over his ears. "I'll take good care of your old friend."

"Don't worry about it, Tommy," Samara said as if she were in a hurry. "When we get to Orangeville, you'll have your friend back."

McQueen extended his hand toward Miles. "God luck, Son. Give 'em hell."

Samara grabbed Miles by the arm. "Come on, book boy. Let's get this thing done."

Tommy reached up for his hat that was no longer on his head and flexed his wrist like he was tipping it. "Good Luck."

Samara and Miles walked downriver. McQueen and Tommy waited until they were out of sight, then they crossed the left branch of the river, walked up the right branch, and headed toward Orangeville.

CHAPTER 27

Samara walked with a swift step and Miles trotted behind her. When they got to where Samara figured Sproat would be, she stopped and surveyed the area. Cattails that once lined the shore were almost completely under water. Their pointy tops bent in the current and struggled to stay above the surface. Like skinny stick people, they seemed to be trying to gulp down a few more rays of life-giving sunshine before they drowned. Along the shore, roots, just below tree trunks were covered with water. They appeared to be wading. But Sproat's men were not to be seen.

"Do you think they already crossed," Miles asked.

"Let me look." Samara scanned the banks of the two rivers. Tall sections of grass stood upright; and last year's fallen leaves were still crisp, brown, and undisturbed. "They couldn't have crossed here," she said. "Those fat slobs would have left deep footprints in the mud and a trail of garbage."

In the distance, a high-pitched voice drifted across the river.

"That's Sproat," Miles said. "I wonder how he got off the steam car platform."

"I don't know, but he's here." Samara studied the raging river. It was narrower than it was downriver, but it still ran deep and strong. "Too bad we couldn't get them to try and cross here."

"Even if we can't get them to cross here, we'll have to do something to make them follow us upriver and then keep them mad enough to cross both rivers."

345

From across the river, a loud base drum boomed. Sproat's men bobbed their heads in time with the same monotonous bass beat, not once or a few times, but over and over and over. And they walked like zombies, hypnotized by the brain-numbing beat.

Samara tilted her head away from the noise. "Sproat must be afraid Indigos are close. Just because he has a big plastic cone on the drum that amplifies the sound, he mistakenly believes Indigos are afraid of the loud bass noise."

Miles gestured toward the noise. "When he brings his drum he always brings big barrels of beer. His men tow them like cannons."

In thought, Samara nodded. "I've seen those barrels before. It seems like beer is the most important thing of any of his conquests."

"Unless someone points them in the right direction and supplies them with an endless supply of beer, his men aren't much good."

"It must make them feel like they never left home. That beer gives them a sense of security."

Miles nodded in agreement and replied with a playful look on his face. "You spill his beer and he'll be plenty mad."

Samara's eyes shone with mischief. "Stay here, Miles. I'll be right back."

Using her super speed, Samara ran upriver; and with her super strength, she swam across. Then she made a wide circle and came up behind the advancing army of slobs. Twelve men wearing dirty baseball caps that were turned to the side, were in front of two fifty-liter barrels of beer on two-wheeled trailers. A pole with a T was attached to the center of the pair of wheels and allowed men to stand abreast, in front of the T, and push. Although there were six men on the push-T's of each barrel, they lagged behind. Out of Sproat's view; each man tried to let the others push most of the load.

"Start pushing," one man complained.

Another man stepped forward but only placed his relaxed hands on the push-T. "I'm pushing. You're the one that's loafing."

"This thing's too heavy," another man grumbled. "We should stop and lighten the load."

"That's the best thing I heard all day," another man said.

"Yeah," another man chimed in. "One good drink will lighten this thing just enough."

Up ahead, Sproat ordered the drummer to stop and shouted back. "Come on, you big half-wits, get that beer up here."

All the complainers quit slacking and pushed on the shaft. The beer barrels moved with ease, and they were rapidly gaining on Sproat. Sproat shook his heavy head with approval and signaled the drummers to hit the drum again, and harder.

The volume of boom-booms increased.

Samara picked up a pointed rock, did an end run, and came up behind the last barrel of beer. As Sproat's men pulled the barrels and bobbed their heads to the thump of the boom-booms, they didn't hear or see Samara.

Thunk! Boom! Right in beat with the loud boom booms, she crashed the point of the rock into the side of the beer barrel. The wood cracked, but Sproat's men didn't hear it.

Wham! She hit it again. Snap! The wood cracked, more.

They still didn't hear.

Beer flew out the cracks in the wood and spumed into the air.

Before Sproat's men could figure out why they were being sprayed with beer, Samara ran back into the cover of the forest and watched.

Sproat's men stopped pulling the broken beer barrel; and as if it were escaping gold, they frantically tried to place their chubby fingers over the beer-spewing cracks.

Beer sprayed high up into the air and came down onto the backs of the other men pulling the lead barrel. They turned back, dropped the pull shaft, and went back to help. Samara dashed to the lead barrel and thrust the rock into its lower end. This time, on the first hit, the wood on the back of the barrel broke and opened a big hole. Like water busting out the bottom of a broken dam, beer flew out and gushed over the ground.

More beer sprayed on the pullers and drenched their feet. The loud boom-booms of the drum continued to block out conversation and chaos. Sproat and the others didn't look back. Samara, didn't run. She stood and made faces at them.

They still didn't look back

She picked up a rock and fired it at the big drum. It hit the leather skin and rocketed right on through. Half the pounding noise faded. Sproat turned toward her. She fired another rock. It thunked into the huge amplifying cone. With the next boom-boom, the cone buzzed with an irritating sound and went silent.

Now, when Sproat raised his voice, he could be heard. "She broke our speakers." He looked to the broken beer barrels spewing beer. Horror filled his face. He screamed. "She broke our beer barrels! Get that little bitch."

Sproat's army turned and looked back. Fountains of their lifeblood, beer, fizzled into the air and fell on the ground where it could not be drank or enjoyed. Like someone had just killed their only child, a great sadness filled their eyes.

Then panic struck.

A hoard of men ran toward the spewing barrels. Some took off their baseball caps and tried to fill them. Others pulled the puller's hands away from the holes in the barrels and put their eager opened mouths into the foaming, beer streams. Others elbowed their way to the barrels, cupped their hands, and tried to catch the flying beer sprays. They all tried to drink every last escaping drop, but none had sense enough to grab a tankard or a container to catch the beer. When all the beer had been lost on the ground or had been sucked up by the army of vacuum-cleaner-like mouths, an angry protest erupted thought the ranks.

Suddenly, they realized that Samara was the one person responsible for the unnecessary ruination of their happy inebriated state. Calls for her death thundered through the trees. She let herself be seen, and mocked them saying, "What's the matter? Are you little babies going to cry over a little spilt beer?"

Like heavy wheels on a steam car, they lumbered after her, picking up speed, and firing their antidote guns. Even though she was immune

349

to the poison antidote bullets, she didn't want to take the time to pull them out. She ran, but just far enough ahead that their antidote bullets fell to the ground before they hit her. Making sure they were watching, she dove into the river and began to swim across. Halfway across, she turned. Treading water as if there were no current, she motioned to Sproat's men. "Come on in," she taunted. "The water's fine."

With antidote bullets, intended for Samara, flying over their heads, two of Sproat's men waded into the water. When the swift moving current was up to their waist, they couldn't stand up. They tumbled over and sank into the swift water. Making feeble strokes, they tried to keep their heads above water.

Their efforts were useless.

The current was too strong for their skinny arms and balloon-shaped bodies. Like round oversized bobbers on a broken fishing line, they went downriver at a fast float. When they hit a twin whirlpool, like heavy round rocks, they plopped under the water and never came back up.

Samara walked ashore on the other side and Miles was waiting. "They look pretty mad," he said. "Did you break the beer barrel?"

"No." Samara smiled a big satisfied grin. "I broke both of them."

Miles beamed with satisfaction. "Way to go. Now they're twice as mad."

Like spoiled babies in a hissy fit, Sproat and his men bunched up along the riverbank. They shouted and waved their fists in the air, making their ruddy alcoholic faces flush to high-blood-pressure pink.

Some aimed their antidote guns and shot across the river. The bullets landed in the swift water.

The earth shifted. The water in the river surged into a huge rolling wave. It swept onward dragging anything in its path. Right after three boats, one green, one yellow, and one blue, zipped past, the wave tore a huge pine tree from the shore and flung it downstream.

After the wave subsided, an iodine scent filled the air. On the side of the shore where Sproat and his men stood, a huge decomposing clump of dark-green seaweed sat on the shore.

One of Sproat's men, wearing a dirty-white chef's hat, walked up to the seaweed, bent over, and picked up a long strand of it. Shaking it in his hand, he turned toward Sproat. "Captain Sproat!"

Talking to two other men, Sproat didn't turn around.

The man with the seaweed persisted. "Captain Sproat!"

Sproat turned and growled at the man. "What do you want?"

"Do you want me to cook this Spanish?"

Without examining the seaweed, Sproat waved his hand down. "Go ahead, cook anything you want."

The man bent over, scooped an armful of seaweed, and walked away.

Samantha bent over and picked up a rock. "Let's rile them up." She flung the rock high into the air. It traveled in an ark over the river and clunked down at Sproat's feet. He motioned behind him. Two of his men, lead a dog, on a leash, up to him.

Samara turned toward Miles. "If that dog can hunt he'll pick up our scent. Even if we get them to cross the river, our plan might not work."

"Maybe if you get them mad enough they'll try to cross here."

Samara threw another rock. This one bounced once and veered into Sproat's foot. He grabbed his foot and pointed to the river. In his high-pitched voice, he shouted at the dog, "Kill!"

Miles's face filled with confusion. "What's he doing?"

"He wants the dog to swim across and attack us."

Again Sproat pointed across the river and shouted, "Kill!"

The dog tucked its tail between its legs and didn't move. Sproat kicked the dog. It whined in submission. He picked it up and threw it into the river. It landed in a calm spot where it tried to swim back to shore. Sproat threw rocks, sticks, and anything he could find at the dog. It winced with each painful hit. With sad pleading eyes, it gave up trying to swim to shore. It turned from Sproat's ignorant cruelty and dog-paddled toward the center, where the current swept it to a whirlpool. It paddled faster. Its paws chopped the surface, but it was a losing effort. Its head bobbed up a few valiant times. It was in antidote bullet range. Samara wanted to swim out and save it, but if she did, a shower of antidote bullets would hit the dog and kill it anyway. The dog slipped under the water and was gone.

Across the river, Sproat's men patted Sproat on the back; and as if he were some kind of hero, they cheered.

"I usually have a conscience," Samara said in a mad rage. "But sending Sproat and his whole rotten army to the bottom of the river wouldn't bother me one bit."

With tears forming in the corners of his eyes, Miles stared at the swirling water where the dog had gone under.

Samara looked into Miles's face. It showed hate and pity.

"That was probably a nice dog," Miles said, and stood there like he was in a trance.

Samara pulled on his arm. "Let's get this show on the road."

Making sure Sproat and his great army followed, they started upriver. Along the way, Samara threw rocks at Sproat. At points along the riverbank where only his head and shoulders could be seen, Miles pulled Tommy's hat down over his ears, crouched down, and duck-walked.

On the other side of the river, Sproat and his army of men followed like they never followed anyone in their lives: noiseless and beerless.

CHAPTER 28

Huffing and puffing, McQueen danced around the rocks and ran along the grassy shore of the river.

Tommy followed at a hectic pace. Between gasps, he managed to blurt out, "Hey, slow down."

McQueen slowed to a trot. "Okay, I guess there's no hurry."

Right before a sharp turn, the river narrowed and the water calmed. Tommy stopped. "Can we cross here?"

McQueen stepped into the calm water. "If we keep going upriver, we'll have a longer walk. Let's try it."

Taking careful steps, Tommy eased his little legs into the water.

With Tommy at his side, McQueen started across the river. When the water was up to Tommy's waist, McQueen grabbed him by the arm. "I don't know if there are drops off, but hang on."

Tommy took one step and went under. McQueen pulled him up. "It's too deep."

"My feet are killing me," Tommy said. "Let's swim across."

McQueen looked into the water. Broken trees with pointed ends, pieces of buildings, and other debris floated past. In calm water he could save Tommy if something happened; but the thought of having a tree root or a sharp board sang onto them and pull them under without Samara around to pull them out, was not encouraging.

He pulled on Tommy's arm. "Let's go upriver a little more."

Just as they were about to step back onto shore, the water level dropped. The river suddenly became a little crick.

Tommy looked At McQueen.

McQueen looked at Tommy.

Both had questions in their eyes.

Tommy jerked with fright. "Snake!"

McQueen turned and looked down. A rattail and its dead Pygmy's body appeared in the muddy canal bed.

Tommy's face paled. "What's going on?"

Trying to ease the pain in his heart from seeing the dead Pygmy, McQueen rubbed his chin and swallowed. "I hope it's not what I think it is." He started across the muddy canal bed.

Tommy gestured toward the dead Pygmy. "Should we burry him?"

McQueen violently shook his head. "I'd like to but they might be killing more. If we hurry we might be able to save some." He continued across the canal. "Come on, let's go."

On the other side of the canal, McQueen broke into a trot and Tommy lagged behind. When McQueen came to the bottom of a tall bank of yellow dirt, he stopped and waited for Tommy to catch up.

Huffing for breath, Tommy stopped at McQueen's side. "What's the big rush?"

McQueen looked up. The yellow bank of dirt had held here, but he didn't know if the dam had. He didn't answer Tommy's question. He pointed to the top of the bank of dirt. "It should be right over that ridge."

Tommy scrambled halfway up the bank and looked back at McQueen.

The earth shifted and a tremor passed beneath their feet.

McQueen moaned. "Now what?"

Tommy opened his mouth to answer, but the ground under his feet collapsed. Before he could cry out, he fell to the ground and the breath was knocked from his lungs. He dropped down the slope amid a cascade of stones and dirt. As he bounced and tumbled, newly exposed rocks pummeled him from all sides. All he managed to do was protect his face with his arms. At the bottom of the bank of dirt, he tumbled to a stop.

McQueen rushed over to him and looked down. "You okay?"

Tommy felt his body. "I might have a couple of black and blue marks tomorrow, but I'll be just fine."

McQueen reached down and helped Tommy stand up. "You want to take a break?"

Tommy took a few deep breaths. "We can't. We got Pigmies to save." He turned and scrambled up the side of the bank that had not collapsed. When he got to the top, he stopped and waved for McQueen to come up.

McQueen climbed the bank, but he climbed it slow and methodically. Knowing what he would see, he delayed the inevitable by moving slow.

When he was at Tommy's side, he looked over the ridge. The small boats that had zipped here and there around the lake were no long floating. He slumped down. The beautiful reservoir that the Pygmies had carefully constructed to be in harmony with nature and enhance the earth's recovery had been replaced with a vast sludge flat. The only sound was a single fly buzzing. Everything else was dead.

McQueen whistled with one long exhausted breath and shook his head in sorrow. "Now we know why that little canal turned in to a raging river."

In a voice filled with awe, Tommy asked, "What happened?"

"I'm not sure. Maybe the dam was destroyed by some monstrous storm, or maybe the water companies didn't want the clean water to cut into their water sales. Maybe Sproat's scabs found the dam and blew it up."

With a sad defeated tone to his voice, Tommy said, "It doesn't really matter how it happened. It's gone now."

McQueen nodded in sad agreement and looked at what looked like a huge empty sewer pit. The vast expanse of water had gushed from the gigantic reservoir. Now, only a little stream of black sewer water flowed down a narrow ditch. All around this, what the deep water had concealed was exposed. Dead fish lay here and there. Beer bottles, cans, plastic containers, bags, and every type of garbage imaginable was sticking up out of the mud.

At the sides of the broken dam, great power plants partially covered with lead that would have produced electricity before the magnetic fields had gone haywire, sat idle. Below lingering wisps of smoke, it was as if a giant foot had mashed houses and meeting halls into the ground. They were nothing much more than splinters. At the base of a smoldering mountain of garbage, green trees still grew and flourished, but without the lifeblood of water they would soon dry up and die. Their beautiful limbs would turn skeletal black.

If this wasn't the work of Sproat and his men, it had to be people just as awful, or worse.

McQueen knew the only hope was the orange turn. With a slight spark of hope in his chest he turned to Tommy. "I wonder if Samara and Miles got Sproat's men to cross before the water went down."

CHAPTER 29

Samara arched back to throw another stone. The water in the raging river dropped to the level of a stream. Now that the roar of the river was gone, all became quiet. Then, like the high-pitch of a swarm of bothersome mosquitoes, the obnoxious voices of Sproat's men became loud and irritating. Charging across the riverbed, their sickening threats echoed through the trees.

Samara ran.

Miles followed.

Samara looked back to see if Miles was following fast enough. He was. Sproat's men were far behind. Samara held out her arm and signaled for Miles to stop.

He did.

"If we get too far ahead," she said, "they'll lose sight of us. Let's wait for them to catch up."

Miles huffed in deep breaths. "Good idea," he said between huffs. "Let me catch my breath."

After an hour of waiting, Sproat and his men could not be herd. Searching the forest for signs of movement, Samara paced from one tree to another. She saw no one. "Maybe we'll have to go back and find them."

"Wait!" Miles held up his hand.

An army of Sproat's men came crashing through the trees.

Samara put her hand of Miles's shoulder. "You think you can go slowly enough for them to follow us now?"

Miles grinned. "No problem."

They took off running at a slow trot. Sproat's men picked up their pace and followed. Up ahead, behind a stand of skinny trees, a band of Sproat's men jumped up and leveled their antidote guns at Samara and Miles. Samara turned to her right. Another band of men jumped up with guns drawn. When she turned to her left, Sproat came walking out of the brush waving his hands in a halting motion. "No need to shoot, men. They're not going anywhere. And besides, they're going to tell us where McQueen hid that key."

Miles vehemently spit the words out, "We're not telling you a thing."

"Go ahead don't tell us," Sproat smugly said. "When your stupid father finds out you haven't returned, he'll be back to get you."

"You're the one that's stupid, Miles protested. "There is no key. There is no treasure."

Sproat shook his finger in Miles's face. "Don't tell me that, you little creep. The whole world knows your worthless father has horded a great treasure for himself."

"That's a lie," Miles said and tried to reason with Sproat. "You're already a rich man. You control everything. What more do you want?"

I want a nice place to live, too. I want to live in an ocean of blue grass. I want to be the Chief Earth Officer."

Surprised, Miles stared at Sproat.

Samara cocked her head in amazement. She couldn't believe a person could be so stupid. "Money can't fix the earth's problems."

Sproat wagged his head with lofty tilt. "It may surprise you, Miss Prissy, but I don't care about the earth's problems. It's lost anyway. When it dies, I'm going to die with it. But, in the meantime, I'm going to enjoy what little time I have left."

"But there is no treasure," Miles whined.

"How would you know?" Sproat shot back. "You're just a kid." Your old man just wants to keep the key and the treasure for himself. While we worked and slaved, you and your old man lived in luxury for seventeen years."

Miles's face turned hard with anger. "If you would have tried to save the earth, you could have been Chief Earth Officer.

"I should have been the Chief Earth Officer years ago. Your greedy father just didn't want to share the wealth and the power. Without that key he's nothing."

As if he were flicking garbage at him, Miles jerked his opened hand toward Sproat. "He doesn't need a key to do anything."

Sproat raised his hand to strike Miles.

Samara cleared her throat with a threatening tone.

Sproat lowered his hand. "We don't need people like your father running the world."

As if he were about to throw up, Miles jerked his head back. "Like you have done a better job? If Samara hadn't busted your beer barrels, at this very moment, you would be drunk on your feet."

Acting as if he didn't hear Miles's remark about being drunk, Sproat waved it off. "It's all your old man's fault. He's the one who lied about the blue grass. He's the one who exposed the fake virus and then said it wasn't fake."

"If you weren't so stupid," Miles's said and tightened his fists. "You would know that the virus was created for the good of the world. It is the only way to keep the pig people like you from destroying what little livable land is left."

As if he were shooing a flock of flies, Sproat waved his hand. "I've heard it all before." He shook his chubby fist at Miles. "Just tell us where he's at, and tell us where he hides that key."

"If there *is* such a key," Samara said, "how do you know McQueen has it?"

"It was written in the old stones of life that a man with three, would be entrusted with the key. Before he became Chief Earth Officer, McQueen had three sergeant stripes. He is the one who has the key. The stones of life tell us so."

Miles lifted his hand and pointed his finger at Sproat. "But you were one of the protesters that claimed the stones of life never existed."

Sproat hesitated and said, "Even though I have never seen such stones, I know they can tell the future."

"Don't be ignorant," Miles said and flicked his wrist at Sproat. "The only people who can predict the future are the gifted Indigos."

As if he were caught in a lie, Sproat's face reddened. "Maybe that's where I heard it." As if in thought, he lowered his head. After a moment he looked up. "Everybody knows he has the key. Everybody can't be wrong."

"Why not? They were all wrong about the blue grass."

"Because the majority rules," Sproat said, and his red face distorted to a scowl. "The majority is always right."

From out of the forest a voice rang out. "Not this time."

It was Samara's brother, Hack.

A conglomeration of Indigos poured from the forest and surrounded Sproat's army. Sproat's men tuned and drew their guns.

Sproat held up his hand and shouted to his men. "Wait until my command, then open fire."

Antidote guns cocked and anxious fingers feathered triggers.

Hack defiantly smiled at Sproat. "Do you really want to do that?"

Sproat drew back and lowered his hand. "We all want that treasure," he reasoned. "It doesn't matter how we get rich, just that we do. Why don't we band together and get it?

Miles protested. "Why do I have to keep telling you? My father has no key to a treasure."

"Oh, but he does have a key." Sproat shot back. "If we have to, we'll kill him to get it."

Fire filled Mile's eyes. "You touch my father and it'll be the last person you ever touch."

Grinning and snickering as if the situation were amusing, Sproat said, "No need to get angry, son. Your father's life can be spared. All he has to do is give us the key."

Hack held up his hand. "Sorry, Sproat, but it doesn't work like that. There has to be two keys. Two people have to do the turn."

Sproat rubbed his chubby face, and his forehead wrinkled as if her were in pain. "Well, who has the other key?"

"It could be anyone of us," Hack said. "It could be Miles. It could be me. It could be anyone of your men."

Sproat glanced at his men. They lowered their antidote guns. "I would know if it was one of my men."

"You don't know that," Hack said. "Why do you think we never killed anyone? You and your great army may have already killed the only other person who can do the turn."

"Anyone can turn a stupid key," Sproat said and his men raised their guns.

"Maybe just any one can turn the key, but when the DNA doesn't match up, the ship full of treasure will not come up out of the ground."

As if he didn't like what he was hearing, Sproat vigorously shook his head. "Just how long do we have to wait until this great other person shows up?"

"No one will know who the other person is until the time just before the turn." Hack gestured to Sproat's men. "If anyone is killed here, the key could go with them. The ship will be lost."

Sproat signaled for his men to lower their guns. "Well let's go and find McQueen."

Miles looked at Samara. She knew from the look in his eyes that he wanted to send them in the wrong direction. She put her hand on his back. "Sorry, Miles, but before it's too late for anyone to be saved, I think it's time for us to solve this key and treasure problem."

Miles slowly shook his head. "Okay, let's go."

Burke walked from behind the tree where he had been hiding and walked up to Miles. "Way to go, old buddy. I knew you'd see it my way."

Miles didn't exchange looks or acknowledge Burke's presence. He turned; and lagging behind the others, he slowly walked upriver toward Orangeville.

CHAPTER 30

Above the vast drained and destroyed reservoir, McQueen turned to Tommy.

It was time.

"Tommy," he said, "I have to tell you something."

With a disgusted look, Tommy turned toward McQueen. "Things can't get much worse. Go ahead."

"You know the story about the treasure and the key?"

"Everybody knows that old tale."

"McQueen clinched his teeth and continued. "It isn't a tale."

Tommy's round eyes opened wide. "What?"

"There is no treasure, and there is no key."

"So what's the big deal?"

"The key covers a magnetic chip. Augur, the mega mutant, gave me the key to use when the last hope of saving the earth was near."

A look of relief, then excitement dawned on Tommy's face. "Augur left you the secret? Will we finally get rid of the scum on this planet and get it back to a livable state?"

"I think it's too late. I have to do the turn."

Tommy's little forehead wrinkled with wonder. "What are you talking about?"

"Only two people, one male and one female have chips. The turn cannot be done without one or the other. It must be done together."

"So who are these two people?"

McQueen placed his hand on the chip sewn in the waist band of his underwear. "I'm the male. I don't know why I was chosen." He took his hand off the chip. "I wish it had been someone else."

"No other male is qualified," Tommy said. "But who is the female?"

A feeling of loneliness came over McQueen. "I always thought it was Danielle." He wiped his eye. "But if she were the one, the ship that can take us to a new planet is lost."

"Wait a minute," Tommy said with a quizzical glance. "Did you say ship?"

"Yes, there is a ship, the last and best of the Darth Disk series."

"It doesn't matter what series it is. Nothing can get through the space junk."

"This ship can. It is covered with layers of ceramic Kevlar."

As if it were the barrel of a gun, Tommy stuck out his finger and poked himself in his chest. "Like a bullet proof vest?"

"Not quite. The space junk will blast off the ceramic Kevlar layers and hopefully it won't get through to the main body of the ship."

"In other words," Tommy said with wonder, "it's a one shot deal. If the ship gets through, no one's coming back."

"But even if it can get through, there is still a problem."

"What problem?" Tommy asked with a pained expression on his face.

"Only the two selected people whose DNA match can do the turn. They have been given the power to choose a group of people to fly from this diseased planet and begin again in a new land."

Tommy jerked his hand downward with disgust. "I could have stayed in the Grotto. Underground I would have been safe."

"I wish that were true," McQueen said. "But the pig people are off the blue grass. They'll find the entrance, and that will be the end of the Grotto."

"You mean I came all this way for nothing?"

"That's why I didn't tell you sooner. If the other person is dead and you knew it, you wouldn't have come with me. I couldn't have come here without my best friend and the first person I have chosen to go with me."

The start of a tear formed in Tommy's eye. "Let's not get mushy. We still have a chance. We'll just have to find the other person who can do the turn."

McQueen stared at the desolation of the reservoir. "And what if we can't find her?"

Tommy shrugged. "We'll just have to go back to Blue Town. We'll have to get the people back on the blue grass."

McQueen sighed with defeat. "Maybe if we just tell them the truth, this time they'll understand. They'll stop destroying the earth."

"It won't matter if they understand or not," Tommy said, and his eyes swept over the mud filled reservoir. "If they want to live, they'll have no choice."

As if he were holding a heavy weight, McQueen extended his hand, palm up. "That will be a big job." With a vigorous shake of his head, he added, "An impossible job."

Tommy made a face that shown with disagreement. "But you seem to forget what your father told us years ago when we were just kids."

McQueen's father had shown Tommy and McQueen many things that had saved their lives; and he had made them the men they had become; but McQueen couldn't remember what Tommy was referring to. "What did my father tell us?"

"Do you remember when we were digging the secret underwater tunnel and we wanted to quit?"

McQueen nodded. "I thought I was going to die from exhaustion. How could I ever forget that?"

"And you remember that I said it was impossible to build such a tunnel?"

Nodding, McQueen rolled his hand. "Keep talking."

"Your father said, 'There is nothing that can't be done. Some things just haven't been tried yet.' Don't you think we can try to save the earth?"

McQueen felt the pain of great conflict in his head. He wanted to save the earth. He wanted to get the pig people back on the blue grass. He wanted to educate them, somehow show them, somehow train them, to live with the planet, not on it; but with people like Sproat running the earth, he knew the only hope was to go to another planet. He knew Tommy wanted to stay and fight, but it was useless. The ship and the turn would be best for all concerned.

"At one time, we might have saved the earth," he said. "But that was before it was ruined beyond repair. All the people I trusted gave me false reports. We can't fix something that's impossible to repair."

369

Tommy let his arms fall to his sides. "Maybe you're right."

"Sure I'm right," McQueen said to help confirm the decision in his own mind. "After we're gone, Sproat and the pig people will be free to die in their own filth. And the universe will be rid of an incurable cancer."

"But the Dinkies aren't pig people," Tommy protested. "And all life is precious."

"Sure it is," McQueen said. "Don't confuse the issue. Sproat and the pig people destroy life. They are only getting back what they have sown."

Tommy turned to McQueen in exasperation. "But what about my Dinky friends?"

McQueen felt sadness for the Dinkies. "I hate to leave them behind, but if we have to, we'll go back and you can select a few to go with us."

Slumping, Tommy shook his head in disagreement. "We can, but they have been lied to, too many times. I don't think anyone will believe you. None of them will come."

"We can't just stay here and die. If we find the other person who has the chip, we'll pick a few good people and get out of this dump world."

Tommy turned his back to McQueen and held his hand to his ear. "Listen."

McQueen stood perfectly still and listened. The sound of Sproat's army of fat feet shuffling through sticks and leaves crinkled through the air.

McQueen assumed a defensive posture. "If they eliminate us, we won't have to worry about the turn or anything else."

Like a traveling circus, Sproat's army appeared at the tree line.

Preparing to run, Tommy began swinging his little arms. "Let's get out of here."

McQueen pointed to the vast mud of the drained reservoir. "Sproat had brought too many men. The only way out is across the reservoir. If we go that way we'll sink in muck like that wild boar did."

Tommy jerked his head to his left. "Let's go that way."

"We'll never get down that." He looked toward where the dam had been. The concrete that once held back the huge body of clean water was broken and jagged. Sharp rocks and pointed steel rods stuck out like deadly spears. What was left of the dam looked like it had been blown up. It was a sheer cliff."

Tommy looked to his right. "Maybe we could run along the shoreline."

McQueen turned toward the right and took one step. Indigo people with gold feathers in their hair, led by Hack and Samara, filtered out of the trees and walked along the shoreline. Miles wasn't with Samara. McQueen hoped he was still alive. Although the Indigos wouldn't kill them, if they tried to escape along the shoreline, it would be like running through an Indigo obstacle course.

McQueen nodded with confidence. "Maybe we can talk our way out."

Scanning the area with wary eyes, Tommy took in the multitude of Indigo people coming toward them. "I think we have a chance. It looks like the whole fam damily's here."

"Too bad some of your Dinky friends aren't here."

"I wouldn't be surprised," Tommy said. "Sludge always has a way of showing up."

While the caravan of Sproat's men waited, Sproat and a few of his men walked up to McQueen and stopped.

Behind them, little feet tramped on loose gravel.

McQueen and Tommy turned toward the sound.

From up over the ridge, where Tommy and McQueen had entered the dam, two Dinkies were walking across a short stretch of gravel. It was Yellow Ring and Sludge. They carried walking sticks that looked like weapons. Although they were walking on clean dust-free gravel, when their feet hit the stones they created puffs of yellow dust that resembled little clouds of gold.

When they got close Sproat held up his hand like a traffic cop. "That's far enough."

Sludge and Yellow Ring stopped and looked to Tommy. Tommy smiled at them and said, "Well, if it isn't the gold dust twins."

Yellow Ring smiled and pointed to Tommy's head. "Well, if it ain't the hatless wonder."

As if he had just remembered he didn't have his hat, Tommy reached up and placed his hand on his head.

Yellow Ring chuckled.

Sludge didn't smile. He looked at the ruined dam; and with a bewildered look on his face, he asked, "Is this Orangeville?"

"This was Orangeville," McQueen said flatly.

As if he was placing all the blame on Sproat, Yellow Ring glared at him, but talked to Tommy.

"See, I tole you they would die in their own crap. They blew the whole place to smithereens."

"Shut your stupid mouth," Sproat said, and stared at the fake mouth on the back of Yellow Ring's neck. He pointed to it. "And I mean both of them."

His men laughed with the vicious pleasure of ignorance.

Yellow Ring lifted his walking stick and held it high, ready to strike. "Look, balloon-butt face, I'll talk any time I want to talk."

Sproat waved him off and walked up to McQueen and Tommy.

Tommy disfigured his face. Imitating Sproat, he talked with a high pitch voice. "Hey, fat boy, your scabs left a few trees standing. Are you sure you don't want to go back and get more pig people and destroy the place completely?"

"Very funny, you dumb Dinky," Sproat snapped back. "Your kind shouldn't be here anyway."

McQueen stepped forward with a threatening posture. "He'll go anywhere he wants. He's my friend."

Sproat tried to puff up his chest, but only his belly expanded. He wagged his chubby finger at McQueen. "As Chief Earth Officer you're not permitted to associate with Dinkies. You should be brought up on charges."

"While we're at it," McQueen said. "Let's do it right. For the disregard you have for your fellow man, you should be arrested for impersonating a human being."

Yellow Ring and Sludge laughed and walked toward Tommy. Sproat lifted his hand for them to stop, but lowered it. They walked past Sproat's threatening arm and stopped at Tommy's side.

Sproat became calm, almost docile. "Now, now," he said and shook his finger with a playful gesture. "No need to become hostile. We can all be friends." He extended his hand.

No one shook it.

He continued to hold it out. "I'm sure there is enough treasure to go around."

McQueen looked at Sproat's hand but didn't shake it. "There is no treasure."

"Sure there is." Sproat lifted his hand and motioned to one of his men.

The man pulled Miles from behind the group of men and presented him to McQueen.

"We found your son wandering around." Sproat smiled a self-satisfied grin. "We knew you would be worried about him, so we brought him here."

Miles stepped next to his father. "That's not true, Dad."

McQueen placed his hand of Miles's shoulder. "It doesn't matter. You're here now."

"That's right," Sproat said. "Everything will be just fine. We'll all be rich."

Tommy stepped to Miles and held out his hand. "Can I have it back?"

Miles pulled Tommy's floppy hat from his back pocket and handed it to Tommy. Tommy immediately placed his hat on his head and breathed a sigh of relief. "Thanks' Miles, I really missed this thing."

McQueen's ear caught the faint sound of music.
He looked toward the sound.

In the distance, a stand of black bony trees stood at the base of the smoldering mountain of garbage. Like a song in the night, pipe organ music drifted through the air and echoed off the mountain.

All eyes turned toward the sound.

As if they were a herd of sheep being herded by an extinct border collie, the entire group of people gravitated toward the echo. After they rounded the garbage mountain, with sudden puzzlement, they stopped.

An open-ended, square building, with a corrugated silver roof, sat in the center of a field of bright orange grass. Despite the weird setting, inside the building, a tall orange man, in a white flowing robe, sat in a plush, red leather chair at a brass pipe organ, playing church music. As he gracefully pressed the immaculate, white keys, the translucent fingernails on his long fingers flashed silver. Below, his orange feet pumped pedals sending air to the brass tubes.

Perplexed, Tommy turned toward McQueen. "Are we dreaming?"

"Maybe," McQueen said. "That guy looks like something mutated his skin."

As the approaching group's legs swished through the orange grass, the orange man turned. When the group stopped in front the open ended square building, the orange men smiled a welcoming smile. As he did, the sides of his long drawn face looked like they were being pressed in a wine press.

"He doesn't have any hair," Tommy said, "and his face doesn't look too good. Look at those eyes."

Twice as big as Tommy's, the orange man's almond-shaped eyes gave off a clear glow; and his black irises broadcasted a deep dark feeling.

As the organ music filled the air, Samara wedged herself between McQueen and Miles and softly placed her hand on McQueen's arm.

Wondering if she could be the other person with the key, McQueen studied her face.

A tear formed in her eye.

Softly, she said, "I think he's the turn man."

"Maybe he can tell us who the other person is."

Samara lifted her hand from McQueen's arm, extended her finger, and tapped her belt. "He knows."

The orange man stopped playing, turned his head toward Samara, and nodded.

McQueen glanced at the orange man and then looked at Samara. "Are you the one?"

Samara lowered her head and looked up. "Yes."

To make sure of what he was hearing, McQueen stopped breathing.

He stepped closer. "What?"

Samara reached out and placed her hand back on McQueen's arm. "I would have told you before, but I couldn't be sure I could trust you. But now it doesn't matter, there is too much at stake."

"That's right," Sproat interrupted. "There is a lot at stake."

Tommy faced Sproat like a little angry bee. "Tell it like it is, Sproat. You only want to be rid of

McQueen. If he leaves the planet, you'll be in line to be the next Chief Earth Officer."

Sproat's face puffed up and became pink. "So what? You little creep," he yelled, but glanced at the orange man and lowered his voice. "There's nothing wrong with a man wanting to better himself."

"That's true," Tommy said. "Too bad you'll never do it."

Sproat ignored Tommy's remark. As if he were the spokesman for everyone gathered there, he stepped forward and shouted at the orange man, "We're here to do the turn."

Yellow Ring waved his stick in the air. "Show us the treasure."

The orange man tilted his head upward. The white clouds remained, but the sky turned from blue to orange. The corrugated silver roof of the open ended building flew up, rumbled through the air; and a few meters away, it slammed down onto the orange grass.

The crowd reacted with a collective intake of breath.

Amazed, Tommy's mouth dropped to his chest. "How did he do that?"

The orange man pivoted his plush leather chair until his back was facing the crowd. Then he looked to the orange sky. With his palms toward the three walls of the building, he straightened his arms. The walls of the building fell outward, eased down onto the orange grass, and sent up clouds of orange dust

As the dust settled, the orange man pointed to the huge mountain of smoldering garbage.

Sounding as if it were coming from the bottom of an abyss, his deep voice echoed from his cavernous chest. "The turn cannot be accomplished until the mountain of filth is moved."

McQueen cringed under the sound of the powerful voice and didn't speak.

"We're not garbage men," Sproat protested. "But we'll supervise the others." He looked at Yellow Ring and Sludge. "Especially those two."

Yellow Ring scowled. "You couldn't supervise your own rear end if you had both hands in your back pockets."

"That's the kind of a remark I would expect from a Dumb Dinky with two mouths." Sproat gestured toward the garbage mountain and made shooing motions with his hand. "Now let's be good little Dinkies and get to work."

Yellow Ring and Sludge didn't move.

The orange man swiveled his chair around and faced the crowd. "You believe you can live as you chose," he said, sounding more than a little annoyed. "My time here is limited. If you all work together you will be able to move this filth before I must go."

Placing his hands on his hips, Sproat assumed a posture of authority. "What do *we* have to move it for?"

The orange man looked at him with indifference. "The ship you are looking for is below. It cannot rise until the filth is moved."

"We don't care about a ship," Sproat said. All we want is the treasure."

"Yeah," Yellow Ring said. "Just show where it's at."

The orange man turned his head in a playful tilt and winked at Sproat. "The ship will reveal the greatest treasure known to man."

"Then all my men are going on that ship," Sproat said. "I'll need all the help I can get to load it and come back."

"It's your call," the orange man said with a wave of his hand. "Whatever you are going to do, do it quickly. When the sun goes down, I will be gone."

"When will you be back?" McQueen asked.

As if he didn't care whether they moved the mountain of garbage or not, the orange man eased back into the softness of the plush chair. "When would you come back to a warped clump of insanity?" He began playing the orange organ.

Hack looked at Sproat.

Sproat looked at Hack.

McQueen raised his arm and gestured toward the mountain of garbage. "This is a huge task, and we don't have much time. Let's all work together and get this done."

The group took a few steps toward the mountain and stopped.

"Come on," Sproat said. "It's the greatest treasure known to man. There's enough for all of us."

His men waded into the garbage pile and began picking up garbage, carrying it fifty meters away, and dropping it."

Hack looked at Samara. "Now we know there is no treasure, but if we don't move this garbage the orange man will leave. We'll be stuck on this planet forever." He raised his hand. "Come on, Indigos. Let's show them how to work."

The Indigos rushed to the pile of garbage. With their super speed and super strength, like whirlwinds, they picked up huge chunks of garbage and toted it onto the new forming mountain. With each trip they made, the orange man increased the tempo of the music. When Sproat's men made a trip, he slowed the music to a labored almost guttural sound. When Yellow Ring, Sludge, and Tommy made a trip, he played merry-go-round music.

Hours passed. The sun began its slow roll. When it touched the horizon, Sproat's men pulled the last scrap of garbage to the new mountain.

After everyone brushed themselves off, with faces alight with hope, they stood in front of the orange man.

Like a whistle stopping after it had signaled quitting time, the orange man stopped playing the organ; and while sitting in his chair, he turned toward the gathered crowd.

"Okay, we moved your garbage," Sproat said. "Now let's do the turn."

Standing before the orange man, McQueen held his hand on the key in his waist band. "But we haven't picked the people who will go on the ship."

"You're not picking anybody, "Sproat said. "I'm going first and all my faithful men are going, too."

Hack stepped forward. "You can't go. You have ruined this planet. We can't let you ruin another one."

Samara put her hand on her waist and nodded her head in agreement.

The orange man stood up so fast that the back of his knees banged into the front of the chair. As if it were made of light-weight material, the heavy chair went skidding across the orange grass. He turned toward Sproat and Hack. "You should not fight like little children." He lifted his long arm and pointed to McQueen. "You!"

McQueen understood. He stepped to the pipe organ.

The orange man pointed to Samara. "You!"

Samara stepped to the pipe organ and stood by McQueen's side.

It was time to do the orange turn.

CHAPTER 31

McQueen placed his hand on his waist but did not take out the chip. "I cannot do the turn until I am assured that only the people Samara and I choose are the ones to go on the ship."

With a cocky demeanor, Sproat nodded. "I just knew you'd pull something like this." He motioned to his men. Bring out the barrel.

The six men, who had been pulling one of the beer barrels Samara had smashed, ran into the trees and disappeared. When they appeared again they were pulling a huge barrel on two wagon wheels through the orange grass.

Samara looked at Miles. "I wonder how I missed that one"

Miles watched the approaching barrel. "Maybe they carry a spare."

Yellow Ring turned to Sludge. "They can't do nothin' without getin' drunk."

Sludge heaved a sigh of frustration. "They have to turn everything into a circus."

"Wadda ya expect?" Yellow Ring said, "They're nothing' but a bunch of clowns."

With Sproat growling at Yellow Ring, six men pulled the barrel and stopped it in front of him. Sproat smiled at McQueen and pointed to the barrel.

His men opened the lid.

Danielle, McQueen's wife, was inside. Her eyes were dark and sunken from starvation. Her black hair was matted and filthy. But her inner beauty shone through.

McQueen started toward her. "You're alive!" he shrieked with so much emotion that his voice cracked.

For a moment, Miles broke free. "Mom!" He lurched toward the barrel, but Sproat's men held him and his father back.

"Let her go," Tommy shouted so loud the veins in his neck stood out.

Sproat's men held her in the barrel.

She couldn't get out.

McQueen felt like he had just awoke from a nightmare where he had been just going through the motions of living. Now he felt a new inner strength. Now he felt like fighting. But he couldn't shake Sproat's men. He wanted to hold Danielle. He wanted to make sure she was real. He kicked and struggled.

He couldn't escape.

His voice took on the whine of a starving dog. "Danielle!" he pleaded. "Are you all right?"

Inside the barrel, Danielle nodded her feeble head. With a hoarse voice, she rasped out, "I'll be okay. Don't do the turn. If you do, they'll kill you and me, too."

"Go ahead don't do it," Sproat said, and lifted his arm.

His men put the lid back on the barrel.

Danielle's weak screams of protest came from inside.

McQueen looked at Samara. "I have no choice. We must do the turn."

Samara looked into McQueen's eyes. "If the new planet is advanced, Sproat and his men will not be able to destroy it."

"I surely hope so," McQueen said. "But it only takes one bad Sproat to ruin a new world."

Samara turned toward the barrel. "I'll not do the turn until she is released."

Sludge weaved his way through Sproat's men and placed his walking stick on the lid. "Let her out," he demanded.

Sproat's men pulled Sludge away. As if he were unwanted garbage they threw him to the ground.

As he struggled to his feet, Sproat kicked him and let out a huge horse laugh.

Sludge stumbled and fell.

Samara stepped between Sludge and Sproat. "You're three times as big as he is. Stop it, you Neolithic creep." She bent over, helped Sludge to his feet, and brushed him off. Then she aggressively leaned toward Sproat. Do you always have to be vicious and predatory?"

Sproat irreverently looked away, smiled at his men, and signaled them to let Danielle out.

They opened the lid.

Danielle crawled out of the barrel and tried to stand up but rag dolled.

Her legs buckled under her.

Miles and Tommy ran to her sides, held her arms, and lifted her to her feet. With slow measured steps and with the help of Miles and Tommy, she struggled toward McQueen and the orange organ. When they were five meters away, she reached for McQueen. Her face showed deep pain.

McQueen reached for her.

Three of Sproat's men stepped in front of McQueen. Another three pushed Miles and Tommy away and held Danielle back.

"Not until after the turn," Sproat said and pointed to the orange man.

A blossoming of a bright orange light rose from behind the orange man. Rising, it grew into a mesmerizing awesome sight and hovered in the sky above him. Enthralled by the apparition, the crowd stood, rooted in place. The orange man turned his palm up. As if he were summoning a higher being, he stretched his hand toward the sky.

Somehow McQueen and Samara knew it was time to take out their chips. McQueen looked at Miles. "Give me your knife."

Miles reached into his pocket and pulled out his knife. Sproat backed away. Miles handed the knife to McQueen. McQueen slipped the blade into the sewn waistband, cut out the key and held it in his hand.

Samara reached in her belt and pulled out the lead key that encased her chip.

With uncontrollable excitement in his voice, and his finger shaking, Sproat pointed to the keys. In his high-pitched voice, he screeched, "That's the keys. We're in the money now."

The Orange man stared at Sproat and then at the keys. Samara took her key and pushed the flat surfaces sideways. It opened. The yellow chip appeared. She took it out and held it in her hand.

Out of the corner of his eye, McQueen watched Sproat. Like a little kid on Christmas morning, his face beamed with joy and anticipation.

McQueen wondered how any man could be so controlled by material things. Greed and power was a terrible thing and Sproat had both. McQueen hoped the new world could change or eliminate people like Sproat.

Sproat waved the back of his hand with encouragement. "Go ahead do the turn," he cried. "I can't wait."

Hack glared at Sproat. "You have it all wrong, Sproat. There is no treasure."

Sproat's face saddened.

Yellow Ring jerked his hand toward the organ. "Quit lyin'. Everybody knows there's a treasure."

Sproat's face beamed back to its excited state. "Just do the turn. You'll see."

"Don't you know?" Hack said, flashing Sproat a castigating look. "The orange turn is the path to a new world, a world free of pollution."

"Don't feed me that crap," Sproat shot back. "You know as well as I do that without pollution there is no money to be made."

Hack menacingly inched toward Sproat. "Ignorance like that is what rules your kind." He raised his fist.

Sproat cowered.

"That is why we had to keep pushing you pig people back to where you came from."

Samara held up her hand.

Hack lowered his fist.

Samara looked at Sproat with pleading eyes. "I'm sorry, but we don't need your kind swarming on board any ship. You'll only contaminate a new planet."

Sproat's face turned hard and mean. "Shut up! Just do the turn."

The orange man smiled and held up his hands in a welcoming gesture. McQueen slid his key sideways and slipped out his red chip.

"The chips ain't the same color," Sludge said, wormed his way through Sproat's men, and pointed an accusing finger at Sproat. "What did you do? Ruin the chips, too?"

Annoyed, Sproat elbowed him away.

As if they were before a minister at a wedding, Samara and McQueen held out their hands and presented the chips. The orange man gently cradled their hands in his. Then he placed the chips between their two fingers, and gently placed them next to the inserting slots. The chips glowed orange.

"Red and yellow make orange," Miles said. "Everything is going to be okay."

The orange mad nodded in approval.

As Samara and McQueen waited to be given permission to insert the chips and do the turn, the orange man pulled his hands back and smiled. With his hands spread and his palms up in the air, like a Messiah he said: "You have banded together in search of a great treasure. You can do this. And when you do, you will discover the greatest treasure you were ever given."

As if he were angry because he wasn't the center of attention, Sproat tried to change the subject. "When the history of this day is written, it will show that it wasn't right for superior warriors to work beside Indigos and mutants."

The orange man looked annoyed. "It doesn't matter who's right or wrong," he said and waited for his words to sink in. "There is a better way for you people to live."

Hack turned to his band of Indigos. "After the turn, there will be a better way."

Nodding, the orange man assured them, "After the turn, all danger shall vanish from the earth."

Chuckling, Tommy pointed his finger at McQueen. As if he just had to get the last word in, he said, "It's your turn."

McQueen smiled a slight smile. Keeping his hand and the chip next to the slot, he turned toward Danielle. Their eyes met. Even though her body was frail and skeletal, he could feel her love. "Where we are going, you'll be able to regain your strength."

Danielle smiled a reassuring smile. McQueen knew that even if Sproat killed her, she wanted him to do the turn and go to a better world.

McQueen turned back toward the orange man and placed his arm around Samara's shoulder. She placed her arm around his waist. Together, they slipped the chips into the slots. With heads bowed, they looked up at the orange man for permission to proceed.

The orange man nodded.

Samara and McQueen turned their wrists and did the turn.

Supreme silence hovered over the crowd. Not even a bird chirped. All was still. All was calm.

Everyone waited in strained silence.

Nothing happened.

388

"What's going on?" Sproat yelled and rudely broke the calm. "Is this all a joke?"

Yellow Ring jerked his walking stick toward Sproat. "You're the only joke here."

"And a bad joke," Sludge added. "Everything you touch turns to crap." Almost as an afterthought he added, "Why did you blow up the dam?"

"It taught you people a lesson," he said with arrogance in his voice. "In the future, if somebody doesn't want me to enjoy something, I'll make sure nobody enjoys it."

A skinny Dinky with glasses raised a stern finger. "You destroyed a valuable source of drinking water."

Sproat turned and waved his hand at the Dinky. "So what?' We have all the water we want in the ocean."

The dinky kept his gaze locked on Sproat. "Only if you like dying from the red bloom algae."

Sproat looked back with an unfriendly expression on his face. "Nobody can die from red water."

The Dinky pressed on. "At first, people only got sick when they ate shellfish contaminated with red tide toxin. After you dumped more chemicals and radiation into the ocean, the red blooms wiped out all coastal residents."

For a moment, it seemed Sproat was thinking about it, but he shrugged. "Just another dumb Dinky talking about something he has no knowledge of. Red water is just as safe as regular water."

"The next thing you'll be telling us is that blowing tops off mountains to get coal didn't cause the water to turn black and the streams to run yellow."

Sproat gestured to the mud flat. "Blowing up mountains was necessary, and a little dam being blown up didn't hurt a thing."

The orange man placed his fingers on the keys of the organ. No sound came out.

Yellow Ring pointed his walking stick at the orange organ. "If that thing's broke" — he whipped around and thrust the point of the stick at Sproat — "when you blew up the dam, you broke it."

The crowd began to grumble. Beneath their feet, the earth rumbled.

Sproat opened his mouth to speak, but shut up and watched.

The whole crowd gasped, shut up, and stared in wonderment.

In the silence, the earth moved in front of the organ. Next to the mountain of rotting garbage, the ground opened. Gigantic doors swung open and flopped onto the ground. A cloud of red and yellow dust puffed into the dry air and turned orange. Then, out of an ancient underground silo, a dull orange spaceship, the old Darth Disk series, the size of twenty steam cars, rose. In a crescendo of claps and cheers, the crowd whopped its approval. Suddenly they went silent. Filth had seeped down from the mountain of garbage and streaked down the sides of the orange disk. Along its underside, unkempt rusting pipes looked to be in a tangled mess.

Alarm and shock traveled through the crowd.

The people began to talk:

"That ship is in bad shape."

390

"Will it work?"

"We have three Dinkins. They'll clean it up."

"Clean it up with your big fat mouth."

Then the crowd began to argue.

"I'm going first."

"No, me. I deserve to go more than you do."

"No you don't. You're just a pig person."

"I'm Indigo. All Indigos will go."

"They gotta have somebody dat has brains," Sludge said. "All Dinkies gotta git on."

The orange man did nothing to stop the arguments.

He pointed to the ship.

Sproat was the first to step forward. "Can we get on now, sir?"

The orange man didn't answer. He smiled an all-knowing s smile and touched the last key on the organ. Bright blue electrical flashes danced over the surface of the ship. It glowed from dull orange to yellow, then red, then eye-blinding, bright-neon orange.

The crowd stepped back from the sulfur odor and the heat. The ship hissed like the long sigh of a defeated warrior. The ceramic Kevlar layers softened and melted. Then the ship disintegrated and fell into a heap of smoking ashes. The crowd recoiled with surprise. Confused and scared, they had been caught off balance.

Yellow Ring waved the smoke from the front of his face and pointed at Sproat. "See I tole you so."

As if it were a delayed reaction, the crowd gasped in horror.

Sproat placed his hands on his flabby hips and assumed a posture of superiority. "Is this the great secret of the orange turn?"

A mix of anger and confusion lined Samara's face. "We can't get off the planet. How will we repopulate a new world?"

McQueen wanted to know the answer, too. This orange man had to have a superior intelligence. He destroyed the ship for a reason. He would have a magic solution. He would have a way to save the earth. McQueen waited for him to speak.

But Tommy spoke first. "You said that all danger would vanish from the earth. What happened?"

The orange man's facial expression remained the same; there was none. Maybe this all happened to soon," he said. "You people got to talk yourselves into a new way of life, because down deep inside you have shown that you just don't care. He gestured to Sproat's men. Your bloated stomachs advertise the most despicable merchandise a man could peddle: Complacency, the narcotic of weakness." With his great almond eyes gleaming with tears, he pointed to the crowd. "Not one person here is innocent." He swung his arm in a great arc. "You have *all* destroyed the natural earth and all her gifts."

Objecting, Hack repeated Tommy's statement. "But you said that all danger would vanish from the earth."

With a look of compassion and concern, the orange man looked down on Hack. "All danger *has* vanished from the earth." He made a fist, held out his thumb, and pointed to himself. "For *us*."

With his mouth agape, Hack stared at the orange men. "What do you mean *us*?"

The orange man pointed his long, translucent, finger-nailed finger at Hack. "You and the others have shown that you are not ready to control your world." His voice pulsed with violence and raw power. "We cannot let you contaminate our orange grass world. Now the threat to our world is gone. The danger has vanished from the earth, vanished from the universe."

"But we were chosen," Samara pleaded. "Weren't we ready to go to another place?"

A puzzled look came over the orange man's face. "No one of this world is ready. We feel that you will never be ready. When you were permitted out of your world, you left bags of disease-carrying excrement on our world. You sent crude rockets and exploded bombs on our world. When you trespassed into our domain, you put up flags and made claim to what wasn't yours."

"But we can change," Samara pleaded.

"Yes you can," the orange man said. "It is not too late, but it will take thousands of years."

Hack took the gold feather from his hair and waved it in the air. "We have worn these gold feathers in support of the earth. Couldn't you take one of us with you just to show us what to do?"

"Displaying feathers or waving flags are only symbols of man's own folly and despair. Don't pretend to be innocent or ignorant. All of you people have always known what to do. You just haven't done it. By your actions, you have shown that greed and self-satisfaction are more important. Now that you have buried yourselves to the very brink of extinction you want someone else to dig you out so you can do it again."

Hack bent his knees and dropped to an almost kneeling position. "But couldn't you save us just this one time?"

"We saved your race once before." A look of disgust and determination haunted the orange man's face. "We are not here to do it again."

McQueen held up his hand. "What do you mean, again?"

The orange man cast a cold eye on his audience. "We gave you this little planet when you destroyed your old planet."

McQueen shook his head. "But we never had another planet."

"If you wouldn't have destroyed the stones of life, you would have known that your race came from the planet you murdered. The dead red planet."

McQueen paused and the name of the planet burned in his brain. "Was it Mars?"

The orange man didn't answer and continued. "The earth man is unfit to inhabit the earth or any other planet." He flashed a discouraged face. "Your race has not learned to live with the planets. You kill everything you come into contact with. You are not taking your death and destruction to our world again. This time, there will be no exceptions. Not one of you will ever put another planet to death."

McQueen opened his mouth to speak, but Hack interrupted. "But there should have been a sign to show us what could happen."

With disbelief, the orange man's almond eyes opened wide. "How many signs do you need? When there was no decent water to drink, wasn't that a sign something was wrong? When you had no clean air to breathe, wasn't that a sign something should be changed? When fish and wildlife grew three heads, wasn't that a sign something should stop?"

The earth shifted. The crowd of people swayed. Some stumbled to the ground but managed to get to their feet.

The orange man continued. "You have dumped millions of gallons of crack water into the veins of the earth and caused the ground to shift under your very feet. What have you done to correct it? You have pumped more poison into the earth, released methane into the atmosphere. Your disregard—"

"You are wrong, sir," A pig person, dressed in a finely tailored suit coat, abruptly interrupted and took off his fedora.

All eyes turned toward the pig person. He lifted his hand, smoothed his fresh haircut back, buttoned the top button on his suite coat, and adjusted his red tie. "With all due respect, sir," he said with an air of superiority. "You are wrong. I am a representative of the Pleasant Gas Company. We have consulted with high councils. We have brought the matter to the Friends of the Earth Corporation. All sides agree that scientific proof shows that a little water dumped down a hole never hurt anyone. We need that gas to keep warm. And besides, global boiling is not a serious danger to humanity." As he lifted one finger to emphasize a point, his pig-like eyes narrowed and brought a hard edge of brutality to his face. "Sure, a few weak inferior people have died." He spat out. "But that was only Nature purging the excess population. We should let Nature decide if people are strong enough to live."

"Damage to the ozone layer is manmade," the orange man shot back, very fierce now, his skin a faint yellowish orange. "You are one of the men with a fluid tongue and facile mind. You understand what is right and wrong, but you put it into words beyond immature people's understanding. Your words have been betrayed by the results of your actions."

A phony, innocent look clouded the pig person's face. "What actions?"

"Don't act innocent!" the orange man roared back. "While the earth crumbles before your very eyes, you continue to spread disinformation."

The pig person arrogantly lifted his head. "Humans breathe out carbon dioxide, so it must be good for the earth. There is nothing to worry about. We all know global boiling is nothing but a bunch of old tales cobbled together a couple of thousand years ago by some lazy people trying to make money off of people who didn't want to work."

Sludge flared up angrily. "What are you? Some kind of nut? I work every day. The earth has got hot. Now we got droughts. Now we got forest fires. Now we got dust storms. We got fire tornados, and now we got cold places that used to be nice and warm. And in case your great scientists haven't noticed, hurricanes and tornados are now an everyday thing."

The pig person sagged and tilted his head to the side. "Come on, now, my little Dinky friend, "he said with fake compassion. "You don't really believe that?"

With hate-filled eyes, Tommy roared at the pig person. "The Friends of the Earth gave your companies one break after another." He waved his hands feverishly. "You are one of the egotists who are paid high salaries to promote lies. For years your campaigns have cause people to duck the issues and avoid making hard choices. Every study your corporation does is flawed. Even when a little of the truth was exposed, it confirmed things looked bad when they were far worse."

The pig person turned toward the crowd and smiled. "The next thing you'll be saying is that this orange man can play the tuba with his butt."

No one laughed.

Seeming oblivious to what Tommy said and not getting and expected laugh, the pig person calmly waved his hand down. Anyway, no one believes anything a dumb Dinky says?"

"Perhaps you will believe what I say," the orange man retorted sullenly. "Your ancestors were given the secret of the midnight crystal. If they would have used it peacefully, you would have no need for other energy. But, instead, in a single night they blew the land of Mu off the face of the earth." He waved his hand in the air. "You have knowledge of clean wind power, but because it was free and you couldn't charge people for it, you increased carbon dioxide emissions, increased dangerous levels of hydro fluorocarbons, and heated the atmosphere."

397

"That wasn't us," Sproat objected. "Why blame us for something we didn't do?"

"We believed you people would change with time. It is thousands of years later, and you people haven't changed one bit. You were given more than ample food to sustain your bodies. For amusement, you created wheelbarrow people. You were given nuclear power and what did you do with it?" He gestured to three squinty-eyed pig people with deformed faces and arms. "You filled the atmosphere with radiation and mutated the gene pool of thousands." He slowly turned his head from side to side. "Look around. There are many visible reminders of the ignorance of the people who caused the destruction of another planet, and there are signs that it is happening again."

Hack straightened his shoulders and stepped forward. "What Sproat has done is not our fault."

The orange man defiantly folded his arms tightly across his chest. "As long as it continues to happen, it *is* everyone's fault. Once again you people have come to believe that it is not what is right or wrong that matters, but only what you can get away with. Money begets followers. If used correctly it can create a good world for all. You have used money to proliferate evil. This ignorant greed caused dead planets. It is not wanted in our world or other worlds."

Hack looked up, his eyes misting. "But we'll change."

Hack's remorse had no effect on the orange man. He raised his voice. "Again, you have done what you have always done. You have made your world what it is. Now you want to place the blame on someone else."

The crowd began to grumble. Then one by one, and in no order, they spoke out.

"We don't need some orange kook telling us what's right and wrong."

"It's still our planet. We have the authority. We'll give the orders."

"That's right. We tell the people what is really right.

"Pig people are like sheep. They're better off when they do what we tell them to do.

"Don't waste your time on that crap. "

"It's all a lie. He still has the treasure."

"I tole you, you don't know nothin'."

As if they appeared out of midair, seven rat-tailed Pigmies stood next to the orange man and hissed through their buck teeth.

As if it were an angry ocean, the field of orange grass rolled violently.

Cowering under the threat, the crowd of people mumbled amongst themselves.

McQueen raised his hands above his head and shouted. "Shut up!" His voice was so loud it thundered and echoed over the ruined reservoirs. "Let the man speak!"

Yellow Ring put his hands over his ears.

The orange grass became calm.

The others shut up.

The orange man gazed over the crowd.

Strange silence filled the air.

With absolute authority in his voice, the orange man spoke. "You do not live long enough. Your ancestors lived six hundred and eight hundred years.

After seventy years your brains begin to develop, but if your poisoned world doesn't kill you, you are put into a community and terminated with a neutron wave. You could not obey ten orders written in stone. Now you must obey an eleventh order."

Shocked McQueen jerked back. "Eleventh order? What Eleventh order?"

The orange man lifted one arm and softly said, "You must stay on the blue planet."

Sproat's men released Danielle. She elbowed her way through the men in front of McQueen.

McQueen saw her and reached out.

They met and embraced.

When they kissed her lips were dry and cracked, but McQueen felt the magic. It was still there. Sproat and his scabs hadn't erased the love they had for each other.

As the orange man smiled down on them, a tear formed in the corner of Samara's eye.

McQueen drew away from Danielle and looked into the orange man's almond eyes.

The orange man spoke in a gentle voice. "When it is time for a being to do it, no man can avoid what he is supposed to do."

McQueen saw the truth. He knew there was no magic plan to save the earth. There was no easy way out. It would be business as usual. He would have to get the world to change, again.

He raised his hand in a salute to a higher being and turned to the crowd. "We must be more like these lost bewildered guardians of tomorrow." He gestured to the Pygmies. "We can orchestrate ourselves to be what we can be, not as we are. We have taken so much from the earth. When we stay on the blue grass, if it isn't too late, maybe we can save a portion of the earth's life-giving properties."

Sproat broke out in a furor of resentment. "That's hog wash, McQueen. It's been too late for years. We ain't getting back on that blue grass," He motioned to his men. "Grab that orange freak." His voice rose to an excited high pitch. "He said he would show us the way to the greatest treasure known to man. He lied."

The orange man shook his head. "The greatest treasure known to man is all around you."

Sludge looked around. "I don't see no treasure."

The orange man pointed to the lakebed. "Your treasure is there. Perhaps you do not realize that dumping lethal chemical into rivers and streams ruined it." He waved his arm in an arc. Perhaps you have tasted dirty air so long you have forgotten what fresh air is. Your treasure is the land that feeds you and the air you breathe. Your treasure is what gives you life."

Seething with frustration, Sproat turned to the crowd. "This orange freak's lying. He has another ship to get out of here. We'll make him give it to us."

The Pigmies didn't curl their tails into a threatening S or hiss, and the orange man didn't brace himself in defense. As if he were looking into Sproat's soul, he just stood and stared.

Sproat's men lunged forward.

With lightning-swift reflexes, he thought he had lost, McQueen stepped between the men and the orange man.

The men came to an abrupt halt.

401

"Go on!" Sproat shouted to his men with his excited voice rising to a high pitch. "Don't let McQueen scare you. Throw him out of the way." He jerked his fist at the orange man. "Show McQueen and that orange freak who runs this place."

The orange man's stare concentrated on Sproat.

Sproat's voice rose to an even higher pitch. "What are you looking at, freak?" he squeaked out.

Twisted sticks of blue lightening filled the orange sky.

Sproat's face filled with pain. He grabbed his own throat, and opened his mouth to speak. Nothing came out. The orange man continued to stare. Clutching his throat, Sproat dropped to his knees.

One of Sproat's men stepped toward the orange man. "You're killing him. Stop!"

The orange man turned his attention to the man. The man staggered and reeled back. Disoriented, he fell to his knees. The orange man let his eyes travel over the crowd. As if they had been sentenced to hang and the rope around their necks had just been slipped tight, the worst of Sproat's men held their hands in front of their necks. Squealing, they slowly walked to the garbage mountain. Once there, they stumbled a few meters up the mountain. Then, one by one, as if they knew they belonged there, they leaned forward, fell, face-first into the garbage, and lay still.

McQueen stared at the orange man with disbelief. "What kind of a man are you?" he wanted to know. "Everyone can change. They shouldn't be murdered."

402

The orange man turned his head. With a quizzical look to his face, he said, "I have not ended their lives." Although his hands were nowhere near the organ, it thrummed a spooky low bass tone. Without missing a beat, the orange man continued. "When life destroys life, it is no longer a part of the nonphysical wheel of life. It ceases to be life. When the psyche realizes this, as a learning process, and for the good of the wheel, it eliminates the lifeless."

Suddenly, unlike the usual sad feelings McQueen had experienced when someone had died or was killed, he felt nothing but good in his heart. He turned toward Tommy. "I wonder why I don't feel bad."

Tommy shrugged. "I don't know. "Maybe it's planned obsolescence."

Sproat stayed on his knees. With each labored breath, his huge belly heaved up and down, and his eyes grew wide with fright. The orange man smiled down at him. With dazed lifeless eyes, Sproat got up off his knees and walked to the mountain of garbage.

The orange man held out his arm and gestured toward Sproat. "When pushed too far, life will take measures to correct the wrong done to it."

Sproat plopped into the garbage. In one last desperate attempt to gain material wealth, he clutched the garbage that was his execution place. Clawing downward, his trollish figure ceased breathing.

The pig person, with the red tie, removed his fedora, lowered his head, and spoke softly. "He was a magnificent liar, but now he will matter to no one and count for nothing."

Whirling wisps of white smoke swirled in the distant gray sky. Although the field of orange grass remained calm, the sound of a new wind swished through the tops of the black skeletal trees.

As the sky suffused to a bluish gleam, the orange man faced the people. "In the end—" He paused and pointed to Sproat and his fallen men lying in the garbage. "In the end, we will all become what we are."

Tommy turned toward McQueen. "What do we do now?"

McQueen looked off into the now distant blue sky. "Change the earth."

For a moment the rattails of the Pigmies curled into threatening S shapes. But then, smiling buck tooth smiles, they dropped their tails to the ground, turned, and walked away. They escorted the orange man through the field of bright orange grass. At the end of the field, as they eased into the dense foliage, the pigmies' rattails snaked through the struggling plant life and vanished.

ACKNOWLEDGMENTS

This story couldn't have been written without the help of
Gary Vath, the Marine who stayed to the end.

and

Sparky: Man never had a better friend.